Max Robinson

Penguin Books

Outrageous Behaviour
Best Stories of Morris Lurie

Morris Lurie was born in Melbourne,
Australia, in 1938, to which city he returned
in 1973, following seven years abroad, mostly
in England, Denmark, Morocco and Greece.
He is married, with two children, and is a
frequent visitor to New York.

His stories have appeared in many leading
magazines, including *The New Yorker,
Antaeus* and *The Virginia Quarterly Review*
in the USA; *Punch, The Times* and the
Telegraph Sunday Magazine in the UK; and
in Australia in *Meanjin, Overland* and *The
National Times*. They have been much
translated and anthologised, and broadcast on
the BBC.

Also by Morris Lurie

Novels

Rappaport (1966)
The London Jungle Adventures of Charlie Hope (1968)
Rappaport's Revenge (1973)
Flying Home (1978)
Seven Books for Grossman (1983)

Stories

Happy Times (1969)
Inside the Wardrobe (1975)
Running Nicely (1979)
Dirty Friends (1981)

Pieces

The English in Heat (1972)
Hack Work (1977)
Public Secrets (1981)

Plays

Waterman (1979)

For Children

The Twenty-Seventh Annual African Hippopotamus Race (1969)
Arlo the Dandy Lion (1971)
Toby's Millions (1982)
The Story of Imelda, Who Was Small (1984)

◆ *Outrageous Behaviour*

◆

◆ Best Stories of Morris Lurie

Penguin Books

Penguin Books Australia Ltd,
487 Maroondah Highway, P.O. Box 257
Ringwood, Victoria, 3134, Australia
Penguin Books Ltd,
Harmondsworth, Middlesex, England
Penguin Books,
40 West 23rd Street, New York, N.Y. 10010, USA
Penguin Books Canada Ltd,
2801 John Street, Markham, Ontario, Canada
Penguin Books (N.Z.) Ltd,
182–190 Wairau Road, Auckland 10, New Zealand

This selection first published by Penguin Books Australia, 1984

Copyright © Morris Lurie, 1969, 1975, 1979, 1981

Typeset in Century Old Style by Dudley E. King, Melbourne

Made and printed in Australia by
The Dominion Press–Hedges & Bell

CIP

Lurie, Morris, 1938–.
Outrageous behaviour.

ISBN 0 14 007097 4.

I. Title.
A823'.3

Again, to Ian Catchlove, who selected

◆ *Acknowledgements*

◆

◆ Of the thirty stories in this book, nine are from *Happy Times* (Hodder & Stoughton, London, 1969), nine are from *Inside the Wardrobe* (Outback Press, Melbourne, 1975), nine are from *Running Nicely* (Hamish Hamilton, London, 1979), and three stories are from *Dirty Friends* (Penguin Books, Ringwood, 1981).

◆ Contents

◆

♦ My Greatest Ambition

♦ My greatest ambition was to be a comic-strip artist, but I grew out of it. People were always patting me on the head and saying, 'He'll grow out if it.' They didn't know what they were talking about. Had any of them ever read a comic? Studied one? *Drawn* one? 'Australia is no place for comics,' they said, and I had to lock myself up in the dining room to get some peace. My mother thought I was studying in there.

I was the only person in my class – probably in the whole school – who wanted to be a comic-strip artist. They were all dreamers. There they sat, the astronomer, the nuclear physicist, the business tycoon (on the Stock Exchange), two mathematicians, three farmers, countless chemists, a handful of doctors, all aged thirteen and all with their heads in the clouds. Dreamers! Idle speculators! A generation of hopeless romantics! It was a Friday night, I recall, when I put the finishing touches to my first full-length, inked-in, original, six-page comic-strip.

I didn't have the faintest idea what to do with it. Actually, doing anything *with* it hadn't ever entered my mind. *Doing* it was enough. Over the weekend I read it through sixty or seventy times, analysed it, studied it, stared at it, finally pronounced it 'Not too bad,' and then put it up on the top of my wardrobe where my father kept his hats.

And that would have been the end of it, only the next day I happened to mention to Michael Lazarus, who sat next to me at school, that I had drawn a comic-strip, and he happened to mention to me that there was a magazine in Melbourne I could send it to. We were both thrown out of that class for doing too much mentioning out loud, and kept in after school, to write fifty eight-letter words and their meanings in sentences – a common disciplinary action at that time. I remember writing 'ambulate' and saying it was a special way of walking. Do I digress? Then let me say that the first thing I did when I got home was roll my comic up in brown paper, address it, and put it in my schoolbag where I wouldn't forget it in the morning. Some chance of that. Lazarus had introduced an entirely new idea into my head. Publication. I hardly slept all night.

One of the things that kept me tossing and turning was the magazine I was sending my comic to. *Boy Magazine*. I had never bought one in my life, because it had the sneaky policy of printing stories, with only one illustration at the top of the page to get you interested. *Stories?* The school library was full of them, and what a bore they were. Did I want my comic to appear in a magazine which printed stories, where it would be read by the sort of people who were always taking books out of the library and sitting under trees and wearing glasses and squinting and turning pages with licked fingers? An *awful* prospect! At two o'clock in the morning I decided no, I didn't, and at three I did, and at four it was no again, but the last thing I saw before I finally fell asleep was Lazarus's face and he was saying, 'Publication!' and that decided it. Away it went.

Now let me properly introduce my father, a great scoffer. In those pre-television days, he had absolutely nothing to do in the evening but to walk past my room and look in and say, 'Nu? They sent you the money yet?' Fifty times a night, at least. And when the letter came from *Boy Magazine*, did he change his tune? Not one bit.

'I don't see a cheque,' he said.

'Of *course* there's no cheque,' I said. 'How can there be? We haven't even discussed it yet. Maybe I'll decide not to sell it to them. Which I will, if their price isn't right.'

'Show me again the letter,' my father said. 'Ha, listen, listen. "We are very interested in your comic and would like you to phone Miss Gordon to make an appointment to see the editor." An appointment? That means they don't want it. If they wanted it, believe me, there'd be a cheque.'

It serves no purpose to put down the rest of this pointless conversation, which included such lines as 'How many comics have *you* sold in your life?' and, 'Who paid for the paper? The ink?' other than to say that I made the phone call to Miss Gordon from a public phone and not from home. I wasn't going to have my father listening to every word.

My voice, when I was thirteen, and standing on tiptoe and talking into a public phone, was, I must admit, unnecessarily loud, but Miss Gordon didn't say anything about it. 'And what day will be most convenient for you, Mr Lurie?' she asked. 'Oh, any day at all!' I shouted. 'Any day will suit me fine!' 'A week from Thursday then?' she asked. 'Perfect!' I yelled, trying to get a piece of paper and a pencil out of my trouser pocket to write it down, and at the same time listening like mad in case Miss Gordon said something else. And she did. 'Ten o'clock?' 'I'll be there!' I shouted, and hung up with a crash.

It hadn't occurred to me to mention to Miss Gordon that I was thirteen and at school and would have to take a day off to come and see the editor. I didn't think these things were relevant to our business. But my mother did. A day missed from school could never be caught up, that was her attitude. My father's attitude you know. A cheque or not a cheque. Was I rich or was I a fool? (No, that's wrong. Was I a poor fool or a rich fool? Yes, that's better.) But my problem was something else. What to wear?

My school suit was out of the question because I wore it every day and I was sick of it and it just wasn't right for a business appointment. Anyway, it had ink stains round the pocket where my fountain pen leaked (a real fountain, ha ha), and the seat of the trousers shone like a piece of tin. And my Good Suit was a year old and too short in the leg. I tried it on in front of the mirror, just to make sure, and I was right. It was ludicrous. My father offered to lend me one of his suits. He hadn't bought a new suit since 1934. There was enough material in the lapels alone to make three suits and have enough left over for a couple of caps. Not only that, but my father was shorter than me and twice the weight. So I thanked him and said that I had decided to wear my Good Suit after all. I would wear dark socks and the shortness of trousers would hardly be noticed. Also, I would wear my eye-dazzling pure silk corn yellow tie, which, with the proper Windsor knot, would so ruthlessly rivet attention that no one would even look to see if I was wearing shoes.

'A prince,' my father said.

Now, as the day of my appointment drew nearer and nearer, a great question had to be answered, a momentous decision made. For my father had been right. If all they wanted to do was to buy my comic, they would have sent a cheque. So there was something else. A full-time career as a comic-strip artist on the permanent staff of *Boy Magazine*! It had to be that. But that would mean giving up school and was I prepared to do that?

'Yes,' I said with great calmness and great authority to my face in the bathroom mirror. 'Yes.'

There were three days to go.

Then there occurred one of those things that must happen every day in the world of big business, but when you're thirteen it knocks you for a loop. *Boy Magazine* sent me a telegram. It was the first telegram I had ever received in my life, and about the third that had ever come to our house. My mother opened it straight away. She told everyone in our street about it. She phoned uncles, aunts, sisters, brothers, and finally, when I came home from school, she told me.

I was furious. I shouted, 'I told you never under *any* circumstances to open my mail!'

'But a telegram,' my mother said.

'A telegram is mail,' I said. 'And mail is a personal, private thing. Where is it?'

My mother had folded it four times and put it in her purse and her purse in her bag and her bag in her wardrobe which she had locked. She stood by my side and watched me while I read it.

'Nu?' she said.

'It's nothing,' I said.

And it wasn't. Miss Gordon had suddenly discovered that the editor was going to be out of town on my appointment day, and would I kindly phone and make another appointment?

I did, standing on tiptoe and shouting as before.

The offices of *Boy Magazine* were practically in the country, twelve train stations out of town. Trains, when I was thirteen, terrified me, and still do. Wearing my Good Suit and my corn yellow tie and my father's best black socks and a great scoop of oil in my hair, I kept jumping up from my seat and looking out of the window to see if we were getting near a station and then sitting down again and trying to relax. Twelve stations, eleven stations, ten. Nine to go, eight, seven. Or was it six? What was the name of the last one? What if I went too far? What was the time? By the time I arrived at the right station, I was in a fine state of nerves.

The offices of *Boy Magazine* were easy to find. They were part of an enormous building that looked like a factory, and were not at all imposing or impressive, as I had imagined them to be. No neon, no massive areas of plate glass, no exotic plants growing in white gravel. (I had a picture of myself walking to work every morning through a garden of exotic plants growing in white gravel, cacti, ferns, pushing open a massive glass door under a neon sign and smiling at a receptionist with a pipe in my mouth.) I pushed open an ordinary door and stepped into an ordinary foyer and told an ordinary lady sitting at an ordinary desk who I was.

'And?' she said.

'I have an appointment to see the editor of *Boy Magazine*,' I said.

'Oh,' she said.

'At ten o'clock,' I said. 'I think I'm early.' It was half past nine.

'Just one minute,' she said, and picked up a telephone. While she was talking I looked around the foyer, in which there was nothing to look at, but I don't like eavesdropping on people talking on the phone.

Then she put down the phone and said to me, 'Won't be long. Would you like to take a seat?'

For some reason that caught me unawares and I flashed her a blinding smile and kept standing there, wondering what was going to happen next, and then I realized what she had said and I smiled again and turned around and bumped into a chair and sat down and crossed my legs and looked around and then remembered the shortness of my trousers and quickly uncrossed my legs and sat perfectly straight and still, except for looking at my watch ten times in the next thirty seconds.

I don't know how long I sat there. It was either five minutes or an hour, it's hard to say. The lady at the desk didn't seem to have anything to do, and I didn't like looking at her, but from time to time our eyes met, and I would smile – or was that smile stretched across my face from the second I came in? I used to do things like that when I was thirteen.

Finally a door opened and another lady appeared. She seemed, for some reason, quite surprised when she saw me sitting there, as though I had three eyes or was wearing a red suit, but I must say this for her, she had poise, she pulled herself together very quickly, hardly dropped a stitch, as it were, and holding open the door through which she had come, she said, 'Won't you come this way?' and I did.

I was shown into an office that was filled with men in grey suits. Actually, there were only three of them, but they all stood up when I came in, and the effect was overpowering. I think I might even have taken a half-step back. But my blinding smile stayed firm.

The only name I remember is Randell and maybe I have that wrong. There was a lot of handshaking and smiling and saying of names. And when all that was done, no one seemed to know what to do. We just stood there, all uncomfortably smiling.

Finally, the man whose name might have been Randell said, 'Oh, please, please, sit down,' and everyone did.

'Well,' Mr Randell said. 'You're a young man to be drawing comics, I must say.'

'I've been interested in comics all my life,' I said.

'Well, we like your comic very much,' he said. 'And we'd like to make you an offer for it. Ah, fifteen pounds?'

'I accept,' I said.

I don't think Mr Randell was used to receiving quick decisions, for he then said something that seemed to me enormously ridiculous. 'That's, ah, two pounds ten a page,' he said, and looked at me with his eyes wide open and one eyebrow higher than the other.

'Yes, that's right,' I said. 'Six two-and-a-halfs are fifteen. Exactly.'

That made his eyes open even wider, and suddenly he shut them altogether and looked down at the floor. One of the other men coughed. No one seemed to know what to do. I leaned back in my chair and crossed my legs and just generally smiled at everyone. I knew what was coming. A job. And I knew what I was going to say then, too.

And then Mr Randell collected himself, as though he had just thought of something very important (what an actor, I thought) and he said, 'Oh, there is one other thing, though. Jim, do we have Mr Lurie's comic here?'

'Right here,' said Jim, and whipped it out from under a pile of things on a desk.

'Some of the, ah, spelling,' Mr Randell said.

'Oh?' I said.

'Well, yes, there are, ah, certain things,' he said, turning over the pages of my comic, 'not, ah, *big* mistakes, but, here, see? You've spelt it as "jungel" which is not, ah, common usage.'

'You're absolutely right,' I said, flashing out my fountain pen all ready to make the correction.

'Oh, no no no,' Mr Randell said. 'Don't you worry about it. We'll, ah, make the corrections. If you approve, that is.'

'Of course,' I said.

'We'll, ah, post you our cheque for, ah, fifteen pounds,' he said. 'In the mail,' he added, rather lamely, it seemed to me.

'Oh, there's no great hurry about that,' I said. 'Any old time at all will do.'

'Yes,' he said.

Then we fell into another of these silences with which this appointment seemed to be plagued. Mr Randell scratched his neck. A truck just outside the window started with a roar and then began to whine and grind. It's reversing, I thought. My face felt stiff from smiling, but somehow I couldn't let it go.

Then the man whose name was Jim said, 'This is your first comic strip, Mr Lurie?'

'Yes,' I said. My reply snapped across the room like a bullet. I was a little bit embarrassed at its suddenness, but, after all, wasn't this what I had come to talk about?

'It's very professional,' he said. 'Would you like to see one of our comic-strips?'

'Certainly,' I said.

He reached down behind the desk and brought out one page of a comic they were running at the moment (I had seen it in the shop when I'd gone to check up on *Boy Magazine*'s address), *The Adventures of Ned Kelly*.

Now, Ned Kelly is all right, but what I like about comics is that they create a world of their own, like, say, *Dick Tracy*, a totally fictitious environment, which any clear-thinking person knows doesn't really exist, and Ned Kelly, well, that was real, it really happened. It wasn't a true comic-strip. It was just history in pictures.

But naturally I didn't say any of this to Jim. All I did was lean forward and pretend to study the linework and the inking in and the lettering, which were just so-so, and when I thought I'd done that long enough, I leaned back in my chair and said, 'It's very good.'

'Jim,' said Mr Randell, who hadn't spoken a word during all this, 'maybe you'd like to take Mr Lurie around and show him the presses. We print *Boy Magazine* right here,' he explained to me. 'Would you like to see how a magazine is produced?'

'Yes,' I said, but the word sounded flat and awful to me. I hated, at thirteen, being shown round things. I still do. How A Great Newspaper Is Produced. How Bottles Are Made. Why Cheese Has Holes And How We Put Them In.

And the rest of it, the job, the core of the matter? But everyone was standing up and Mr Randell's hand was stretched out to shake mine and Jim was saying, 'Follow me,' and it was all over.

Now I'm not going to take you through a tour of this factory, the way I was, eating an ice cream which Jim had sent a boy out to buy for me. It lasted for hours. I climbed up where Jim told me to climb up. I looked where he pointed. I nodded when he explained some involved and highly secret process to me. 'We use glue, not staples,' he explained to me. 'Why? Well, it's an economic consideration. Look here,' and I looked there, and licked my ice cream and wondered how much more there was of it and was it worth going to school in the afternoon or should I take the whole day off?

But like all things it came to an end. We were at a side door, not the one I had come in through. 'Well, nice to meet you,' Jim said, and shook my hand. 'Find your way back to the station okay? You came by train? It's easy, just follow your nose,' and I rode home on the train not caring a damn about how many stations I was going through, not looking out of the window, not even aware of the shortness of the trousers of my ridiculous Good Suit.

Yes, my comic-strip appeared and my friends read it and I was a hero for a day at school. My father held the cheque up to the light and said we'd know in a few days if it was any good. My mother didn't say much to me but I heard her on the phone explaining to all her friends what a clever son she had. Clever? That's one word I've never had any time for.

I didn't tell a soul, not even Michael Lazarus, about that awful tour of the factory. I played it very coolly. And a week after my comic-strip came out in print, I sat down and drew another comic story and wrapped it up and sent it to them, and this time, I determined, I would do all my business over the phone. With that nice Miss Gordon.

Weeks passed, nearly a whole month. No reply. And then, with a sickening crash, the postman dumped my new comic into our letterbox and flew on his merry way down the street, blowing his whistle and riding his bicycle over everyone's lawns.

There was a letter enclosed with my comic. It said that, unfortunately, *Boy Magazine* was discontinuing publication, and although they enjoyed my comic 'enormously', they regretted that they had no option but to return it.

My father had a field day over the whole business but no, no, what's the point of going over all that? Anyhow, I had decided (I told myself) that I didn't want to be a comic-strip artist after all. There was no future in it. It was risky and unsure. It was here today and gone tomorrow. The thing to be was a serious painter, and I set about it at once, spreading new boxes of water colours and tubes of paint all over the dining room table and using every saucer in the house to mix paint. But somehow, right from the start, I knew it was no good. The only thing that was ever real to me I had 'grown out of'. I had become, like everyone else, a dreamer.

◆ *Home Is*

◆ He lived in New York and in London and on the isle of Rhodes, and in Paris there was always a room for him at Peter Stein's place with a view of grey slate roofs and the Seine, and in Prague Bob Turner who taught English at the University liked to have him but he sometimes chose a hotel (Bob's children were nice, but he didn't like having to tiptoe around when they were asleep), and in Beirut and in Istanbul and in West Berlin and in Rome he always stayed in hotels, though he had friends, good friends, in all these places, and he had friends in Athens too but he preferred the Gran Bretagne, and now, as the plane he was in touched down on Rhodes, he closed the book he was reading (poems: *For the Union Dead*) and sat back and waited for the plane to stop. He closed his eyes. And when he felt no movement he opened them and unlocked his seat belt and reached up for his hat and then made his way along the aisle and down the steps and smiled at the hostess and then he looked up and for a second he was completely lost.

It was no place Max Gottlieb had ever been in his life before.

And then it was Rhodes.

It lasted a second, no more, but it was immense, gigantic, and it took all the strength out of his legs and he almost collapsed. One second. For one second he hadn't recognized Rhodes, this airport, trees, these hills, where he had been so often, so many years. It was like walking through the door into your bathroom and finding yourself in Africa. Or on the surface of the moon.

Christ, I'm going crazy, he thought.

He shook his head and whistled phew and blinked in the sun. It was gone, but for a few seconds more his legs felt funny as he walked across the tarmac to Customs.

Someone was waving. At me? he thought. Who – ? *Sylvia*. Of course. And Larry. He'd cabled them from Athens that he was coming. I really *am* going nuts, he thought.

'Hi!' he called, and waved back.

He showed his passport and went through the gate and they came up to him and Sylvia gave him a hug and a kiss on both cheeks and Larry slapped him on the back.

'Max. Welcome home. Max, you're looking marvellous. Good trip?'

Sylvia so exuberant, Larry his smiling self.

'Oh, beautiful, beautiful,' Max said. 'Sylvia, you're four times as brown as when I left. *Five* times. What have you been *doing*, treading grapes in the sun or something? Larry, how's the painting?'

'Oh, so-so, you know. Just dabbling.'

'I *bet*. And winning prizes and getting commissions and making thousands every day. Oh, here come my bags. I'll just get this thing stamped and we can get out of here. *Air*ports, my God.'

'The car's right out front,' Sylvia said. 'Larry, don't just *stand* there. Help Max with his bags, that's what you're here for.'

'That's the style,' Max laughed. 'Earn yourself a handsome tip. Hey, careful with that bag. It's full of Greek cakes and nylon shirts.'

'Oh Max, you're gorgeous,' Sylvia said.

'The pearl of the Adriatic,' Max said.

They squeezed into the front of the Farrell's Citröen – one of those small ones with bug eyes and a canvas roof – with the luggage bouncing in the back. Larry drove and Sylvia sat in the middle and Max lit a cigarette and oh these hills and trees he loved so much, goodbye New York for ever, who needs it? – they swerved around a peasant girl on a donkey, Larry blasting on the horn and the girl sitting sidesaddle and her legs pumping up and down as the donkey trotted along – and again, for a second, the strangest feeling came over him. Where am I? What am I doing here? But he had no time to think because Sylvia, as usual, was talking non-stop.

'How was London? Brilliant? We've been reading all about it in the papers. The *theatre*, my *God*. The things we're missing. Did you see *every*thing? That new thing, what's the name of it – Larry, what's that absolutely brilliant play the papers have been full of? Oh, he doesn't remember a thing. Old age. Max, you were in Berlin too, oh you lucky thing. Did you go into East? How was it? Opera? My *God*, they're foul beasts but they do have the most fantastic opera. Max, hey, you're not listening to a *word* I'm saying.'

'Oh . . . what? Sorry,' Max said. 'All this flying.'

No, he hadn't heard a word. He had been looking at his face reflected in the windscreen. Thirty-five, and still so boyish. Dark, sad eyes and that intense look. But not quite as intense as it had been ten years ago. A little rounder, a little softer. A different intensity. The poet was gone. And in his place?

'Max, I want to hear absolutely everything. Before you tell *any*one else.'

'What? Oh.' Wake up, wake up, he told himself, what's wrong with you? And he did, all at once, he became his old self, Max the raconteur, charming and casual, full of fun. 'Well, before I forget,' he began, 'Ziggy sends you his love and – '

'*Ziggy*. How nice.'

' – *all* the plays in London are awful, completely awful, you have no idea, and – '

The poet had become a gossip. This was Max Gottlieb, aged thirty-five. And inch by inch, one inch at a time, carefully, he opened the glittering bag of talk and news he had brought with him from the theatres and parties of Europe, trinkets and pearls and tantalizing first inches of multicoloured ribbon – carefully, it had to last for two months. There was love from him, regards from her, stories and jokes and first views of new places and new people, while the bays of the isle of Rhodes opened up before them, the purest sand, the sea that unbelievable blue, and on the slopes of the hills the olive trees so gnarled and centuries old on their pockets of land so small amongst the rocks and the houses so simply white.

'Oh, I must tell you about a party Freddy gave. Someone brought a horse and – Wow, look at that!'

They had taken the final turn and there was the Acropolis and the white village of Lindos, which many say is the most beautiful in all Greece.

'Go on, about the horse,' Sylvia said. 'What horse? *Hey!*'

'Ssh,' Max whispered. 'The view.'

It affected him like this every time he saw it, every time he came back. Five years now, going on six. 1961. The year his father died (and the poet too, but he didn't know that then). Max the millionaire on his first world trip.

There were four of them, Roger and Viv and that girl with the red hair – What was her name? Lester? No . . . and Max, and they were doing the Greek islands, really doing them. Hydra and Mykonos, Patmos and Samos, Santorini, Crete, and from Crete they flew to Rhodes because Roger said there was a famous Acropolis there, shouldn't be missed, and as soon as Max saw it, and under it that nestling village like a handful of sugar cubes in the sun – drunk admittedly, the four of them in the back of a cab, Roger and the girl with the red hair on the jump seats and all of them laughing for no real reason at all – he decided, I'm buying a house here, and he did. Lindos.

Houses were cheap then, not that it mattered, and he bought a small one overlooking the bay and for three months he had Greeks working non-stop knocking out walls and installing a bathroom and a kitchen and putting up bookshelves and building benches, while Max made a whirlwind trip through Europe and came back with chairs from Denmark, Spanish rugs, knick-knacks from Liberty's in London, a German stereo, and a superb print of the defeat of Napoleon at Waterloo for the wall above the mantelpiece.

'This is home,' he said, and he had almost decided to get rid of his apartment in New York and his mews flat in Chelsea (which he'd only had for six months) and stay forever in this Greek paradise when he woke up one morning with a great desire for green fields, country lanes, German beer, mountains and snow, and he flew to New York (it was summer there) and stayed for three months. Theatres, parties, old friends, new places.

And after that, to cool down, a month in Paris, which was just as hectic.

Then he came back, stayed two months, and left again. And he had been doing this ever since.

'Here we are,' said Sylvia. 'Larry, get the bags.'

'Ah, isn't it wonderful,' said Max.

It was different every time, and always the same. Donkeys, and black-clad women filling their waterjugs at the fountain and old brown men sitting in the sun and everyone talking and making a noise. The same, and so different. Tourist buses and hundreds of Swedes and souvenirs for sale everywhere you looked. There was none of that when he had first come. There were only the Farrells and the Dutch painter (Rembrandt, everyone called him, and my God, weren't his paintings awful!) and an old English lady with a houseful of cats – and now every second house had a painter or a writer or a millionaire, or a beatnik who wanted to be any of these in it, and there were two restaurants where before there had been none, and there was a pavilion on the beach and all the Greeks spoke English. Well, the dozen words they needed to sell their wares. A dozen words of Italian and Swedish and German and French. The international gibberish of the merchants of Europe.

'Max! Welcome back!'

Toby, who was from California, a painter with a small talent and the right connections and a taste for whisky but a nice guy, slapped him on the back.

'How long are you staying this time?'

'Who knows, who knows?' Max said. 'Maybe for ever.'

'It's the same old Max,' Toby said. 'Listen, come around. Say, six? Have a drink.'

'Sure,' Max said. 'Look, I must go up to the house. See if it's still there.'

'See you,' Toby said.

Max paid a woman to look after his house while he was away. She opened the windows and dusted and when he cabled that he was coming back (to the Farrells; they told Ilena) she washed the floors and made up the bed and picked fresh flowers for the vases and the bowls and bought food and filled up the refrigerator. She lived across the street from Max's house, and she was there in her doorway as they came along the street, Larry with both bags, Sylvia still talking, Max trying to listen and not hearing a word.

'Ilena!' he said, seeing her, and embraced her and kissed her on the cheek.

She was an old woman, and shy, and she had nothing to say but her eyes twinkled with delight. How long has she been standing in her doorway waiting for me, with the key in her hand? Max thought. Oh, she's marvellous. Ilena. Ah.

'Larry,' he said, 'give me that bag,' and there, in the street, he opened his bag and took out a tablecloth of the finest lace and blushing for no reason that he knew, he gave it to Ilena and kissed her again.

'*Efharisto, efharisto,*' Ilena said. Her face glowed like the sun, and to hide her embarrassment she made a great business of fitting the key in Max's door and then she stepped aside and they went in first and she quietly followed.

The house was exactly as he had left it, filled with sun and flowers, a bottle of wine and six glasses on a tray on a table on the terrace, the wine cold and the bottle beaded with water, and beside it plates of honey and jam and nuts, sweet things, the traditional greeting.

'Well, you're home,' Sylvia said. 'Again.'

'And let me tell you,' Max said, 'it's great to be back. Home.'

'Home is where your friends are,' Sylvia said, smiling broadly. 'Oh, before I forget, you're having dinner with us tonight, okay?'

'Well, yes,' Max said. 'But to tell you the truth . . . '

'Sylvia,' Larry said. 'Come on, let's go. I'm sure Max wants to relax by himself for a while.'

'Oh, no, no,' Max said. 'Please. Have a glass of wine. I'm not tired or anything. Hell, a seasoned traveller like me.'

'No, Larry's right,' Sylvia said. 'You do look a bit drawn and quartered.'

'*Sylvia,*' Larry said.

'I know, I know,' Sylvia said. 'I'm going right home to read my Book of Etiquette. But dinner, Max, if you can. About eight?'

'Eight,' Max said.

Alone, he sat down on the terrace and lit a cigarette but after two puffs he threw it away. He stood up. The sun was high in the sky and a white yacht was anchored in the very centre of the bay and there was a blue flag flying from it. Max took off his jacket. Suddenly he felt very tired, a wave of tiredness he was completely unused to, and he closed his eyes and stood for a minute just like that, not thinking anything, just slightly rocking on the balls of his feet.

Hey, boy, what's wrong with you? he asked himself.

He left his jacket on the terrace and went through the lounge into the bedroom and sat down on the edge of the bed and, hardly able to keep his eyes open, he pulled off his shoes, then remembered his hat and took it off and let it drop on to the floor, and a minute later, in his clothes, he was asleep.

He slept for six hours and when he awoke it was night and quiet and he felt an enormous sense of peace, a peace so total, so complete – and then it was gone. He became aware of the wooden beams on the ceiling, the top corner of a wardrobe, the curtains by the sides of the window billowing in a breeze. And for a second he panicked, and then he knew where he was. He switched on the lamp by his bed. He sat up. A rooster was crowing madly in the night. For a minute his head spun with a hundred things, not one of which he could put his finger on, and then he remembered that he was supposed to be eating with Sylvia and Larry tonight – and drinks with Toby at six – but he knew it was too late even before he had looked at his watch. He lay back on his bed. He didn't feel particularly hungry. He'd see what Ilena had put in the fridge later on.

A moment of peace, a second of panic – it was like that every time he woke up, all that week, and the next, and the week after that. For a few seconds, before he was properly awake, he was somewhere else, in great peace, but where? Peter Stein's in Paris? Prague? And of course it was so simple but it took him nearly a month before he pinned it down.

Each night when he went to bed, after a day of gossip, reading, sitting in the sun, drinking, talking, he thought about those seconds of peace he would feel when he woke up, and when those seconds came, each morning, oh so short, he tried to prolong them, to suspend himself in them, so he could examine them, but each morning they lasted just two seconds, three, never more. As soon as he became aware of that great peace, before he had even opened his eyes, it was gone, and in its place, blind panic. Then nothing.

In the fifth week it came to him, so simple, so obvious. For two seconds, every morning, he was in his father's house, twenty-five years ago, in his room at the end of the house that looked out on the garden and the fruit trees, New England sky, birds in the trees, the first birds of the day, and the house silent with his parents sleeping. Home. That room he had known so well, photographed on his brain. The ceiling sloping, timber, sixteen planks, and twenty planks on one wall and fourteen on the other wall, and the yellow door. Now, he could still see the lamp, his books, his clothes on a chair, the view from his window, the tops of the trees, bare in winter and in summer green and full. And then his mother getting up and walking in her soft slippers down the hall to put on the coffee for breakfast. While his father still slept.

Home.

Then they went to New York and for a while they lived in Chicago, and then his father went to Rome for a year and they went with him, and they holidayed that year in Venice, in rooms filled with the smell of the sea. Old rooms, yellow plaster, ornate on the ceilings, chandeliers, tiled floors, marble, cold to walk on, cracked.

Then three apartments in New York, each time richer, larger, and then his father's heart attack, and his mother's small apartment, but he didn't move in with her. For various reasons. Beginning and ending with the feeling that she didn't want him to.

The next morning when he awoke, those seconds of being home, that peace, were not there. *Not there.* Nor were they the next morning, nor the morning after that, nor after that, and not for the next ten days, and on the fourteenth day Max awoke with a great and sudden urge to see a friend in Copenhagen, oh that lovely city, so human, so minutely detailed, the ivy growing on the walls and the pigeons waddling unafraid under your feet in the squares.

He left immediately. There was a plane going to Athens at two, and he phoned and booked a seat. Then he saw Ilena and told her he was flying off again (he laughed and shrugged his shoulders) but would be back soon, as always, he always came back, and then he saw Larry and Sylvia and Toby and a few other friends, and at twelve he was in a cab and on his way to the airport.

He got there in plenty of time, and after the passport formalities he stood with his bags one on either side of him, and lit a cigarette and watched the mechanics refuelling the plane. Then he checked his bags and sat out in the sun with a cup of coffee and waited for two o'clock.

There were less than twenty people flying to Athens, and Max was the first on board. The air inside smelt stale and of plastic and synthetics and the seats looked tired. He moved down the aisle, looking for his seat. It was by a porthole. He put his hat up on the overhead rack and sat back, and all at once he felt relaxed and completely at ease, in this shoddy, soiled, stale, winged metal tube, which was throbbing and the props turning and the light on saying Fasten your seat belts please, and he did, and here, on the way to Athens, on the way to Copenhagen, to Paris, to London, on the way to anywhere at all, he felt, at last, completely at home.

The Day the Bottom Fell Out of Yugoslavia

♦ *The Day the Bottom Fell Out of Yugoslavia*

♦

♦ Every time I cross a border, my usually calm, sane, logical, honest mind changes into an IBM machine. It ticks, whirrs, buzzes, calculates, balances, measures, weighs, while the Customs ask me the usual questions and I answer like a parrot. Whisky? Two hundred bottles. Cigarettes? One. Cameras? Tape recorders? Ammunition, matches, livestock, pets? No, no, no, no, no, no. No? They let me pass. I am harmless. I cross into the new country and pull over to the side of the road. The cells of my brain are tumbling like a wire barrel of monkeys. *I'm working out money.* I start with dollars. I throw them into sterling. I click them into Australian pounds. I change gears and reverse into the last currency, lights blazing. I throw out a signal to Hong Kong. I remember Port Said. And finally it's done. I can usually manage it on five sheets of paper, using two pencils and my leaky pen, in eight minutes flat. Then I buy a beer.

I came from Greece to Yugoslavia on a Friday afternoon. I made my calculation. I noted prices. My fears flew away on the wings of the rate of exchange. I was suddenly loaded. I drove towards Belgrade, inflated with buying power, singing opera at the top of my voice.

The country was beautiful, almost like springtime Switzerland, with wide brown rivers and the road tunnelling under the mountains. I raced a steam train. I passed farmers driving loads of hay, their wagons decorated with painted flowers and horses and scenes of the hunt. I stopped and photographed them and told them I was an Australian and we smoked cigarettes by the side of the road.

I slept that night under a tree in a field, by a quacky, green village. A farmer's wife sold me milk. The price was ludicrously low. I offered her more but she wouldn't take it. She waved me happily on my way.

It was three o'clock when I got to a town called Nis. Everyone was promenading, and I followed the crowd. We crossed over a brown river and passed through a pair of massive gates and I found myself in an old Turkish fortress, now a park. People were drinking beer and eating ice cream at small tables. Everyone was dressed in his Saturday best. Lovers strolled arm in arm. Soldiers strolled in groups. Children ran about, playing. I decided to spend an hour or two, stretching my legs, strolling, breathing the fresh air of this town.

Then I came to a long, old building with many doors. One of them was open. There was a poster advertising an art exhibition next to it. I went down three steps under an arch into the foyer of the room.

There were two girls sitting at a table.

'Is it free to come in?' I asked.

They looked at each other.

I pointed to myself and then I pointed to the gallery (which seemed, from where we were, cavernous and dark) and then I made signs of walking and then I lifted my eyebrows up in a big question. Yes, yes, yes, they smiled and nodded, and, putting on my best gallery manner (hands behind back, feet at right angles to one another, head angled forward like a crane), I went to the first picture.

The top of my head blew off. It was just this side of magnificent. Or maybe the other side. I blinked, trying to clear my mind of countless Bruegels and ad-infinitum Van Goghs and Rembrandts without number and the soundless explosion of Baroque space in a dozen palaces and galleries where footsteps sounded apologetic and no one coughed, I shook my head free of a hundred Greek athletes and their flawless, blank-eyed stare, and I looked again. It was like Turner. It was more than Turner. It was a painting in an impossible-to-capture green, lit up with its own sun, a fabulous city, a legendary place, a myth, a vision. It was dated 1965. I couldn't read the painter's name. The painting was fantastic. Shattered, I moved on to the next.

It was terrible. It was the kind of painting I used to do around the time my father discovered the word bum. It was tired, it was murky, it was corny. I felt instantly happy. The Yugoslavs had no right blasting me out of my senses with a fabulous painting. Who were they, anyhow? How come I'd never heard of them? Why did my *Concise History of Art* not give them even a passing nod, if they were so good?

And then the next painting lifted me six feet off the ground. It was the same green, the same sun, the same light, the same impossible sky, right there before my eyes.

Now I forgot all about my pose and my poise and my gallery manner and I ran around the gallery like a dog let off its lead. Half the paintings were worse than awful, but the others – ! I didn't know which one to look at first. I stood in front of one and craned my head to look at another. I ran over to it. I spun around. I twisted. I sweated. And then I noticed that a girl was standing next to me, smiling.

She was one of the girls who had been sitting at the door.

'Good?' she said.

'They're wonderful,' I said, forgetting all rules of bartering and trade. 'They're really marvellous.'

Her smile showed that she understood. In fact, she seemed ecstatic that I liked them. She clapped her hands together. She kept touching me on the arm and saying, 'Good, good.' She was past thirty, in a dark-blue polka dot dress, and, but for her wedding ring, looked to me like those girls past thirty who throw themselves on young men. Her friend, who was young and beautiful, was still at the table.

I cleared my throat. I became deadly serious. All eagerness (I hoped) went out of my eyes.

'Are – these – paintings – for – sale?' I asked. 'I – would – like – that – is – I – would – like – to – *inquire* – about – the – price – of – certain – of – them?'

Berlitz would have shot me. The girl gave me a blank look. Her mouth and her eyebrows said, What? I don't understand.

'Look,' I said, and took out my folder of traveller's cheques (not an easy task; I wear them wrapped around my handkerchief, weighted down with keys, in the thief-proof bottom of my bottomless trouser pocket). 'How – much – *money* – are – these – paintings?'

She took my traveller's cheques and looked at them.

'Pounds,' I said. 'Pounds *sterling*.'

'English?'

'Yes. Actually, they're not money, that is, they are, but, well, they're *better* than money, because you can't *lose them*, well, you can, but if you do – '

I tried to convey that picture in the advertisements of a traveller's cheque happily ablaze ('Try this test!') and no one overly concerned.

'English?' she said.

I nodded yes. She ran back to her table and then came to me (submerged in that limpid green, happily drowning) with a pen and a piece of paper already covered with figures.

'Yugoslav. Dinars.' She drew a circle around a figure, the price of the painting. My IBM machine started whirring.

'May I?' I took the paper and the pen and in a minute had scribbled fifty figures of my own. Then I looked at the girl and pointed to her figure and then to the painting before which we were standing, and she nodded yes, and then I turned the piece of paper over and calculated it all again, but the figure was still the same. Ten pounds. *Sterling!* Nothing at all!

'I – would – like – to – buy – *two*,' I said, pointing to myself, then to two paintings, then to my traveller's cheques. She took the paper and wrote another figure, but my mind was already away. *In the private collection of,* a small brass plaque flashed inside my head. I could hear people knocking on the door of my home. I could see my name in italics in all the good books.

The girl handed me back the paper. Two paintings cost twenty pounds!

Without words, I said, Don't bother wrapping them up, I'll just take them off the walls just as they are, I'll slip them under my Greek jumper and warm them with my Greek tan and quietly tiptoe out, ta ta, thank *you*, but the girl seemed to be nodding no.

'What?' I said.

'Sunday,' she said. She took my hand and showed me ten o'clock on my watch. 'Painter, here, Sunday, you,' she said.

Desperate now, I rummaged in the back of my brain and brought up some old schooldays' German. She countered with broken French. Her friend joined us. Somehow we seemed to get across. I was to come back on Sunday morning and the painter would be there and we would discuss the business of the paintings then. Did he, the painter, speak English? No. Did he speak German? No. Did I speak Russian? No. Did I have any special plans for the evening? Well, no. Would I like one of the girls to walk around with me and show me Nis? Certainly, yes! I got the wrong girl, I got the one who was past thirty with the polka dots and the wedding ring and the way of always touching me on the arm, while the other one, the lovely one, the one with the dark hair and the deep eyes, went back to her table. Why is it always like this with me?

'My name, Anna,' the past-thirty girl said, and I told her my name, and then we stepped out into late-afternoon Nis.

We sat at a small sidewalk café and ate ice cream. Anna asked would I like to go to a film.

'In English?' I asked. In Athens I had sat through a French film with Greek subtitles and I wasn't going to do that again.

'Sure,' Anna said. 'English.'

The film was a bad Robert Mitchum movie I had seen five years ago, and the people were queueing and pushing in the street and there were no more seats left. It had started to rain. I pretended to be disappointed.

'Will you eat with me?' I asked Anna. I mimed a knife, a fork, a wide-open mouth, an upended glass.

While we ate, my IBM was ticking over and over, clicking and double-checking, and every time I consciously turned it off, that green, those paintings, those fabulous cities, flooded my brain.

'How – much – is – this – car?' I asked Anna, pointing to a Fiat and taking out the pen, the paper, the traveller's cheques. She calculated. I fell off my chair.

Two hundred pounds!

'For you, not so much,' she said. 'Is big tax.'

It was incredible. I asked about everything.

'How – much – does – a – doctor – earn? A – *doctor*?'

Two pounds!

We walked in the street. I stopped in front of a shop and pointed to a pair of beautiful, handwoven leather shoes.

'How – much – are – these – *shoes*?'

One pound!

When finally I fell asleep that night I was a multi-billionaire and I dreamt about gold and yachts and a villa by the sea and my father in a white silk suit and a long flight of marble steps with me at the top, fanned by slaves, in a mist of Havana smoke, my feet never touching the ground.

I was up at eight and I walked twice round the walls of the old Turkish fortress, just to make sure it didn't go away. At nine I bought coffee and hot rolls and smoked a cigarette. At ten, on the dot, I was at the gallery, as nonchalant as nonchalant can be.

Two painters were there, the bad and the wonderful. I shook hands with them both. The bad was a large thick-set man with grey hair brushed back at the sides and a double-breasted suit. He looked like a Mexican banker. I found it slightly embarrassing to have him there, because it wasn't his paintings I wanted to buy.

The wonderful painter was called Dragon. (His surname, I'm afraid, has disappeared.) He had black hair and dark, soft eyes and was wearing a soft brown suit and a white shirt open at the throat. His hand, when I shook it, was frail and warm. (The bad painter's had been as solid as a plaster cast.) His smile was modest and reserved.

We sat down amongst the paintings, smiling at each other, offering each other cigarettes, while Anna ran out and came

back with beer and *slivovitz* and biscuits and cakes. We sprea
them out on another chair. We toasted each other, we drank an
we ate. I told them I wasn't a painter. I was going to England.
drew a map. I had come from Greece. I drew a map. I wa
Australian. I drew a map. What was I going to do in England?
shrugged. We smiled, and drank more beer and more *slivovit*
and ate more cakes and more biscuits.

Then we walked round and looked at the paintings. I tol
Dragon which ones I wanted to buy. He showed me the ones h
liked, and, as is often the case when a painter shows you his ow
work, they were the least interesting ones. I kept changing m
mind and saying I wanted this one, no, this one, well, maybe tha
one, and each time I would change my mind Dragon would lowe
his eyes, like a bashful child. I somehow managed to convey t
him my gallery-going odyssey, the paintings I had seen, th
galleries I had visited all over Europe, and that I liked hi
paintings, loved them! best of all. The bad painter kept noddin
his head.

I told Dragon that I wanted to get to Belgrade before dark, bu
he said, no, no, I must come to his house, I must meet his wif
and see his children, I must eat with them, I must drink mor
slivovitz and we must talk.

'You don't want me now,' Anna said, and I said, 'Don't b
silly,' and the four of us squeezed into my car and we drove t
Dragon's house.

Dragon lived on the fourth floor of a large new block o
apartments. The stairwell smelt of paint and wet plaster. Ther
were no numbers on the doors. And there was no lift. My hea
was heavy with *slivovitz* and Dragon kept pointing to the floo
above and we were all laughing as we trudged up the stairs.

His wife was beautiful. She had the whitest skin, and her hai
was red and brown and fell over her shoulders. She gave me a
mannish handshake. We tumbled inside.

In the manner of all wives, she apologized for the state of he
house, nodding her head, excuse me, excuse me, it is Sunday
morning, I did not know, ushering us along the hallway and into
the lounge and sitting us down, that is, sitting me down, putting
me on the sofa and bringing me a cushion, is this enough? giving

me another, while I kept smiling my *slivovitz* smile and blazing my Greek tan all round the room. Before I was properly sitting, Dragon had brought out a blue china pot and a half-dozen cups, tiny things, and began to pour. It was *slivovitz*, of course. The first cupful disappeared inside me. Immediately my cup was refilled. A beer was put into my other hand. The Mexican banker painter offered me a Yugoslavian cigarette. Anna touched me on the arm.

Dragon's wife brought in the children to look at the man who was buying the paintings. They were in their pyjamas. The boy hid behind a chair. The girl was like a marble doll with rouged cheeks. She was still asleep.

Dragon sat down cross-legged on the floor and then immediately got up and ran out of the room. He came back with an enormous canvas. It was a fine abstract. Then he ran out again and brought in another. He ran out five times and the room was filled with paintings, propped against the chairs, the table, the walls, all abstracts. They were the work of his students. Two of them were wonderful.

'Good?' Anna kept asking me and touching me on the arm. I kept my eyes riveted on her wedding ring. She wouldn't stop smiling at me.

Then Dragon got out his books of art, his prints, and we leafed through them. We said Good to the good ones, No to the others, agreeing on practically everything. Picasso? *Very good*. Matisse? Well, sometimes good. Then he turned a page and there was a Turner burning barge. I waited. Dragon said, '*Very good*,' and I was as happy as I've ever been. I told Dragon that *he* was like Turner, *he* was just as wonderful, *he* understood about light the way Turner did. Down went his eyes in that modest look. The bad painter quietly nodded his head, acknowledging his position in the presence of the great. Dragon proudly refilled my tiny blue cup.

Then we ate. We ate leisurely and happily. There were new potatoes and chicken livers in a sauce and a crisp salad and a hot pudding with ice cream, deliciously cold. The coffee was strong and fragrant. I sneaked a look at my watch. It was three o'clock.

'Oh, I must go,' I said. 'I must get to Belgrade before dark.' Everyone looked at me. I took out my folder of traveller's cheques. Dragon's wife cleared away the dishes. I took out my pen and paper. The little marble girl was playing with her pudding. Dragon sat her on his lap. I began to explain what wanted to do.

I would come back to Yugoslavia in four months' time, on my way back to Greece. I would pay him now. I explained again about traveller's cheques, how they worked. Dragon had never seen them before. I told him that he could exchange them for the currency of any country he was in. He could change them for dollars or pounds or francs.

'I will go to Paris,' he told me. 'In the spring.'

'You haven't been to Paris?'

'No,' he said. 'From Yugoslavia it is very difficult to go. It is hard to get money to go.'

I could see him in Paris, and the excitement his paintings would cause, and greedily, I couldn't help thinking how the paintings in my possession would soar in value and worth.

I passed him the paper and pen. I asked him to write down the exact price of the paintings I wanted.

He wrote down a figure. I looked at it. There was something wrong.

My IBM equipment digested it, spewed up the result, sucked it back again for a recheck, but all the time I knew it was no good. Doctors didn't earn two pounds in Yugoslavia. Shoes cost more than a pound. Cars were astronomically expensive.

'Oh,' I said to Dragon, and to Anna, and to the bad painter. 'We made a mistake.'

It was a simple mistake. A decimal point. The paintings were a hundred pounds each.

I wrote on the paper and showed them the mistake. I showed them again. I pointed to Anna. Dragon didn't understand.

I felt gritty and dirty. I crossed off a nought and pointed to Anna. She looked terrible. She wouldn't look at me. I looked at Dragon's soft eyes and I disappeared inside them. I could see his spring in Paris fading away like a dream. I wanted to be a hundred miles away, to have never seen those paintings, to have never met these people. The bad painter was as silent as a rock. I wanted to give Dragon all my money, to take off my watch and throw it on the table before him, to give him my cufflinks, my tie pin, but it was no good, and we all knew it. The sun had gone out of the afternoon.

I explained again how much money I had and how much I had thought the paintings to be, and how I could not buy them. I covered four sheets of paper with my apologies. Dragon asked did I want the paintings cheaper, and I said no. They were worth more than a hundred pounds and I had been foolish and I couldn't pay even that. I put my traveller's cheques back in my pocket, like a thief, and stood up.

Dragon and his wife and the two children and Anna and the bad painter all waved as I went down the stairs, but it was a sad wave, and for all my smiling and theirs, I tried to look as though I wasn't running away. I had taken away something from Dragon that I had had no right to do, and there was nothing I could say that would restore it.

I drove through Nis and across the brown river to the gates of the Turkish fortress. I wanted to look one last time at Dragon's paintings, but the gates were locked, and I got back in my car and drove to Belgrade, hard, not taking my eyes off the road, not singing a word.

I am writing this in Copenhagen. It is summer. Rain is falling. The slate roofs across the courtyard from my room are wet and shiny, and the blinds on all the windows are drawn. The ivy on the houses and the lawns in front of the churches are green, but it is not the same green, not the right green, not Dragon's green.

Next to me is a newspaper which says that the dinar has taken a calculated tumble. Yugoslavia is now twenty-five per cent cheaper. *Slivovitz* is five shillings a bottle. Dubrovnik is lovely in the spring. Bled is unforgettable. A hundred pounds sterling is now eighty. My IBM goes click, click.

I will be there before you.

◆ A King of the Road

◆

◆ You can lead a horse to water, but you can't make my father buy a car. Master psychologists have tried. For example, my mother. 'Abe, let's buy a car,' she says. 'I don't need it,' my father says. 'What for?' And he takes down our perfectly all right toaster from its shelf and gets busy on it with the small screwdriver which he always carries, and at such moments, when he's fixing, no one talks to him.

We move forward a month. Picture a spring night, a star-crammed sky, a black Pontiac stopping at our front gate. My father gets out first, then my mother. My mother tells Uncle Sam for the twentieth time to thank Tzila for the wonderful supper, really, she shouldn't have gone to all that trouble, and then, catching up with my father, who already has his key in the front door lock, she says, 'See how it is when you have a car? Right to the door.' 'A nice lift,' my father says.

How long does the water-on-stone treatment take? I lie in my bed and listen to it happening, drip, drip, at the other end of the passage, in my parents' bed. A month, two? Time doesn't mean anything. Occasionally I hear a loud 'No!' and from its violence I know that things are about to happen.

And they do. One Sunday morning, when I have stewed in my bed past the point of pleasure, I get up and my father is not at home. 'Where's dad?' I ask my mother. For every Sunday for as long as I can remember, my father has been out in the garden, either mowing a lawn or pulling up weeds or just standing and thinking about one of those two. 'Don't bother me, can't you see I'm busy,' my mother says. She has taken out all the cutlery and is lining the drawers with new white paper, a thing which she does only for *pesach*, or if someone spills something in a drawer, but never at any other time. No answer. I make a breakfast. An hour later my father comes in, looking flushed. 'Well?' my mother asks. 'I don't need a car!' my father says. 'What for?' The driving lessons have begun.

The next Sunday I am awake at seven, dressed in five minutes, sitting on my bed and then standing up and then sitting down again, a thousand times, waiting for my father to go out and begin his lesson. I hear a car toot. My father is in the kitchen, drinking tea, and I hear the cup fall from his hands, with an enormous sound, as though every piece of china in our kitchen has been broken, and then I hear him moving quickly down the passage, fumbling with the front door, the door slamming, and then my father's steps running down the path. I am out, also running, but quietly, and from the front room window, concealed behind the drawn blind, I see everything.

There is a short, bald man sitting at the wheel of a large green car. He sees my father. He slides over on the seat, leans over and opens the door, and my father gets in. They talk for a long time, the man pointing, my father nodding. Then the car starts. My father's face is a study of concentration and terror. He looks at the bald man. The man points to something. My father does something with his hands, then puts them both on the wheel, high up, and I see – or feel – how white his knuckles are. Then the car begins to move.

It shoots forward, stops, bounces, seems to come back, then forward again, up into the air, over to one side, and I hide my face. And when next I look, the street in front of our house is empty.

I run outside, forgetting all caution, all stealth. And I am just in time. The green car is at the very end of our street, where it meets the main road, and it's not moving. I watch it, and it seems to stand there for ever, hours, while my heart waits too. Then suddenly it is gone, as though wires have jerked it round the corner, and I breathe out.

I don't bother to wait around to see my father drive back. Everyone has difficulties at the beginning, I rationalize, it's only natural, after all. But something has died inside me. When he comes back from his lesson I am mowing the lawn and frightened to look him in the eye. I mow like a madman, front *and* back, and then I start on the weeds, and the only thing that stops me finishing them is my mother calling me in to lunch. Never again do I go out to see the lesson begin, not once.

Once again time has no meaning. Months pass, one after another, and it is as though my father has always gone for driving lessons on a Sunday morning, I can't remember a time when he didn't. And when my Uncle Sam drops around and says to my father, 'So, you're taking the lessons, uh?' and slaps my father on the shoulder, I leave the room.

Naturally, it's me who brings in the letter with the picture-window envelope and my father's name typed inside. 'Ah,' says my father, getting his toaster-fixing hands to it as though it was the last *latke* in the world, while I feign indifference. But at the dinner table I am spared nothing. The talk is all of licences, only of licences, and this licence, my father's, is held up and waved and shown and finally my father lets it out of his hand for just a few seconds and lets me hold it. 'Nu, scholar,' he says, 'can you read it?' and snatches it away before I have even had a chance to focus. 'You know how long it took Max Lazarus to get this, this piece of paper? Nu? Ten months! Ha! And about his wife I'm not even going to mention.' While my mother, the master psychologist, serves the soup and says not a word.

Now the talking in bed starts again, the soft voices in the dark, the whispers, and then the loud 'No!' while I lie in bed and strain for details. But this time there is no secrecy.

My father announces, the next night, that he is going to buy a car, he has decided, even the colour he knows. Blue, in two shades, the lighter one on the top, like the Finkelsteins have. Well, not exactly like the Finkelsteins have, theirs is the old model, already out of date. 'Tomorrow I put down my name,' he says, looking already a good three feet taller than he actually is. 'Eight months,' he says to me. 'For such a car, you have to wait eight months. Don't worry, I'll get it in six.'

Once again I lose track of the time, but as the months creep past, and speed, and lunge forward, and relentlessly advance, I keep surprising my father, sitting all alone in the front room with the light off, his licence held in both hands, his eyes riveted to it. 'Oh, I'm sorry,' I say, having switched on the light, 'I didn't know you were . . . I wanted to hear something on the radio.' 'I don't want the radio!' my father shouts, and stands up and lunges out of the room, putting the licence away quickly inside his wallet, pushing the wallet down deep inside his trouser pocket, then standing in the passage, not knowing where to go.

This happens again and again, maybe four times. As the time for the car's arrival draws near, my father grows more and more quiet. To speak to him is at your own risk. Even my mother, that master psychologist, can't draw near. 'Abe, maybe you should have a few more lessons, to brush up,' she says. 'You know, to get the feel.' 'No!' my father shouts, and it is only his iron will that keeps him from taking out his licence at the table and staring at it.

Then one night, a Thursday, the phone rings. My mother answers. I hear her talking for a half minute, and then she says, 'Just a minute, I'll get him,' and then she calls out, 'Abe, for you! The car!'

My father scrambles to his feet and his face is flushed and ashen at the same time. He holds the telephone receiver as I saw him holding the wheel of the green car for his second lesson. 'Hello?' he says, in a voice I have never heard him use before. 'Tomorrow? All right. I'll – yes . . . ' and the phone falls from his fingers.

'Tomorrow,' he says to my mother, who is standing a foot away, about six inches from me.

'Well, ring up Sam and tell him to go with you,' my mother says.

'I don't need Sam,' my father says. 'I can drive.'

'The city traffic, Abe,' my mother says, and my father says, 'You call him.'

My mother dials, and gets, of course, Aunt Tzila, who is always first to the phone. 'Tzila?' she says, 'the car has arrived. What? Yes, we just heard, now on the telephone, they rang us up, it's ready.' 'Nu?' says my father, suddenly impatient. 'C'mon, let me speak.' And he takes the receiver out of my mother's hand while she is in the middle of a word, explaining that it is a two shades of blue car, like the Finkelsteins', but, naturally, a new model –

'Tzila?' my father says. 'Thank you, thank you. Naah, I'm not excited, what's a car? It's a machine, that's all. Yes, a blue, two shades, that's what I ordered. Blue is a good colour, you don't have to wash it so much. Ha ha, yeah . . . Listen, is Sam there?'

There is a pause for some seconds while Aunt Tzila calls out to Sam that he's wanted on the phone, it's the car, it's arrived, a blue one, two shades.

'Hello, Sam,' my father says. 'Listen . . . yeah, tomorrow. Listen, Sam, maybe it would be a good idea if . . . ah! There? In the showroom? Four o'clock. Come a bit earlier, so we can . . . Four o'clock? Nu, good. What? Just a minute, I'll put her back on, she's standing right here. Four o'clock, all right?'

And he gives the phone back to my mother, so she can speak some more with Aunt Tzila, and then, unable to employ his iron will a second longer, he plunges his hand into his pocket, draws out the wallet, with loving care unfolds the licence from its place inside, and studies it, really studies it, until he looks up and sees me watching him. 'You haven't got any lessons?' he shouts at me, and I flee to the sanity of my room.

Four o'clock the following afternoon I am already standing outside our house, waiting. And so is everyone else in our street. Somehow the word has spread. All the street is in their gardens, or standing and talking, looking nonchalant, but I know what they're waiting to see. Even Mr Pinter, who hasn't spoken to my father in four years, after some difference of opinion which time has long obliterated, is there.

Only my mother won't come outside. 'I'll come, I'll come,' she says to me, but she stays inside.

It is half past four. The street is still empty of the car. Now, if anything, there are more people than ever, and their nonchalance has gone. For all their talking and occasionally laughing, I can feel an electric tension in the street. In just a few minutes, a second, one beat of my heart . . .

And then the car appears.

We see it turning slowly into the street, two shades of blue, my father at the wheel. It makes an elaborate turn, and then pauses, and begins again. The street is quiet.

'Mum!' I call out, but she is already there, by my side.

'*He's* driving,' my mother says. 'Why isn't Sam driving?'

But it is my father at the wheel. Sam is sitting next to him, a separate shape.

'Mum,' don't worry,' I say, or shout, or something, running out into the street, then back on to the nature strip, then out into the street again.

The car comes closer. It is moving as quietly as a stream of oil, as slowly as a dream. Now it is close enough for me to see my father's face. It is like a tomato, the sun, beaming, shining, bursting, and his smile is enormous. I have never seen my father look so radiant, like a king on the field of battle when the enemy has fled.

My father smiles to everyone, on both sides of the street, as he drives his brand-new car. He smiles to Mr Pinter, who shrinks, to the two ladies at number twelve, to the Obers, the Winters, to all. And then I see Uncle Sam lean over and say something to him and point at something inside the car and my father looks down for a second and does something with his hand and then looks up again, his face serious now for a second, though still bright red, and then the smile comes back, and now he is almost at our house and beginning to turn – our gates are open, the garage yawns wide – and his smile is still enormous and in this fashion my father drives into our fence.

'Oh!' gasps my mother, inside her throat.

The car shakes, shudders, stops. A door flies open. My Uncle Sam is out. 'Nothing, nothing,' he says, and he is running to the front of the car, bending to see what has happened, looking up at my mother, then back to the front of the car, then at my father, who hasn't moved. He sits, his hands still on the wheel, the colour draining out of him, like a stone.

'My God!' says my mother, a hand to her heart.

'Don't worry, don't worry,' Uncle Sam says, and he runs around behind the car and comes up and opens the door on my father's side.

'I'll fix it,' he says. Like a stone, my father gets out.

Now, expertly, in a flurry of gears, looking at no one and at everyone, craning his neck to see behind him, sitting up straight, moving like a machine, he shoots the car back, corrects its angle, and whips it up our drive and into the garage.

I run to see what has happened. My mother is a step behind me. My father stands on the nature strip, not moving.

Uncle Sam is out of the car, the keys in his hand. He has a kind of smile on his face. 'Ah, it's – ' he starts to say, but we push past him and rush to the front of the car and stare at it.

There is a dent in the front bumper about the size of a pea.

'My God!' says my mother, again and again, over and over, shaking from side to side, as the old Mrs Fisher does on Yom Kippur, totally immersed in her prayers.

Uncle Sam stands with the keys in his hand and doesn't know what to do. He begins to say something, 'Ah, believe me, *my* first car, you should have seen how – '

He stops. No one is listening to him. My father has come up the drive and is standing next to him, looking at the car but not going around to see the front of it.

'The fence is all right,' he says.

Finally my mother is persuaded to come inside, what's the point of standing here? 'I'll have a cup of tea,' Uncle Sam says, smacking his hands together, smiling, but no one is fooled. I am sent to close the front gates.

My mother makes the tea and Uncle Sam tells us all, at least three times, how it was with his first car, why, this is nothing, not even an accident. And my father drinks his tea and doesn't say a word. Nor does my mother. Both my parents are deep inside themselves.

When Uncle Sam has gone – 'Don't worry, Abe,' patting my father on the arm – my mother suddenly comes alive. 'Go in your room. It's enough for one day,' she says to me, and she closes the kitchen door and – but I'm not sure about this – locks it.

Then I hear their voices, now loud, now soft, and then my mother opens the door and goes to the telephone, closing another door so I can't hear what she's saying, and then when she has finished there she calls me to come out.

We eat in total silence, not a word. When we are drinking our tea, my father says, 'I'm selling the car,' and then picks up his cup and ends the matter with a loud sip of his tea.

The next morning, before eight, two men come and take away the car. I watch them signing papers, and then they hand my father a cheque, and he puts it inside his wallet and shakes their hands and goes out with them to the garage, but that part I don't watch. Who wants to see a brand-new car, two shades of blue, being driven away at eight o'clock on a sad Saturday morning? No one.

By Sunday, my father is already boasting of his fine sense of business. Because there is a waiting list, it seems, and so many people desirous of possessing this model, these people are willing to pay quite a certain amount more than the car actually costs, for the privilege of immediate possession.

'Don't worry about me,' my father says. 'I know how to make a good business. Who needs a car anyhow? What for? You have to wash it, oil it, insure it, what for? What's wrong with the bus? Here, take a look at this cheque, you ever seen such a figure? Uh, scholar?'

And my mother, the master psychologist, smiles and says, 'I'll ring up Tzila. Maybe Sam will take us, we'll go to the beach.'

◆ Fenner

◆

◆ Exactly at midnight Fenner, in pyjamas, bursts out of the house. A light rain is falling. There is no moon. He comes down the back stairs in his gardening boots, feet crashing, laces cracking, then out across the yard, stepping carefully to avoid the puddles, this week's *New Statesman* wedged under his arm, airmail edition, fragile, like an insect's wing, his cigarettes and matches and the tomato-red kitchen alarm clock all somehow clutched with one hand to his body, the other frantic hand closing the gap where his pyjamas gape, catching the wind. Against all reason, on this black night, he is frightened above all else – more than of falling, more than of getting wet, more than of dropping things – of being *seen*, by next-door Alf or snoopy Miss Williamson over the back fence, his vicious neighbours huddled under umbrellas, he imagines, spying, eyes like slits, tut-tutting, nodding their heads. A black tree smacks him with water. The back door slams shut on its spring, with a crack like a cannon. Fenner runs with his pants hoisted high, milky calves bobbing like ghosts in the night.

He drops his glasses. A cat flashes past – that mean cat from two houses down, a neighbourhood spy, sleek with heat. He bends, stumbles, his face wet, detours round a tree, ducks under the washing hanging wet on the line, sad sagging underpants dismally hanging, stretched and shapeless, alongside those of his wife and the endless garments of his children, like a waterlogged carnival, deserted and grey. A burst, a spurt, a final effort, and he's at the garage, panting, by the side door. What now? He has no free hand with which to grab the handle and wind is whistling and rain is dropping down the back of his neck. He juggles the clock, squashes the cigarettes, fumbles with the matches, and somehow seizes the knob. A fast, hard turn to the right. A push. Nothing happens. The door is, of course, swollen in its frame, stuck, and then a great fall of water comes down from the spouting above which is clogged with leaves and probably a tennis ball and drops with unerring accuracy down his thin, cold back. Oh, he moans, absolutely helpless.

Frantically, he rearranges his objects, freeing his other hand, knees tight together to keep his pyjamas up, afraid to turn the knob again. What? His mind is a spinning blank. Desperate now, he closes his eyes, and turns and doesn't care about the gape in the front of his pyjamas and he butts the door backwards with all his strength. Down comes more water from the spouting, the door crashes open, and Fenner flies backwards inside. Down goes the alarm clock, bouncing on the concrete floor.

Then everything goes, the cigarettes, the matches. His pyjama pants slide slowly down his thin, white legs, but Fenner is past caring. For a whole minute he doesn't care about anything at all, not a thing, standing in the dark with his pants down, his mouth open, wind whistling and the *New Statesman*, completely forgotten, still wedged tight under his arm. Made it, he says. Then suddenly, out of nowhere, he has a fear of the night, of the dark, of the black swinging shapes of trees and of someone suddenly stepping out of the dark and grabbing him, and he rushes to the door, insanely, hearing his pants rip, not caring, and slams it shut, shooting the bolt home as fast as he can. Safe! Safe? Heart still pounding, he searches for the light switch, can't find it, *can't*, his hand groping up and down the wall, and then it clicks on. The room lights up, pale yellow. Fenner breathes out.

Well, he says. He turns around. He sees his bed standing in the middle of the room, just where they put it this morning. It is made up ready for sleep, the pillow plumped, one corner of the covers neatly turned back. His slippers are on the floor, peeping out. The yellow garage light dangles over it on its dusty cord. It looks so sad here, so out of place, this half of the bridal pair, so sad it hurts him to look at it, to see it here, in the chaos of the garage, sadder than a mockery, sad beyond words.

He bends down and pulls up his pants. Then he bends down again and picks up his cigarettes, then his matches. He is so weary, standing here, the *New Statesman* forgotten under his arm. He remembers the clock – oh – and even before he looks to see where it is, he can picture the scene when he brings it inside in the morning, broken. It dropped, he will say. How? his wife will ask. How can you drop a clock? How can you let a thing like that go? Oh, Brian. Then she won't say anything, not another word, not a sound, while he sits bent at the table and she puts the inevitable breakfast in front of him, porridge, toast, one egg, tea. Never anything different. Then, quite casually, she will pick up the broken clock and say something about how much it will cost to repair, and where's the money to come from, and the money for the broken clock will suddenly blossom into the money for clothes, and curtains, and God knows what else, while Fenner swallows his breakfast completely without appetite. And then, if she goes on for just one second more, Fenner will rear up from the table, shouting, slapping down his fork, his chair falling over and the baby crying. Can't I eat just one breakfast in peace! he will shout, and stamp out, slamming the door, and storm to the morning train with no breakfast in his stomach, no lunch in his bag. When he comes home there'll be a note. I'm at mother's. Two days later she'll return, and they'll start again.

I'm sorry, I'm sorry, he says, now, his wife so fragile in his mind, and why do we fight all the time? He sits down on the edge of the bed and heaves a great sigh. He blinks, hardly able to keep his eyes open. His bottom lip hangs down like a flap. He hasn't the faintest idea what to do. Then – a miracle! – he hears a ticking, loud and strong, and there by his foot is the red kitchen clock, not a mark on it, not a crack, the hands fixed in a smile at ten past ten. Thank God for that, he says, and bends to retrieve it, the *New Statesman*, still unnoticed, poking up as he bends.

Fenner takes a cigarette from his squashed pack and puts it in his mouth. The sound of the match is enormous and he looks up, half expecting someone to be there, investigating the noise. No one. A cloud of smoke drifts up past the light. He looks down at his boots then lifts his pyjama pants to see if there is mud on them, expecting the worst. There isn't. He sits, too tired to think, staring at the odds and ends piled around the walls of the garage. No car. Newspapers, string, the lawn mower, gardening tools, boxes and boxes of bottles. In one corner, filled with wood, stands the carton the television set came in, three years ago. Nothing ever thrown out. On the bench by the furthest wall stand the tins of paint and congealed brushes left over from the last time they painted the house, Fenner wobbling on the ladder and his wife having to get up and finish the eaves because he'd had enough, there was paint in his hair and he knew he was going to fall down. That was when they had two children. Now the fourth less than a month away and the house needs painting again. Fenner yawns, and his eyes fill with tears. He hasn't slept for three days.

He tried to sleep today, at lunch time, feeling foolish on the train going to school with a blanket over his arm. He ate his dry cheese sandwiches and apple quickly and all alone in his small square office and then sat down in his armchair and put his feet up on his stool and covered himself with his blanket and tried to sleep, but his head kept falling forward with a jerk and each time that happened he woke up. Then, almost in a stupor, he spread newspapers on the linoleum and took off his shoes and undid his trousers and laid himself down, with two volumes of an encyclopaedia for a pillow, and the blanket over him. And he slept. There is no lock on Fenner's office door, and at half past two the headmaster came in because Fenner's class was screaming and throwing books, and he found Fenner there, lying on his back with his mouth wide open and snoring and one black sock poking out from under the blanket with a hole in it, like a cartoonist's symbol of poverty. Fenner! the headmaster shouted, what's the meaning of this? and Fenner, at first not knowing where he was and seeing only this dark shape bending over him, had let fly with his fist and at the same time screamed, jumping to his feet, ready for anything. The headmaster fell back. He is a small man, almost sixty, and has not had violent physical contact with anyone for nearly forty years, and with Fenner lunging at him, he was terrified. But only a fraction as much – though in those first few seconds he had no idea – as Fenner. Oh, said Fenner, and rushed out to quieten his class. Open your atlases! he had commanded, and immediately the class fell silent, and then someone handed him the note. *Psst!* it began. Fenner blushed to the roots of his hair. The class roared.

The beasts, says Fenner.

Last night he had rebelled and made a scene. It can't go on! he had screamed. I'm going mad. Ssh, his wife had whispered. You'll wake the baby. Wake the baby? he had roared. Is it asleep? It's just lying there ready to bawl its lungs out as soon as I get into bed. Brian, please, his wife was near to tears. You can move into the garage tomorrow. We'll put the bed in there. Hah, he had snorted, the garage. Not on your life.

This morning, before the neighbours were up, Fenner and his wife had carried the bed across the yard. The two children ran around them like puppies, and inside the baby cried. Daddy is going in the garage, daddy is going in the garage, daddy is a car, beep beep, honk honk. Stop it! Fenner yelled. Go inside! And they carried the bed in through the big front lift-up door and then Fenner's wife sat down on it, and Fenner felt sorry for her, so large with her pregnancy, her face so without colour in the morning light. He wanted to sit down next to her and tell her everything was going to be all right, to hold her hand, to kiss her cheek. He felt great tenderness for her, achingly so. Instead, unable to find the right words, he had slammed down the door so that the neighbours wouldn't see him in his pyjamas and his wife in her nightie, with the huge swell of her child so obvious, and then gone inside, dressed quickly, and hurried off for the train.

This is absolutely disgraceful, Fenner, the headmaster had

said, afterwards, after school, the headmaster safe behind his massive desk. Explain yourself. It's the baby, sir, Fenner had told him. We've had the doctor, but he said it's best to let him cry. Oh, I'm sorry to hear that, said the headmaster, but he will never forget Fenner lunging at him with his pants open and no shoes.

The baby, the baby! says Fenner. I don't need the baby for an excuse. If he doesn't like the way I – oh, what?

For a minute he hates the headmaster and the mean, spiteful politics of the school, thinking of Gallagher who got that promotion and hasn't got a brain in his head and . . .

But he doesn't want to think about that. He shakes his head. Not knowing what to think about, he suddenly notices the long ash on his cigarette and he looks around, wondering where to butt it. His wife always makes sure that there's an ashtray on the small table on his side of the bed, and he's lost without it. Everything is wrong. The cigarettes he has ground out on the floor of this garage are countless, but his wife swept it clean this morning, while he was at school, and somehow he can't throw a cigarette down on the floor next to the bed where he is going to sleep. He stands up, aware that this is ridiculous, but still he does it, going over to the bench and crushing out the cigarette on a paint tin lid. Now I'll sleep, he thinks, clomping back to his bed in his old gardening boots, the laces trailing on the concrete, and then, for the first time, he feels the *New Statesman* under his arm, doesn't know what it is, and panics. For one hopeless moment he thinks that it is a huge bat that has attacked him in the side, flown down from the roof, a maddened thing, and he almost screams, slapping at it wildly, and then he realizes what it is. He gives a small laugh and takes it out from under his arm, battered. He sits down on the bed and smoothes out the pages. The habit of reading. He turns the first page.

But his eyes refuse to focus and anyhow he always reads by the light of the lamp on the small table next to his bed, his wife usually already asleep, her back curved and turned away. Sometimes, while he reads, she turns, her feet touch his, and all the warmth she has held cradled against her body flows out and touches him, and then, usually, he puts his paper down, or his book, and reaches up and turns off the light and slips down under the covers and sometimes his wife, even though asleep, sneaks her arm around him and holds him close and maybe, maybe, she is not completely asleep at all, but waiting for him, now, with all the children asleep and not a sound in the house, not a sound anywhere.

Brian, he hears his wife say.

He lets the paper drop. He sits for a while, not thinking about anything, shoulders sloping, back bent. Then he blinks and sees himself sitting there and winces, somehow ashamed. And at once that makes him think of the letter from Mark that came this morning from San Francisco, five wild pages scrawled in Magic Marker, bright red – Mark! Mark Stevens. They sat next to each other in school and then Mark sailed for Tahiti to become a painter, head filled with Gauguin and images of tropical sun, wildly excited on the ship when Fenner went to see him off, Mark shouting drinks for everyone and throwing streamers as the ship sailed away. And when the letter came from San Francisco this morning, with the baby crying and his wife looking so pale, somehow Fenner couldn't show it to her, couldn't let her read how Mark had sold four paintings and was thinking of going down to Mexico for the winter and had just got a commission to illustrate a book and there was a drawing in bright red Magic Marker of the house he was living in, on the side of a hill, and three quick drawings of cats, which Mark always loved. He just couldn't show it to his wife, and slipped it into his pocket and didn't say a word. But when he came home from school he got down the old school magazines and there was Mark sitting next to him in the photograph of the class, his hair standing up at the back and his teeth flashing white, and there next to him was he, smiling like a fool.

Why don't you come? Mark had asked. Jesus, you'll have a ball.

What'll I do there? Fenner had asked. I don't paint.

Just wait'll you get out there, you'll see, Mark said.

No, no . . . Fenner had said. I don't think so.

He thinks about that for a minute, the ship, Mark's wild excitement, and then, sadly, he bends down and picks up the alarm clock. He sets it by his wristwatch, and then puts it back on the floor, where his hand will be able to reach out and turn it off in the morning. He stands up. He blinks, trying to measure the distance from the light switch back to the bed, so he won't kick the clock. Then he bends the cover further back, hurries over to the switch, and then very carefully comes back in the dark, trying to tiptoe in his huge gardening boots.

He sits down on the edge of the bed. The boots drop. His feet swing up and duck under the covers, and then he's in, snuggling down. For a second he thinks, are there spiders here? Will things drop on me in the dark? And then his mind is away. He experiences that child's pleasure of being in your own bed, safe and warm, in a strange place, sailing tucked up in a stormy sea, snug and warm in a dangerous jungle, lions roaring, deliciously wrapped up in some arctic waste with snow pelting softly down.

He stretches, and then curls. And all the meagre, mean, spiteful politics of his school fade away, cease to exist, because Mark, his friend, is going to Mexico – Mexico! – and writes to him in bright red Magic Marker with drawings of houses and cats.

Dear Mark, he sees himself writing, *what's all this crap of bending your talents to the commercial whims of some publisher? Paint what you want to paint, don't* . . .

Then his mind drifts off and he dreams of how his wife once was, and he was, when he first saw her, tying her laces on the tennis courts behind the church where later they were wed, ten years ago, September, October . . .

Birds walk on the tin roof, scratching with their feet. The alarm buzzes but he doesn't hear it. Then his children come banging on the side door, laughing and happy, unable to get inside. Fenner sits up, and the morning rushes in through the big front lift-up door, catching him in his pyjamas with his hair on end, for all the neighbours to see.

♦ Good People in the House

♦ I once had a landlady in Copenhagen called Mrs Rasmussen, and I have known happier times. Mrs Rasmussen is ho ho. She sleeps in a room with a grand piano and she has gold teeth. The first time I saw her I had just come up the four flights of stairs to her front door with two bulging bags, a typewriter, a flapping Burberry, a slipping tweed hat and a heavy cold. And close to total breakdown. 'Ho ho,' she said. She led me along a corridor, crammed with furniture, to the room for rent. It was two o'clock in the afternoon, and I went straight to bed. The next thing I knew the room was full of people. I sat up, blinking. They were Japanese.

How many times have I woken in strange rooms in cities not my home to unfamiliar ceilings and odd-coloured walls? In Athens I stayed in a *pensione* with a damp smell of bodily functions and suspicious blankets and in Belgrade in rooms where old men coughed right through the night and in Berlin there was a flashing neon sign and no blind, and in Copenhagen everything should have been fine, I was invited to stay with an architect and his wife, a large white apartment, children playing on the rugs, sunshine and coffee, but suddenly, out of the blue, the wife locked herself in the bathroom and wouldn't come out and her husband, a quiet man with a beard as neat as moss, said I had better leave. Immediately.

Who can explain such things? In Copenhagen, that picture-book town? With its copper spires, canals and pigeons, blue eyes and ivy, colour and clean design.

The next time I awoke in my room in Mrs Rasmussen's apartment, two Swedes were standing at the foot of my bed. They were enormously tall, thin and bony, their wrists poking out of their jackets, no colour in their eyes. 'Ho ho,' said Mrs Rasmussen, and out they went, without a word to me. Then she came back. 'I will make you coffee,' she said. The blind was down and I didn't know whether it was night or day. Hawaiian music poured into my room. Someone was singing. Then back came Mrs Rasmussen, smoking a cigar.

It must have been morning, because this is how Mrs Rasmussen begins her day, with coffee, a cigar, and her record from Honolulu on the record player. She went there once, after her husband died, and pronounces it, 'Honowooloo.' Her hands flutter, her rings twinkle, light catches her spectacles, in their bamboo frames. Cigar smoke and perfume at eight in the morning. Even with a cold it comes through.

'Mrs Rasmussen,' I said. 'Who were all those people in my room?'

'Ho ho, you are not like Irving,' she said. 'Irving is bad.'

She sat herself down on the bed and patted my head, smiling widely, and carefully tilting up her head to blow her cigar smoke away from my face. Coffee steamed in a white pot on the table in the middle of the room. She poured two cups, bitter and black. I could hardly taste mine, but its warmth was welcome. The Hawaiian music, that acoustical throbbing, that electrical mockery of lagoons, coral strands and palms, pounded on.

'What you think about black men?' Mrs Rasmussen asked. Quickly she smiled, sipped her coffee, puffed her cigar. 'You think the black man is all right? I have never had a black man in my house before. What you think, I can trust him?'

'Who?' I asked.

'Oh, that Irving,' she said. 'Ho ho, he is funny. Always sleeping. Yoo hoo, Irving!' she suddenly called. 'Are you sleeping?' There was no reply from Irving, whoever he was. Mrs Rasmussen turned back to me. Another pat on the head. More of the gold smile, then a hasty puff, a quick sip, the faintest giggle.

'Mrs Rasmussen,' I said. 'I've got a cold. Who were all those people in my room?'

That made her stand up, and for some reason she wouldn't look me in the eye. She giggled, and fussed with my blankets, straightened my lamp on the table, bent down to pick a thread off the rug, and then, quickly now, she loaded up the coffee tray, and was gone.

I lay back and thought about nothing at all. Then suddenly the door opened again and back came Mrs Rasmussen with a vacuum cleaner. She moved the chairs, pushed the table, jerked up the blind, the vacuum cleaner roaring and Mrs Rasmussen flicking at everything in sight with a feather duster and not once looking over at me. She didn't say a word. She scrupulously avoided my eyes. And then out she went, leaving me with the sun spilling on to my bed and a million motes of swirling golden dust and a pain like every door in the world slamming banging inside my head.

The next morning began with three Germans.

They came before eight. I sat up, my mouth open, eyes still glued with sleep. 'Ho ho,' said Mrs Rasmussen. She opened my wardrobe and patted the chairs and flung open the window to show them the view. 'Hmm,' said the Germans, then out they went. Ten minutes later in came a Greek. 'What?' I cried. Mrs Rasmussen's gold teeth flashed like jewels at the opera. I sleep naked and it is a measure of my desperation that I flung back my blankets and leapt to my feet. The Greek's mouth fell open. Mrs Rasmussen ran. 'Get out!' I shouted to the Greek. I looked around desperately for my underpants. The Greek ran. I heard the front door slam. Mrs Rasmussen's door was closed. I knocked. Then the Hawaiian music started. I pounded on the door, standing in my underpants, nose running. No reply. I could hear her in there moving around. I grabbed the door handle and twisted it. Locked. Behind her door, Mrs Rasmussen began to sing.

The next morning she didn't come in with coffee and the smoke of her cigar, and I rode into town with a clear head, the tram pleasantly swaying round the bends and the ivy on the walls of the buildings past which we raced like the banners of the victorious, celebrating the triumph of justice and right, beauty and good. Pigeons waddled in the squares, totally unafraid, practically underfoot, puffing up like little explosions at the very last moment. Flags flew over Tivoli and the sky was blue. No one had gold teeth and no one was locked in a bathroom and when I got back to my room there was a negro sitting in my chair.

'Hi,' he said. 'I'm Irving. Just having a look at your books. Man, you really read, don'cha?'

I sat down and offered him a cigarette. 'No, don' smoke,' he said. I asked was he holidaying in Copenhagen. 'Yeah, man,' he said. 'Havin' a ball,'

So then I asked him what he was, what he worked at. He had enormous hands, and a loose, totally relaxed way about him. He could have been anything, a jazz drummer, a truck driver, a clerk in a shop. He had on a white shirt and a tie, and his trousers were sharp and slim.

'Well, I'm studyin', ya know. Law. In New York. Ever been to New York?'

'No,' I said.

'Well, look me up when you do,' he said. 'Pleased to meet you any time.' He fished in his trousers, brought out a bulging wallet, and from it extracted a card. 'That's me,' he said, pointing to the name with a long, thick finger. Irving Stoller, Student of Law, I read. 'Man, you really have a lotta books here, don'cha?' He was up again, off his chair, walking round my room in his loose, totally relaxed way, peering at my books. He picked one up. He was as loose as a cat. His shirt flowed on his back.

'Hey, what's with this Mrs Rasmussen?' I asked him. She was out, and the apartment was pleasantly quiet. No cleaners roared, no Hawaiian guitars pounded between the crammed walls. 'She keeps bringing people into my room,' I said.

'Yeah?' said Irving. 'Man, don'cha let her do *that*. She tried to do that to me. Man, you gotta lock your door. Don' let her do that to *you*, man.'

The idea of Mrs Rasmussen bringing people into my room seemed to have upset him considerably. His loose, relaxed look was gone. His face was screwed up, his body tight, his hands holding one of my books poised, motionless.

'But what's she doing?' I asked. 'Who are they?'

'Man, I don' know *what* she's doin',' he said. 'She's alla time showing her rooms to new people. Man, she's neurotic, if you want my opinion. She don' know *what* she's doin'.'

He looked so annoyed that when I smiled – I didn't know what else to do – it felt like the wrong thing. 'Well,' I said, 'I've told her that I'm staying here for two months, and as long as she leaves me alone, I don't care if she's as neurotic as a bat.'

'Yeah, well you better lock your door, man,' said Irving. 'Don't let her in, see?'

So I locked my door. I don't like living behind a locked door. There is something furtive about it, something wrong. A locked door is not a home, and the next afternoon when someone knocked, I opened my door at once. In came two Italians in striped suits and Mrs Rasmussen with her fluttering hands and smile of gold. In she flew, smelling like a flower. 'Mrs Rasmussen!' I said. 'I want a word with you.'

'Ho ho,' she laughed, trying to brush past me.

'Mrs Rasmussen,' I said, not budging. 'Why are you showing my room to these people? I've told you I'm staying two months.'

Again she tried to get past. She wanted to open the wardrobe, to fling up the blind, to pat the chairs, to demonstrate the springiness of the bed, the whole bag of tricks, as before, but I wouldn't let her. I had her in a corner and there was no way for her to get out.

'Ho ho,' she laughed, and tried to pat me on the head, but her eyes were nervous, I could see, behind the bamboo frames, and her ringed fingers trembled with agitation.

'I want good people in my house,' she said. She shot a defiant look into my eyes, then her eyes flicked away.

I stared at her and didn't say a word.

Her tongue flicked over her lips. She went into a great routine of blinking. She laughed, Ho ho. I didn't move a muscle. I stared straight at her, my face five inches from hers. For a minute I thought she was going to collapse.

Then back came the charm. 'Ho ho, you are a good boy,' she said, 'not like Irving.' And up came the hand to pat me on the head. I ducked. Mrs Rasmussen sailed free. The Italians stood and looked down at their pointy shoes and didn't know what to do. 'Ho ho,' said Mrs Rasmussen, and flew, *flew* out of the room. I turned to the Italians, my face stone, and out they went too, heads down, a look of incomprehension and deep shame on their faces.

She knocked again the next morning and I could smell fresh coffee, her peace offering, but I didn't open the door. 'Yoo hoo!' she called. 'Are you in there?' She rattled the door handle. 'I have coffee for you!' she called. I told myself to behave normally, to make as much noise as I wanted, to ignore her, but for some reason I couldn't. I sat in my chair and didn't so much as turn over a page of my book. Minutes passed. And then I heard another door opening, and at once the Hawaiian music, super loud, came pounding into my room.

An hour later she knocked again. 'I must clean your room!' she called. The Hawaiian music was still going strong and there wasn't a hope in the world of doing any work. I couldn't think. There was no escape. I opened the door and in she swept, vacuum cleaner howling, feather duster flicking, blankets flying, the chairs dancing through the air and all my books falling over on the shelves. 'Ho ho,' she laughed, and half an hour later, when she finally left, I was a ruin. I took a tram into town, that fairy-tale town where Hans Christian Andersen read his stories to golden-locked children, where the shops are gay and flags and barges toot down the canals, but this time it was just another aimless city. I wandered in parks, stared at buildings, and it was four o'clock before I felt relaxed enough to try again.

Up the four flights of stairs I went and put my key in the door. 'Come in, come in!' called Mrs Rasmussen. She had obviously heard me at the door, and her head was poking out of her room

into the corridor and I didn't have a chance. 'Yoo hoo!' she called.
'I have coffee for you!'

So into her room I went. All the blinds were down, a lamp was
burning, and the room was thick with cigar smoke. On a bright
June day. The lamp and the smell of smoke with the sun shining
outside seemed sinful and bad, but in a funny way. There was not
that debauched smell of an all-night poker game that has turned
its back on sunshine and air, but the giggly badness of children
playing some forbidden game with all the blinds down so no one
can see.

'*Guten tag*,' said a little old man in a green cardigan.

'Good afternoon,' I said, extending my hand.

'Pleased to meet you,' said a woman dressed in grey. She had
grey hair, brushed tightly back, grey eyes, and a grey well-cut
suit.

What? I thought. 'Hello,' I said.

'Ho ho,' said Mrs Rasmussen. 'You must all meet my good
boy. He is not like Irving. Yoo hoo, Irving! Are you sleeping?'
Mrs Rasmussen was dressed in a dipping frock that was all
spangles and glitter. Her hair was a bright orange. Her glasses
were not quite straight on her face and she was wearing only one
shoe. She was drunk.

'Dubonnet?' said the little old man in the green cardigan.

'Please sit down,' said the woman all in grey, speaking very
clearly and evenly, and moving over on the sofa to make room
for me beside her.

'Ho ho, we are all drunk,' said Mrs Rasmussen. 'Now I will
play for you.'

There was about three square feet of space in Mrs Rasmussen's
room and she almost fell going over to the piano. She bumped into
the coffee table, giggling, into a chair, saying Ooh, into a writing
desk, laughing, into a standard lamp, which rocked and swayed,
like Mrs Rasmussen herself, and then with a crash down she sat on
the stool in front of the piano. It was a grand piano, and how it had
ever been brought into that room I don't know. It was covered with
photographs, ashtrays, bric-à-brac, two lamps, three lace doilies,
and a whisky decanter set into a model of an antique car. Mrs
Rasmussen adjusted her glasses. There were photographs and

postcards all over the room, on every horizontal surface. Mrs Rasmussen cleared her throat. The walls were covered with paintings, men with moustaches, little girls with dogs, flower arrangements, and one huge painting of a doe dipping its nose into a crystal clear lake, in which were reflected Alpine peaks, pines and snow, and a log cabin with a twist of smoke curling up from its chimney. Mrs Rasmussen turned the sheets of music propped up and sagging before her. And then, with all the style of a concert pianist, she poised her hands over the keyboard, tilted up her chin, sniffed, and began. Out spilled the notes, out they flowed, and at first I didn't know what she was playing. Her rings flashed. The keys were like water under her hands. They spilled and splashed. Then she opened her mouth, the music took shape, and in a high clear voice, her fingers rippling over the keys, Mrs Rasmussen sang.

> Some enchanted evening
> You will see a stranger
> You will see a stranger
> Across a crowded room.

'Ah,' said the little old man in the green cardigan. 'Dubonnet?'

'Please,' said the woman in grey, making more room for me on the sofa.

Crooo-ded rooooom,' sang Mrs Rasmussen.

And I, of course, was the stranger. I began to wonder how I was going to get out. I smiled at the woman in grey, I smiled at the little old man, who promptly lifted up his eyebrows and the Dubonnet bottle, and refilled my glass, and Mrs Rasmussen played on. She was in a trance. 'Some Enchanted Evening', with no effort at all, no visible break, no pause, no respite, flowed into and became 'I Could Have Danced All Night'. The woman in grey leant forward and offered me a cigar. She lit it with a lighter shaped like a woman's leg. She offered me a plate of biscuits and cheese. She poured coffee for me. My hands were filled, a smile was stretched across my face, and I could feel my nose starting to drip.

And then, with a crash of chords, Mrs Rasmussen's playing stopped. I put down my cigar and dived for my handkerchief. Mrs Rasmussen stood up, beaming, and bowed.

'Hilda, that was very beautiful,' said the woman in grey.

'Ho ho,' said Mrs Rasmussen. 'Now we hear my music from Honowooloo.'

Back she swayed, crashing into the coffee table, into the lamp, into the writing desk, into the chair, to the record player in the corner. The turntable was under the television set, and you had to stoop to get to it. Mrs Rasmussen, her face bright red, stooped, puffed, and then with a grunt sat down heavily on the rug. She rolled, helpless, laughing. She bumped into a large vase, one of a pair that stood on either side of the television set, and I braced myself for the inevitable tragedy of spilled water. There was no water. The flowers were plastic. 'Ho, ho,' laughed Mrs Rasmussen, her dress way up and the underpinnings, straps and clasps, elastic and lace, showed cruelly against her white skin. 'Oh, let me,' I said, trying to rise, but there was no room. 'Please,' said the woman in grey, motioning for me to resume my seat. Mrs Rasmussen struggled up, her Hawaiian record in her hand. 'Ah!' she cried. The needle scratched and bounced across the record, skittered and skipped.   'Dubonnet?' said the little old man, refilling my glass.

And then the music came on. It had never been so loud.

'Oh, Honowooloo!' cried Mrs Rasmussen. She lifted her arms over her head and swayed on the rug, her hips shaking and rolling. My smile was like a badge of deceit stretched across my face. I tried to look away but there was nowhere to look. There was too much furniture and I was hemmed in.

'Oh, I must make another trip!' cried Mrs Rasmussen. 'Tell me, where should I go? Oh, I don't like Copenhagen in the winter, it is so cold.'

She patted me on the head and I was powerless to resist.

'Greece is nice,' I said, idiotically.

'Oh, but I must have nice people in my house,' cried Mrs Rasmussen. 'Where can I find them? How can I go?'

'Fly,' I said, and the little old man gave me my fourth refill of Dubonnet.

'Oh, I must have good people,' Mrs Rasmussen wailed. She looked quite unhappy. 'Oh, my husband, what would he think if he could see? Hilda, he would say, what are all these people in the house? Black men! Oh, ho ho, he would not know what to say.'

She took a quick sip of Dubonnet. She grabbed my cigar, which was lying in an ashtray, and puffed on it furiously.

'Quick,' she said to me. 'I will show you my house, where I used to live.'

Over she swayed to the writing desk, rocking and bumping. Drawers flew. Papers and cards spilled on to the carpet. 'Ah!' cried Mrs Rasmussen. 'Now you will see.'

Back she came with a photo album, her fingers flicking through the pages.

'Here,' she said. 'Here is where we once lived. Is it beautiful?'

They were colour photographs of a large white house set in rolling green lawns. Dense old trees. A curving drive. Three photographs were of interiors, a stately dining room, the chairs grouped sedately around an enormous table, a chandelier glittering overhead. There was a plush bedroom, and a vast hall with a staircase winding up and out of sight.

'I see,' I said, and where, I wondered, had Mrs Rasmussen's money gone? Who had her husband been, and what was his business that they lived in such style? The chairs in the photographs, I saw, were the ones now crammed into this small room. The writing table, the sofa, the grand piano, the rugs, the paintings, the chandeliers, all this splendour was now packed into a small apartment on the fourth floor in an ordinary street in Copenhagen, and how had Mrs Rasmussen's life turned to bring her here?

'Oh, I must make a trip, I must,' said Mrs Rasmussen. She was like an animal trapped in a cage. Her eyes darted furtively to and fro. 'Good people, good people . . . ' she moaned. And then a wild look came into her eyes and she shouted, 'Irving! Are you still sleeping? Come,' she said to me, 'we will see if Irving is still asleep.'

She took me by the hand and I had no option but to come with her along the corridor to Irving's room.

'Yoo hoo!' she called. 'Irving! Are you sleeping? Oh, he is always asleep,' she said to me. 'I cannot make the room. Yoo hoo! Irving!' She rattled the door handle, there was a click, and the door swung open.

The blind was down, the room was dark, and Irving was in bed. The room smelt strongly of Vicks.

'Man, what's goin' on?' Irving said.

His voice was thick with cold. His eyes were wet and sleepy. Mrs Rasmussen had obviously woken him up.

'Ho ho,' laughed Mrs Rasmussen and swept into the room. Up flew the blind. 'You are always sleeping, Irving,' she cried. 'I must make the room.'

'Oh man, I gotta cold,' Irving moaned. 'Why you comin' into my room now?'

'You are always sleeping,' said Mrs Rasmussen. She swept around the room like a zephyr, pulling at chairs, pushing Irving's table, shaking the curtains, blowing at objects on his dresser.

'Now listen here,' said Irving. 'If I wanna sleep, that's my business. You got no right comin' into my room. Man, you're neur*otic*.'

'Ho ho,' laughed Mrs Rasmussen. 'You are always talking so funny.'

'Jeez!' said Irving, and started to get out of bed. Mrs Rasmussen looked alarmed, and I made my escape.

There is a great charm to Copenhagen in the summer, it is a rare town built to a human scale. The buildings don't impose and the girls smile at you in the street. What did it matter that the little old man in the green cardigan had moved in and shuffled around in his battered slippers offering me Dubonnet in the morning and trying to corner me in the corridor and smiling and talking endlessly in German though I kept shaking my head and saying I couldn't understand a word he was saying? Mrs Rasmussen had somehow become more tranquil. True, she still burst in with her vacuum cleaner and mop, but the calls for coffee were less frequent and the Hawaiian music softer and not played so often. True, sometimes she rattled my door handle and called out, 'Yoo hoo! Are you in there? Are you writing about me?' She rattled Irving's door handle too. He was always asleep during the day, but at night he would come out of his room dressed in his suit and a clean white shirt and go off for the night. Girls, jazz! He was, as he said, having a ball. And I was working well. The skies were blue.

One night I came home late from a movie and there was Irving sitting in the corridor. He was sitting on a suitcase. There was another suitcase next to him. When I came in he stood up and there was an angry look in his eye.

'Man, I thought you was her,' he said. He sat down again. He stared at the floor.

The apartment was dead quiet. You could hear the trams rolling in the street four floors down.

'She threw me out,' Irving said.

He looked up at me and his face no longer had the stamp of anger, not the slightest trace. He was like a little boy who has been punished and doesn't know why. He looked unfathomably sad.

'Go an' take a look in there,' he said, pointing to his room. I did. There was no mattress on the bed, just the bare springs, and the room, though it still had its wardrobe, table, dresser, chairs, looked as empty as a room can look.

'She jus' waited till I was gone and then she jus' packed ev'rythin' up,' Irving said. 'What she wanna do that for? I'm paid up. I told her I was leavin' *tomorrow*. She knew that. I'm going to Barcelona.'

This last he said so sadly, in a voice so forlorn, that an image of Barcelona, a city I have never seen, rang like a chord inside my head. The way he said it, sitting so sadly with his shoulders slouched down and his head hanging low, it was as though he had uttered the name of that city, that goal, we shall never see.

'Jeez!' Irving cried. Back from Barcelona I snapped. He was up now, angry as a bull. He smashed his fist into the wall. 'Man, what am I gonna *do*?' he cried.

'Where is she?' I asked.

'I dunno,' Irving said. 'I thought you was her.'

I took out my cigarettes, forgot he didn't smoke and offered him one, and then we stood in the corridor, outside Irving's empty room, and waited for Mrs Rasmussen to come home.

She came at one, laughing and drunk. We heard her key in the door and Irving stood up. She swept open the door, stepped inside, her head high. To Irving she seemed to give only the most passing glance, to me, nothing at all. It was only when she came to Irving's cases, and couldn't pass, that she paused.

'Mrs Rasmussen!' Irving shouted. 'I wanna talk to you!'

'I'm very tired,' Mrs Rasmussen said. She raised a leg to step over Irving's suitcase. Then she wobbled. Then she giggled. I thought she was going to fall.

'Now listen here!' Irving shouted. 'Why you thrown me outta my room? I tol' you I was leavin' *tomorrow*!'

Mrs Rasmussen turned.

'I only want good people in my room,' she said.

'What?' Irving roared.

'You were asleep all the day and I could not clean the room.'

'Jeez!' Irving shouted. 'If I wanna sleep, that's my business. What right you got takin' out my mattress and packin' my bags and jus' throwin' ev'rythin' out?'

'I must have good people in my house,' Mrs Rasmussen repeated. She looked over at me, but she didn't see me. She didn't see anything. Her eyes were bright, wild and mad.

'You got no right!' Irving shouted. 'I paid you till tomorrow and you got no right to throw me out, see?'

Mrs Rasmussen shook her head as though this whole business was most disagreeable to her. She fumbled with her handbag. 'Here is your money,' she said, and dropped a note on to the floor.

Down it fluttered, and for a minute there was no sound at all in the corridor of Mrs Rasmussen's apartment. I stared at the note as it drifted to the floor. Irving was frozen. Mrs Rasmussen had her head up high, like a duchess. She turned to go, her business done, but Irving's suitcase was still in the way. And then Irving grabbed her.

He took her by the shoulder and spun her around. 'Man, you are neurotic!' he screamed in her face. 'Neur-otic! Ya hear that? Neur-*otic*!'

Mrs Rasmussen's mouth fell open and she started to blink. Her mouth moved to say something but nothing came out. All at once she looked very frightened, the hard, glittering glaze of madness broken. I stood very still and didn't know what to do.

Then she laughed. 'Ho ho,' she said. 'You are funny, Irving. I have never had a black man in my house before. Ho ho.'

Her teeth shone and the hallway light caught her bamboo-framed glasses. She was miles away. Irving's hand fell away from her shoulder. Mrs Rasmussen turned and stepped over the suitcase and went down the corridor to her room, swaying and giggling, in another world.

She unlocked her door, stepped inside, quietly closed the door behind her, and then we heard the Hawaiian music, softly, drifting up the corridor in lapping waves. We stared, Irving and I, down the empty corridor along which she had passed. A minute passed, two, and then Irving took a step forward and shouted with all his might, 'Man, you are NEUROTIC!' He stood like that for a full minute, his face filled with fury, his body as tense as a spring, but there was only the Hawaiian music, no other sound. Then he looked down, defeated, and then he slowly turned to me. 'Help me with my bags, will ya?' he said. 'I gotta find myself a hotel.'

I carried his luggage down the stairs and waved down a cab and the last I saw of Irving was his sad face in the window of the cab driving off into the Copenhagen night.

I worked, all that week, with my door locked, opening it for no one. She didn't come in to clean the room. She made no offers of coffee. She played no music and she went out every night. A week passed, then another. She grew bolder. I passed her in the corridor and she said, 'Ho ho, it is good without Irving, no?' I didn't say a word. And at night I thought of her throwing me out of my room, and the streets of Copenhagen at night with the wind blowing and nowhere to go, and how I hadn't lifted a finger to help Irving. I saw the architect's face with its neat beard, and his mouth moved in my dreams and always he said the same words: 'You must leave. Immediately.'

Into Irving's room she put a Frenchman who worked in the city and went out every night. I hardly saw him. The little man in the green cardigan went away and no one saw him go, and the morning after he left the woman who owned the corner shop knocked on the door and said he had left this address and an unpaid bill for three hundred kroner. Dubonnet. Mrs Rasmussen refused to pay it and slammed the door. I went back to my room and locked the door and at another time it might have been funny, but I kept thinking about Irving.

And then I received a letter from a friend in Sweden. 'Stockholm is out of this world!' he sang. 'The girls are unbelievable and leaves are falling and the whole town's turning gold. Come!'

I knocked on Mrs Rasmussen's door. She was wearing a floral robe and her hair was lifeless, mousy, and tied up in a net. She looked like what she was, a middle-aged widow, alone in the world. There was no sparkle in her eyes. Her gold teeth were dull. Her furniture-crammed room was as melancholy as a back room in a junk shop. But then Irving's sad face, wide-eyed, unbelieving, flashed before me. I wasn't fooled. I made my voice as hard as nails.

'I am going to Stockholm,' I said. 'I am going for two weeks, and I want to leave my room just the way it is. I've paid my rent for a month, and when I come back I'll stay for another two weeks. Is that all right?'

'Stockholm is lovely,' Mrs Rasmussen said.

This is no place to talk of Stockholm and its waters, its islands and its mist, though the girls were golden like the leaves and as profuse. Brown farmhouses, sweeping green fields, the air like crystal . . . another time, another time. I stayed for two weeks, and then started back for Copenhagen, my head filled with song, and I felt with a pang the pain of leaving when the ferry tooted and I stepped away from Swedish soil.

Copenhagen had put on another coat. The winds were sharper, and the ivy on the buildings, red now, rippled, as though alive. I paid off the cab and went up the four flights of stairs to Mrs Rasmussen's front door.

It was after midnight and there was no sound in the apartment. I turned on the hallway light. It was as crammed with furniture as ever. I picked up my mail. I heard a tap dripping slowly in the bathroom. I got out the key to my room and put it in the lock. I turned it, opened the door, and switched on the light. I stepped inside and then there was a rustle of movement and a girl sat up in my bed. Her eyes were wide open and her hand was up to her mouth. She wasn't wearing a thing. She was as black as night.

'Oh!' I cried, stepping back.

'Ho ho,' said Mrs Rasmussen, coming into the room.

♦ The Larder

♦

♦ The people who didn't go to the reef crowded around to see what the others had brought back. 'My goodness,' said one of the old ladies who hadn't gone (she had come for a rest, and was a little bit frightened of boats and water and all that stepping up and down), 'what are they?' She peered down at one of them, blinking. It lay on its back, on the grass, the creature tucked up inside its shell, only the tip of its claw visible, quite harmless, but the old lady wouldn't touch it. Some of the others were crawling about on the grass. The island dog sniffed at them and barked. 'Aren't they beautiful?' said the people who had brought them back, pushing them with their feet when they tried to creep away too far, out of the circle of light. Forty people had gone to the reef, and they had brought back almost a hundred shells. The tide was in, so the boat had been able to tie up at the quay, and they had stepped straight ashore, laughing, flushed with sun, exhausted, the usual tourists. When the tide was out, you were brought in by flat-bottomed barge, a slow and tiring business. The tide went out almost half a mile. It was night now, quite dark. The bells for dinner sounded through the trees. 'Is it safe to just leave them here?' the people who had brought them back wanted to know, because they were hungry and wanted to go in for dinner. 'Safe as houses,' said the guide. 'Turn them over, they won't get far.' So they turned them over and left them there on the grass, some of them wriggling, most of them still, with the island dog sniffing and growling and running around them in the night.

They talked about them over dinner, proudly. 'Oh, I brought back *nine*,' one of them said. He laughed. He was a real-estate agent with a huge face, loose jowls, shaggy eyebrows, his shirt open at the throat and his corduroy jacket loosely thrown over his shoulders, leaving his arms free while he ate. 'Don't know what the hell I'm going to do with them all, but there they were, free for the taking, you can't pass up a chance like that. Damn rare. Chance of a lifetime. God knows when I'll be in these parts again. Well, see that lady over there? – with the glasses? She brought back *twelve*. Love to see her getting all those home, ha ha. One of them about the size of this table.' 'Really?' said a lady who hadn't gone. She was a schoolteacher. 'That big?' 'Naah,' said the real-estate agent, laughing, his mouth full of food. 'I'm joking. But pretty big, all the same. About like this.' He showed her with his hands. She narrowed her eyes and shook her head. 'What *are* they exactly? What are they called?' she wanted to know. 'Don't ask me,' said the real-estate agent. 'Beautiful things, though. When you turn them over. Smooth as silk. You have to take the things out of them though, otherwise they really stink up the place.'

They had crawled quite far in the morning, some of them off the grass and onto the gravel paths, and a few of them even further and in amongst the trees, but they were all found and all brought back. The larger ones hadn't moved at all, their silk-smooth purple and mauve underside still pointed up to the sky. In some of them, the creature had come quite a way out, and you could see the pink of its body past the claw. But they all ducked back into their shells as soon as they were touched, except for the very tip of the claw, for which there was no room in the shell. They were lightning fast. They had already started to smell. A few of them looked dead.

The owners of the shells gathered around them, poking them with their feet, picking them up, turning them over, comparing shells, boasting of their own. But a few of them, seeing them now in the sun, appeared slightly embarrassed. They had brought back so many! Yesterday's enthusiasm hung on a thread. In the bright morning sun, under the palms, you could see how ugly they were, spiky, as rough as rocks, crawling slowly on the grass. But their undersides, in the morning sun, were more beautiful than ever.

A few of them set straight to work to get the creatures out. The others watched, not knowing what to do. It was hard to get hold of the claw, and even when you did, it was impossible to pull the creature out. It hung on grimly, locked inside its shell. You could pull them out about an inch, no more. And once you let go, the creature would hastily withdraw, and that was that. It wouldn't venture out again, unless you left it alone for over an hour.

'Bastards, aren't they?' said the real-estate agent. He had sat himself down on the grass and had one in his lap and was scratching away at the creature with a long-bladed knife, trying to gouge it out. 'That's awfully cruel,' said the schoolteacher, and shuddered. The real-estate agent laughed. 'Naah,' he said. 'They don't feel a thing. Larder of the earth, the sea. Man's richest feeding ground. There's plenty more where this came from, and getting this fella out won't make any difference at all. Pity they're not edible though.' He continued gouging with his knife, squinting in the sun, enjoying his work.

It was impossible to get them out with knives and sticks. Someone tried a fishhook but that tore through the creature, which quickly withdrew, leaving a wet colourless smear on the shell. Wire was useless. Throwing them about on the grass didn't do anything at all. Putting them in water to coax the creatures out and then using a knife was a waste of time. It was half-way through the morning and no one had succeeded in removing a single one.

But they kept at it, undaunted. They sat about on the grass, under the trees, smoking cigarettes and trying everything they could think of and calling out suggestions to each other. 'Why not just leave them in the sun?' someone suggested. 'Let the ants eat them out.' 'They'll smell for months,' was the reply to that.

Then someone hit upon an idea. Everyone gathered around him and he explained it. 'Fishing line,' he said. 'Make a noose around the claw and then hang the shell up and the weight of it will drag the things out.' He showed them how. In thirty minutes they had hung them all up. They hung them from shrubs and from low branches and from railings. Everywhere you looked there were shells hanging. The method began to work at once. You could see the shells inching down to the ground, the creatures stretching, more and more of them coming out, pink in the sun. In ten minutes, some of them had pulled out as much as six inches, thin and pink, with the shell swaying under them. The owners of the shells watched, fascinated, until the bells rang for lunch, and then they went off to wash their hands and to eat.

All through lunch you could hear the shells dropping, plop, plop, softly on to the grass, regularly, one after another. You could see them lying on the ground through the windows of the dining room, like coconuts, except for the spikes. And you could also see those that hadn't yet dropped, hanging low, the creatures stretched to a foot and more, the shells swaying and rocking under them though there was no wind.

The people who had hung them up were very happy at lunch. 'There goes another!' they called out, each time one fell to the ground. There was a lot of laughing and joking. They made bets to see which ones would drop first. The fishing line idea, they agreed, had been a stroke of genius.

By the time the main course arrived, they had all dropped. The grass was littered with shells. Those that had fallen with their undersides up shone in the sun. Most of them fell the other way, rough side up, the way they had looked on the reef, where you could hardly tell them from rock, except for the movement.

Then the birds came. They came just as the dessert was being served. They wheeled in the sky, scores of them, their wings flapping, screaming, crying, swooping down with their beaks open, flashes of white and grey, with red legs and orange beaks. They came for the things on the fishing lines, hanging from the trees. You could smell the things through the open windows of the dining room, as rank as the sea, salty and foul. The attack of the birds was sudden and swift. It was all over before coffee.

After lunch, the people who had brought the shells back from the reef collected their shells and stacked them up outside their rooms, ready to take home with them. It was wonderful, they said, how cleanly the creatures had come out. The shells were not harmed at all.

They left the next morning, early, while the tide was still in. They took about twenty shells with them. They took only the smallest ones, those about the size of your hand. They were a good size, they said, for your mantelpiece. The others were ludicrous. They laughed, imagining them in their homes. Anyhow, they couldn't possibly fit them all into their luggage. The shells they didn't want they left outside their rooms. After the tourists had gone, the unwanted shells were pushed into a pile and thrown away, like the unwanted shells of the week before, and the week before that, and the week before that.

In the afternoon, a fresh boatful of tourists came in. They had come to swim and to drink and to laze in the sun. But already they were eager for their trip to the reef. They had been promised a treat. Their trip to the reef would take place on the day of the lowest tide of the year.

◆ The Card-Players

◆

◆ Polish Rummy, a Continental card game of chance and skill for two to six players, using two full packs (with jokers), is being played in the kitchen of our Melbourne suburban house by my father and his fifteen-year-old son. It's my deal. We've won one game apiece. Tension is high.

'Deal,' says my father.

He is impatient. Understandably. I am a slow, awkward shuffler, cards falling all over the place whenever I attempt some speed. Fancy ripples, as practised by my champion card-playing aunts, are beyond me, so far. Even with sleek, new, plastic-coated cards, which these are not.

'I haven't finished,' I tell him, attempting one more shuffle, which does little to rearrange the order of the cards. They must be years old, these cards. (The nine of spades has a corner missing, which you can spot a mile off, and for the two of diamonds we use a blank.) They feel like chunks of felt in my hands, absolutely refusing to slip properly.

'It's enough,' my father says. 'Come on.'

'Here I come,' I announce.

I straighten up the edges of the deck with a series of taps on the edge of the table, and then, with studied nonchalance, I slide the cards out to the centre of the table for my father to cut.

'Cut,' I tell him.

But what's this? My father, a minute ago so eager, is suddenly boredom personified. He leans back in his chair. He yawns. He hums or moans a snatch of some inner melody. Then, with all the time in the world, he reaches out a lazy hand for the deck, cuts, hardly looking at the cards, gives me a small mocking smile, then leans back again, this time with his fingers laced.

Uh-oh. He's playing tricks. And we were getting along so nicely.

'Hey,' I practically shout. 'You're supposed to take the bottom card.'

'Don't tell me the rules,' he snaps. 'Deal.'

What's happening? Doesn't he want to play? Well, if he doesn't that's all right with me. I've got plenty of other things to do. The card-playing was his idea, not mine. I'm supposed to be studying, if the truth be known.

'Wake up,' he says, again with a flick of impatience.

I take a deep breath. I look at him. His maroon jumper spotted with stains. The most rumpled shirt collar in the history of the world. And trousers of unbelievable bagginess, fortunately this minute out of sight. You should hear the dramas when my mother tries to get him to change his clothes.

'Well?' he says.

I deal. Plop, plop, one card at a time. The great card-players, my aunts, always do two, skimming them out fast and low, a bare inch at most off the top of the table, winging them in with uncanny precision, right where they want them. Not me. I like to take it slow.

It's quiet. There's hardly a sound other than the soft fall of the cards as I deal them out. Eight, eight. Nine, nine. It's early, not yet eight o'clock, just we two here, my father and me. My mother has taken my five-year-old brother off to an uncle's to be fitted for a school suit. The suit fitting will take ten minutes – it's probably over by now – but afterwards comes the real business of the visit: the cups of tea, the slices of cake, and the talk. Oh, the talk. When my mother gets together with her family, it never ends. Two hours at least. More likely, three. While my brother sits there going out of his head. My father was supposed to go, too, but at the last minute changed his mind. They're not *his* family. He can't stand all that talk.

'Okay,' I tell him, the dealing done.

He seems to be in no hurry to pick up his cards. His usual style is to grab them up as they come, getting them in order in his hand quickly, eyes narrowed with concentration. He is at his most serious at such times, each in-coming card a matter of life and death. The trouble is, his face is transparent, he can't conceal his disappointment or joy, frowns and smiles chasing each other madly across his wide face, and when he picks up a joker everyone knows. He beams like the sun. Lately, he has developed a new technique. When a joker comes, he gives a cry of glee, plants a happy kiss on the card, and then pastes it on his forehead, high up (have I mentioned he's practically bald?), a taunt and a crown. My mother's family, with whom he usually plays, can't stand this sort of clowning and berate him loudly. He doesn't care. He has other tricks, too. For my Aunt Milly, who is an enormous deliberator, he has a range of snores, from a small oink to a long deep buzz, to impress upon her the passing of time. For Sonya, the chain smoker, he has throat clearings and coughs. In tense moments, when everyone's waiting for his move, he likes to stand up and readjust his trousers. He is a singer, too, and a foot tapper. This is when the game's going well. When he's losing, he's surly.

'Sometimes I seriously wonder why we let you in the game,' my Aunt Sonya says.

'Ah, where's your sense of humour,' my father says, scowling, looking angry.

Inside my father, who is a small, round man, there is a gunfighter, a cowboy, a tall, bronzed, weatherbeaten man of action, and what he would dearly love to do, when playing with my aunts, is fix them with a steely eye, challenge them coolly with an 'Are you calling me a liar?,' and then, moving quickly but deliberately, knock the table across the room with one powerful flick of an arm, cards and money flying, let loose with a few shots, and then, unruffled, calm, with the smoke of battle still hanging in the air, give his gunbelt an arrogant hoist and slouch over to the bar for a slug of rotgut whisky. Neat.

Why does he play with them? Well, who else is there?

However, he's not playing with my aunts tonight. He's playing with me – a nice, friendly father-and-son game in our shiny bright kitchen. For pleasure. No money involved.

I look up from my hand and see that he hasn't even started to pick up his cards.

'Are you playing,' I ask him, 'or not?'

'I can beat you with one hand tied behind my back,' he says (this is the gunfighter talking), and again there's the mocking smile. But at least there's some action, too. He straightens up in his chair and begins to scoop up his cards.

His eyes narrow. The cards flick into place. He gives a grunt of satisfaction, then a sour moan, another grunt, a smile, a frown. He has all his cards now. He regards them narrowly. I wait. It's his go. Suddenly he throws them all down and falls back in his chair.

'Misdeal,' he says.

'What?'

Another one of his tricks!

'I had fourteen cards,' he says.

'You didn't even count them!'

He smiles.

'I didn't like the look of them,' he says. 'Deal again.'

'Oh, for God's sake!'

I throw my cards down, too. We glare at each other. What's going on? This was supposed to be a nice, friendly game.

'Deal again,' my father says.

There is a challenging look in his eyes. We sit, neither of us moving. What do I do now? Stand up and storm out? One point I've never been able to work out about my father: Does he like me?

He's always yelling at me. I'm dumb. I don't study enough. Then, when I win a prize at school or get terrific marks for something, he changes his tactics completely. He switches to the physical side. 'Why don't you ever mow the lawn?' he yells. And then, just to show me, he runs out and does it himself, charging up and down with the hand mower, in no time at all bright red in the face. Actually, he loves it. He loves to sweat. He rips off his shirt, exposing his muscular arms and chest, wheeling around in his singlet and his baggy pants, cut grass flying up like a fountain, with my mother looking horrified and calling out, 'Sam! For God's sake, everyone can see you! Put on your shirt!' His happiest days, he has told me a million times, were when he worked in a quarry in Palestine, hewing out massive blocks of stone in the sun. 'Ah, but what would you know about that,' he says to me.

Does he like me? Look, we're playing cards. Or are we?

My father has a finger in his ear. He's wiggling it up and down. He takes it out. The cards lie all over the table.

'Well?' he says.

'Are you going to play properly?' I ask.

'I'm playing, I'm playing,' he says. 'Come on.'

'Okay. But no more tricks.'

Once again I scoop up the cards. They're in an incredible mess from having been thrown down all over the place. He watches me as I sort them out. I try to do it quickly, to get some life back in the game. He doesn't say a word. I go into my routine of clumsy shuffling. Still not a word. I slide the deck out to the middle of the table. He cuts, slipping out the bottom card, not looking at it. I start to deal. He watches the cards as they come his way, but doesn't pick them up.

'Come on,' I say to him. 'I've got a fantastic hand.'

'Is that so?' he says, and reaches for his cards. He starts to move quickly, giving little grunts.

'Here,' he says, throwing down the eight of hearts.

We start to play.

The object of the game is to get rid of all your cards, making sets and runs – if possible, doing it all in one shot. I need about five cards, unless I rearrange them all in some other way, which I haven't yet properly worked out. Ah. I pick up a three of clubs. Things are looking good.

My father studies his cards. He has to throw one out. He's taking his time. The pause lengthens. Has he forgotten it's his shot?

'Your go,' I remind him.

Still he doesn't move. Nor does he seem to be thinking all that much. With my father's transparent face, you always know what's going on.

'You're to throw out,' I remind him again.

He looks at me, just for a second, then down at his cards again. He breathes out, noisily, through his nostrils, almost a sigh, his mouth a glum line. He moans, deep in his throat. He blinks. Then he throws his cards down, all of them, just lets them fall, pushes his chair back from the table, and walks out of the room.

Where's my father going? For a second I think it's the bathroom, but no, he goes right past. He's in the hall. I hear the click of a light switch. Then another. He's going into the living room.

But he doesn't sit down. I don't hear any grunts, or the creak of his favourite chair. Nothing. Not a sound. Then I hear the click of the light switch again – he's turned it off – and then a door opening and another light going on. The front bedroom. But he doesn't go in. He must be standing in the doorway, doing I don't know what. Another click. He's turned the light off. Now he's just standing there, in the dark, while I sit in this bright kitchen, still foolishly holding my cards.

I look up. The cupboards are works of art. My mother had them done last summer, spending a fortune on a Polish painter who, for some obscure reason, only worked at night. 'A real craftsman,' my mother said proudly. 'Who cares what time he works?' The painter was a tall, thin man who wore a black beret, working till two or three each morning, taking innumerable breaks for coffee and cigarettes, stepping back every five minutes to appraise his work. I've never seen anyone so fussy. It was as if he were painting a mural, and not a cupboard door. But look, the cupboards shine like mirrors. There's not a brushmark to be seen. It took him four weeks for a job that he could have done in one. He didn't mind. 'What else is there to do?' he once said to me. 'When I go home, I sleep. I sleep all day.' And then, lighting another cigarette and staring away into space, 'There's no life here. Nothing. Nothing at all.'

I sit holding my cards, listening to my father moving around the house. I can hear him going from room to room, turning on lights, switching them off, with long, empty pauses in between. He's in the hall again. I can hear him coming this way.

I look up, and there he is in the doorway, both hands deep in his trouser pockets. He looks, all at once, very small. And suddenly very tired. Is something wrong? Is he sick?

Impossible! My father is as strong as an ox. Except for his kidney stones, but he's always had those. 'From those oranges in Palestine,' my mother says. 'Rubbish!' says my father. What harm is there in an orange?' And then he gets carried away with memories of those old days and starts to boast. 'A dozen at a time!' he shouts. 'Real oranges! Not like you get here.' I think he gets incredible pains, but he never says a word. That's not his style. 'Don't worry,' he said, when he came back from a check-up last week. 'They're not going to bury me in this country.' He laughed. He told one of his famous coarse jokes. But I think he has to go back again.

He's not looking at me. He doesn't seem to be looking at anything. It's so quiet I can hear him breathing – those deep, sigh-like breaths through his nostrils, his mouth still a tight line.

I don't know what to say. I look away.

He comes into the room. He stands by the table, looking down at the cards. He sniffs. He breathes out. One hand comes out of a pocket and falls onto the back of his chair. A long pause. Then, at last, he pulls the chair out and sits down.

He rubs his face, pushing his cheeks in hard. He blinks. And then something seems to flick across his transparent face – a decision, a thought. He gives a mock smile. He scowls.

'Well, why are you sitting here like a stone?' he says, with his old impatience. 'Deal.'

◆ French Toothpaste

◆

◆ My toothpaste is made in France. *Société Parisienne D'Expansion Chimique*, it says on the tube. *Pâté Gingivale Spécial*. It is pinky-red. They didn't have my usual brand. It has turned my toothbrush pinky-red, too. My toothbrush is British. Kent. Tipped nylon. M.

Isaac Shur, thirty, sometimes happy, sometimes sad, a playwright and a poet, came, after many stops, to the house of a friend in Lindos on the isle of Rhodes, and sat in a white upstairs room that stared out at the Acropolis and the remaining third of a Greek theatre, and there, on an April afternoon, the sea almost white, and only one cloud in the sky, one only, like a puff of cannon smoke, slowly drifting, he lit a cigarette and made an inventory.

Stukas. Greek cigarettes. Are they named after German fighter planes, and is this Greek humour, to forever set them alight? My typewriter is Italian, my handkerchief is Swiss, my shoes are Danish, my cigarette box is from Yugoslavia. Hand-made. The lid squeaks. Listen.

Instead, he heard the braying of a donkey. There is nothing so laborious, so seemingly painful, as a donkey's bray, and Isaac Shur waited and thought about nothing until the donkey had run down, pumped out its last sounds, and all was quiet again. It was very quiet. The donkey's braying, though it had finished, seemed, to Isaac Shur, still to exist, and he saw it, like a puff of smoke, like that one cloud in the sky, running down the cobbled streets, under the houses that arched over, wheeling and turning, between the white-washed walls, skin over skin over skin of white, forever peeling, down steps, turning corners, and then suddenly breaking out of the labyrinth of streets and bursting into the *platia*, expanding, rising, over the fountain and over the trees, out to sea, free. Then, in his mind, it rose, higher, higher, became blue, and disappeared.

My watch is Swiss, but bought in Singapore (he continued). My camera is Japanese, bought in Hong Kong, paid for in American dollars. My string vest is Austrian. My shirt is Spanish, trousers British, the sweater from Scotland, my socks bought on a ship and not labelled. It was raining in Vienna. Who was it with blue eyes?

My wallet is Egyptian, my towel is made in the USA. The film in my camera (Japanese) is English. My soap is Pears Transparent Soap. My razor blades are Canadian, the shaving lather American but made under licence in England. From Oslo, Jerusalem, Fez? Nothing.

He looked at his suitcases and noted where they were made. He read the labels on all his shirts, on his underwear, inside his hats. The umbrella was bought in England, but there was nothing written on it to say that it had been made there. He lit another cigarette. Stuka. With an English Brymay match. Average contents 54. Large. Then he went downstairs.

The friend in whose house he was staying was in Athens, and had phoned that he would be returning in a day or two, Isaac Shur summoned to the post office by a short, stubby Greek, the postmaster's assistant, and speaking into that telephone on the wall and old women and children standing quietly and not saying a word, waiting for the day's mail to be distributed, and listening to Isaac Shur. The telephone, Isaac Shur saw, was made in Germany.

The house of Isaac Shur's friend is large, built around a courtyard, the courtyard paved, as are all courtyards in Lindos, in black and white river pebbles, as smooth as old coins, stood up on end and arranged in traditional patterns, and Isaac Shur noted that in one corner the pebbles had come away and were lying loose, flat, like spilt beans. On the walls of the house are prints, by Matisse, Picasso, Delacroix, Van Eyck, and suddenly Isaac Shur thought of his belt. That's made in Italy, too, he remembered. Bought in Florence. At a street market. And my stud box, too.

He stood in the courtyard and looked up at the white, puffy cloud in the blue sky, and then he looked at his watch. The band, he thought. The band was nylon. Bought in Gibraltar. Made in Japan. Seven minutes past five. He had been invited for drinks at five o'clock by a painter from Rio de Janeiro. He decided to take his umbrella. The door to summer is not quite open in April in Lindos, and the seemingly peerless blue sky clouds over in minutes and the streets run with rain. Umbrellas are cheap here, he thought. Also Scotch and petrol. But the Greeks, he thought, don't drink Scotch, and racket around on motorbikes and scooters that sound as though they are being run on the lowest octane fuel.

He took his umbrella and locked the door and walked to the house of the painter from Rio de Janeiro. 'Come in!' the painter called, and they sat up on the painter's roof and drank gin and orange and looked out across the roofs of the village, the Acropolis over to one side now, the Greek theatre hidden, at the sea. It had changed colour, completely, as the sea does here, particularly in these months before summer. Now it was slate grey, and darkening fast. Isaac Shur found himself staring at the painter's espadrilles and wondered were they Spanish or from some place else.

The gin, he saw, was Gordon's London Gin, and the orange juice was in a Johnnie Walker bottle, from which the label had been removed. The painter told Isaac Shur an amusing story about a Frenchman in Athens who had been swindled buying what he thought was an old Greek coin, and Isaac Shur smiled, and when the painter bent down to refill his glass, Isaac Shur leant forward and tried to see the label inside the collar of the painter's shirt, but he couldn't quite make it out. The writing on it didn't seem to be in English. Rio, he thought. And at once a strange feeling came over him, not at all pleasant, not exciting, not that bustling, tight, nervous feeling he would have had three years ago thinking about Rio, South America, any place he had not been, and he immediately looked up at the sea and drained his mind of all thought. The sea was almost black.

At six, though the sky was still bright, it had become chilly, and they went downstairs and sat in front of the fire the painter's maid had prepared earlier in the day. That fire is Greek, Isaac Shur thought. Made in Greece. Made from trees grown on the isle of Rhodes and burning Greek air. 'What?' he said, when the painter asked him a question. 'Sorry, I . . . '

He went, at eight, to the house of a writer on the other side of the village, where he had been invited for dinner. He passed an old Greek with bent legs in corduroy breeches and high boots and nodded to him. The man was so old, tall and stooped, big knuckled, enormously moustached, that Isaac Shur thought for a second that he was in Russia and that this was a peasant from Georgia, where people live so long, he remembered. Georgia? Old age? He came out of a street and into that small square where the tourists never penetrate, with its old tree and wooden benches and a sign for beer clumsily lettered on a wall. Fix. Which had once been Fuchs. He thought about the beers he had drunk, Greek beer, Italian beer, Tuborg and Carlsberg in Copenhagen, Amstel in Rotterdam, Shlitz, Guinness in Dublin in a smoky pub where they turned the pot to form an initial in the froth that lasted all the way down, John Courage in Kent, sharp and bitter Australian beer, Tiger beer in Hong Kong, but the names of the brands in Yugoslavia, Budapest, Vienna, Berlin he couldn't remember.

Copper bells tinkled in the street that led up to the Acropolis, the street for tourists, and in another month this street will be crowded with Germans and Swedes, fat women bouncing on donkeys, sitting astride on the hard wooden saddles, the Greek boys running them up, laughing all the way. Rugs and plates hang on the walls, but it is too late in the day, too early in the season. '*Cali spera*,' a woman with a water jug said to Isaac Shur. Good evening. He mumbled something in reply. I'll need sandals, he thought, if I decide to stay here. Made in Greece. I don't have anything made in Greece. Except for the Stukas, which don't really count.

The writer had prepared a bean soup, and then chicken, and they ate by the light of lanterns, the writer playing for Isaac Shur the latest jazz records which he had received only a day ago. During the meal, Isaac Shur heard the wind rising, and he wondered was it going to rain. 'These records are from America?' he asked. 'Yeah,' said the writer. 'Oh, and you should have seen the rigmarole I went through at the post office to get them. Wow. I – ' But Isaac Shur wasn't listening. That rug is Turkish, he thought. And these plates are – he carefully lifted his up and read what was written under it – Arabia Pottery. Made in Finland. He read, over and over, the label on a jar of marmalade that was standing on the table. Dundee Orange Marmalade. Dundee and Croydon. Made from sugar syrup and Seville oranges. Net Weight 1 lb (454 g). Dundee Orange Marmalade. Dundee and Croydon. Net Weight.

He left at twelve and walked back to the house where he was staying. He passed no one. It had rained, and the cobbles were slick and black. He unlocked the door, left his umbrella in the courtyard, leaning against a wall, and went upstairs to the white room with the view of the Acropolis and the remaining third of the Greek theatre, where he would sleep tonight, and sat down at the table and stared at his typewriter. Made in Italy. He lit a Stuka. Brymay Matches. He turned in his chair and stared out of the window. The street lights in the village twinkled and lit up patches of white wall, but over the village they cast a haze and the Acropolis was invisible against the night sky. Isaac Shur stood up, cigarette in hand, and went outside. He looked up at the sky. It was clear, and he could see stars, but not as many, he knew, as he would see when the electricity went off. The moon was not yet up. He threw his cigarette down into the street below and went back into the room.

At one o'clock, the electricity in the village went off and Isaac Shur sat at the table in the dark and didn't move. He wasn't tired. His head felt clear, but not with that tingling sharpness that preceded creative thought. When that happened, when he was on the brink of a poem, or a scene, then his brain was as sharp as a fragment of silver paper in the wind, it rustled, clicked, spun, crackled, and he heard voices, music, he saw immense colours, and his hands trembled with excitement. But not this time. This time the feeling was quite different. My shoelaces are Portuguese, he thought, and then he went through all his possessions again, French, English, American, Dutch, over and over, shirts, trousers, luggage, typewriter, shoes, and when he had gone over the list three times, he said 'Stop!' out loud, but he couldn't. Made in Spain, said his brain. Made in Vienna, Made in Japan, Made in USA. *Pâté Gingivale Spécial.* Pears Transparent Soap. Quink.

The village, without electricity, looked brighter and whiter lit by the stars. The moon, Isaac Shur saw, was up. There was no sound in the village, none at all. The sea was invisible, a black hole. The wind had dropped away. Isaac Shur sat without moving at the table in the upstairs room of his friend's house. Then a rooster began to crow.

It crowed on the other side of the village, past the picture theatre and the church, a long way away, and yet its sound was clear. It crowed all alone, and Isaac Shur could picture it standing in a dark yard under a peeling white-washed wall, crowing with all its might. 'Cocka-doodle dooooo!' Its cry, to Isaac Shur, seemed filled with panic and alarm. It crowed again and again, each time exactly the same cry, with a pause between, but there was no reply.

And then, from the other side of the village, almost next to where Isaac Shur was sitting in the dark, another rooster answered the cry.

They alternated, first one, then the other, across the village, the first still crowing in exactly the same way, in the same terrified, panicked tone, and in the pauses, the second rooster answered.

Then a third rooster began, then a fourth, and to Isaac Shur there came all at once an image of these roosters crowing in the night. He saw the first one waking, alone and afraid under the stars, and calling out in terror, 'Is there a God? Is there a God?' his cry waking a Catholic bird who crowed, 'Hail Mary Mother of God! Hail Mary Mother of God!' Then a Greek Orthodox bird woke and crowed with all its might, 'Hail! Hail!' waking a fourth, 'Amen! Amen!'

A fifth bird joined in, a sixth. 'We believe! We believe!' they crowed. 'Father, Mother and Holy Ghost!' 'Amen! Amen!' shouted a donkey. 'Hallelujah!' crowed the rooster right by Isaac Shur's window. 'God! God!' barked a dog.

By now every animal in the village was awake and shouting, Jewish birds, Church of England, Presbyterian, dogs of all faiths, congregations of chickens, Mormons, Quakers, roosters from every church. They crowed to the sky, 'Hallelujah! God! Hail Mary and the Holy Ghost! Amen! Amen!' and the sound of their belief was enormous.

Then Isaac Shur heard doors slamming, feet running, tins crashing against walls. 'God! God!' barked the dogs. 'Hallelujah!' crowed the cocks. And on and on they went, ten minutes, twenty, the dogs barking without pause, the roosters crowing with all their might. More doors slammed open, more tins crashed, there were shouts, calls. And then, one by one, slowly, the voices fell silent. Three dogs barked, then two, then one, and then right round the village the chorus died, first this rooster, then that, and the last sound of all that Isaac Shur heard that night was the first rooster, on the other side of the village, past the picture theatre and the church, still crowing alone and afraid, 'Is there a God? Is there a God?'

And then, at last that rooster too fell silent.

♦ A Social Life

♦ Here four days and still a virgin. Haven't played tennis, haven't played golf. Rain every night. Hear it lashing the windows, driven by wind, sitting up in the lounge watching my friend Raymond Raveck dying a slow death. But we came for girls! Nurses, secretaries, university student girls with long blonde hair! No. Raymond the poker king is being unthroned, never getting a card, never raking a single pot. There he sits in his Cary Grant attire, eyes tight with smoke, his steel-blue jaw like a rock over which waves are breaking, going downhill.

And who could have planned it better?

One, we are in an acknowledged sure thing place. Deep in the mountains, fifty miles from town. No one has ever left this guest-house the same as he went in. There's something in the mountain air that does the trick.

Two, I am in the company of the great Ray. He's the only definite non-virgin I know.

Three, we have cigarettes, money, a huge bottle of Johnnie

Walker whisky, and a double supply of contraceptives to get us through the week.

But here I am, four days gone, in six weeks I'll be seventeen, and the contraceptives are untouched. If only he'd win a game. A single hand.

My mother worries that I don't have a social life. I admit it. I suffer, slightly, from shyness. That's why I need the great Ray. He's a year older than the rest of us at school. Drives his father's car. Smokes Camels. Runs a poker game behind the bike sheds. Features almost weekly in the photographs on the social page with his arm around a different girl each time at weddings, engagements, barmitzvahs and other social affairs. In the company of anyone else, the issue would be problematical, but who could fail guided by Ray?

But the cards say no. I wake up in the morning to a wondrous view of mountain steaming with cloud, it's like the trees were on fire, and everything smelling wet and fresh, the grass, the gravel, the trees all around, but before my heart gets a chance to leap I look over at the other bed and there lies Ray, looking yellow and bleak in the morning light, pasty, snoring, in need of a shave very bad, and somehow I can't help but feel sorry for him. The gong goes for breakfast and out I sneak.

Four days come and gone.

Dear mum, I'm having a wonderful time.

I am seated in the dining room with two fussy parents and their untrained children. The little girl won't eat. The little boy has to go to the toilet. You've just been! Crash goes his cornflakes onto the floor. Parents both red in the face. Asking me politely to pass the sugar, pass the toast. Making me red in the face too. Hear that embarrassingly enormous sound? That's me sipping my tea.

After breakfast I take a walk to ease my grieving heart. Two girls are playing tennis, hopping like birds on their long legs in short tennis gear. Last night a marvellous girl was playing carpet bowls, her knees a fabulous sight. Why don't I talk to them? I need Ray. Why? Well. Because.

But Ray is going downhill. He hasn't won a single pot.

And then I collide with a girl in a corridor. She seems to have blonde hair. 'Whooo!' she says. And there sneaks out from my flustered mouth the following incredible words: 'Hey, wanna play golf?'

Golf?

We hire clubs and climb to the first tee. My trousers are baggy with golf balls, the kit and kaboodle of this ridiculous game I have never before played bouncing all over my back, me tied up with straps and this girl swinging free beside me, hair streaming in the wind. Her name is Denise. Here all week? Yep. Who are you with? Just me. My heart takes a small leap. She has never played golf before in her whole life. Good.

I allow her the courtesy of first swing at the ball. She drives it forward a mighty eight inches. 'Can I have that one back?' she asks. 'Sure,' I say. Her second hit is double her previous distance, a considerable achievement. Divesting myself of the golf bag, I put down a ball, assume the proper golfing stance, and swing.

In no time at all I have created a turbulence of air around my ball, despite which, for some reason, it refuses to move. Not an inch. Clods of turf zoom through the sky. REPLACE ALL DIVOTS says a sign. Then I at last find my distance, connect (with that satisfying sound known only to true sportsmen), and away goes my ball, never to be seen again.

'Terrif!' cries Denise.

We make it to the third tee before admitting to fatigue. 'Man!' cries Denise, and falls to the grass. I let go my golf bag. Down it goes, gratefully dead. I crumple peacefully by its side.

We are in long grass, Denise and I. There is a stand of pines behind us. A long way down the hill I see a train chugging over a bridge, trailing carriages, puffing steam. It's like a scene out of a movie. We are in a hollow of hills. The sky is alive with clouds. The guest house is on the other side of the river, a long way away, but level with our eyes. Denise's are slate grey. 'What a brothel,' she says.

She looks into my eyes, cool as can be. This, I know, is the moment I have waited seventeen years minus six weeks for. I look back. I suffer, as I have said, from shyness. But now? I feel an enormous urge to blink, and do, snap! goes that invisible line tying our eyes together. I look away. Then someone yells, 'Fore!' and the next thing I know something is flying over my head like a maddened bird and there is a great sound of crashing and smashing twigs and other wood in the pines behind us. 'Jesus!' I cry, and leap to my feet.

We go back to the guest-house, neither of us saying much, if anything. Half-way up the gravel drive Denise yells, 'See ya!' and off she runs, legs flipping out sideways as she goes. When I get to the room, Ray is still in bed.

It rains all afternoon. I spot Denise in the dining room but she leaves before me, and when I come out she's nowhere around. I challenge a precocious seven-year-old to a game of carpet bowls, smoke a few cigarettes, and the day is gone.

Back in the room, I discuss the evening's tactics with Ray. He is getting dressed. He has poured us two huge shots of his Johnnie Walker and I sit on my bed, glass in hand, watching him get dressed. He starts to shave. He has stripped down to his shorts in front of the washbasin, giving himself the steely eye in the mirror above it. From time to time he takes a deep puff on his Camel and swigs down some Johnnie Walker. I am still in my corn yellow sweater and grey trousers. I don't go in for all this dressing up.

Ray and I have the best room in the whole guest house. It's separate from the main block, that's its beauty. It's all alone, down a path, hidden by trees. Ray has used this room before. 'No one can hear ya in here,' he told me. 'Great for private parties.' A wink. The bottle of Johnnie Walker stands prominently displayed on a bedside table. Beside it, two cartons of Camels. In the drawer beneath, the contraceptives. We have made of this room a real place for men, filled it up with the smell of smoke, spiced it with alcohol. Ray begins to lather up.

'Going to the dance tonight?' I ask him. There is a dance every night, in the pavilion at the bottom of the front garden. Everyone goes.

'Take a look,' says Ray.

'There are some not bad girls around, Ray,' I say.

No reply.

'See that one playing carpet bowls last night? In the light blue dress.'

I hide in my heart all knowledge of Denise.

'She's nothin',' says the great Ray.

'Well, I don't know,' I say, watching Ray scraping away at his chin. Ray has this really heavy shadow.

'She's with her mother,' says Ray. 'Nothin' doin'.'

Ray takes about three hours to shave off the lather. When he's finished, he looks the same as before, but with a shine. He walks over to his bag and takes out his after shave and applies a liberal dose. The smell of it fills the room.

Then he starts to get dressed. Out of his bag he takes a blinding white shirt. He has a whole supply of them, a fresh one for each night. He clicks on a pair of cufflinks, each one as large as the face of my watch. He slips into a pair of jet black trousers. Before my eyes he is changing into Cary Grant. He knots a deep purple tie. 'Ya seen my shoes?' he says, stepping around all the clothing – all his – which is on the floor. He finds them and gives them a wipe with his bed cover. They gleam like mirrors. Then he gives his hair a careful comb, slips on the jacket of his suit, gives himself a final over-the-shoulder look in the washbasin mirror, shoots his cuffs, and then picks up his cigarettes from the bed.

'Let's go,' he says.

We do the usual round of all the usual places. Down the long corridor to the front foyer, passing on our left, through a bank of windows, the guest-house swimming pool. Dismal grey in the rain. There are some people in the foyer but Ray gives them only a cursory glance. He opens the door of the card room and pokes his head inside. The room is filled as always with middle-aged Jewish mothers, dealing with fingers heavy with rings, extravagantly dressed, smoking non-stop. The ashtrays are jam-packed with lipsticked butts. The card room air reeks of perfume and smoke. One of the mothers looks up from her cards, her face creased with annoyance. 'Come in or get out!' she snaps. 'You're making a draught!' We get out.

We try next the lounge. A log is burning nicely in the huge brick fireplace, the older group of guest-house guests crowded around it, warming their bones. They sit slumped like sacks in the overstuffed armchairs from which they are inseparable. The marvellous girl with the fabulous knees is sitting on a straight-backed chair reading a book. She looks up as we come in.

'Nothin',' says Ray. 'Let's go down to the billiard room.'

We cross through the recreation room. Two men are playing table tennis, huffing and puffing good naturedly as they hurl themselves at the ball. Children are making a train out of chairs at the far end of the room. There are three girls in a corner quietly watching the table tennis. They look across at us. Ray doesn't even give them a glance.

We go out through another door, into another corridor, then down a flight of steps, through another door, and we're at the billiard room.

Ray drifts in. In his right hand he holds a cigarette. His left is in his trouser pocket. 'Hiya, men,' he says. 'How's tricks?'

There is a certain sort of person who, on Yom Kippur, cruises in his father's car from shul to shul, lining up the talent. Here are two of them. Jerry and Sam. They are the villains who, for four days, have been fleecing Ray, my friend.

'Hi,' I say.

They bestow upon me a pair of weak smiles, in passing, as it were. They are not my kind of people.

'Playing tonight, Ray?' Sam asks. He is artistically draped over the billiard table, cue in hand, mid-shot.

'Try and stop me,' says Ray.

'Good,' says Sam, and with a click pockets the red ball.

I sit down on the wooden bench that runs along one side of the billiard room and take out my cigarettes.

And why am I wasting my time in this stuffy room, watching this game of show billiards? That's the way they play, Jerry and Sam. All show. Denise is probably sitting around somewhere, wondering where I am. Click goes Sam, scoring a showy cannon.

But I continue sitting and smoking and watching Jerry and Sam showing off with their cues until the gong sounds for dinner. I stand up. The mountain air does something all right. Makes you hungry. And now there's all the rigmarole of dinner. Pass the bread. The little girl was in tears last night. She said the soup tasted funny. Which it did.

'Coming up, Ray?' I say.

'Yeah,' he says. 'See ya, men.'

'Bring your wallet,' says Sam, and out we go.

After dinner, Ray and I take our coffee in the lounge. The older guests are back in their armchairs around the fireplace, recovering from the heavy meal. Newspapers sag in their hands. Then I spot Denise and take over Ray to be introduced, slightly annoyed that I have to have him with me, but at the same time needing him.

But Ray doesn't seem particularly interested. Thank God.

After about an hour, we hear the band down in the pavilion starting up. Three female musicians and an old man.

'Wanna go to the dance?' I ask Denise. 'Ray?'

'Sure,' he says. We run through the rain.

This guest house in the hills is a great place for honeymooners. They surface at night for an hour or two, and here they are, swirling around the dance floor, cheek to cheek, Denise and Ray and I squeezed into a booth at the side of the dance floor. The band is really corny. Every second thing they play is a novelty number, probably because so many parents are here with their children. A father glides past with his ten-year-old daughter, looking smug. Ray lights a cigarette. 'Wanna dance?' I ask Denise. 'Love to,' she says. Out onto the floor we go.

We have picked a nice quiet number. The lights are down low. Denise's hair brushes past my cheek. My hands feel clammy. I look over at the table, seeking Ray, for reassurance. He's staring straight ahead, cigarette between his lips, that famous steel-blue jaw of his looking darker than ever.

Somehow we get through five numbers non-stop, Denise and I. Nothing is happening. I feel as though I'm going to drop dead. 'Had enough?' I ask Denise. 'Man!' she says, blowing hair out of her eyes. We go back to the table. Ray is not there.

I try a couple more dances with Denise, but I'm much too nervous. It's all me, I know. A couple of times I've tried dancing closer, and her body has said yes. But I let go. Seventeen in six weeks' time. What's wrong with me?

When we go back to the lounge, the game has already begun. Ray and Jerry and Sam have moved a table into their usual spot, right in the middle of the lounge, directly under the phony chandelier. Ray sits immaculate in his jet black suit, his cards held low, his jaw tucked in. He could be winning or losing, but I know he's going bad. I know the look.

We watch the game till nearly twelve, Denise and I. Ray doesn't win a single pot. He keeps taking notes out of his genuine alligator skin wallet, each time shooting a nervous look inside to see how much he's got left. He deposited an envelope full of cash at the front desk the day we arrived. That was to pay for the room.

'Queens,' says Sam, and rakes in a pot.

Denise yawns. 'I think I'll go to bed,' she says. 'Oh,' I say. She seems to be lingering. Ray has just been dealt three nines. 'Well, goodnight,' she says. He's got two aces as well. 'See ya,' I say. She goes out through the lounge door. I feel lousy. And slightly stupid. 'Raise ya ten,' says Jerry. 'Ten more,' says Ray. 'The same,' says Sam. Not a superfluous word. Thin streamers of smoke hang in the air between the cards and the chandelier. 'See ya,' says Ray. Four kings. Ray's face is a sinking ship.

Six days come and gone. Me and Denise? Nothing. A walk by the river. Nothing happened. A walk into the township. The same. Another game of golf? 'Not in the mood,' said Denise. The Johnnie Walker is half gone and the contraceptives remain untouched.

And still Ray continues to go down. He has taken the envelope from the front desk. And gambled it away. He has borrowed from me. He exists on IOUs. His face is a sad sight.

It's Friday night. Tomorrow we go home.

I sit on my bed, watching Ray go through his dressing-for-dinner ritual. Rain is falling. It's very quiet. My whisky has a sour taste.

'Ya better spread the word,' says Ray. 'I'm going to swim in the pool. Midnight. Five bob to watch.'

I canvas the guests at dinner. Everyone seems delighted with the idea, but cash seems to be short. I approach the old guests in their armchairs around the fire. They seem uninterested. I try the Jewish mothers in the card room. 'You're making a draught,' says the same lady as before.

Before the big swim, Ray and I go for a long walk. Rain beats down on our heads, but we refuse to run. Ray is tight-lipped and withdrawn. We walk all the way to the township and then back.

At half past eleven, Ray and I go into the changing rooms by the pool. No one has appeared as yet. Silently, Ray strips off his clothes. It is freezing cold, and he wraps himself in a towel.

'How much did ya get?' he asks.

'Five and seven,' I tell him.

'The bastards,' says Ray.

Exactly at midnight, Ray steps out to the pool. He is stark naked. I come out after him and see that everyone has turned up. Denise is here. The marvellous girl in the light blue dress is here, even the middle-aged Jewish mothers have temporarily abandoned their game. A gasp goes through the crowd at first sight of Ray. He looks to neither left nor right. Straight-backed, head up, he mounts the edge of the pool. He stands, for a second, poised. The pool has not been cleaned out since last summer, if then. Cigarette packets bob in the green scum. The surface is dotted with rain. Back go Ray's arms and without further ado into the water he dives.

A cheer rises from the crowd.

Everyone is excited now, crowding to the edge of the pool. Ray swims with powerful strokes, cleaving the foul water. It takes him seconds to get to the far end. He turns, flipping under the water. Back he comes, the same as before, his powerful arms showing no sign of strain. I stand with the towel, ready. Ray's hands touch the edge of the pool by my feet. He's done it. The crowd is screaming jubilantly now. Ray pauses for a second, then up he comes. A sodden leaf is plastered to the top of his head.

'Champion!' screams a table-tennis player.

'Quick, get into this,' I say to Ray, spreading out the towel.

But he ignores me. He walks straight past. I run after him into the changing rooms, the towel in both hands, like a bullfighter. Behind us, the crowd is really screaming now, but I don't bother turning to look.

I run after Ray into the changing room and slam the door. Ray is standing in the middle of the room, on the concrete floor, looking stunned. I put the towel around his shoulders. He can hardly speak. His teeth are chattering like dice in a box.

'Bastards,' he finally says.

I watch him drying himself, not knowing what to say.

I can hear great sounds of splashing and worse. I go to the door and take a look. It's incredible. People are hurling themselves into the pool, screaming and laughing like loons. In goes Denise, fully clothed. In goes the marvellous girl in blue. In goes the table-tennis player, shooting up water.

'They're all jumping in,' I tell Ray.

'Yeah,' he says.

'Oh, here's the money I collected,' I say, suddenly remembering.

'Keep it,' he says, tight lipped.

More people seem to be jumping into the pool, but I can't be bothered going to watch. I stand and look at Ray. He is getting into his jet black trousers. His legs are not properly dry and the trousers cling. He fumbles with his cufflinks. He can't undo his tie.

'I'll have to phone my dad,' he says. He looks down at the ground, not at me. 'I'll tell him I lost my wallet. Ah, he'll never believe it.' He looks totally defeated.

'You want me to speak to him?' I suggest.

'Naah,' he says. 'What's the use?'

Fully dressed now, he sits down on a bench and lights a cigarette. He keeps staring down at his feet.

'Let's go into the lounge, Ray,' I say. 'Warm up by the fire.'

'I'm not going out till every one of those bastards has gone,' he says.

We sit for half an hour, Ray still shivering, smoking cigarette after cigarette, not looking at me. The noise in the pool dies down. After a while, there's only the soft sound of falling rain.

'They've all gone, Ray,' I tell him, coming back to the door.

'Ah, shut up,' he says. 'Leave me alone.'

Even saying that he won't look at me. I start to say something, then think better of it, and leave him there, still sitting, head down, smoking yet another cigarette.

Back in the lounge, it's as though nothing has happened. A couple of old-timers sitting in armchairs, yawning, getting ready for bed. The card-players are finishing off for the night. There is a quiet game of darts going on in the recreation room, which I watch for a while. Then I go down to the billiard room, where a

couple of pros are playing. I watch that for a while. It's after one
I decide to go to bed.

Down the long corridor. Past the pool. Out the door and down
the path. Under the trees. I open the door and on Ray's bed is
Denise with her legs in the air.

Once more down the long corridor. Into the foyer. Out the front
door. The gravel crunches under my shoes as I go down the hill. It's
not raining just this minute, but the trees are dripping. I can hear
the river rushing behind the trees, high with September rain. Legs
in the air. The great Ray. There are no lights showing in the
township, not a single one. Legs. I walk through the township as far
as the bridge, and then I start back.

Ray is asleep when I get back. I knock on the door first, just to
make sure. Then I go in.

The great Ray. He looks pasty, exhausted, the shadow on his
jutting jaw almost pure black. I consider packing my bags and
just going, out on the road, walking till I drop. Maybe I can hitch
a lift. Who drives on that road at this time of night? I sit down on
my bed and study the face of the great Ray.

I consider driving a small hole into every one of his
contraceptives.

I consider pouring his whisky down the drain.

I see myself flinging his Camels, one at a time, out into the
rain. There they go, little white soldiers!

I kick off my shoes.

We're going home tomorrow. I kick off my trousers. Ray and I
on the bus. Off with the jumper and shirt. Depleted. Each in his
own way. And just before I fall asleep, I think of the great Ray in
the phone booth talking to his father. 'I lost my wallet, dad.'
That's worth a small smile, and on that note I fall asleep.

♦ American Shoes

♦

♦ We open our story on a Saturday afternoon at the Commonwealth Hotel in Port Augusta, known to the local drinkers as the Crazy Cottage, where the owner, a tall, gaunt woman of forty with red-rinsed hair hanging down like string is playing the violin. She once gave recitals in the capitals of the world, winning renown for her Bach, but now her eyes are mad. She is accompanied by a short, fat man on trumpet, and a fourteen-year-old boy on drums. The trumpeter has a drinker's nose, a drinker's watery eyes, and his face, as he plays, is on fire. The boy has black hair plastered down hard with water or oil, and his drumming is loud, flat and even. He stares straight ahead, deadly serious, never smiling. They are playing popular tunes, the violinist sawing frantically, bony elbow flying, and stamping a foot. The place is packed and in an uproar. Everyone is shouting. Harold Singer, who is twenty years old and five hundred miles from home, is sitting with a battered ex-boxer, a tall Dutchman, and a once-professional con-man with a mouth full of silver teeth. The boxer is pummelling Singer with talk of the ring.

'Hey, ya heard o' Blue McDonnell?' he asks.

'I don't think so,' says Singer.

'I fought 'im,' says the boxer. 'Knocked 'im clean out o' the ring. Yeah! Ya heard o' Stan Davis?'

'I really don't know too much about boxing,' Singer says.

'What about Tommy Muldoon?' says the boxer, unperturbed. 'Little runty fella with sandy hair. Fought 'im twice. First time he practic'ly killed me, second' time I 'ad 'im in one. Yeah!'

'Is that so?' says Singer politely, trying to conceal his unease. The boxer frightens him. He is a small, surly man with little yellow eyes set close together and eight teeth missing in the front. His face and hands are battered with sun and bumpy with scars, and he seems to Singer a man capable of anything. Singer takes a quick sip of his beer. The boxer leans in close, breathing hard, his yellow eyes not leaving Singer's for a second.

'Ya heard of a guy by name of Steve Mansfield?' he says, jabbing Singer with a finger.

'Well . . . ' says Singer, 'the name . . . rings a bell . . . '

'Ah, leave him alone, Mick,' says the Dutchman. 'He's only a boy.'

'Shut up, Lofty,' the boxer snaps.

The Dutchman laughs. He is having a fine time. Yesterday he was broke and today he's drinking jugs of beer. He is a big man, six feet three or more, with happy blue eyes and protruding teeth like dirty piano keys. His long legs are sprawled out in front of him like pipes, his pants stretched tight and halfway down his right thigh an unnatural bulge showing. There is something wrong with his privates, caused, the Dutchman told Singer, by an accident on the railway line a week ago involving, somehow, a handcart, two forty-four-gallon drums of petrol, a train and a cook. 'Look,' said the Dutchman to Singer, indicating his melon bulge, 'I don't think it's natural to be like this. All blown up like a rock. It's not right. Ha! But you should see that cook! The train went bang! he shoot up in the air and when he come down he started to run and I never seen that fella again! That cook!'

'How about some more beer, Mick?' says the once-professional con-man with the silver teeth.

'What?' says the boxer, and Singer takes this opportunity to turn away, away from the boxer and his probing yellow eyes. He looks around the room. The décor is Victorian, dim, with heavy hanging lamps on chains and ferns in brass pots by the walls. The walls are covered with paintings, stiff and formal portraits of men with moustaches, sleek racehorses, views of trees, mountains and skies, all brown with age like gravy. Between them and above them, the walls show wallpaper mildewed and stained like old maps.

Singer sees his mother's face and quickly looks somewhere else.

His eyes alight on a woman sitting at a table to his right. She has enormous breasts and a huge face like a moon on which has been painted a cupid's bow pair of lips. She sits comfortably with her feet wide apart and a large handbag over one arm. With her is a little whippet of a man wearing a wide-brimmed grey felt hat. The man's face is serious and white. He takes quick, nervous sips of his beer, his eyes glued to the woman's breasts. The woman, as Singer watches, laughs. The breasts quiver and lunge. The man leans forward anxiously, mesmerised by the bouncing flesh. A chair crashes to the floor as a drinker at the next table stands, but the little man with the grey hat doesn't move. Singer gets a sudden picture of the breasts bouncing free, jumping absolutely and completely out – and then what? What will her little friend do then? Singer is sure it is all about to happen, when suddenly the woman turns and looks at him, catching him unprepared. He blushes furiously and quickly looks away, but not quickly enough. 'Wanna come upstairs, son?' the woman shouts at him. 'Show ya a good time, ha ha ha!' 'Marge, ya're all tit,' someone shouts back. 'Watch yer language!' yells the woman. 'Where do ya think ya are, at home? Ha ha ha!' Singer, flustered, flees to the band.

He is just in time to see the owner throwing down her violin. She slams it down on top of a piano, her eyes bulging. Then she sits down at the piano and starts to play. She plays with considerable force, her fingers stiff with rings and banging like hammers. Singer stares at her, amazed at her fury. No one else, he sees, is paying her the slightest attention. In the shouting room she can hardly be heard. Singer has never been in a place like this ever before in his life.

'Hey,' says the boxer, jabbing Singer with a finger, 'ya ever heard of a fighter by name of Snowy Edwards? Helluva fighter, strong as a bull. Yeah! Ya heard o' Percy Blake?'

'I don't think so,' says Singer.

'Yeah? What about Mitch Flanagan?'

Singer tries to smile, blinking into the boxer's broken face.

'Me and Mitch fought it out once,' says the boxer, but Singer doesn't hear the rest. He is all at once back in the changing rooms under the grandstand at the local football field, where he slept last night in his sleeping bag on a hard wooden bench, climbing in through a window after it was dark and waking up at five in the morning to hear a strange sound. The wind has come up, but the sound is more than the wind, and for a minute Singer is terrified. It is like a horde of frantic birds. He runs outside and sees the grandstand above bedecked with pennants and flags, flapping and fluttering in the morning wind, and he thinks of funerals and death.

'Ya know Buddy Kelly?' says the boxer, and Singer sees his mother, and he feels himself sinking, filled with fear.

She is sick, she is very sick, and why Singer has run away he doesn't know. He left suddenly, thumbing rides with cars and trucks, not sleeping, going as far as fast as he could. All the way to Port Augusta. The last town before the desert.

'Another jug, Mick,' says the con-man, banging the boxer on the arm.

'Yeah,' says Mick. He scowls, but at the same time looks proud as he brings out of his trouser pocket a roll of notes two inches thick and clumsily peels one off. He flicks it to the centre of the table, and then leans back in his chair, his yellow eyes skimming around the shouting room.

'Look at all that money,' shouts the Dutchman. He gives Singer a broad wink. 'Happy, boy?' he asks. 'You like the Crazy Cottage? It's a good place.'

'It's fine,' says Singer. 'It's very nice.'

The Dutchman was the first person Singer spoke to in Port Augusta. He met him two days ago, leaning up against the bar in the front room of this pub. 'I'm looking for a job,' Singer told him. 'You know where there's one around?' 'You got money to buy me a beer?' the Dutchman asked. Singer had – and has – five traveller's cheques at the bottom of his pack, and five pound notes in single notes in various pockets. He took out a crumpled note. 'That's all I've got,' he said. The Dutchman grabbed it and waved it in the air. 'Over here!' he shouted at the barman. 'My friend's buying!' The pound went fast, Singer trying to find out about work but getting nowhere. 'You got any more money?' the Dutchman asked. 'No,' Singer said. 'I have to get a job.' 'Come back Saturday,' the Dutchman said. 'My friend Mick'll be here. He'll fix you up.'

A pound down the drain, Singer thought, and the next place he went to was the Government Employment Office, where he should have gone first, and there a man told him that the only job available was fettling, repairing track, out in the desert. 'Pretty tough,' he said, looking hard at Singer. 'Gets hot. They're all alcoholics out there. Only place a drunk can get a job. They won't hurt you, but my God, they'll drink the spirit out of your lamp. Where you from?' he asked, and when Singer told him, he shook his head. 'You better go home, son,' he said. 'This is no place for you. Go home.'

There's a clock on one wall and Singer, looking up, sees that it's after four. He has been here for nearly two hours, drinking the boxer's beer, and the subject of jobs hasn't even come up.

'Have another drink,' says the Dutchman, refilling Singer's glass from a new jug.

'Ya know Sydney at all?' the boxer asks Singer, looming up again, his face only inches away. 'There's a bastard of a town. I had some times there though. Me and four girls in a hotel, best in town. Yeah! We done everything! Just won a fight. Feeling great. Those women! They was all over me. They go mad when they see blood. Ya can't keep 'em away. Yeah! They tear ya t' pieces, do anything ya care to name. And when ya lose and don't get a penny, they wouldn't look at ya in the street. Wouldn't spit on ya. Yeah! That's the truth.'

'What I really want,' says Singer, made bold by beer and the flying minutes on the clock – it has suddenly become five o'clock – 'is a job. Do you know where there's one going?'

'What kinda work?' says the boxer.

'I don't care,' says Singer. 'Anything.'

'Yeah?' says the boxer, his little yellow eyes boring hard into Singer's. 'What sort o' work ya do back home?'

'Well,' says Singer, and feels sweat breaking out on his brow – he can see I'm a student, he thinks. He can see I've never done anything. He can see I'm Jewish. 'I worked for a while with a firm of shopfitters,' he says.

'Yeah?' says the boxer.

'Got into a bit of trouble,' says Singer. 'You know.'

'Ya got any money?'

'No,' says Singer. 'Not a penny.'

'Okay, son,' says the boxer. 'You come with me. I'll fix ya up. Listen. Ya ever come across a fighter by name of Ronnie Smith? Big Ron he was called. Had a reach on 'im like a bloody crane.'

'I don't think so,' says Singer, but the boxer doesn't stop. Name follows name. Beer follows beer. Singer, suddenly a shopfitter with a background of trouble, lets himself go. He stares into the boxer's broken mouth and hears the thud of leather on flesh and the roar of the crowd. Up and down the coast of Australia he goes, girls screaming, blood spurting onto the canvas of a hundred rings, in Melbourne, Sydney, Brisbane, Adelaide, in bush towns, at carnivals, in smoke-filled private clubs. Exhibitions, contests, grudge fights, title bouts. In and out of taxis he leaps, into plush hotels where everyone bows and knows his name, in cheap anonymous rooms where from behind the thin walls comes the sound of old men coughing all night. Vast sums of money magically appear, mysteriously fly away. Champagne explodes from icy bottles, red-lipped girls do amazing things. The boxer's chin is wet with spittle, cigarette after cigarette hanging from his cracked lips, and when next Singer looks up, it is six o'clock. And the place is in turmoil.

'That's all for today, ladies and gentlemen!' the owner is shouting, her violin tucked under one arm. 'Drink up and get out! But don't forget to come back! Non-stop entertainment guaranteed!'

Singer stands up, dazed with beer. Everyone is standing, but no one seems to be leaving. Everyone is shouting and waving money in the air. Singer sees waiters rushing from table to table, loaded down with boxes of beer. Everyone is buying, for the long drought of Saturday night and all day Sunday. Singer has never seen anything like it. 'Over here!' Mick is shouting, waving his roll. Singer watches as he buys four boxes of beer, a dozen bottles in each, two bottles of whisky, and a gallon flagon of sweet sherry. 'Okay,' he says. 'That should do. Let's get outta here.'

They are outside. Singer is amazed to see the sky still blue and the sun burning down. He blinks, sweating, and rubs his eyes.

'I want a taxi,' the boxer mutters.

In the bright light of day he is a smaller man than Singer thought, with short bowed legs and a fighter's sloping shoulders and low neck. He stands, his whisky bottles jammed into the pockets of his jacket, the gallon of sweet sherry under one arm, squinting angrily down the street.

'You come with us, boy,' the Dutchman says to Singer. 'We gonna have a party. Okay, Mick?'

'Where's ya gear, son?' the boxer asks.

'It's at the police station,' Singer says.

'Them bastards!' He scowls and spits into the street.

'Hurry, boy,' says the Dutchman to Singer. 'We be right here.'

Singer is off, running. The police station is halfway down the street, next door to a bank. A sergeant at a desk nods as Singer comes in, and Singer goes along a corridor, then through a door to the yard at the back. This is the gaol, a large barred cube like a cage at a zoo, open to the sky. The floor is concrete. There are buckets and long wooden benches, nothing else. A man with a stubbly grey beard stands at the bars as Singer hurries past, the man's eyes red-rimmed and empty. Singer goes through another door, collects his pack, and hurries back the way he came, head down as he passes the prisoner.

They are in a taxi and about to leave when Singer comes running back. The Dutchman throws open a door and Singer squeezes in, his pack on his knees. The taxi is hot inside, and smells of scorched plastic, dust and sweat. The windows are so dirty Singer can hardly see out. Next to him, the con-man lights a cigarette.

They travel for ten minutes and then Mick leans forward and jabs the driver on the shoulder.

'Right here,' he says.

Singer struggles out, banging a knee. He sees a cluster of huts, with bright tin roofs and yellow wooden walls. There are about thirty of them, grouped together on a low pocket of land down from the road and next to the railway line. He hoists his pack onto his back. A train begins to shunt along the line, appearing and disappearing between the huts.

He waits for Mick to pay the driver, and then follows him down, his pack bouncing on his back. Mick unlocks the padlock on the door of his hut, kicks the door in with his foot, and then goes in. The con-man follows, then the Dutchman, and then Singer, first taking off his pack.

There is a bedroom, a kitchen, and one other room. The kitchen is filled with empty bottles, yellowing newspapers, rusty tins. There is a black stove in one corner, shiny with grease. The bedroom is dark, and all the other room has in it is a broken chair, and an old calendar nailed crookedly on the wall by the kitchen door. Singer puts down his pack.

'Here y'are, son,' says the boxer, and hands him a bottle.

'Thank you,' says Singer, and sits down on his pack. The Dutchman lowers himself carefully to the floor, and then sits, his back against a wall, his long legs sprawled out in front of him. He gives Singer a happy wink. The con-man takes a bottle of beer and goes out. Mick sits down on the broken chair and lights a cigarette. He stares at the floor, his brow furrowed. Suddenly he looks up at Singer, his yellow eyes burning.

'Where ya reckon I got these shoes?' he says, jabbing a foot at Singer. 'Take a good look.'

'Sydney?' says Singer.

'Sydney be damned! They're from New York! America! Yeah! Listen, ya heard o' Bing Crosby? The singa fella. Well, I been to his place. He lives on a big ranch. I put on a little exhibition for 'im. Yeah. He ain't a bad fella. Knows how t' treat a man. Not tight with his dough like some. I got these shoes in New York. I been all over the place. Been to Italy, been to France. Come here,' he says to Singer, standing up. 'I'll give ya a little lesson, teach ya how t' fight.'

'Easy, Mick,' says the Dutchman.

'Ah, I ain't gonna hurt 'im,' growls the boxer. 'Come 'ere,' he says to Singer. 'Get yer hands up. Now watch.'

Singer takes up a position, but before he can think, Mick has thrown his arms around him and is squeezing him hard, breathing in his face.

'Yar!' he grunts. 'Spit in 'is eye! Chew 'is ear! Keep movin' so the ref. can't see. Yar! Yar!'

Singer is helpless, his arms pinned to his sides.

'Stomp on 'is foot!' grunts Mick, stomping hard on Singer's foot. 'Keep turnin' round! Don't let 'im get free!'

Singer is terrified, he can't do a thing, but all at once the boxer breaks his grip, takes a fast step back, grunting and snorting, and then lets fly with a flurry of punches, hitting Singer on the arms, chest and in the stomach, Singer gasping and trying to step back.

'Mick,' says the Dutchman. 'Leave him alone, he's just a boy. Drink your beer.'

'Ah,' Mick growls, the fire dying in his eyes. He falls back onto his chair. 'Soft,' he mutters. 'Get yerself killed.'

He drinks from his bottle, and then lights another cigarette.

'When were you in America, Mick?' Singer asks, trying to act as though nothing has happened.

'I been all over,' Mick says. 'Fought in England, too. I done all right. See this hand? That's the one shaken by Bing Crosby himself. In person. He ain't a bad fella. Not like some o' them. Yeah!'

Singer upends his bottle, but drinks very little. The beer tastes warm and sweet. He's not going to find me a job, he thinks. But how do I get out of here?

The con-man comes back, and stands in the doorway, a fresh bottle in his hand.

'The party is about to commence,' he says, flashing his silver teeth. 'Guests are reminded to kindly supply their own drink.'

'Jeezus!' cries the boxer. 'Them bastards'll drink every drop I got! Lofty, get on yer feet. We gotta hide some of this stuff.'

The Dutchman stands up, smiles at Singer, then carries a box of beer and the flagon of sherry into the bedroom, where he pushes them under the bed.

'Come on, boy,' he says to Singer. 'The party is starting.'

'I'll be over in a minute,' says Singer. 'I just want to do a few things first.'

'Touch me stuff and I'll kill ya,' the boxer says, jerking his thumb at the bed.

'Next door, boy,' says the Dutchman. 'You'll hear the noise.'

Singer is alone.

He thinks first of fleeing, taking his pack and going – but where? Another night in the changing rooms, with the pennants flapping in the wind? And what if someone finds me there, he thinks. He looks at his watch. He sees, with surprise, that it is after eight o'clock, and he feels instantly hungry. He had coffee for breakfast, nothing for lunch, nothing but beer all afternoon. He unstraps his pack and takes out a piece of cheese and some black bread, bought two days ago, both now hard and dry. He washes them down with beer. Then he lights a cigarette, takes out from his pack his pen and a writing pad and sitting on the pack he begins a letter to his brother back home.

I'm in Port Augusta, he writes. *I might take a job here for a while, I'm not sure. Or I might go on to Alice Springs. It's very hot here. It was ninety-three degrees today. How is mum? Tell her not to worry about me. I am going to*

What? he thinks. I am going to what?

He sits and stares at the pad on his knee. Then he looks up and stares through the open door at the sky, criss-crossed with washing lines. An angry shout followed by a burst of laughter comes from the hut next door. Jesus, thinks Singer, and closes his eyes. Then he opens them, stands up, tears the page he has written on off the pad, screws it into a ball, goes to the door and throws it out into the night. They're singing in the hut next door now, a dozen voices belting out a drunken song. Singer thinks again of fleeing, grabbing his pack and running away, and for two minutes he stands, head down, undecided. Then he looks up, pushes his hands deep into his pockets, and steps out of the hut to the party next door, for where else is there to go?

Just one more thing about this night: at two o'clock, Singer can take no more and slips back to the boxer's hut. He is woozy with beer, hoarse from too many cigarettes, his face aches from smiling into drunken faces, and he unrolls his sleeping bag on the floor and in five minutes is asleep. At three the boxer and the Dutchman come in and wake him up. The boxer is very drunk. He sits down on the broken chair, a bottle of beer in one hand, a cigarette in the other.

'What're ya sleeping for?' he says to Singer, and then sees Singer's pen and pad. 'Listen,' he says. 'I want ya t' write me a letter. Yeah. To my sister. Bev.'

Singer sits up, rubbing his eyes.

'I'll tell ya what t' say,' the boxer says. 'Tell 'er I'll be round one o' these days. Yeah. Ask 'er how she is. How ya keepin', Bev? Write that. How are the boys? Listen. Tell 'em t' stay away from the fight game. Write that. Stay away. It's a mug's game. Stay outta it, ya hear? It's a game for flamin' mugs. Yeah! They're good boys, they don' need all that. It's a mug's game, it's a racket.' He says this over and over, tears running down his battered cheeks and chin, until the Dutchman taps him on the shoulder and says, 'It's all right, Mick, it's all right,' and the boxer staggers off to bed.

Our story takes a skip of three weeks. Singer is now in the employ of the railways. He is at the butt-welders, close to a hernia. Here, forty feet lengths of rail are being welded three together, and it is Singer's job to push these hundred and twenty feet lengths of rail down a slide. 'Crack 'em like a whip, boy!' the foreman shouts at him. 'Keep 'em moving!' He shows Singer how, grabbing one end of a rail and whipping it backwards and forwards so the whole length comes alive and slips like a snake down the slide, but when Singer tries it, nothing happens. The sun beats down on his head. Black spots dance in front of his eyes. His hands tremble and shake. 'Put yer back into it!' the foreman shouts.

Singer lives in another colony of huts in another part of town, sharing a hut with a drunken Czech. Night after night the Czech tells him the story of his life, something about respect and a bad woman and three or four gaols, while Singer waits for a letter from home. Nothing comes. Will I go to Alice Springs? he thinks.

'Ya'll die there, son,' the boxer tells him. 'Sun's so hot it'll fry ya brains like eggs in a pan. Yeah!'

The boxer seems not to be working. Singer bumps into him occasionally in the wide street of the town, with its verandah posts and row of pubs like a set for a western film. Mick looks each time shabbier and shabbier, his cheeks grimy with beard. 'Lend us a quid, will ya, son?' he asks. His fat roll of notes has gone.

One night, lonely and bored, Singer drops in at Mick's hut. The Dutchman is there too, and a young man named Howard with a bright red face and thick nearly-white hair like straw.

'How do you like the railways, boy?' the Dutchman asks Singer.

He is as jovial as ever, stretched out comfortably on the floor, a bottle of beer in his hand.

Howard is reading *Time* magazine. Singer met him at that party three weeks ago. He is a university graduate, and was just about to take up a position in a pharmaceutical firm when he suddenly left home and came here. He seems to Singer highly intelligent, but he drinks. He makes no bones about it. 'I'm a boozer,' he says. And when he asked Singer what he was doing here, Singer was vague, he couldn't tell him about his sick mother, he shrugged, looked away. And then wished he hadn't, that he'd told Howard everything, but now it's too late.

'Hello, Mick,' Singer says.

Mick doesn't look up. He is drinking wine and looks surlier than ever. All at once he stands up, shoulders hunched, and leaves the hut.

'What's wrong with him?' Singer asks.

'Ah, don't worry about him,' Howard says. 'Ya on the booze yet?'

'I'm not really a drinking man,' Singer says.

Singer stands one afternoon on a hill with his back to Port Augusta and before him the desert. He watches a truck moving out into the desert, raising a long plume of dust. After a while the truck is out of sight and all he can see is dust. Then that goes too. There is nothing to see, the view to the horizon is featureless and flat, hazy in the sun, but still Singer stands. He lights a cigarette and tries to focus his thoughts. I can't go home, he thinks. I can't go home yet. I just can't.

There now enters the scene, dancing in, wearing shiny black shoes with pointed toes, a dapper little man with a pencil-thin moustache and sparkling eyes. His name is Harry and he is a liar.

He moves into a hut two down from Singer's and hangs up a sign saying *Haircut 2/-*. This is cheaper than the barber in town and Singer goes to have his done.

'I've seen some bad places,' says Harry, dancing around Singer with his scissors clicking, 'but this is the worst. Just a minute, I'll show you my map. It's all there. How do you like it in the back? Short? Up high?'

He gives Singer a few more clips, and then leaves him, with only one side done and hair creeping down Singer's shirt under the tatty towel Harry has spread over his shoulders, and on one knee he bends down and slides out from under his bed a small suitcase which, with a neat flip, he puts onto the bed, his thumbs, at the same time, clicking open the catches. Up flies the lid. 'It's all here,' says Harry, opening up on Singer's lap a large map of Australia.

'You name it, I been there,' says Harry, dancing back a step, hands on hips, rocking proudly on the balls of his feet.

'What's this?' says Singer, trying to free a hand from under the towel with which to point. A snip of his hair rolls down from the towel and explodes soundlessly in the middle of Western Australia, creating new rivers and roads. Harry dances back to Singer's side.

'That?' says Harry. 'Lost four hundred quid there. See? *Lost £400 – poker.* Everywhere I go, I write down what happens. See? *Worked for butcher.* That was at a slaughter-house. Good work. Wasn't there long, though. It's on the map. *2 months.* Got into a fight with the foreman. I don't like being pushed around. I broke his nose, collected my pay, and took the next train south.'

I'll bet, thinks Singer. 'Is that so?' he says.

'See that?' says Harry, pointing to a tiny inscription in the middle of New South Wales. *'£1200. Two-up.* Got into a little school there, cleaned them all out. Had to fight my way out of the place, they was so mad.'

Wow, thinks Singer, what a liar, but he doesn't look up, frightened his eyes might betray him. He peers at the map, trying to decipher some more of the writing which is scrawled everywhere.

'I've got a map of New Zealand and a map of Japan,' says Harry. 'Won't show them to you now. Take hours. See that line? That's where I sailed, on the way to Japan. Had a little Swedish skipper. Tight with his money. The food was so bad, one day I went up to him and said, "Listen, I can't eat that stuff any more. I notice you don't eat it. How about some real food for a change?" Well, he didn't say anything, but when I went down to eat that night, there was that same lousy food. The skipper was eating steak. Well, I grabbed him, took him up on deck, and hung him over the side by his heels. When I pulled him up, he gave me his steak. Ate well the rest of the voyage. The skipper stayed out of my way. He knew what was good for him.'

'Hmm,' says Singer, pointing to another inscription. 'And what's this?'

'That?' says Harry, dancing in closer to look at the map. '*Shearing. Horse.* Oh yeah. That was up north. Queensland. Fella up there thought he'd have a little joke. "See that horse?" he said to me. "Tame as a milking cow. Gentle as your own mother. Get on and I'll teach ya how to ride." He thought I'd never been on a horse before. So I got on. Well, the second I was in the saddle, the damn thing started jumping and careering all over the place. I tell ya, if I hadn't been able to ride, that horse would have broken my neck. You can bust up your insides on a horse like that. Well, I stayed on for a while, and when I'd had enough, I got off and went over to that joker and said to him, "I suppose that's your idea of a joke. Well, I don't." I knocked out three of his teeth. He didn't know what hit him.'

Singer looks up, attempting a smile. There is something about this Harry he doesn't like, and not just the obvious lies. He looks at his watch and feigns surprise. 'Hey, it's seven o'clock,' he says. 'Can you finish me up, I have to see someone.'

'Sure,' says Harry, dancing in. 'Won't take me a minute.'

The following day, while Singer is washing his shirt in the communal laundry, another facet of Harry's character is revealed. The small dancing man has been not only a shearer, a butcher, a sailor and a gambler, but a man of the ring.

'Yeah,' says Harry, throwing his shirt into the tub next to Singer's, 'I've been in a few fights in my time. Professional. I'm not talking about the others. Won some big purses too. All in a day's work.'

'Do you know a boxer by the name of Mick Sullivan?' Singer asks. 'A small guy. Little yellow eyes.'

'Mick Sullivan!' cries Harry. 'Jesus! I haven't seen him in years! Know him? I fought him. Hell of a fighter. One of the best.'

'He's in town,' says Singer.

'In Port Augusta?' says Harry, and Singer blinks, amazed to see such coolness. What a fantastic bluffer, he thinks.

'You know the Crazy Cottage?' he asks Harry. 'He goes there a lot.'

'Listen,' says Harry, 'next time you see him, tell him I'm here. Wait a minute, wait a minute. Tell him I'll be in the Crazy Cottage Friday afternoon, four o'clock. I'll buy him a beer.'

'Okay,' says Singer.

'Mick Sullivan!' cries Harry, dancing back with his shirt from the tub. 'This'll be an event.'

That night Singer goes around to Mick's hut to tell him his old boxing friend Harry is in town and wants to meet him. Singer doesn't know what kind of reaction to expect from Mick, but he feels excited, he's not sure why.

But Mick, when he tells him, seems hardly interested. He is drinking port. The hut smells of it, sour and thick.

'Friday,' says Mick, not looking up. 'I'll be there.'

There is no enthusiasm in his voice, no surprise. He seems to Singer to be more morose than ever, his head down, his face dark, and after twenty minutes of surly silence, Singer says good night and goes back to his own hut, feeling off balance and ill at ease.

The next day is Thursday. Harry has his chair out in the sun, in front of his hut, and is sitting listening to a portable radio, his dapper feet crossed.

'I've seen Mick Sullivan,' Singer tells him. 'It's all arranged. Four o'clock tomorrow.'

'Fine,' says Harry. 'Sit down. What have you been doing? I haven't had a decent conversation all day.'

Singer sits down on the step outside the barber's hut and lights a cigarette.

'You been here long?' Harry asks.

'About a month,' says Singer. 'I'm thinking of going to Alice Springs.'

'The Alice,' says Harry. 'Good place. Matter of fact, I'm planning to go there myself. Gonna drive up. There's a sweet little car going for thirty quid I've got my eye on. Needs a bit of fixing up, but I can handle that, no trouble. Worked in a garage once, I ever tell you? When are you thinking of going? Might take you along.'

Whoops, thinks Singer, his heart suddenly beating fast.

'I'm not sure,' he says, not looking at Harry. 'In about two weeks, I think.'

'I'd better get onto that car,' says Harry. 'A bargain like that doesn't lie around too long.'

'Well, I think I'd better be off,' says Singer, getting to his feet. 'Got some things to do.'

On Friday, Singer finds himself passing the Crazy Cottage. It is half past four. They won't be here, he thinks, going in. Well, certainly not Harry.

But they are. Mick and Harry are sitting side by side under a painting of a race horse, ferns in brass pots on either side of them, like a tableau. This is the room where the mad violinist plays on Saturday, but now it is completely quiet, a different place. Mick and Harry have two glasses of beer on the table before them, and a plate of sandwiches, so far untouched. Mick looks very serious. Harry is smoking a cigarette.

'Hello, Mick,' says Singer, smiling broadly. 'Hello, Harry.'

'Go away,' snaps Mick, his yellow eyes hard and vicious. 'Beat it.'

'Yeah,' says Harry. 'Leave us alone.'

Singer retreats.

That night Singer goes over to the barber's hut to see what it was all about.

'Mick Sullivan?' says Harry. 'That wasn't Mick Sullivan. Jesus! I should have broken his nose for using the good name of the man.'

'What?' says Singer.

'Just a bum,' says Harry. 'Using Mick Sullivan's good name. I should have broken his face for him.'

He says it with such conviction that Singer begins to doubt his picture of the barber. A liar? He looks quickly at Harry's hands, which all at once seem to him strong and hard, a fighter's fists. But what about that business of hanging the Swedish skipper over the side by his heels? he thinks. That can't be true. Then he sees the way Mick and Harry were sitting side by side at the Crazy Cottage, so calm and solemn, and he doesn't know what to think. What were they talking about? Why did they tell him to get out?

'Just a bum,' says Harry, and Singer knows he will get no more from the man. The matter is closed.

'I had another look at that car today,' says Harry. 'Gave it a good going over. Not much needs doing, a lot less than I thought. We'll be out of here in a week. The Alice! Wonderful time of the year to be heading up there. Hot? Yes, it is. But it's a dry heat. A man can work in that kind of heat, it's the humidity you've got to watch. I've worked in a hundred and ten. And let me tell you, you won't find a better beer-drinking climate anywhere in the world than you get up in the Alice.'

'Sounds good,' says Singer, looking over his shoulder.

Any moment now, thinks Singer, he's going to ask me for that thirty pounds, and then what will I say? A flat no? It won't be easy. I'll tell him I've already booked on the train. I'll tell him I'm going with a friend.

But the next afternoon, as Singer is going past Harry's hut, he notices that the haircut sign has gone. The door of the hut is closed, but through the window he sees a big man lying on the bed, a big man wearing a dark blue suit staring up at the ceiling and smoking a cigarette.

Where's Harry? thinks Singer.

'It's like that out here,' the man in the hut next to Singer's tells him. He is an old railway man with tufts of hair growing out of his ears and brown spots on the back of his hands. 'Fella takes off in the middle of the night, ya never see him again. Maybe he heard someone was in town he didn't particularly want to see. Maybe the police. Harry, eh? Yeah. They just go. You'll never see him again. Why, he bite ya for a couple of quid?'

'No,' says Singer, 'he didn't. He didn't ask me for a penny. That's the funny thing.'

That night, yet another night of loneliness and boredom, fears and doubts, Singer goes around to see Mick. He has nowhere else to go. The Czech in his hut has embarked on a bout of heavy drinking, reeling around and cursing and throwing bottles at the walls. There are no letters from home. It is a hot night, the sky crammed with stars, the smell of desert in the air.

Alice Springs, thinks Singer, why do I want to go to Alice Springs? He sees his mother's face and flushes with shame and guilt. He has to close his eyes. His stomach tightens into a knot. He hurriedly lights a cigarette and to keep from going around in circles, he concentrates on Harry and Mick and all the stories he's heard.

There is no light showing in Mick's hut. The door is closed. Singer knocks. There is no reply.

'He's gone,' says a voice, and Singer turns to see Howard sitting on the step of the next hut, a bottle in his hand. 'Took off last night,' Howard says. 'Don't know where. Into the desert, I suppose. That's where they all go. Want a drink? I've got some cold bottles inside. Sit down. I won't be a minute. Been a bastard of a day, hasn't it?'

It remains now only for Howard to tell the end of the story. He goes inside his hut and comes back with three bottles of cold beer and sits down beside Singer, on the step.

'The local constabulary paid us a little visit last night,' he says. 'Two of them. Plain clothes. They drove right up here, in a big black car, right up to the door of Mick's hut. Mick was sitting on his step, like you and me now, not doing a thing. One of them stayed in the car and the other went up to Mick, said a few words, and then they both went into Mick's hut. Closed the door. They were in there about half an hour. Then the policeman came out, looked around, nice and casual, and then he got back into the car, and they drove off. Nice and slow. Then out came Mick, and Jesus you should have seen him. That copper made a real mess of him. There was blood everywhere. He'd just about torn off an ear.'

'Why?' says Singer.

'Well,' says Howard, 'the coppers said Mick had a gun. That's rubbish. That's a straight lie. He didn't have a gun and they knew it. They just wanted an excuse to beat him up, that's all. They don't like Mick around here. Anyhow, when I went over, Mick told me to go away. He said he was all right. He didn't want me poking my nose in. Well, that's his business, but Jesus you should have seen the way he looked. I've seen some guys beat up round here, but never like that.'

'But what was it for?' Singer asks.

Howard takes a slow drink from his bottle before replying. 'They don't like Mick round here, that's all,' he says. 'He's been in too much trouble for their liking. He once killed a man, you know that? A sailor. Did it for ten quid. That was back in the days when he was a standover man. Beat up anyone for a tenner. Break a leg for another five. He must have beaten up that sailor a bit too hard. He was in gaol for eight years.'

'I thought he was a boxer,' says Singer.

'Did he tell you that?' says Howard. 'Naah. He was never a fighter. Not professional, anyway. Might have been in a couple of fights when he was a boy, same as a lot of them, but he was never a real boxer. Our friend Mick was a common gangster, a standover man. That's all.'

And what am I? thinks Singer, riding to Alice Springs on the train. From the windows of the train he looks out on river beds run dry, broken trees, boulders, mile after mile of sand, as he speeds into the desert, the final retreat. What am I? he thinks. What am I? There looms up before him the boxer's broken face, and he looks into the small yellow eyes, but they're blank, there's no expression, all he can see in them is his own face. He unstraps his pack and from the bottom takes out his five traveller's cheques and he fingers them like the end of a string tying him to his home.

◆ Repository

◆ I live in the seventeenth century. My business is with angels and saints. Also with virgins, trees and water, skies, mandolins, lutes and fruit. Occasionally with dragons. More often with gondolas, horses, dogs. When he spoke to me, my eyes were four inches from a madonna, moving slowly over her rapturous face. She held me transfixed. Such calm beauty! Such serenity! Such inner light! He spoke the one word that could draw me instantly away.

'Domenichino?' he said.

I turned. I knew him, of course. That is, by sight. Perhaps we had even nodded to each other. But we had never spoken. He was just one of the many people I saw every day, out of the corner of my eye, here at Sotheby's, and at Christie's, and at the two or three other auctions where I do my business. A vague face. A presence. Nothing more than that. I live, as I say, in the seventeenth century, and the only people I really see are Reni and Feti, Luca Giordano, Guercino, Sirani. Even the auctioneer is nothing to me but a cold eye. But I looked at this man now, as

closely as I had been studying that madonna. There seemed to
be a smile playing about his lips.

'Could be,' I said.

He smiled now, openly.

'Ah!' he said.

He wasn't one of the big dealers, I knew that much. Neither
am I, for that matter. Far from it. When a picture moves over
four hundred pounds, I say goodbye. My budget keeps me down
mostly to drawings – where I'm quite happy, let me quickly add.
I do all right. I've only been in this business for about four years.
I used to be a teacher. I do better than *that*, let me tell you. We
don't starve. And there's always the hope that one day I'll
stumble onto something, spot something that no one else has
seen, or anyhow doesn't recognize for what it is. And then! But
until that happens, I'm quite content to earn a living, to look,
learn, adore. And hope.

And this man? This vaguely *untidy* man in his grey
double-breasted suit, white shirt, striped tie, an
unremarkable-looking man in every way. He looked nearly fifty,
fifteen years older than me. Perhaps he was more. Grey-green
eyes. Brown hair, quite a lot of it. But nothing out of the
ordinary, nothing you'd remember or note. He looked at me, still
smiling, as though he knew that he had spoken the very word
that I had been thinking, and now he seemed to lean towards me,
as though we were partners in some conspiracy.

'Do *you* think it's a Domenichino?' I asked.

He shrugged. But still with that smile.

I sensed that there was something that he wanted to say. I
turned back to the painting. The madonna was on her knees.
Three cherubs or angels circled over her head. Through an
arched doorway or window there was a view of trees, water and
sky, such as you see in a thousand paintings, the usual backdrop
of the period. Not a large painting. In need of cleaning, a certain
amount of restoration, as most of them are. Who could say what
lay under the centuries of grime? If it was a Domenichino, it was
worth twenty thousand, at least. If not – what? Five hundred?
Perhaps half that. I went back to the madonna's face, but where
a minute ago it had radiated such beauty, now it was as impas-

sive as a mask. It wasn't even a face any more. It was just a surface of paint. At my back I felt the presence of the grey-suited man, looming behind me like a dark cloud, taunting me, pushing me to a decision.

'No, I don't think so,' I said, turning back.

'Of course it isn't,' he said. 'It's not severe enough. Look at those cherubs. Domenichino would never have allowed them to roll around like that. Look!' He stabbed the picture with a finger. He seemed to be suddenly angry. His face was red. And then, just as suddenly, he relaxed, and smiled, apologetically, as though ashamed at this display of emotion.

I looked at him again. There was something in his eyes, or behind them, but what it was I couldn't see. Why was he speaking to me?

'You're interested in Domenichino?' I asked.

'No,' he said. 'Not particularly. I think he was a capable enough painter, a *useful* painter for the period, but where's the drama? Where's the true feeling? No,' he said. 'Give me Caravaggio. Any day.'

Now it was my turn to say, 'Ah!'

'You like Caravaggio?' he said.

'Of course,' I said. 'Who doesn't?'

'A gambler,' he said. 'Possibly a murderer. Certainly a brawler, a fighter, fast with his fists. And his knife too. A lightning-quick temper. A pederast. Look at the way he painted his boys, in his early works anyhow. A despicable man, a ruffian, a gangster no doubt, but ah, his pictures! And I don't mean just the *light*, though God knows that'd be reason enough. But look past the light. Look at the hands, the feet, the faces, the *suffering*! He understood people. He had the insight of a true saint. Can you imagine what pictures he might have produced in another time, a freer age, when a man wasn't strangled by the church? Where do you eat?' he said to me suddenly. 'I usually go to an Italian place around the corner. Do you know it? We admire their pictures, it seems only right to eat their food.'

'Beckett,' he said. 'Ernest Beckett. Sorry, I should have introduced myself before.'

I told him who I was. We ordered our food. He recommended the veal but took lasagna for himself. A carafe of the house chianti. He lit a cigarette while we waited, but didn't speak. I tried to see into his eyes, but carefully, of course, not staring. They were different now. For the moment, there was nothing there.

Beckett ate quickly, as though the food were an obstacle to be removed before he could get down to business. Which was . . . ? I busied myself with my veal, which was very good, and waited for him to speak.

He finished before me. He took a sip of his wine and lit another cigarette. Then he frowned, as though deciding something, and put his cigarette down.

'Are you happy?' he asked me.

I smiled.

'What do you mean?' I asked.

'You'll never make any money there,' he said, jerking his chin in the rough direction of Sotheby's.

'Well,' I said. 'I do all right. Nothing fantastic, of course, but –'

'But one day you'll stumble onto something.'

'Well, perhaps . . . '

A tax inspector, it suddenly occured to me. No, I've seen him too often. A tax inspector wouldn't hang around auctions every day. I tried to remember if I'd ever seen him buying anything.

'But will you know it when you see it?' he asked.

Now he looked angry again – not like the last time, not as openly as that, but the anger was there.

I finished my veal and reached for my wine.

'Here,' said Beckett, refilling my glass.

'Authenticity,' he said. 'That's what everyone wants. Cast-iron proof of who painted the picture. But you can't have it. They didn't sign their pictures, most of them. And even where they did, who knows? Maybe that's all they did, sign their name. And then pat the student who had painted it on the head and go off to collect their fee.'

'Of course,' I said. 'But –'

'You're going to tell me about experts,' he said. 'Don't bother. I know about experts. I know a woman in Capri who has a Reni which is a Reni as surely as you and I are sitting here, and yet there's not one expert who will even hint as much. Why? Because the inferior copy *they* said was a Reni hangs in New York! Even Berenson, the great Berenson,' he said, his voice filled with scorn. 'Listen. There's only one way to know if a painting is authentic, and that's to *become the painter*! You have to be able to move your hand over the canvas and feel *his blood* in your fingers, *his brain* telling them where to move!'

He was very excited. That thing was in or just behind his eyes again.

'Caravaggio,' he said softly.

He was a chameleon. He seemed to change by the minute. Now he was quiet again, but more than quiet. He was anonymous, in his grey double-breasted suit, vaguely untidy, tired, old.

'Do you dream,' he said suddenly, changing again, leaning close to me across the table, 'of one day finding a Rembrandt in a junk shop for fifteen pounds?'

He's going to sell me something, I thought. And smiled, crediting his salesmanship.

'Who doesn't?' I said.

He leaned back in his seat, lacing his fingers across his chest.

'Tell me what you'd do,' he said.

'If I saw a Rembrandt?'

He nodded.

'Well, I wouldn't do what most people would do. I wouldn't run all around the shop looking at everything *but* the painting. I'd go straight up to it. Declare my interest. Why beat about the bush? The owner's reaction could tell me more than the painting itself. I'd ask the price. Get that settled straight away, so there could be no argument later. Then I'd study the painting. Ask to take it outside. Get it into the light. I'd study the condition of the canvas, the frame . . . everything. I don't know Rembrandt all that much, I'm an Italian man myself, mostly Venice, but for – fifteen pounds did you say? – how could you go wrong? I'd buy it, of course.'

Beckett smiled.

'And if there were two?'

'I beg your pardon?'

'And if there were two Rembrandts in the shop?'

'Two? Well, I'd buy them both.'

'And if there were three?'

His face was suddenly very close. That thing that was in or just behind his eyes was obvious now, almost completely revealed. His eyes looked straight into mine.

'Let's say,' he said, 'you were in Naples. You had a few days up your sleeve. You hired a small car, a Fiat. You decided to drive down to the south, just for a look, not aiming for anywhere in particular. Just south. Calabria, let's suppose. There's an auto-strada, of course, but you left that almost at once. You weren't after speed or easy driving. You were enjoying yourself. You went onto secondary roads. Even smaller. Rutted roads. Cart tracks. Round about four in the afternoon, let's say, you even became lost. Not seriously lost – you knew you would ultimately find your way out – but suddenly something happened to the car. The axle. Hmm?'

'Go on,' I said.

'A farmer came. You explained the situation as best you could. You speak Italian? Neither do I. Not enough, anyhow. The farmer nodded, looked, nodded again, crawled under the car. Then he went away. About an hour later he was back, this time with ropes and two horses. He towed you to a village. There was a blacksmith. He could do a temporary repair, enough to get you back to Naples. You watched for a while, and then you went for a stroll. A hot day, of course. It's very hot down there. Pretty soon you had to sit down, have a drink.'

Beckett reached for his cigarettes on the table. I watched him light one. His hands had a tremor, or perhaps I imagined that. He blew smoke and then leaned close again.

'It wasn't much of a place,' he said. 'A few houses, a square, a small church. The women all dressed in black. Some children playing in the dust. Chickens, dogs. You sat down at a café, the only café, outside, and ordered a campari. You sat there for an hour. It was pleasant enough, but you were becoming impatient. Was the car going to be fixed in time for you to drive somewhere decent, get a good hotel? You stood up. The waiter was an old man, probably the owner of the place. He was inside, reading a newspaper. You went in to pay. And then you saw, hanging on the wall next to a fly-specked calendar and an advertisement for some drink or other, a painting of two young men sitting at a table playing dice and you knew at once that it was a Caravaggio.'

Beckett took a quick pull on his cigarette, his eyes still fixed on mine. I didn't say anything.

'How did you know?' he said. 'Because you've *lived* Caravaggio, you know everything about him, you know how his mind worked. Every time you stand in front of one of his paintings, you *are* Caravaggio! *You* painted it! And this was a Caravaggio. You knew it in your blood.'

'I see,' I said.

'You pointed to the picture,' Beckett went on. 'You asked if it was for sale. Of course it wasn't. It was a decoration. It was in the family. It had hung there for years. Very old. Let's skip the details. Finally the owner said so-and-so many lire, about sixty pounds. You pretended to be horrified. So much! You finally agreed on thirty. You shook hands. You took the painting outside and studied it in the light, but you hardly needed to do that. You *knew*! Your hands were shaking. You had trouble keeping your heart quiet, but somehow you did. A Caravaggio for thirty pounds! Imagine! You went back inside to pay, and there was the old man, holding a second Caravaggio in his hands.'

Beckett paused for a second – for dramatic effect? For breath? I couldn't tell. His face was still close to mine, almost too close to see.

'From his bedroom,' Beckett went on. '*Very* old. You could hardly breathe. It's a dream, you thought. It's a trick. You asked to take it outside. Three leering men with bad teeth. Murderers. Thieves. An incredible painting. It was as real as the first. How? you asked yourself. How can there be two Caravaggios here? But he was in a lot of places, of course. All over Italy. Malta. Fleeing for his life. Hiding. No one knows exactly where. Perhaps he painted them here. Your brain went round and round, but it didn't matter, your blood said *yes*, this is a Caravaggio! You went back into the café, and there was the old man holding a third.'

'A third?' I said.

'And a fourth,' said Beckett. 'And a fifth.' His face came even closer. It was very red. 'Can there be five? Can there be five

Caravaggio paintings in a dirty little village somewhere in Calabria? Is it possible? Boys, saints, madonnas, fruit, grinning thieves! And all the time that old man standing there and smiling – why? Was he beaming with joy to have made more money in ten minutes than he made in a year? Or because he'd tricked you, he saw your excitement, he knew you were a fool? Can there be five?'

'No,' I said.

'Even if you knew in your *blood* – '

'No,' I said. 'It's not possible. It's against all logic. Two, perhaps. Not three. Certainly not four. Five? Unbelievable! I mean, consider the law of diminishing returns . . . '

'So what would you do?' Beckett asked me.

'What would I do? I'd say it was the sun. I'd say it was the heat. I'd say it was the tension of being in a strange place, your car broken down, a lot of things. What would I do? I'd get the hell out of there as fast as I could.'

Beckett stared at me. His face was terribly red. There seemed to be tears in his eyes. And then I saw that he wasn't looking at me, he was looking through me, as though I wasn't there, as though I didn't exist. I saw that thing in his eye, that thing that had been there all the time; it was naked now, clearly in the open, released from its repository behind his anonymous face, and I knew what it was.

I looked away.

◆ What is My Secret Identity?

◆

◆ There is someone in the phone booth
taking off his clothes. I don't know how he does it in the confined
space. I wait around in the corridor for him to have done (I want
to call my plumber), smoking cigarettes and drawing profiles of
Dick Tracy on the wall. I do them very well. I can't seem to get
out of the habit. I don't know where I picked it up. I have quite a
sizeable area covered before the booth bursts open and a streak
of red and blue shoots out. It is Harris from Accounting but he
looks fine. He runs nicely down the corridor and disappears into
the men's room. If I had X-Ray vision I could tell you what he is
doing in there, but I haven't, so I can't. I step into the phone
booth. My wrist radio is playing soft jazz.

Harris's clothes are all over the floor and I try not to stand on
them as I dial. He takes a size 16 shirt, I observe. His tie is draped
nonchalantly over the receiver. His shoes are neatly placed side
by side just inside the door. There is a window in the phone booth
which looks out onto the street. While I wait for my plumber to
answer, I see three men dressed like Batman, Captain Marvel and

the Green Lantern walking towards the bank. The man who is Batman has his hood pushed back. He has curly red hair and is smoking a cigar. It must be hot in a hood, I think. The Green Lantern has a large stomach like a melon, and his pants have creases in them around the knees. He doesn't seem to know what to do with his hands. He has no pockets, of course. Finally he clasps them behind his head, and he walks into the bank, just like that. The man who is Captain Marvel is carrying a pigskin attaché case. That is, it looks like pigskin from here. It could be a synthetic.

Just as my plumber answers the phone, there is a tap on the phone booth door. It is Harris, wearing a bathrobe. 'May I?' he says, and I open the door and he takes his clothes out. There is a hard look in his eye. He gathers up his clothes quickly, grunting as he bends down for his shoes. His cape flashes red but he doesn't say a word. 'Yeah?' says my plumber. 'C'mon, I haven't got all day!' 'It's about the hot water,' I tell him. I notice that I have written HOT WATER!!! on the cover of the phone book, with a speech balloon around it. The words are coming out of Dick Tracy's mouth.

'So?' says my plumber. 'It starts hot and then goes cold and then comes hot again, like that, over and over,' I tell my plumber. 'Not only that, but there's a strange taste of brine.' 'Holy Moley!' says my plumber. 'You be home tonight? Round six?' I look at my wrist radio. Then I remember and take out the pocket watch my father gave me from the lefthand-side pocket of my vest. It is round and smooth and warm in my hand. 'Yes,' I tell him. For some reason there are tears in my eyes. 'I'll be there before you can say Shazam,' he says, and hangs up.

As I am stepping out of the phone booth, Lucille Meadows from Research comes past, carrying an armful of folders. 'I know your secret identity,' she whispers. Her eyes twinkle behind her tortoiseshell frames. My mind spins and races and tries to remember a Christmas party and a dark corner behind the filing cabinets, but the picture is not clear. I walk on. When I am halfway down the corridor I turn and look back. She is still there, gazing in my direction, her head dreamily on one side. 'What did she mean?' thunders through my head. Lucille Meadows sighs, and then blushes, and then walks quickly away. Her heels tap like machine guns on the cold corridor floor. I continue on to my office.

I am about to push open the door of my office when some sixth sense warns me it's a trap. I get out my ballpoint pen and hold it like a dagger and then count three and kick the door open with my foot and step back, breathing hard. The office appears empty. I edge in sideways, ready for anything. 'Great Scott!' says a voice and I spring to face the speaker.

Rawlins, my assistant, is sitting at his desk with his feet up, reading a newspaper. 'You took me by surprise,' he says. I grope my way to my desk and sit down. When I am sure that Rawlins is not looking, I take out my handkerchief and mop my brow. I light a cigarette. 'What's news?' I ask Rawlins. 'Here, I've finished,' he says, and throws the newspaper over to me.

The Russian Premier is issuing a five-speech-balloon warning. The war news is full of BLAM! and WHUPP! and KACHOW!!! I skim down the page to where it says To Be Continued and put the newspaper down, wearily. I gaze out of my window. A Bat Signal is feebly trying to make itself seen in bright daylight. I feel old and tired and take out my father's pocket watch and run my fingers over its smooth surface. His long-ago face seems to swim before my eyes. He looked like Sigmund Freud . . .

Then I see that it is almost one o'clock. 'Great Scott!' I think. The meeting with Sinclair is at one! I gather up the necessary papers, straighten my tie, and go out along the corridor to Sinclair's office. The afternoon is as still as a day in the country. Somewhere far off a police siren wails.

I knock on Sinclair's door and hear a voice say, 'Come in.' I go in. Sinclair is sitting at his desk, writing quickly on a large sheet of paper. He circles the words with speech balloons, effortlessly and efficiently. He has great style. 'Won't be a minute,' he says. 'Sit down.'

I sit down and once more admire Sinclair's office. He has taste. Mona Lisa wallpaper. A Campbell's Soup paperweight. A Batmobile desk lighter. An original Steve Canyon framed on the wall. An antique grandfather clock.

'Right,' he says. 'Let's go. The others are waiting.' He steps into the grandfather clock. I follow him.

◆ Happy Times

◆

◆ 'Be nice,' says Fine. Then he opens the door and runs down the stairs from his flat to Martin Black's waiting car at the kerb. He comes down too quickly, but he can't help that. His smile is like neon, and he can't help that either. Down he comes, the road this Saturday night like a river of chrome, and Martin Black's shiny car parked at the kerb. Everyone is going somewhere, the river of chrome flowing in both directions, noisy, fast and hard, though on its fringes the springtime trees are shooting up first leaves, as down comes Fine, skipping the last two stairs, bounding through the gate, one hand in his pocket, the other swinging free. 'Hi!' he says, to everyone, Martin Black, Evelyn Gold, Madeline – Madeline! He opens the back door, his neon smile quite enormous now, pokes his head in for the first look in two months and eleven-and-a-half days at the girl he loves. Madeline. There is a flash of black. He feels the canine nip of teeth on his brand-new suit, bought this very morning. 'Jesus!' he cries. 'Quick, we're late,' says Martin Black. Fine falls inside, the car already moving, bumps his head, catches his sleeve in the door as, with a crunch of gears, Martin Black's shiny car flows into the river of chrome.

But dogs don't matter. Martin Black doesn't matter. Nothing does. Madeline! At last, beside her! 'Hello, Madeline,' says Fine. '*Sssh*!' she snaps. 'What?' says Fine. 'You're upsetting Froggy,' she says. Her arms are around the dog, holding it tight. 'Ha ha, hello, Froggy,' says Fine, extending a warm hand. 'How are you, old dog?' 'Oh!' cries Madeline, as Froggy breaks free and lunges at Fine, who gets his hand out of the road just in time. 'Jesus, what's wrong with *him*?' he says. 'Don't swear. And don't move!' Madeline orders. In the front seat, Martin Black gives two toots on the horn for no reason at all and then turns around with a pleased smile on his wide face. 'Ev'rybody happeeey?' he asks.

'I saw the most *mar*vellous little bag this morning,' says Evelyn Gold. 'Did you, my love?' says Martin Black. 'And not *really* all that expensive,' says Evelyn Gold. All that Fine can see of Evelyn Gold is a tower of hair and a side slice of face, the one visible eye heavily encased in lash obviously not of her own making. Evelyn Gold and Martin Black! Madeline's friends. All those fights with Madeline. 'They're my friends,' she would say. 'If you don't like them –' Martin Black, a doctor, with his wide shoulders and thick, curly hair, and Evelyn, made out of paint. He feels, now, looking at her, his face going tight and his mouth turning down. *Be nice! Be nice!* he commands himself, and right then Evelyn Gold half turns, acknowledging his existence for the first time with a bland smile, and asks, 'And how are you?' 'Okay,' says Fine. 'Good,' says Evelyn Gold, already turned back. 'Oh, and absolutely *gorgeous* shoes,' she continues. 'Terrif!' says Martin Black. 'Hey, can't I move at all?' says Fine. 'No,' says Madeline.

'Okay,' says Fine. And really, it doesn't matter being wedged up tight against the door in Martin Black's car with his hands tucked out of sight so a crazy dog won't bite them, no, these things don't matter. Not now. Not after all this time. He can feel himself trembling electrically, his mouth dry with excitement, his heart beating. He smiles over at Madeline. 'Anyhow, how are you?' he asks. Froggy growls. 'I *told* you not to move,' Madeline says. 'I didn't move,' says Fine. 'Well, your voice is upsetting him,' says Madeline. 'Jesus,' says Fine, but softly. 'Can't I even talk?'

'Hey, anyone heard anything about this film?' asks Martin Black. 'I heard it's terrific,' says Madeline. 'Glenn Ford.' Froggy, in her arms, lies quiet, eyes closed. Fine, getting needles in one side, leans ever so slightly forward to get more comfortable, and immediately the dog's eyes snap open and his mouth curls back in a growl. 'Sssh,' says Madeline, softly, to her dog, and to Fine she gives a hard look. He eases himself back as best he can, stealthily almost, an inch at a time, but his neon smile, despite everything, still flashing. His face is beginning to ache with it. It just won't go. To suppress it, he bites his bottom lip. 'Rita saw it and she said it was beautiful,' says Evelyn Gold. Fine can resist no longer. The film they are driving to see is *The Four Horsemen of the Apocalypse*, remake, with Glenn Ford, and normally wild horses couldn't drag Fine to such a film. Awful! 'Well, if you want to, you can come to the drive-in with us,' Madeline had said. It was the first time he had heard her voice in over two months. 'With Martin and Evelyn,' she said. 'Yes,' Fine said. After two months and eleven days. Yes. Hoping against hope, dizzy with excitement.

But Evelyn Gold! He can't resist. 'All the critics said it was dreadful,' he says, releasing that small arrow. 'Oh?' says Evelyn Gold. Her reply is ice, her armour is intact, and Fine, knowing he shouldn't have said a word, feels the colour rising in his face. He closes his eyes and opens them very slowly, lingering as long as he dares in neutral blackness. I need a cigarette, he says to himself. He looks over at the dog, then at Madeline. Don't move! her hard eyes say. And once more he closes his eyes and this time opens them even slower.

She is different, completely different. Her hair is different. Up. It used to be down, and soft, and now it's up and somehow brittle and hard, not to be touched. She is like Evelyn Gold, her friend. Fine, sneaking a look, sees the public nakedness of her neck, and it used to be white and private and mine, he thinks, and the remembering of that stabs him. He looks down into his lap, but immediately over at Madeline again, irresistibly drawn. Her eyes! Like Evelyn Gold's, they too are lash encased. Her face is a different colour. Her smell is not her smell at all. She used to smell of Breck shampoo and smoke, Fine remembers (another stab), woodsy, just washed, and he remembers how she once had a shot of his pipe (another stab), and puffed on it professionally (stab), not really like a man but not like a girl smoking a man's pipe either. 'Too rich,' she had said, handing it back. Stab! Stab! He looks away and out of the window.

They are driving away from the city and out through the suburbs, right out to the scraggly fringe with its empty lots and old horses chomping the grass, to where the drive-in is. Everyone in the car is talking except Fine, who is determined this night to let nothing upset him, and he swings his head back from the window, feeling already, just by having looked out, that he has damaged something. His neon smile begins to flicker again, the colour up in his face. He reaches for his cigarettes. The dog growls. 'I'm just getting a cigarette,' Fine says. 'Well, don't,' says Madeline. 'What's *wrong* with him?' Fine asks. His cigarettes are in a brand-new case he bought this morning, plus a Dunhill lighter, foolish things, but somehow this morning he had to do something, and he rushed into the city in a cab and bought a suit, well, because he *needed* a new suit, but somehow that wasn't enough, so he bought a shirt, socks, cufflinks, a tie, overspending and the purchases not making him happy, but somehow all necessary. For tonight. No, not *just* for tonight. For Madeline? No! For? He feels, now, overdressed, awkward and ridiculous, wearing a brand-new almost-silk dark suit to a drive-in theatre, and in great need of a cigarette.

'Froggy got locked in the garage,' Madeline says. 'Didn't you, Froggy? Poor doggie. He was in there all night and all day without any dinner and we didn't know *where* he was. We thought a big, bad man had stolen you away, didn't we, Froggy?' She cradles and rocks the dog, soothes it, pets it, despite which the dog keeps one eye open and fixed on Fine.

'Gee, that's awful,' says Fine. His voice sounds, to him, like tin.

Martin Black cuts in front of a white Mercedes, at the wheel of which sits an old lady, sedate and pink, Black giving two more toots on the horn and swinging right in front of her. Fine closes his eyes again. All the windows are up tight, and the air is thick and brassy. Evelyn's scent is as sharp as a cat, Madeline's also rich and wrong, and Martin Black has been liberal with after-shave. Fine can smell the dog too in this humidor of a car. He feels the beginnings of claustrophobia, those first pricklings. He looks over at the window, but can imagine what will happen if he winds it down. Back swing his eyes to Madeline's white neck. What if I touch it? he thinks. Something shrinks inside him.

'Hey, we're there!' says Martin Black. 'Ev'rybody happeeey?'

They turn, now, off the main road, following arrows and lit-up signs, black trees on either side silhouetted against the sky, and ahead of them the winking red lights of a car, and suddenly the screen hoves into view, a three-quarter view, the road winding, and Fine can see at once that the film has begun. Faces flash and swim against the sky and figures strut in glorious colour, like a dream in the night. 'It's started,' Fine says. He hates coming late, to any film, even a bad one. 'It's only the beginning,' says Evelyn Gold, her tone icy condescension, as Martin Black slows down for the ticket box.

Martin Black winds down his window. 'Four,' he says. 'And a dog, ha ha.' Fine reaches for his wallet. The dog snarls and starts to move in Madeline's lap. Fine freezes, and looks over desperately at Madeline. Her face says nothing. 'Relax,' says Martin Black. 'I'll fix it. Pay me later.'

Down the road they go, cars in front of them and cars behind, all moving slowly, and attendants in white dustcoats waving torches and looking harassed and irritable. Saturday night; and Fine remembers dozens of Saturday nights, and week nights, always with Madeline, in her father's springy Ford. And the last time he went to a drive-in it was with Madeline, and he looks over at her now, to see if she is remembering too. Nothing. She is facing dead ahead with her dog in her lap and her eyes frozen hard inside her lashes.

'Lots of people are missing the beginning,' says Evelyn Gold.

They creep along, and now Fine can see the screen all the time, huge heads, mouths moving and no sound at all. Inside the car, no one is saying a word. Fine can feel his heart beating and his hands feel hot and wet.

The car in front of them turns off to the right, its rear red light winking, and an attendant in a white dustcoat swings his torch in an arc, signalling for them to follow. Martin Black winds down his window again. 'We're going to the restaurant first,' he says. 'What?' says Fine. 'We haven't eaten,' says Madeline. 'Oh,' says Fine.

There are cars lined up for the restaurant too, at the back of the field, a bright cube of light and darkness all around it. Fine sees that it's full of people, queueing and pushing, and now they're facing away from the screen and he can't see the film at all. 'Wait here, kids,' Martin Black says. 'I'll get everything. Won't be a minute, okay?' Out he jumps, then leans back in and gives Evelyn a kiss on the cheek and then off he runs, and Fine sees his wide shoulders pushing through people and then he's gone.

'I'm *aw*fully hungry,' says Evelyn Gold. 'So am I,' says Madeline. 'I *love* eating in the drive-in, don't you?' says Evelyn. 'De*lic*ious smells.' And on and on they go, Fine not knowing what to do, because no one is talking to him, and anyhow he wouldn't know what to say if they did. He feels the need of a cigarette badly. He looks out of the window and then back again, at Evelyn, trying to smile at her and show interest in her chatter, and at Madeline, cradling her dog. Nothing. Time drags. Fine feels as though he has been sitting in this car for ever. One leg has gone completely to sleep. He suddenly becomes aware that he has been staring at Madeline, at her new face, her swept-up brittle hair, her glittering cold eyes, and when something stabs him deep inside his stomach, he doesn't know what it is. Love?

'It's no use,' Madeline had said. 'We'll be friends. I'll phone you in two months. Don't phone me. I'll hang up if you do.'

Why does Evelyn Gold always have to be around? Fine thinks, still staring at Madeline. And if she wasn't? His hand, in his mind, reaches up and touches Madeline's white neck, and her face, in his mind, swings around to face him. Angry. He blushes and stares at the crowd, trying to find Martin Black.

And at last, at last, back he comes. His hands are filled with food on paper plates, with plastic spoons, straws, knives and forks poking out of his top pocket, his side pockets bulging and that smile on his wide face. 'Food!' he announces, and the dog growls, and in through the window the plates come. A smell of fat and chips fills the car. 'That's yours,' says Martin Black to Evelyn, 'and that's yours,' to Madeline, 'and this is for me.' 'Oh, Evelyn,' says Madeline, 'can you hold mine for just a minute? Froggy! Be*have*!'

Now the car is full of plates. 'Here,' says Evelyn Gold, and passes one to Fine. 'Oh, that's yours,' says Martin Black. 'Oh,' says Fine. 'Hold mine,' says Madeline, passing Fine her plate. 'Hold tight, kids, we're off!' says Martin Black. 'Just a minute,' says Fine, not ready, but no one hears him.

The car shoots forward, Fine holding on to two plates and feeling something wet on his leg. 'Here we go!' says Martin Black, and down a row of cars they go, looking for a space. There isn't one. Martin Black goes right to the end of the row, and is now in an impossible position and has to back out. 'Oops, ha ha,' he says, and Fine feels something roll off a plate and on to his knee. Potato salad. He shifts uncomfortably, trying to see if his trousers are marked, but it's too dark. The car backs laboriously, Martin Black's head craned around to see. 'Can't see,' he says to Fine, and Fine, trying to smile, sinks down lower in his seat.

Down another row they go, Fine down low and only the tops of cars visible to him, black and shining in the night. 'Hey, there's one!' says Madeline, pointing. 'Got it!' says Martin Black. 'In we go.' He swings the car around, doesn't make it, the car up a slope now and Fine hanging on to the plates for dear life. Martin Black tries again, his hands slapping on the wheel and no other sound at all in the car. 'Right!' he says, not making it again, backing, slapping the wheel, grunting, laughing, 'Ha ha, next time, kids,' and at last they're in. 'Wow!' he says. 'The sound, the sound!' says Evelyn Gold. 'Right you are, sweetie,' says Martin Black, winding down his window and reaching out for the speaker. 'Quickly, quickly,' says Evelyn Gold, 'we're missing bits.' 'Here you are, love,' says Martin Black, 'how's this?' He hangs the speaker on the steering wheel, switches it on, and at once the car is filled with sound. Filled! The sound is enormous. Fine blinks. No one is turning it down, no one is complaining. It's deafening. Is it going to be like this all night? His ears ring.

'Now,' shouts Martin Black, twisting and turning, 'who wants a knife?' 'Oooh, please,' says Madeline. 'I think this is yours,' says Fine, handing back her plate. 'Froggy, be still!' says Madeline. 'Coffee for ev'rybodeeey!' shouts Martin Black, and out of his bulging pockets it comes, in sealed cups, sloshing inside. He hands one to Fine without a word. 'Thank you,' says Fine. The movie booms. Fine juggles his plate. Froggy eyes him, growling in his throat.

'Ev'rybodeey happeeey?' sings Martin Black.

Fine looks down at his plate. There are three coloured scoops of ice cream, and a froth of cream speckled with nuts. He doesn't have a spoon. The lid is off his coffee, and he feels the paper cup squashing in his hand.

He looks up, not knowing what to do. They are right over to one side of the field, up close, and all he can see is the top third of the screen, at a distorted angle. And then Evelyn Gold slides over to sit tight next to Martin Black and now all Fine can see is the two black blobs of their heads and hardly any of the screen at all. He struggles to sit up higher, the dog growls, he feels the ice cream slipping around on his plate, which is wilting, folding up in his hands, already wet and sticky, and the coffee sloshing dangerously around in its cup. He closes his eyes, and then – no! – decides that he just won't he bothered with the film at all, won't even *try* to see it, what's the use? He hasn't the faintest idea of what's going on, and even if he sits up as straight as he can, craning his neck, he still won't see more than half the screen. Two Horsemen of the Apocalypse. He looks over at Madeline, and she is eating quite calmly, watching the film, blinking with interest. And, as he watches, she scoops up some ice cream in her plastic spoon and offers it to her dog. 'Here, Froggy,' she says. 'Lovely.'

It then occurs to Fine, desperate now, that the only thing to do is to wind down his window and throw all this rubbish out. He inches his hand over to the handle, and slowly, furtively, starts to wind it down. Down it comes, one inch, two, and suddenly Evelyn Gold turns, not really in his direction, but enough, and says, 'Oooh, cold.' Fine blushes, caught, and back up the window goes.

His ice cream is a puddle now, slipping from side to side. He takes a sip of his coffee. It is sickly sweet with sugar, tastes of plastic and wax, and is not hot. He bends forward, trying to put it down on the floor, because his plate has folded almost in half and is leaking badly and he hasn't the faintest chance unless he can get both hands to it. He bends, almost has his coffee down on the floor by his shoes, when he feels the plate suddenly lighten, and the ice cream, all three scoops, softly drop on to his brand-new trousers. Over goes the coffee. 'Jesus,' he moans, as coffee seeps into his sock. Madeline shoots a hard look over at him, and then ignores him, stares straight ahead, a look of extreme concentration on her face. Fine, blood red now, his mouth open and the film roaring in his ears, lets go of the plate, just lets go, not caring where it goes, who sees, anything. He breathes out, spent, then in, deeply, his body itching and prickly and never in his life has his claustrophobia been so bad.

He looks at Madeline, imploringly. Nothing. Then he starts to count. One, two, three, four. At six, not giving a damn about any-thing any more, he lunges for the door handle, wrestles it open, bangs his shoulder, leaps out, slams the door and starts to run.

Down through the rows of cars he goes, all black and anonymous, hardly seeing anything, running, making for the restaurant, that bright cube of light. In he runs, panting, to the toilet. He slams the door shut in a cubicle, tears handfuls of paper out of the dispenser, swabbing at his trousers, wiping, but he knows it's no use. They're ruined. When he comes out, his hands are sticky with ice cream and coffee, and when he sees his face in the mirror above the handbasin, as he straightens up, hands dripping, he starts, shocked. He takes a step back, and his mouth falls open. The white, wide-eyed, furious face in the mirror he hardly recognizes as his own.

He blushes, ashamed, then washes his hands, avoiding the mirror with his eyes. Then he looks down at his trousers again. Thank God it's a dark suit, he thinks. Hardly visible. But that doesn't fool him for a minute. Ruined. The crease has gone. On his legs, the cloth feels sticky and wet. The front of the coat is rumpled. A brand-new suit! For a second, he feels like crying. *Don't!* he commands himself. Have some coffee. Yes, he says. Coffee.

He sits down all alone at a table with a cup of coffee and lights a cigarette. Then, after it, another. The restaurant is all glass, and the film, rooms and skies, trains crashing across the screen, floats in the night. He watches it abstractly, feeling that everyone is watching him, everyone knows he has just run away and is all alone at the drive-in on a Saturday night in a ruined brand-new suit with no idea what to do. He goes to the counter for a second cup of coffee, ordering it in a thin, high voice, keeping his head down. He smokes another cigarette, and then, gradually, strand by strand, the strings and tensions inside him part and he begins to feel normal again.

He lights a fourth cigarette. There is almost no one in the restaurant now, only women with tired faces in bright blue dresses cleaning up the tables and an old man in overalls sweeping the floor with a battered broom.

He sits ten minutes more, composing himself. He thinks about the car, Martin Black and Evelyn Gold with their heads together and the sound on the steering wheel booming, and in the back, Madeline. Madeline. Maddy. And her dog. Froggy. He wonders what they are talking about. About him? He sneers, hating them all. And then he thinks, how am I going to get home?

He is miles from a bus, miles from a train. Ten miles to walk. At least. He doesn't even know the directions. What roads? This is a part of the world he has never been in other than by car, Madeline's father's car, never giving a thought to the roads, just drifting, Madeline driving, Fine relaxed on the seat next to her, holding her hand, which she tightened when she wanted him to let go so she could change gears. Driving in the rain to the drive-in, and sitting in the car, the windows all steamed up with breathing and smoke, the windscreen wipers droning and the screen almost invisible. Never many cars there. They didn't care. They sat close, tight, together, and sometimes the sound, never loud, just went off and they knew the movie was over. 'Hey, mister,' she used to say. 'It's all over. Hey, mister, hey, whatcha doing?' Happy times. In the drive-ins. Where else do you go with your girl when you want to be alone?

A woman comes up and wipes his table clean, sweeping crumbs into his lap. 'Sorry, dear,' she says, her face as hard as a brick.

Fine stands up. He lights another cigarette. He steps outside, the screen no bigger than a television set and all the cars bumped up in front of it, like a metallic congregation, worshipping. He thinks and thinks, and knows he has to go back. Or never see Madeline again. And the thought of that – Never! – is like a blow in his stomach. He is trembling. Hey, stop that! he tells himself. He breathes in, drops his cigarette down on the concrete, squares his shoulders, and starts back.

He threads through one row of cars, trying to appear nonchalant, walking quickly, with a sense of purpose, trying not to look at anything.

He crosses in front of a car, bending down low, hurrying. He takes a quick look around to see where he is, up at the screen to get his bearings, then up between two cars he goes, past another, and he's there. He takes another deep breath, reaches over for the handle on the back door, and swings the door open.

A girl, completely naked, leaps up to face him. Her breasts flash white and her mouth is a black hole. 'Oh,' says Fine. Then a man's face appears, but Fine doesn't wait to apologize. He ducks and runs, behind the car, his brain trying to sort out where he is but unable to shake the image of the naked girl. He blinks, trying to remember. Over at the side – right? Two from the end – right? He sees what he thinks is Martin Black's car, but isn't sure. Then he sees another that he is sure is it. He walks over, bending low, trying to make out shapes inside it. He can't see a thing. What kind of car was it? He tries to think. He doesn't know. Licence number? No. He spins around, every car looking like Martin Black's, every single one of them. His back hurts. 'Oh, Jesus,' he moans.

He goes right up one row, too frightened to look properly, then down another, and all the time that naked girl is swimming before him, that violated, alarmed face, that black mouth. His Dunhill lighter chinks against his platinum cigarette case. A car toots its horn at him. He ducks instinctively. And then, without knowing how he got there, he finds himself right over to one side, staring at a lit-up arrow and a sign saying THIS WAY OUT. He turns and looks at the screen. Glenn Ford's face, thin and distorted. He looks over at the field of cars. Dead shapes, shining, in every one of which he imagines a white nude with a black hole of a mouth and swinging breasts, and the picture stabs him deeply. For all the girls are Madeline. He starts to run.

Down the road he goes, past the black trees, running, then slowing down, out of breath, jogging, walking, hands in pockets, his new suit a ruin, all alone on the black road, not knowing where it is taking him. Then the first cars, early starters, come down the road.

Quickly they come, lights like knives, hooting their horns, people yelling and beer cans hitting the grass by the side of the road and bouncing on the gravel. He turns and looks at each car as it comes, mouth open, dazzled by the lights. One, two, three, out they pour. He stumbles, neck stiff from turning, and horribly aware of what each car must see, this lone figure in a dark silky suit, walking home from the drive-in. *Walking.* For no reason at all, he laughs. It's not a real laugh, there's no happiness in it, no joy. But it does something. All at once he doesn't care. Not at all. Not about anything. Not about what *they* think, or anyone thinks. His back relaxes, his neck stops hurting. The cars flash past, hooting and the drivers yelling, but Fine is not turning any more, he's walking straight ahead. With a smile on his lips.

And now the cars are tearing down this road in great numbers, zoom, zoom, endless, as Fine walks, completely relaxed now, one hand in his trouser pocket, the other holding a cigarette, past the black trees. He looks up and sees the screen, still visible, and just at that second it goes blank.

♦ Running Nicely

♦ See them go! Clock their speed! Nightly at ten, the Bornstein boys run together along the quiet streets of suburban Melbourne, a mile and a quarter under the full-leaved summer trees. Here comes Moses, down the stairs from the flat. He's twenty-two, five five and a half, brown hair, dressed tonight in jungle-green shorts (deep pockets, balloon seat) and horizontally-striped (maroon and cream) lightweight Italian mohair shirt, the collar stylishly flared. Brown shoes, blue socks. On his heels comes Ben, twelve, blondish, five eight, crisp and correct in sporting white, save for the soles of his tennis shoes, which pop up brick-red. They jog to the front gate, and from here the run may be said properly to begin.

Go?

'You lock the door?' Moses asks.

'Yes,' says Ben.

'Turn off the lights?'

'Yes.'

'All of them?'

'You told me to leave one on.'

'Where's the key? I don't trust your pockets.'

Moses buries the front-door key in a pocket of his shorts under five ancient Kleenexes, tamping them down for extra security, and then, without further word, is suddenly off, assuming an instant five-yard lead. Ben narrows it at once to two, and, keeping this formation, they head down the road.

They're off!

Not too fast, thinks Moses, pacing himself carefully, introducing the night air slowly into his lungs. Nice and easy, he thinks. There's a long way to go. A lifetime sufferer from flat feet, he concentrates on the proper placement of his toes, affecting a slight springy bounce. He wiggles his arms loosely by his sides. He throws back his head and takes some deep sniffs. Ah! Ah! Ben is a silent white blur in the corner of Moses' eye. Good, thinks Moses, pleased at the running order. A little respect.

Cars zoom. A heavy truck rumbles and roars. Next comes a bus, lit up like a travelling house. Overhead the trees are a sickly yellow from the fluorescent lights on the main road, their leaves like old paper stuck up in the branches and twigs. Moses doesn't like this stretch of the run. He feels exposed. Anyone could go shooting past in a car and see them, running like lunatics in the night. Oh, it's the poor Bornstein boys! What a tragedy! To be orphaned so young! What are they doing, running at this hour? Look how thin they are! Anyone could see them here – Mr Pincus, Mr Sharp, Mrs Goldberg and her three chins, an uncle, an aunt, an old family friend, all those sad faces at the funeral. Moses feels they're all watching, horrified, as he runs with his brother, and he is relieved when he and Ben turn the corner, off the main road, and true suburban night descends.

Now it's nice. The trees are leafier, the street is darker, private, and the roar of the traffic, like the sea, has dropped away; now the only sounds are the fall of their feet and the regular puffing of breath. Ben closes the gap and they run together, side by side.

There is a smell of water in the air here, a smell of flowers and moist earth, but the gardens, as they pass, are dark. Grass is dark. Flowers are dark. The trees are dark, except where at regular intervals the street lights shine through, a row of moons down the length of the street. They run from light to light, breathing easily, and the only other light is the weird flickering blue of television screens, one without fail in every house they pass.

Fools, thinks Moses, and feels a certain pride at how he has weaned his brother, a former three-hours-a-night man, off that awful habit. Not by any stern command – the set's there, and he can turn it on any time he likes – but by getting him interested in other things, widening his horizons. They watch reruns of *Naked City* and on Friday nights an old movie, if there's a good one, but the best evenings are when Ben has finished his homework and they turn on the hi-fi and listen to early Coleman Hawkins, Django and Bird. 'Listen to this,' says Moses, popping on Art Tatum. 'Just listen to that left hand!' And one afternoon, Moses remembers, he came home early from work, and there was the flat filled with his brother's friends, Lester Young soaring, and Ben delivering to his contemporaries an authoritative history of jazz.

There's another corner coming up. Moses feels Ben speeding up a fraction, and paces himself accordingly. They turn the corner in unison, running in step.

There's a cluster of shops here, five stores serving the neighbourhood – there used to be six, but the grocer went self-service and swallowed up the lending library next door – and, as they go past, Moses sneaks a look at himself and Ben, mirrored in the dark windows. Ben, he sees, has his mouth open, but not too wide, breathing easily. He notes the steely concentration in his brother's eyes. A champion! He rejoices, and then almost lets out a small laugh as he sees himself, a crazy hotchpotch of patterns and colours, the collar of his Italian mohair poking up at the back like a foolish bird hanging on for the ride. Then his brother surges ahead five or six yards, and he lets him go. I can catch him in a second, Moses thinks. Let him run a bit.

Look at him, Moses thinks, as Ben flashes past the last shop – a chemist's – his reflection riding over bottles and jars and the faces of beautiful women. Where'd he get that style? Where'd he learn to run so nicely like that? Not from me, that's for sure. The thing is, he hasn't got my flat feet. Thank God.

Running behind his brother, but keeping the distance between them steady, Moses thinks of many things, quickly, one after the other. How his brother is adept at tossing green salads, his French dressing a joy to behold. How his brother dresses neatly, the right tie with the right jacket, the right socks. How he comes home to find his brother has cleaned the flat, straightened the rugs, made the beds. How his brother can tell Charlie Parker from Sonny Stitt with his eyes closed. How his brother is halfway through *Catch 22*. 'You skipping?' Moses asked him. 'Of course not,' said Ben. 'I'm reading every word.'

'You know what you're doing to him,' said Moses' girl, eating dinner at the flat one night. 'You're taking away his youth.'

'What?' said Moses. 'What a load of rubbish. He's an intelligent kid, that's all.'

And he could have said more, but he didn't feel, just then, like getting dragged into it.

A car goes past. For a second, Moses is annoyed. What's this intrusion? But the car is quickly gone, all trace of it, all sound, and once again they run through immaculate suburban night, past the houses with their weird blue lights, past the neat gardens, too dark to admire, under the canopy of black trees and the regular moons of the street lights shining through. And suddenly Moses has a vision. The whole world has been constructed for him and his brother to run through, the trees planted, the houses built, the television sets turned on, the smell of water in the air, even the stars in the sky – everything arranged and set into place, thousands of years of preparation for this moment in time, the whole world dark, at peace, with no sound allowed but his and Ben's breathing and the fall of their feet in the night.

Nice, thinks Moses, running easily.

They're almost at the end of the street now, Ben still ahead. Well, thinks Moses, I'd better catch him up, and he quickens his pace, coming up to his brother in a rush just as they get to Brown Street, where there's another corner to turn. Ben, on the inside, gets around nimbly, not losing an inch, but Moses overshoots, runs with a clump into the gutter and onto the road, and, by the time he has sorted himself out and is running straight again, Ben is fifteen yards ahead, maybe more.

Hey, what's he doing? thinks Moses. It's not a race. We're supposed to be running together. And he speeds up, flat feet thudding the ground, his hands balled into tight fists up by his heaving chest. Here I come, boy! he announces. Watch my speed.

Brown Street is famous in the neighbourhood. Halfway along its length it takes a sudden plummet, a totally unexpected plunge. The incline is fantastic. Children love it. They roar down on their bikes, screams like streamers flying from their mouths. Wheee! Brown's Hill! Race ya to the bottom! The postman hates it, mothers with prams curse it, old people have to pause three times, gasping, as they slowly ascend, and here comes Moses, his flat feet making an unholy racket as he streaks after his sporting brother, all proper toe placement forgotten, his hair standing up wildly in the self-generated wind.

The gap whittles down. From fifteen, it goes to ten, six, two, and – flash! – he's passed him, roaring like an engine, but what's this? he's forgotten the hill, aaarrrhhh, and down he goes, picking up speed by the second, his feet out of control, a terrible mistake. Tree trunks whip past, fences, windows, one street light after another. Moses is a train. Moses is the stagecoach racing driverless to the cliff. How to slow down? How to stop? Impossible. Can't be done. God, thinks Moses, I'm going to break a leg.

Ben is forgotten as Moses charges down the famous hill, insane thoughts of grabbing a tree or suddenly sitting down flying through his head. He's two-thirds of the way to the bottom, and by some manner unknown even to himself has managed to keep upright, when who should pop out from her gate but a little old lady from No. 26, her night of television viewing at an end, time to take the dog for a stroll. Her dog is the size of a handbag or muff, and is attached to the woman by a length of fine chain, and as Moses approaches, puffing like a furnace, the dog whips around and lets out a terrified squeaky bark, like one pump on an old pair of bellows. Reeee! The little lady turns, looks up, and sees, advancing in the night, a wild-eyed maniac streaked with sweat. A rapist! A fiend! Her small mouth falls open. Her rimless spectacles catch a street light and turn dead white. 'Good evening and don't worry,' Moses wants to say. 'I intend you no harm.' But of course he can't. It's all he can do not to crash into her, not to go flying over the thin chain connecting her to her petrified dog, but somehow, miraculously, he veers around, panting madly.

But who is this streaking up behind him? Why, it's Ben, coming up with Olympic prowess, and for a moment, as Brown's Hill flattens, they're together, running side by side. For ten yards, they're neck and neck, but Ben is in fine control and Moses is not, and, almost before he knows what's happening, an assortment of winds escapes Moses' body, five fine blasts, thundering in the jungle green.

'Hee hee,' laughs Moses, and sees on the face of his brother the beginnings of an answering laugh, and, as though to encourage him, Moses laughs again. 'Hee hee, ha ha,' he laughs, and is about to do a 'ho ho' when he sees a look of annoyance flick across his brother's face; then a mask of severe determination descends, and Ben is off, streaking free into the night.

Hold it a second, Moses wants to say, but can't. Something is happening to his lungs. His breath is all over the place. His running rhythm is upside down. 'Ooooh!' he cries, feeling a sharp pain in his side, and then there flashes into his brain the rimless spectacles of the old lady from No. 26, and he begins once more to laugh. 'Ha ha,' he laughs, 'hee hee,' but between each laugh there is a stab of pain, and when he tries not to laugh it's worse. 'Ow!' cries Moses. 'Oooh!' still running, blood pumping in his head.

He stops. His breath is a hot wind through parched lips. Black spots jump in front of his eyes. He stands, hands on hips, bent forward, shot through with pains. When at last he has calmed down enough to look up, Ben is a hundred yards away, running nicely, a crisp white figure diminishing in the night.

'Rat!' Moses calls, mopping his brow with a mohair sleeve. He's wet through. He's hot. His ankles are agony, his thighs throb with aches. 'I'm not running with you again,' he says, and pushing up his sleeves (Italian mohair for running? thinks Moses. Fool! Fool!) he starts again.

It's no good. He can't do it. Something's gone inside. He drops down to a jog, but even that's too much. He wants to sit down. He wants to lie down. He wants to close his eyes. Moses has run this course with his brother two dozen times at least, but it's never been like this before. Even the first time, completely out of training, he managed to jog home. And woke up the next morning full of aches and pains – but during the course of the day they lessened, and that night they ran again, a little faster if anything.

Brown's Hill, thinks Moses. Never lose control on Brown's Hill.

It is all he can do to walk, past the quiet gardens, the flickering blue windows, under the dark trees, but it's not the same any more, it's no longer that special world made for brothers to run in, it's not peaceful and quiet, it's all changed. He looks up and sees that Ben has gone. A champion, he thinks, but doesn't feel happy. He's alone. Stumbling home, he feels, all at once, a fool.

He sees himself – hypocrite! – lecturing his brother on fair play and sporting style. I never made the football team, he thinks. I was always the last one they picked for cricket. Pop goes the bat and out of the sky drops the shiny red ball, right to him with slow-motion ease and – oh – he drops it. The crowd moans. Moses feels his face lighting up with shame, and is thankful for the dark.

He stumbles on, the sweat on his face cooling down. Ahead, through the trees, he sees the main road again, cars and trucks rolling past, their bodies flashing with neon. He takes a breath, then another, and somehow gets running again for this last stretch, where everyone can see.

It's awful. He feels a thousand years old, half jogging, half limping, a ruined, broken man. He is about to give up and walk the rest of the way – what the hell, who cares about the Pincuses and Sharps and Goldbergs of this world? – when he sees his brother waiting for him at the gate. Ben stands there, fresh and straight, in his crisp sporting whites, not a trace of the night's run on his face. Hey, I've never played him Thelonious Monk! Moses thinks. He'll love him. Ben raises both arms in the air, like a Grand Prix judge ready to bring down the winning flag, and not to disappoint him, his heart beating to burst, Moses finishes strong, the last surge of energy summoned up from God knows where carrying him all the way home.

◆ *Warts*

◆

◆ Leo discovered, when he was twenty-five, that his penis had sprouted four warts. They seemed to have come all of a sudden. Yesterday none, today four. God, he thought, and raced to a dictionary. 'Small hardish permanent excrescences on the skin,' he read. 'Protruberances on tree trunks.'

Who can I turn to? Leo thought.

He knew almost no one. He was new in London, a year out of Australia, a year of travelling alone up and down Europe, plus a short stop in the Promised Land. Once a painter, he now worked in the studio of a large advertising agency, drawing cartoon figures for a shirt account. He had been there a month. The morning after his discovery, he tried to introduce the subject of warts into the general conversation in the studio, though steering well clear of any personal mention. 'Hey, I saw this guy with incredible warts on his hand this morning,' he said, trying to be nonchalant. 'On the bus.' Once, when he was ten, Leo had worn his pyjamas under his suit to school, and though they had been well tucked into his socks and he hadn't told a single person about them, by lunch-time everyone in the class knew that Leo was wearing his pyjamas under his suit, and they had swarmed around him, tugging at his trouser legs. Leo could see the same thing happening with his warts. Friends could be merciless. He went back that night to his flat, deep in gloom, wondering had he somehow come in contact with a frog in recent months.

Alone in his flat, he worried about cancer. He pictured skin grafts, hideous pink plastic patches, three months of difficult living with rubber hoses and a small stainless-steel spigot, and maybe even a whole life with a bottle strapped to his leg. But he couldn't see himself possessed of the aplomb to sit leafing through back copies of the *London Illustrated News* waiting for a consultation with his National Health doctor, a no-nonsense man with eyebrows shooting out like tufts of grass. He decided to sit the wart phase out, convincing himself that they'd go as mysteriously as they had come. He changed his soap to a brand that boasted medicinal qualities. He was lavish with talc. A daily check seemed however to reveal no change, but at the end of six months there were seven warts, not four.

I'm dead, thought Leo.

He told himself that the warts were a manifestation of the wrath of God, for having had repeated sexual intercourse with a girl with no love in his heart. Gabriella Rose. Gaby. He went over in his mind all those writhy Melbourne nights with Gaby on the front seat of his tiny car, dodging the gear shift and avoiding the gap between the seats. What gymnastics! He relived zips, buttons, hooks, elastics and rayons, thin cottons, soft wools, and he said to himself, I'd rather not have done it even once than have all these lousy warts. But then his mind added further front seat details and he wasn't so sure.

Always a hesitant goer, he now dreaded public urinals, wherever possible whipping into a booth. Even there it wasn't easy, and when there were people outside waiting, though his bladder was bursting he just couldn't go.

Relax, he told himself. It's a temporary condition.

Eight months after his first discovery of the warts, Leo counted, with death in his heart, the terrible number of ten. And the original ones were growing.

He thought of out-of-town doctors, night trains to Manchester or Edinburgh, but somehow couldn't move.

He thought of flights to Belgium, or Amsterdam, or maybe a Scandinavian doctor, someone who had surely handled this kind of thing before, but the protocol stumped him.

He became a voracious reader of medical books, skimming frantically in book shops during his lunch-hour. But though he came across some rather interesting diseases and conditions, he couldn't find anything even vaguely similar to his own. One lunch-time he found a volume that looked promising, a large book with full-page plates (several in colour) featuring men bent backwards over surgical chairs, but no sooner had he thought, Hey, this might be the one! than a cocky sales attendant sidled up, nudged him in the ribs and chortled, 'Good book, that, heh, heh. You interested in that kind of thing?' 'I was only looking!' Leo had cried, slamming the book shut and running out of the shop, never to return.

Who can I turn to?

He tried to reintroduce the subject of warts, guardedly, in the studio, to see if anyone had new information.

Nothing.

Leo's holidays were coming up, a fortnight in Rome, and he promised himself that the first thing he'd do when he got there was to go to a doctor, someone who had never seen him before and would never see him again. He would give a false name (Steven Fletcher) and pay by cash, on the spot.

But when he got to Rome, he wasn't sure how to go about it. He sat for hours in the Via Veneto, picturing embarrassing scenes with receptionists and nurses, and wild Catholic vengeance with priests rushing in and the Papal Guards, and he flew back to London in the same condition as he had left, hating himself for being so stupid, and blushing like a fury when the hostess asked him if he'd like a drink.

Back in London he sat in buses and worried about his warts. If you knew what I've got, he said in his mind to a girl in a miniskirt with long legs in black lattice-work tights, if you could only *see*, you'd run for your life.

Every now and then there came to Leo the crushing realization that unless he hurried he would never have children. No son. No heir. His line vanished from the face of the earth. What a pointless existence, he thought. What a meaningless life. For months he sunk into a Lost Generation trough.

But somehow he still managed the occasional foray. The flesh might be warty but the spirit still bubbled and boiled.

One night, on a staircase, a German *au pair* girl with a bouncing bottom and mad black flying hair said, 'Oh, what are these?'

'I've always had them,' said Leo, zipping quickly.

He found though that he was steering clear of sexual encounters, making no advances, looking away when girls smiled, and when he studied his warts under a powerful light and saw that they were getting even bigger, he thought, That's the end.

He felt that the whole essence of life had gone, but didn't see how he could withdraw from it. Become a monk? A rabbi? Whoever heard of a rabbi with warts?

One night he went to a party and there got into a discussion on political matters with a tall girl with red hair and a loose bodice, and though Leo felt no particular lust for this girl, in the middle of the conversation, which was covering a lot of salient points, his mind suddenly lost the thread, and he shrunk into himself, felt himself becoming insignificant and small, while inside he roared, How can you have a sensible discussion on Black Power and the emerging African States when you've got warts all over your dick?

He tried hot baths, cold showers, sponges and soaks, but at the end of two years the wart situation hadn't changed. Still ten. Still roughly the same size. Maybe even growing.

They're regrouping, Leo thought, visualizing fiendish cellular activity going on under the skin. They're planning a major *coup*. It's only a matter of time. I'll wake up one morning and find I've been totally engulfed. Jesus, what's the point of being alive?

He went, one day, to buy a suit, but halfway through the fitting he thought, Why bother? With my condition, what's the point? What's the use of me looking good? He went home without a new suit, and the same thing happened to him a few weeks later when he tried to buy a tie.

A peacock with warts, thought Leo, and put down the bright pieces of silk.

It was insane. He didn't know what to do.

A month passed, two. All at once Leo realized that he hadn't worried about his warts all that time. He hadn't given them a single thought. He was learning to live with them. He had warts like some people had blue eyes and that's all there was to it. What was the point of worrying? For a start, they didn't even hurt.

He made love to an outwardly demure girl from Nice who didn't say a word about them.

And again, with a girl from Bristol, who afterwards jumped on him in the bath.

Tact? thought Leo. Or is it, after all, a fairly common thing?

More and more often, Leo realized that time had flown past without a single wart thought. And each time he came down with a crash. I must be completely crazy, he thought. How can I not worry about a thing like that?

He saw life as a long tunnel, full of corners and bends, birth at one end, death at the other, but across his tunnel, somewhere in the future, there was a wall. Any day he would turn a corner and there it would be. Unscalable. Inpenetrable. No children. A living death. That made him depressed, but then he would picture himself being depressed over something that he hadn't even thought about for months, and he felt his depression was melodramatic, and that depressed him even more.

Warts.

There was no way that he could think around them.

They were always there.

One morning Leo woke up with a throbbing pain in his gum and went to see his dentist.

'I don't like the look of it,' said the dentist, tapping Leo with his mirror. 'Looks like some surgery to me.'

'Surgery?' Leo said.

'Periodontal,' he said. 'Have to drain under that root.' He was the kind of dentist who always described, in great detail, everything he was about to do, believing that ignorance bred fear and fear bred pain. 'I'll slice through the gum here,' he said, 'and then poke around up here and here. Hell of a job, actually. Leaves you with what amounts to an open wound in your mouth for about three weeks.'

'Isn't there some other way?' Leo asked.

'I'll give you some pills,' said the dentist. 'About one chance on a thousand they might disperse the build-up, but don't count on it. That thing you've got is pretty fierce.' He gave Leo another tap. 'Thursday morning suit you?' he asked. 'About ten?'

'Do I need to bring a friend?' Leo asked.

The dentist smiled. 'You'll be all right in a cab,' he said.

The morning of the scheduled operation Leo woke up without a single pain, not a throb, not a twinge, and quickly phoned the dentist, telling him he was fine.

'Come in anyhow,' the dentist said. 'Let's take a look.' Leo thought the dentist sounded disappointed, but he knew that couldn't be right.

The dentist looked in Leo's mouth, jabbing and prodding, and then without a word went away and washed his hands.

'Can I go?' Leo asked.

'Keep in touch,' said the dentist. 'Those things have a nasty habit of coming back.'

For a month Leo held himself in readiness, poised for twinges and throbs, but there wasn't a single one. He was the one in a thousand. He was all right. He forgot all about his tooth. He went to a party. A girl with freckles and an outrageous mouth gave him an unmistakable smile, and when he took her outside, she turned instantly grabby. 'Hang on,' said Leo, retreating a step. 'I'm not ready.' It was dark, it was very dark, and the girl was practically on him, breathing hard, when Leo discovered a miraculous thing. True? Really? How? Why? He couldn't believe it. He searched desperately, jubilantly, fingers trembling. 'Hey,' said the girl. Leo quickly lit a match. It went out and he lit another. 'Hey, what are you *doing*?' said the girl. He lit a third. Not a trace! Not a speck! Not even a bump to show where they'd been! Gone, all gone, each and every one! An absolute miracle! 'Hey, you're not – ?' said the girl. 'I don't know what you're talking about,' said Leo, 'but I'm not. Absolutely not. Come here,' he said proudly, 'and see.'

♦ *The Muted Love Song of Edvard Nils*

♦

♦ She was thirty kilometres from Oslo, it was growing dark, she was hungry, she was cold. She had been there for three hours. Cars had been few and now there were none. She began to feel desperate. The country – the sky, fields, trees, the road (there were no buildings, there were no lights) – turned steadily greyer, and began to jump, flecked and grainy, like an old film. She lit a cigarette. At last she saw the high beam of a car lighting up the scratchy sky. She picked up her pack and stepped to the side of the road. She smiled. The car zoomed past – it didn't even slow down – and now she was more than desperate, hungry and cold. She was furious. She threw her pack down in the middle of the road. She sat down on it. She crossed her legs. When she had finished her cigarette, she lit another. Twenty minutes later, a pale grey Volvo lit up the night. She stood slowly up. She didn't wave. She didn't smile. The car slowed down, stopped, and Edvard Nils, a middle-aged Norwegian father of two, leaned across, opened the door, and fell in love with Margaret Lang.

She was twenty-four. We were at art school together. She was tall, with stunning legs, and an intense, serious look. She was short-sighted, but until or unless you knew that, you thought that she was cross and stayed away. I thought she was beautiful. There comes a moment between two people – you know that moment – when you have to speak, and for some reason I didn't, and that moment never comes again. But we were very good friends. Margaret went from art to photography, something happened, and she went to live in Copenhagen. I didn't hear from her for a while, and then from out of the blue I got a letter and decided to try Denmark myself. I found a room not far from the centre of town, we had dinner a few times, and one day when I went to see her, there was Mr Nils.

She had a studio in an old building in one of those streets with a canal running down the middle. It was high ceilinged, with white walls, and danced with patterns of water and light. From the windows you looked straight out into the rigging of boats – masts, flags and ropes. She was photographing an apple, peering short-sightedly into her camera, fussing with the lens. The Rolling Stones were booming on her stereo. Mr Nils stood quietly in a jug by the door.

'He really is a sweetie,' Margaret said to me.

He was long-stemmed, pink and pale blue, expensively delivered to the door only an hour before.

'Oh?' I said.

She told me about him, how she had met him, how he sent her things all the time. Chocolates, flowers, and once a small brooch shaped like a swan.

'You really shouldn't wander all over Europe by yourself,' I said. 'I worry about you.'

'Don't be silly,' Margaret said.

She went back to her apple. I sat down on a low canvas chair and watched her work. She looked very determined and businesslike. She brushed her hair away from her eyes and squeezed the shutter. Once, twice.

Did I really worry about her? She was a rare girl. Nothing frightened her. She went everywhere by herself, a beautiful girl alone in Europe. Once, in Germany, the driver of the car she was in had pulled over to the side of the road and unzipped his pants. 'Don't be silly,' Margaret said. She put a cigarette between her lips and showed the driver how steady her hand was holding a match. 'Get back on the road,' she said, and he did.

I stood up and went over to the door to admire Mr Nils some more.

'Let me know if he makes any trouble,' I said.

She smiled, and I felt like a clumsy boy scout.

'Well, anyhow,' I said.

'You're sweet,' she said, but a week later, when she phoned me, her voice said help.

Mr Nils was in town. He wanted to take her to dinner. He said he was in Copenhagen for business, but she knew he had come just for her, and she felt suddenly unsure. Would I come too? Please.

'I'll bring my knuckle-dusters,' I said, and then wished I hadn't.

We had arranged to meet at a smart new restaurant near the railway station at eight o'clock. I was a few minutes early. I went in, and there was Margaret sitting in a soft leather chair, legs crossed, reading *Life* and smoking a cigarette. She was alone.

'Hello,' I said.

For a second she looked thoroughly startled, and then she saw that it was me and smiled.

'Hello,' she said.

She was wearing a grey skirt and jacket, cut very simply, without frills. She had taken pains with her hair and face. Mr Nils' swan, I saw, rode on her left breast.

'Want a drink?' I asked her.

She nodded, and I ordered two Tuborgs and sat down on a chair beside her. She put down her magazine and stubbed out her cigarette.

'God, I'm glad you came,' she said.

She looked jittery. Was this the Margaret who went all over Europe by herself? I had never seen her like this before. She started to take out another cigarette, her brow furrowed.

'He sent me a box of fruit this morning,' she said.

'How long's he in Copenhagen?'

'Two days,' she said. She sipped her beer.

'Relax,' I said. 'He'll be gone before you know it.'

She tried another smile but it didn't work. She was troubled. I lit her cigarette. I started to say something else, but she was miles away. I took a long swallow of my beer and leaned back in my chair.

It was very quiet. There were two people at the bar, but they weren't talking. It was quiet at the tables too. It was just starting to be that sad time of the year in Copenhagen. Tivoli was closing in another few days, and walking to the restaurant I had sensed a kind of closing down in everything. The Danes were closing down, retreating, putting their friendliness away for the winter. The canals looked suddenly bleak. The sky was empty. I heard a polite cough, looked up, and there was Mr Nils.

'Oh,' said Margaret.

He was a small meek man with pale blue eyes and soft pink skin. He stood in front of us wearing a hat and a plain gaberdine coat that seemed too long for him. His shoes peeped out at the bottom, faultlessly shined.

I started to get to my feet. 'No, no,' said Mr Nils, very softly, motioning me back. I stood up anyhow. Margaret introduced us. He gave me his hand.

'This is that friend I told you about, Mr Nils,' she said.

We stood there. I felt very awkward. Margaret smiled.

'Would you like a drink?' I asked him.

'I have ordered a table,' he said.

'I'll get you a Tuborg,' I said. 'Sit down.' I offered him my chair.

'No, no,' he said.

'Mr Nils,' said Margaret, 'why don't you take off your coat?'

'Oh, I'm sorry,' he said, and began to unbutton it.

'I'll put it in the cloakroom for you,' I said.

'I'll go with you,' Mr Nils said.

It was very awkward. In the cloakroom he slipped off his coat, and underneath was a quiet dark suit. He took off his hat. His hair (there wasn't much of it) was blond, almost white, and immaculately brushed. It looked as soft as a baby's. He started to hand his coat to the cloakroom attendant, then suddenly remembered something, and slipped a small package out of one of the pockets, not quite furtively, but with a shy smile at me as he did it. I tried to smile back. He held the package behind him and we went back to Margaret.

Once again I offered Mr Nils the chair next to Margaret's, but he wouldn't take it. He stood in front of her, looking down, smiling quietly, the package still behind his back. He seemed shy, almost embarrassed. He kept blinking. At last he produced the package, and handed it quickly to Margaret.

'This is for you,' he said.

'Mr Nils,' said Margaret, shaking her head. 'No.'

'Please,' said Mr Nils. 'It is nothing.'

'Don't be silly,' Margaret said.

'Please,' said Mr Nils. 'Just this time. Open it.'

It was a watch.

'You're very sweet, Mr Nils,' Margaret said, 'but I can't take this.'

'Why don't we go and sit down at a table?' I said.

We sat down. Margaret seemed suddenly very gay, but I knew it was determined. She devoted herself to the menu, skimming short-sightedly from item to item. From behind my menu, I sneaked a look at Mr Nils. He wasn't looking at his at all. He was looking at Margaret. He was transfixed. She looked up and he gave her a timid smile. She smiled back, a brilliant flash of teeth, and then dived back to her menu.

'Hey, they've got artichokes!' she cried. 'Mr Nils?'

'I'm not so hungry,' he said. 'Forget me.'

'Mr Nils,' said Margaret, looking stern.

'You order for me,' Mr Nils said.

We ordered artichokes for three, and steaks to follow.

'I would like to buy a bottle of wine,' Mr Nils said.

'O.K.,' said Margaret.

'How long are you in Copenhagen?' I asked Mr Nils.

It was the strangest meal. Margaret made a big business of enjoying her food, whipping off her artichoke leaves, sipping her wine. From time to time she looked quickly up at Mr Nils and gave him a smile. There was no conversation. The waiter came to take away our artichoke plates, and then Margaret saw that Mr Nils had not eaten a thing.

'Mr Nils,' she said.

'I am happy looking at you,' Mr Nils said.

'Now, don't be silly,' Margaret said, and she frowned.

Mr Nils cut a piece of steak, but as soon as Margaret was busy again, he put down his knife and fork and sat as before, smiling at her with his pale blue eyes.

I tried to talk to Mr Nils, but it was impossible. He said yes and no, but he didn't look at me. He didn't give me any of his time. For him, I didn't exist.

The meal went quickly. We had coffee, and then Mr Nils paid the bill. I stood up.

'I'll get your hat and coat, Mr Nils,' I said.

'No, no,' he said. 'I will go.'

'Isn't he a sweetie?' said Margaret, looking at the watch he had given her. 'It must have cost him a fortune. I really shouldn't take it.'

'Then don't,' I said.

'I can't do that,' Margaret said. 'I don't want to hurt him.'

Mr Nils came back, wearing his too-long coat, hat in hand.

'I would like to take you dancing,' he said to Margaret. 'And, of course, your friend.'

'I really must go home,' Margaret said. 'I've got a lot of work to do.'

'Oh,' said Mr Nils.

We stepped out into the street. A wind had come up. The street was deserted. Dry leaves skittered under our feet.

'Only for one hour,' said Mr Nils.

'You're very sweet,' said Margaret, 'but I really must go.'

'Marvellous dinner,' I said to Mr Nils. He ignored me.

'May I take you home in a taxi?' he asked Margaret.

He had his hat on now and he looked very small.

'Mr Nils,' said Margaret, 'you're very sweet, really you are, but you must behave yourself. I want you to go back to your hotel. I'm going to take a tram.'

'It's no trouble,' said Mr Nils.

'No,' said Margaret. 'Definitely no.'

We walked down the street to the tram stop. Mr Nils, I saw, was two inches at least shorter than Margaret. He walked the way he looked, very quietly, almost on his toes.

A tram came. Margaret put up an arm to signal the driver.

'Please,' said Mr Nils.

'No,' Margaret said. 'And I want you to promise me something. Don't give me any more thing. Go on. I want you to promise.'

'Oh, they are nothing,' said Mr Nils.

'Goodnight, Mr Nils,' said Margaret. She put out a hand for him to shake. 'Thanks for the dinner, it was very nice,' she said, and quickly stepped onto the tram. She turned in the doorway, threw us both a big smile, Mr Nils and me, and then she was gone.

'Which hotel are you staying at, Mr Nils?' I asked.

'I am all right,' he said. He looked lost.

'Goodnight,' I said. 'Very nice to meet you.' I put out my hand. His was unbelievably soft. 'Well, I'm off,' I said, and before I could stop myself I gave him a huge smile, and then took off down the street, not quite running.

Margaret phoned me at ten the next morning and invited me to dinner at her place that night. She had a room and the use of the kitchen in what was once a farmhouse on the outskirts of town. The house had a thatched roof, stone walls, and a lovely garden. The owner was away visiting in Malmö for a month. I said dinner would be nice.

'It's only spaghetti,' Margaret said.

'I'll bring a bottle of wine,' I said.

At eight o'clock I stepped off the tram and there was Mr Nils standing under a street light across the street from Margaret's house.

He was wearing his hat and his too-long gaberdine coat, and when he saw me, on the other side of the street, he nodded, but made no move. I nodded back, then nipped through the gate into the garden of Margaret's house, went quickly down the side, and knocked on her door.

She was a long time answering, but I could hear her running around inside. When she opened the door she looked flustered and upset.

'He's outside,' I said.

'I know,' she said. 'He's been there for hours. Quick. Come in.'

I followed her down the hall to the kitchen. The table was laid. There were candles in long holders. I put down the wine.

'He phoned me about five times today,' she said. 'I don't know what to do.'

'Relax,' I said. 'He'll go away. He can't stand there for ever.'

'I know,' she said. 'But – I don't know. He's so sweet. Look at him. Doesn't he make you want to cry?'

We could see Mr Nils through the kitchen window. He seemed to be looking straight at us.

'I'll close the curtains,' I said to Margaret.

'Well, I don't know,' she said. 'Yes, do.'

We stood there, aware of Mr Nils under the street light, quietly watching the house.

'This is silly,' Margaret said, becoming suddenly businesslike. 'Go and take off your coat.'

Margaret's room was quite small, but looked on to the garden. There were photographs pinned all over the walls, some her own, some out of magazines. I took off my coat and put it on the bed. There was a stack of records on the floor by a portable record player. I flipped quickly through them, found one by the Beatles, put it on the player and turned the volume up loud. When I came back to the kitchen, the spaghetti was steaming on the table, the wine was open and poured, and Margaret was at the window, looking out at Mr Nils through a gap in the curtains.

He was there through the spaghetti. He was there through the salad. He was there through the strawberries and cream. Margaret put her coffee percolator on the stove. Mr Nils hadn't moved. I went back to her room and put on another record. When I came back, Margaret was standing in the middle of the room, looking down at her feet.

'This is awful,' she said.

'Do you want me to go out and talk to him?' I asked, hoping she'd say no.

'I don't know,' she said. She stood there, biting her lip.

'Take out another cup,' I said. 'I'm going to bring him in.'

Mr Nils seemed not in the least surprised when I crossed the street and came up to him.

'Would you like some coffee?' I asked.

'Thank you,' he said, and for one insane second I thought he thought I was going to bring it to him. He would drink it in the street, under the street light, to fortify himself for his long vigil, while I waited quietly by his side for the empty cup.

'It's on the table,' I said. He followed me quietly back to the house.

He seemed not at all embarrassed as he stepped into the kitchen, hat in hand.

'Hello, Mr Nils,' Margaret said.

'Can I take your coat, Mr Nils?' I asked him.

'No, no, I am all right,' he said.

'Sit down,' Margaret said, pointing to a chair.

'Thank you,' he said quietly, and sat down, his hat on his lap.

'Mr Nils,' Margaret said, 'you are being very silly.'

Mr Nils smiled. How can I help myself? his face asked. His pale blue eyes sparkled in the kitchen light.

'I'll turn the record player off,' I said, and hurried out of the room.

When I came back, both of them were sitting just as I'd left them, not saying a word. Mr Nils was looking at Margaret. She had her eyes down to her coffee, but wasn't drinking it. I sat down and took out my cigarettes.

We sat with our coffee for what seemed to me hours and hours. No one spoke. Mr Nils was the happiest I'd seen him. He sipped his coffee, he stroked his chin, his eyes not leaving Margaret for a second.

Suddenly Margaret pushed back her chair and stood up.

'I'd better do the dishes,' she said.

'Let me help,' Mr Nils said, also standing up.

'Okay,' Margaret said. 'But then you have to go.'

The three of us stood in the kitchen, washing and drying and putting away the plates, Mr Nils in his long gaberdine coat. In ten minutes it was all done.

It was early, not yet ten o'clock. I had planned to stay another hour, playing records and talking. But tonight that was out of the question.

'I'll get my coat,' I said to Margaret.

We walked down the path through the garden to the front gate, the three of us, Mr Nils with his hat in his hand.

'I'll phone you,' I said to Margaret.

'O.K.,' she said. 'Goodbye, Mr Nils. Please don't phone me any more. Please.'

'I will be in Copenhagen in another two months,' he said.

'No,' Margaret said. 'No.'

Mr Nils nodded, smiled, and then he turned to me.

'I am twenty years too late,' he said, and walked away down the street.

'See you,' I said to Margaret. 'Thanks for dinner.'

'You better take a tram with Mr Nils,' Margaret said. 'Be nice to him.'

He was at the tram stop, patiently waiting. He nodded when I came up.

'Where are you staying?' I asked him. He told me. 'That's just two stops after me,' I said.

'I have two children,' said Mr Nils, and took out his wallet. Two blond faces smiled up at me, a boy and a girl. 'The boy is your age,' Mr Nils said.

'What does he do?' I asked.

'Oh, he is an architect,' Mr Nils said. 'He is in America.'

He angled the photograph to catch the light, and smiled at his two children. I could feel his pride. They were fine children, he was happy with them, he was proud, everything in life was fine, except for this terrible thing that had suddenly happened to him.

The tram came and we climbed on board. Mr Nils insisted on paying my fare and I let him. We rode in silence through the empty streets. When we came near my stop, I stood up. Mr Nils shook my hand. The tram stopped with a lurch and I jumped off. I turned around for a last look at Mr Nils. There he was, wearing his hat. He didn't look happy or sad.

♦ An Immaculate Conception

♦

♦ On a hectic autumn morning in the Portobello Road, Bob and Rosemary Miller paid two pounds for an extraordinary painting. There didn't seem to be anything extraordinary about it then. In fact, just the opposite. It completely lacked the patina of an Old Master. It had no glow of age. It was in every way plain and grey. The frame was cheap. There was no signature. It was a scene of a hill, some trees, a field, a fence, unspectacular in composition, nothing about it hinting of craftsmanship or skill.

'Isn't it the worst thing you've ever seen?' Rosemary cried, delighted. 'Just the thing for the stairs.'

It's filthy,' said Bob. His hands felt gritty holding it.

'All it needs is a wash,' said Rosemary. 'What do you want for two quid? A Gainsborough?'

But it didn't get a wash. By the time Bob had come up the stairs lugging the enormous mirror they had also bought that morning, the painting was already up. Rosemary was not one to waste a minute. They had bought, that hectic morning, a chest of drawers, an umbrella stand, a Japanese fan, a hat rack, ropes and ropes of cheap beads. Rosemary flew around the house like a parrot, positioning their new acquisitions.

They had been married three months. Rosemary was a secretary. Bob was in insurance. They lived in four vertical rooms in Hampstead, five minutes from the Heath. You went in the front door then up a flight of stairs. The kitchen and the lounge. Then up some more stairs. Bathroom and two bedrooms. Another flight of stairs to the attic. The painting hung on the first landing. It was not well lit. It was a grey rectangle that broke an expanse of plain wall, nothing more. It hung slightly crooked on its nail.

And it might have hung there for ever had not Bob come home one evening and found it lying on the stairs. It had fallen off its nail. He picked it up to hang it back and then saw how dirty his hands had become just touching it, and he decided to give it a sponge. He carried it into the kitchen. Rosemary was in the lounge, playing Bach on the stereo.

He happened to turn just before he went into the kitchen, and he noticed how empty the wall above the landing looked, now that the painting was not there. He smiled to himself. Funny how you get used to things, he thought. Even when they're invisible.

He put the painting face up on the kitchen table and filled a plastic basin with hot water. He squirted in some detergent. Then he frothed the mixture up with a sponge, pushed up his sleeves, and sat down to work.

The painting was indescribably dirty. The first wipes with the sponge only smudged the surface, the dirt forming black streaks, but then all at once the painting started to come clear.

'Rosemary!' Bob called. 'Come in here! Quick!'

Rosemary was an excitable girl. She came into the kitchen as though the house were on fire. Her reading glasses were on the end of her nose. She had a magazine in one hand, its pages hanging like the wings of a trapped bird.

'What?' she said. She ran up behind Bob and looked over his shoulder. 'Hey!' she said. 'Isn't it super!'

'Ssh,' said Bob. He was still wiping with the sponge. He had too much water on the painting. It was like a pool. He squeezed out the sponge and wiped the painting over again, and under his hand the painting appeared brand new and crystal clear.

'Hey, it's new!' cried Rosemary. 'What a super fake!'

'Ssh!' He wiped the sponge over the painting once again.

'Neo-realism,' said Rosemary.

It was the strangest thing. It was so clear. The trees, the hill, the fence. There was a little path running under one tree, a thing they had never seen before. It was like looking through a window. 'Look out,' said Bob, and stood up.

'What?' said Rosemary.

He picked up the painting and went over with it to the window. It was five o'clock in the afternoon, a grey day with not much light. But there was enough.

Bob didn't know much about painting, and he didn't know exactly what he was looking for, but he got the painting into the light and angled it around. There wasn't much light, but he saw what there was to see. The surface of the painting was as smooth as a sheet of glass.

They were not great gallery goers, Rosemary and he, but they occasionally went, and Bob remembered, staring at the painting, shifting it slightly in his hands, that even on the smoothest painting, paintings that looked like the pages of magazines, there were always bumps and lumps, though sometimes you had to peer very closely to see them. But here there were none. 'I can't see any brushmarks,' he said.

'Show me,' said Rosemary, crowding in to look. On her face was a look of concern. The same thing that had crossed Bob's mind now came to her.

'Do you think it's a photograph?' she asked.

'No,' he said.

It was too clear for a photograph. Bob moved his face closer. If it had been taken with a camera, he thought, it would have to have been blown up, and there'd be that slight out-of-focus look to things in the distance, but the painting was crystal clear as far into the distance as you could see. And there was something about it, some quality, that was unlike any photograph he had ever seen.

They stood by the window and stared at the painting.

'I'll get the magnifier,' Rosemary cried. 'Wait here.'

She ran out, leaving Bob by the window, still angling the paint-ing in the light, his nose about an inch from the painting's sur-face.

It was incredible. You could see every leaf. The more you strained, the more you could see. But no brushmarks. No sur-face whatsoever. And in the corner of the painting, no signature. Bob turned the painting over and on the back it was plain grey. There were six tacks holding it in the frame on each of the short sides, eight on the other two.

'I can't find it,' he heard Rosemary calling from the lounge. 'It was in the top drawer, wasn't it?'

'Stay there!' Bob called back. 'I'll come in.'

Bob was a careful person, but now, coming out of the kitchen, he did a silly thing. He was very excited, in a strange way, and as he came out of the kitchen he caught the painting on the handle of the kitchen door. The handle struck the painting dead centre. There was a loud bang.

'Oh God!' Bob moaned.

'Darling, are you all right?' Rosemary called. 'What was that bang?'

'Nothing,' he said.

He stood stock still with his eyes tightly closed. I've ruined it, he thought. He was too scared to open his eyes and look. He pictured the painting with a hole gaping in the middle, shattered, smashed.

'Come on, I've found it,' Rosemary called.

'Coming,' he said, and slowly he opened his eyes. He looked down at the painting. Then he looked again. There was no hole. He held the painting up to his face, staring. There wasn't a mark on it. He angled it around. Not a scratch, not a dent. The surface was as smooth as ever.

It must be steel, he thought.

He tapped the painting with his finger. It wasn't steel. The sound was flat and ordinary, as though he had tapped a sheet of cardboard.

'Come on!' Rosemary called. 'Darling, what are you *doing* in there?'

He carried the painting into the lounge. Rosemary was stand-ing in the middle of the room, the contents of two drawers scat-tered on the carpet around her feet: letters, pens, a packet of envelopes, spools of thread, a stainless steel paper-knife, a paperweight, leather boxes from Florence, buttons. She held in her right hand a small magnifying glass. Bob bent down and picked up the knife.

'Hey, what are you doing?' Rosemary asked.

'I'm not sure,' he said, and scratched the painting with the tip of the blade. He did it right over on one edge, almost under the frame. Then he held the painting up under the light and looked at where he'd scratched. There was no mark.

'What – ?' said Rosemary.

'Ssh,' he said, and this time he scratched the painting as hard as he could, pressing down with all his strength on the blade, all the way along one edge, by the frame.

'Darling!' Rosemary cried.

But there was no mark.

'Give me your engagement ring,' he said.

'What?' said Rosemary.

'Quickly!'

He pushed the diamond as hard as he could across the paint-ing, from the top left-hand corner to the bottom right. Then he scratched the other way, making a cross. Rosemary stood with her mouth wide open. Then he looked. No mark.

'Give me the glass,' he said.

He saw the veins in leaves, an ant on a blade of grass, the rust on the nails on the fence under a tree. He saw the grains of sand on the path, each one clear and distinct. He saw grains of pollen drifting through the air. He saw a spider's web, shining like new wire, and in the centre of it a fly, wrapped up, dead.

And no grain, no surface, no distortion, nothing out of focus, nothing blurred. And no mark of any maker.

Rosemary looked at her husband, and for once in her life she was speechless.

'Let's phone up Kevin,' Bob said. 'I want to get this under a microscope.'

'Let's just go,' Rosemary said.

Kevin and Bob had been at school together. Kevin was a dental technician. He lived in St. John's Wood.

They got into the car. Rosemary sat with the painting clutched to her breast, her reading glasses forgotten on the tip of her nose. The car squealed round corners.

'Careful, darling,' Rosemary said, and when the car squealed again, 'The painting!'

Bob laughed. 'Don't worry about the painting,' he said. 'It's indestructible.'

They ran up the steps to Kevin's front door and Bob pressed the bell, praying that Kevin was in. Rosemary stood with the painting still to her breast, panting, as though she had run all the way. They heard feet coming downstairs, and then Kevin opened the door.

'Well, look who it is!' he said. 'What a surprise.'

'We want to use your microscope,' Bob said. He was already inside the hall. Rosemary behind him.

'By all means, old man,' Kevin said. 'What's that you've got there? Old Master, what? Found yourselves a Rembrandt? Hang on, I'll turn on the light.'

Kevin was not married. He lived alone on two floors, and on the ground floor he worked. He turned on a light switch and followed Rosemary and Bob into his laboratory. It was a large room, but it seemed crammed with equipment: grinning plaster jaws, some with teeth, some without, bottles, jars, an oven, balances, and on a long bench an array of surgical steel implements neatly laid out.

'Lucky to catch me,' he said. 'Just about to pop out and do a spot of shopping.'

'How do I work this?' Bob asked, pointing to Kevin's microscope.

'Hang on,' said Kevin. 'What do you want to see?'

'Anything,' said Bob. 'Here. This bit.' He pointed with his finger at random to a spot on the painting.

'I saw a thing in *The Times* last week about Old Masters,' Kevin said. 'Seems they're fetching quite – '

'For God's sake!' Bob snapped.

'Oh, sorry,' Kevin said. 'Won't be a minute now.'

Kevin cleared some space around the microscope and then he slipped the painting under it, Rosemary holding one end, and then he got his eye down to the eyepiece, at the same time adjusting the lens with the thumb and first finger of his right hand.

'Won't take a sec,' he said. 'Get the old eyeball in focus. Here she comes. Stop moving,' he said to Rosemary, and then he fell silent, and seemed to be squeezing himself down into the eyepiece of the microscope, his shoulders hunched over it. He stared, not moving. The laboratory was silent. Then he said, not lifting his eye from the eyepiece, one word.

'Jesus!'

Bob couldn't wait. He pushed Kevin out of the way and got his eye to the eyepiece, and for a moment he couldn't see anything, and then all at once it became clear.

He sucked in his breath.

He saw black fibres in white space. He saw minute cells, amoeba. Dots and specks and circles and lines. None of them moving, all perfectly still.

It was like a slide in chemistry class, many years ago.

'Let me look, let me look!' Rosemary cried.

'Just a minute,' Bob said. He took his eye away from the eyepiece and bent down to see what part of the painting he had been studying. A blade of grass.

'I say, old man,' Kevin said.

'Please!' said Rosemary. 'Let me look!'

Bob stepped away from the microscope. Rosemary bent down and put her eye to it.

'I say, old man,' said Kevin. 'Where'd you get this thing? What is it? When did – ?'

'I don't know,' Bob said. 'I don't know anything. I don't know anything at all.'

Rosemary (says Bob, talking to himself) wants me to phone the newspapers and get experts to come and look at it. She says it must be worth a fortune. She wants to sell it. I don't know. I want to think about it. I haven't made up my mind.

I've put it up in the attic, turned to the wall, because I'm a bit frightened to look at it. Not that there's anything frightening in it – trees, grass, a fence, a field – but I don't know, I somehow feel we shouldn't look at it. It's like having something stolen in your house. Something that doesn't belong to you.

I lie in bed at night and I think of it up in the attic, as clear as a window, perfect, immaculate, a view of a field and two trees and a hill and a path and a fence.

I think about it a lot. Matter can't be destroyed. That blade of grass is real.

Somewhere in the world, I don't know where, there must be a place where you can stand where the painter stood, when he painted it, and if you stand exactly where he stood, your feet where his feet were, your eyes exactly where his eyes were, and if you look where he looked, not an inch higher, not an inch lower, then you will see a white rectangle missing from the landscape, where our painting has been taken out of the world.

◆ Popov

◆

◆ Amongst other things, he claimed to have saved the life of Moshe Dayan. 'Yeah, yeah,' he said, in his thick, abstracted way, slicing a raw onion against the ball of his fat thumb, feeding himself off the blade of his knife. 'On a horse,' he said. How? I wanted to know. And when? When exactly? 'It was a flood,' he said, and gave a low gutteral growl and would say no more, that was the end of it. With the raw onion he gulped cold milk, wiping his knife – a black-handled pocket-knife – on his trousers before clicking it shut and pushing it away somewhere in his suit, and all I could get from my father, afterwards, was that Popov had found Dayan wedged in a tree, wounded and drowning, and had thrown him over his saddle. When? Many years ago. I believed it, too.

On the other hand, there was that time we went to clear weeds from Popov's garden, my father and I, and Popov kept looking over his shoulder at his house. It was a sunny afternoon. All the blinds were drawn. 'She's watching,' he said. He was very nervous. My father swung a mattock and I helped rake up.

Popov didn't do anything. He was too nervous. I never met Popov's wife. 'A monster,' Popov told my father, and then switched to Hebrew – *Ivrit* – and I heard no more.

I never knew him when he was rich, or anyway was too young to notice or remember – Popov's wealth and fall were vague and mysterious things to me, and thrilling too, like the Dayan flood. Understand, this was Melbourne, and I was, I think, seven or eight when Popov first loomed into my consciousness. The black market. The war. A fire. Trouble with the police. Trouble with his wife. His past was an incomprehensible drama, like the first film my mother took me to, when I was six, and all I remember about that to this day are men in overcoats going up stairs and doors banging and an aeroplane in the night. He told the story of his misfortunes in gutteral melodic *Ivrit*, slicing onions and gulping milk, while I stared at his heavy boots. They were probably orthopaedic, I see now, but then they filled me with fear. But there were elements of the great days about him still, even when he sunk truly low. Gold cufflinks. Rings with weighty stones. Silk shirts. The shirts flashed like electricity when he moved, and one in particular I remember, a dark green one, like a storm at sea. This is the one he wore when he dropped in that night on our *pesach seder*. My grandfather used to run them, and when he died my father took over, and in those first years he took them very seriously. He sat at the head of the table on the huge European pillow brought from his bed, enthroned on the feathers like a king. He sang and chanted loudly, and made me do the same. No skipping. No looking around. 'The words!' he snapped, when I fell to whispering, or only moving my lips. 'I want to hear the words!' We were only a small way into the *seder*, at least twenty pages more before we got to the meal, when there was a knock on the door.

There on the mat was Popov, smiling shyly, shuffling his feet. He reached out to pinch my cheek. I fled. Popov followed. My mother was startled, but hid it quickly and fetched another chair. *'Gut yontov,'* Popov mumbled to my father, light from our *pesach* candles turning Popov's glasses to milky discs.

Popov sat down heavily. He had nowhere to go, he said. His wife, that monster, had locked him out. He fidgeted with *matzo* on the table, breaking it into crumbs. 'We are here,' said my father, passing Popov an open book, and loudly and clearly my father began to chant and sing again, very seriously, and Popov, in that deep gutteral growl, slowly joined in. I watched him, frightened and amazed.

He was wearing, as I've said, his dark green silk shirt, but the tie he wore with it didn't match, and neither did his suit. He was lumpy, he was awkward, a button was going here and another missing there, his tie was twisted and the peaks of his collar stood up like horns. But he had obviously made an effort, this was the best he could make himself look, and I wondered (sneaking looks across the table, dropping my eyes quickly down) if even in his rich days he had looked any different. I couldn't imagine it. Popov's cheeks and chin were blue, all that shaving did was impart to them a steely shine, and sometimes a cut. His fingernails were rimmed with black. Black was Popov's motif, his colour. He had a black tooth, in the front. Black hairs crawled down his wrists and along his thick fingers. His boots were black. He took out a handkerchief at one point to mop his gleaming brow, and his handkerchief was black too. He weighed, I suppose, close to eighteen stone, and overflowed his chair at our *seder* table – his arms on the tablecloth kept him secure, and every second sound that issued from his lips was a grunt.

My mother brought around the traditional pitcher of water, the basin and towel. We washed. We ate. Wine flowed. Popov grew merry. Glass after glass flew to his lips. My father was no great drinker, but when he poured for Popov he poured for himself too. My mother didn't say a word but I could see she was annoyed. She had worked for days to prepare the *seder*. I had helped her get down the *pesach* things, the plates and dishes and cutlery and pots that all year lay hidden in a top kitchen cupboard, covered with brown paper. White plates, edged with gold, finer by far than those we ate off all year.

The *seder* resumed. The second part, after the meal, is mostly singing, and now Popov burst forth, thumping the table, and my father, feeling the competition, his cheeks flushed with wine, thundered to outsing him. They raced like trains. The table rocked. Afterwards, when my mother was in the kitchen, they stayed at the table, comfortably sprawled, my father was

'*Chaver'* and Popov was '*Chaver'* too, and at first they laughed and talked loudly, and then it was softer and mostly in *Ivrit*, my father getting that glazed look that alcohol always gave him, and finally it was just Popov, only Popov who spoke. 'We'll go back,' he said. 'Huh, *chaver?* Like it used to be. You and me.' My father didn't say anything, though he nodded a lot, and after an hour or so Popov grunted to his feet and went home.

'A fool!' my father said the next day. He was angry. The effect of the wine could still be seen on him, but it was more than that. Popov was a fool, certainly, no doubt about that, but he had listened. He had nodded in agreement. He had let himself believe. 'An idiot!' he shouted, and planned his revenge. It took him a week.

There is a part in the *pesach seder*, after the meal, when a glass of wine is poured, filled to the brim, and set down on the table, and the youngest born is sent to open the front door. This is the moment when the Messiah will come, Elijah the Prophet, he will come into the house and drink his wine and the dead will rise from their graves and lions will feed with sheep and peace and prosperity will reign over the world, and year after year I opened the door and there was nothing, never a thing. This was my father's revenge: 'We opened the door for *Eliyohoo Hunovee*,' he crowed, 'and in came Popov!' He laughed. He told it to everyone. The story, in place of the dead, was resurrected year after year. It became part of our family history.

They were in Israel together, or Palestine as it was then, Popov and my father, boys together, young men. Or were they? My father worked in a quarry, and in such stories as he told Popov never figured. He raced on a motorbike, he told me, and helped lay the telegraph line from Haifa to Tel Aviv, and one story was how, camped in the desert, he had glued pieces of newspaper to a sleeping friend's glasses and then woken the friend up and the friend clapped on his glasses and thought he'd gone blind. Was this Popov? I don't think so. I think he would have told me if it was.

There were stories of dancing, and eating, and leaping into the sea, and then my father sailed for Australia, frightened, alone. Bad times. No work. He planned to stay here for a year, until things improved, he would save his money, but he never got back. He married. I was born. And Popov? When did Popov come? Did they come together? Popov was a businessman, in those days anyhow, and my father had no time for dealers or deals. Money talk bored him, made him uncomfortable. He fidgeted when finance came up. If he had money in his pocket and a job to go to the next day, he was rich. Whenever there was a crisis in our house, he would plunge his hands into his trousers and jingle his coins – the reassurance of metal and muscle and honest sweat.

When he won at cards he boasted for a week, and showed me the money, over and over, beaming like a child.

But Popov was certainly from Palestine, he knew all the names and places and his *Ivrit* rumbled flawlessly from his lips, but I doubted then, as I doubt now, that he was an old friend. My father was lonely here, lonely and alone all his life, and anyone who spoke *Ivrit* was a friend, a touchstone, a link, and certainly Popov was an idiot and a fool but he spoke the language and ate raw onions and gulped cold milk, Palestinian ways, and so my father sat with him for hours and hours, for years and years, while my mother, who had never been to Palestine, who had no past there, tried to smile and never said a word but was happier when Popov wasn't in her house. She feared him. She feared his talk. She feared, I think, that one day Popov's words would penetrate that final inch and my father would pack his bags and depart, go back, with her or without, either way it would be a disaster, her family were here, her experience of the world was that travel was a calamity, but she needn't have worried. Popov failed. My father never left. He lies buried in a cemetery on the outskirts of Melbourne, a weedy and windy place with a train line just on the other side of a thin stand of pines, and she lies beside him, and when I go there the train shunts past and the wind blows and I pick the weeds away from their gravestones and then I go home.

It is difficult to speak of Popov without making him comical, and I don't want to do that. The onions, the milk, the pocket-knife, the clumsy boots – they surround Popov's performance like a vaudevillian's props, and I don't want them to do this, I don't want him to appear a clown. In a moment I am going to tell you about his taxi, and there is much in this of a music-hall routine, I admit that, after the strippers in comes Popov and brings the house down, but set it, please, in years and years of Popov, slow years, Popov in a deck-chair in summer, under the plum trees in our back garden, his jacket peeled off, his shirt open at the throat, Popov in winter, warming his heavy hands around a glass of tea, Popov talking, Popov grunting, but mostly Popov just sitting, quietly, slumped, fighting off, I see now, his despair. As the years went by he came to our house more and more often, twice a week, then four times, and sometimes more. He had nowhere else to go. And though my father needed him and poured his milk and fetched his onions, sometimes even his face fell when once again Popov stood on our front mat, shuffling his awkward feet. But he never said a word to him, he never once said, Don't come. He listened. Or anyway, he sat.

Now the taxi. This was near the end, when Popov was calling at our house four times a week or more. I don't remember him ever working, ever taking a job, and now his money was running out. He spoke of deals, schemes, one after another he paraded them in the air. And then he decided to buy a taxi. 'You make nice money from a taxi,' he said. 'A foolish business,' my father told him. 'For a start, how many years since you drove a car?' My father had never learnt to drive. Cars frightened him. Even when he rode in one, he always preferred to sit in the back, clutching the door handle, ready to leap out. 'Driving?' said Popov. 'Hah! You never forget. It's in the blood.' 'And your eyes?' said my father. Popov blinked behind his heavy glasses. 'I can see enough,' he said. There was no dissuading him. He had made up his mind. He became excited, and then hard and businesslike, and I caught a glimpse of the old Popov, the black market Popov, cufflinks flashing when he spoke into our telephone. He made a lot of calls. His voice grew harder. His flesh seemed to firm. He was doing something at last. The business of a taxi meant a long waiting list, and then an examination, but Popov bypassed this. He slipped out secret money. He made more calls. On a Saturday morning the taxi was delivered to our house.

Popov arrived. He walked once around the car, a large gleaming black sedan parked in front of our drive, peered at the licence plates, peered at the wheels, and then he climbed in. 'You want to come with me, *chaver?* he asked my father. 'To where?' asked my father. 'Where are you going?' 'A drive,' said Popov. 'A feel.' 'I'll wait,' said my father. Popov laughed, the first time I'd seen him laugh since that *pesach seder*, put the car into gear, and drove straight into a tree.

Popov sailed for Israel. My father went to see him off, and came home moody and depressed, but angry too. 'Who does he know there?' he said. 'Moshe Dayan? They've got enough idiots there already, without another one.' Then a letter came, and with it was a photograph. Youth knows no age, but the woman Popov had one arm around was young, ten years younger than Popov, at least, and pretty too. '*Chaver,*' wrote Popov, 'I'm having a wonderful time. This is my Tzila, who I met on the ship, what do you think?' Popov's black tooth was like a gap in his flashing smile, an insolent wink. 'Foolishness,' said my father, but he took the photograph and put it in his wallet, and from time to time I would catch him looking at it, his face a mask, certainly to me, and the photograph was still there in his wallet when he died and I came to sort through his possessions and belongings. I don't believe in eternal regrets, and I know that when the Messiah comes my father will rejoice that Popov, his *chaver*, went to Israel, where he married again, and got a good job, and lived with Tzila, his faithful wife – still lives, an old man now – happy and at peace in the Promised Land.

♦ The Death of Rappaport

♦

♦ The last time Rappaport was dying, I grabbed a dozen long-stemmed red American Beauty roses and a copy of *Fanny Hill* and got there as fast as I could, damn the expense. I was sweating. It was one of those early spring afternoons that seem to be drizzling with sun. It was exactly the right day to be dying. We would step slowly across the lawns, the grass achingly green, in our dark suits, heads bent, bearing the last remains of Joseph Rappaport, a good man, misunderstood in his own time, now finally at rest.

I rang the bell. The Rappaports' house is huge, composed almost entirely of additions, added-on bedrooms and playrooms and sunrooms and breakfast rooms and television rooms, around no central core. The whole house must have begun with this bell that I was pressing, while inside Rappaport died.

The door opened an inch and a voice said 'Ssh!' Then it opened a little more and I stole inside.

'How is he?' I whispered. And Mrs Rappaport (it was she!) shook her head, gravely, gravely, slowly, from side to side, a performance I could feel more than see, because the hallway where we stood (the telephone room, added last year) was so dark. Five layers of terylene blotted out the drizzling sun.

'For you,' I said, and handed her *Fanny Hill*, and before she could say a word I tiptoed towards Rappaport.

Rappaport!

He was breathing his last on a plump pile of pillows. His eyes were like oysters, watery, tinged with purple. His hands lay lifeless on the blankets, like plucked chickens. His hair was standing up and over his ears like those photos of the old bolsheviks you sometimes come across, and on his chest, where a button had popped, wild woolly hair showed. His pyjamas? Thundering Paisley. I felt like crying.

'Rappie,' I said tenderly, 'I brought you *Fanny Hill*,' and I put the flowers down with great love and care on the end of his bed.

Rappaport smiled. Oh, what that smile must have cost him. It was like yesterday's breeze sighing across the surface of an old pond.

I remembered that pond (slimy, green) into which I had once pushed him, out in the hills, where we had gone to play golf, and I felt a pang of fresh guilt.

I was ready and waiting (I remembered) outside his house at seven in the morning, the sky chalky grey, no wind, revving up the Vespa to keep it going, but trying to do it quietly so his parents wouldn't come out. They used to hate me in those days. They thought I was a bad influence.

Then Rappaport slid out of the house with egg on his chin and a second jumper tied around his middle like an apron (his mother is one of the great knitters), and this he then swung around to cover his behind because I had no special back seat on the Vespa, and we drove off. Forty miles for a game of golf. But when we got to the links what should we find but that it was Sheep Day. Sheep Day! Everywhere we looked there were the little beasts, nibbling at one end, dropping at the other, keeping the course in trim, and that's when I threw him into the pond, because he had the card and should have known, but luckily he had that second jumper, and we drove to the local pub where we sat on the steps and discussed vital issues and related matters, Rappie filling himself with rum to ward off pneumonia, and then we took that deadly road back to town, both singing opera, mostly Verdi.

Rappaport's lips moved.

'I'm not the top of the tree,' he whispered.

'Sure you are, sure you are,' I lied, trying to hide my sadness, my alarm at his condition, which I could feel my face registering. 'Well, maybe not the absolute top, not the towering peak, not the highest bit of the forest, but . . .'

'You don't have to be kind,' Rappaport said. 'I can take it. The truth never hurts.'

The words came out of him one by one, like rope being played out on the side of a mountain, each inch a matter of life and death. It was like a scene from *Dr Kildare*, a programme Rappaport never watches.

'I'm not the top of the tree,' he whispered again.

I nodded. My mind flashed back ten years. Rappaport's head came through a window. It said, 'I'm not the top of the tree.' There was sadness in his eyes, thirst on his lips, and a hot coin in his large hand. I took the coin. That was how we became friends.

This was in the days when I was a Senior, at school, and I knew Rappaport only by his suits. Actually, they were his father's suits, expensively tailored. He was a big boy even then, and I would see him wandering round the quadrangle in those wide-shouldered, wasp-waisted chalk stripes, the school cap perched on the top of his head like a well-aimed bird dropping. 'Dig that crazy kid,' other Seniors would say to me. In the top pocket of every one of Rappaport's father's suits (I was to find out later), there was a note, usually this:

Please excuse Joseph Rappaport for wearing this suit, but his college grey was savaged by a dog and is being mended.

There followed an illegible signature.

I remembered taking the hot coin and buying him a slurp stick. Rappaport ate between three and four hundred of them a year. He was never without one. But his thirst was too great for the Junior queue, and so I, with my Senior privileges, became his friend.

'Does it hurt to talk?' I asked him, now that he was dying, and he moved ever so slightly on his mass of pillows, and dropped his heavy lids. They told the whole story.

'Damn those Huns,' he muttered. 'Damn their black souls.'

I couldn't exactly place the movie.

He was expelled (I remembered) the first time, for picking up Charles Willoughby, the English master, by the seat of the pants and hurling him down the corridor. Rappaport's story was that Willoughby had farted in class. He was reinstated because his mother had arrived in her black Buick and proven that her son had been wronged, mostly by crying in the Principal's office (the Principal, an old cricketer, couldn't stand tears), and he was expelled the second time (and finally) for no great reason at all. He got nought for all his subjects. Tired of academic life, he wrote *Australia was discovered by the Marx Brothers in 1865*, and material of that ilk. This time his mother saved herself the trip. She told her friends that her son had been discriminated against, and knitted him a new jumper. Rappaport went into business.

'There was a Bogie movie on the television yesterday,' I said to Rappaport.

The miles we have driven, the hours we have spent, to view the great Bogart, Rappaport in his chalk stripes, speechless with passion.

'I was too sick to watch,' Rappaport said, and then I knew how serious it was.

'What is it exactly, Rappie? Are you allowed to tell me?'

'We think it's the kidneys,' Mrs Rappaport said. There she was in the doorway, a mountain of grief and held-back weeping.

'We think he picked up one of those modern diseases,' she said. 'From the street. We don't know if he'll be all right ever again, completely.'

I didn't know what to say.

'Mum,' Rappaport whispered. 'Something has happened to my legs. I can't feel them. They're all shot. God, mum, my legs. My *pins!*'

'You see?' said Mrs Rappaport. 'Now it's the legs. Oh, what are you doing with *flowers?* They make *gases* in the air. Oi!'

She swooped them up, like a spinster lurching for the bride's bouquet. She still had, I noticed, *Fanny Hill* clutched in one hand.

In that room of slow, painful breathing, I remembered another room, another death. My own. I had looped the loop on that damn Vespa and woke up in hospital with my skull cracked and all my front teeth in fragments, the Vespa lying in some garage with mechanics walking past and going tut tut. Rappaport had come as fast as he could, with his mother, and she had been about to give me a box of hard chewing toffees when I smiled and she saw my shattered teeth. She dropped the toffees and ran. Afterwards she apologized. Rappaport, when she was gone, had pulled up a chair, and slipped me a paperback *Kama Sutra,* and we had talked dirty until a nurse told him to go home.

'How'd it happen?' he had asked.

'I was singing opera. I guess I got carried away.'

Now it was Rappaport who was dying.

'I'll make some soup,' Mrs Rappaport said.

In a few seconds, that eternal smell of chicken soup began to creep into the room.

'Gee, how'd it happen to you?' I asked Rappaport.

'I don't know, I don't know,' he said. 'I woke up sick. I went to bed healthy and I woke up sick. That's not fair, is it? It's not right.'

'It's immoral,' I said.

'Am I allowed to ask why it happened to me?'

'Sure you can. Sure, sure.' There was a lump in my throat.

Rappaport eased back his head and looked up at the ceiling. A small voice came out of his tired lips.

'Why?' it said.

Then Mrs Rappaport came in with the soup. She sat down on the edge of the bed and began to spoon-feed her son, very carefully, with a tiny silver tea spoon.

'This will make you better, this will make you strong,' she said with every spoonful, while I looked away, somehow embarrassed to see my best friend being fed.

Rappaport, that master of Chinese food! That devourer of pizza! That twiner of spaghetti!

'When's Mr Rappaport coming home?' I asked, just for something to say.

'Ssh!' Mrs Rappaport said. 'We're eating.'

Then the telephone rang.

'Oh,' said Mrs Rappaport, and how quickly she moved, considering her age and shape, putting the bowl of soup and the little silver spoon down on the carpet by the side of the bed and sweeping out of the room, calling 'I'm coming! 'I'm coming!' and then 'Hello?' in the sweetest voice you could ever possibly want to hear.

'I brought you *Fanny Hill*,' I whispered to Rappaport.

'Unexpurgated?' A glimmer of life showed in his sick eyes.

'Of course. Every word.'

'Slip it under my pillows,' Rappaport said, and I slid it away (Mrs Rappaport had dropped it on the floor) deep under the pillows Mrs Rappaport had brought with her all the way from Europe, with the samovar and the silver candlesticks, long, long ago.

'You've got a heart of gold,' Rappaport said.

'You too,' I said.

'Sonya?' we heard Mrs Rappaport saying. 'I didn't know you were back. Are you brown? Holidays, holidays. I don't know where you get the time.'

We listened to Mrs Rappaport being invited to an evening of supper and cards.

'I might be a few minutes late,' Mrs Rappaport said, 'because my son is very sick. Confidentially, we had the doctor – *twice* – and he doesn't want to tell us exactly what it is. Nu, what can you do? I made him a soup. And how is your Benny? Studying, studying. I know. Never home. That's how it is with the young people these days. Well, we'll talk later. Oh –' and she remembered a few other things, and talked for another ten minutes, saying goodbye at the end of each sentence, then remembering something else. Rappaport and I listened for a while, but it was, after a while, really quite boring. We stopped listening.

'What are you doing New Year's Eve?' I asked Rappaport.

He made a terrible dying face.

Rappaport and I have a thing about New Year's Eve. We hate it. We hate *having* to be happy, just because the calendar has turned. We hate the business of the funny hats and the way you have to blow whistles at every policeman you pass in the street, and the way the policemen have to smile.

Last New Year's Eve, I remembered, we took two beautiful girls dancing and dining, and after we'd waved at police cars and burst our whistles and parked the car under a statue of Queen Victoria and guzzled gin out of plastic cups, the girls said, 'Come with us.' We drove to their flat. Rappaport disappeared into a room with one of the girls. I sat in the lounge with her friend. She was not for me. I talked Literature and Movies and The Meaning of Life but there was no fire between us. Hours went by. I smoked innumerable cigarettes. Finally I could stand it no longer. I excused myself from her glacial company and went to the door wherein Rappaport was disporting himself and gave a knock. 'I want to go home,' I said, and Rappaport came straight out. *Straight out!* That's what I call a friend. He drove me home and we listened to *Under Milk Wood* on the stereo, and then we drove down to the beach and looked at the sea until it was time to go to sleep. And not one word from Rappaport about interrupting him and that girl.

Heart of gold.

And if you don't call that a heart of gold, listen to this. One night Rappaport waited in his car while I said goodnight and other things to the local butcher's daughter, a sterling girl. I was in there for four hours, Rappaport giving gentle toots on the horn every hour or so just to keep me informed of the time, just to let me know he was ready whenever I was.

And now he was dying.

'What can I get you, Rappie? What can I bring you, what do you need?'

'There's nothing a human being can do,' Rappaport whispered. Then he added, 'Get the box out from under the bed.'

I knelt down and pulled out the box. It was a large cardboard box, crammed to the top with magazines, *Tatler, McCalls, Playboy, Queen, Esquire, House and Garden*, The *New Yorker*, The *National Geographic, Domus, Elle, Punch, Time, Sight and Sound, Holiday*, everything you could think of, the spoils of a hundred kiosks.

'Take any three,' Rappaport said.

He had never said a kinder thing to me. I almost wept.

Rappaport is the greatest buyer of magazines that I know. He gobbles them up, he devours them, he brings them home by the shining handful, a fresh batch. They cost him a fortune. But he adores them. He craves them. Take them away and he dies.

'Idiot!' screams his father, hurling this week's *Life* across the room.

Mr Rappaport hates his son. For the usual Jewish reasons. His son is not a doctor or a lawyer or any other sort of professional man. He is a bum. And who but a bum would buy such junk?

Mr Rappaport has a sweets factory, and he comes home, smelling of sugar, to find his house littered with double-page cookery spreads, photos of film stars, maps of Turkey, drawings of cars, exposés, inside stuff, on every floor, in every room, and at night, when he has drowned himself in television (nothing else can pacify him) he squirms in bed while his wife sits up beside him with the light on, her glasses slipping down her nose, reading *Playboy* or *Queen*.

'I am trying to see why my son reads them,' she explains. 'What is he looking for?'

'Truth!' says her son, coming in in his paisley pyjamas to snatch the magazine away. 'I'm looking for God. I want to see Him. And when He comes it won't be in a church or a synagogue with all the Jews standing outside on the steps in their new suits talking about business and golf and their new houses. When He comes, it'll be in a magazine. He'll come in full colour in a double-page spread, with the smell of ink rising like smoke, and I'm going to be there when He comes. Understand?'

'No,' says Mrs Rappaport.

'Put out the light!' howls Mr Rappaport. 'A madman! My son is a madman!'

And the next day, while she is taking a pile of magazines out to the garage, Mrs Rappaport will once again peep inside them, to see if there really is something inside.

'I'll buy you some new ones,' I said to the dying Rappaport. 'Which ones would you like?'

'All of them,' he said, his eyes going far away. 'All.'

Suddenly we heard the scratch of a key, and then the front door opening and then slamming shut.

'I'm home!' Mr Rappaport howled.

We could hear him, advancing rapidly. We heard his hat flip to the floor, his bag drop, the thud of his overcoat falling, a succession of groans and grunts as he kicked off his shoes, then other noises, zippings, tearings, and suddenly he was in the doorway, in his striped underwear, red in the face. There was a strong smell of sugar.

'You!' he said, seeing me. 'Don't make him sick!'

It was impossible to reply.

'Two minutes!' Mr Rappaport bellowed, and he was already gone, we could hear water splashing and running in the bathroom, and Mr Rappaport's howl of rage.

'All you have to do is become a doctor,' I said to Rappaport, 'and you'll have his love.'

'I won't use the knife,' Rappaport said. 'I won't cut. I won't put anyone on that table.'

'You can use drugs,' I said. 'Fast acting. Painless.'

'My hands are too shaky. Look at them. Are these the hands of a surgeon? Shot to hell, that's what they are. Shot to hell.'

'Ssh, Rappie, relax. You'll be back in the shop in no time at all. You'll be top of the tree. You'll grow. You'll reach the sky.

Rappaport's shop. He went into business straight after school. His capital was the single, solitary, lone thousand which he had in the bank from his *barmitzvah*. He went out one day and bought three hundred blue bottles, sixty-two old handset telephones, and a brass bed with stripes and stars on it and a barebreasted woman riding in a chariot drawn by four proud lions. Who from my school has done half this?

'A thousand? The *barmitzvah* money!' Mr Rappaport roared. 'What madman would sleep in that bed? Good God in Heaven, I have given birth to an idiot!'

'The bed cost me four dollars,' his son told him quietly. 'I still have nine hundred and sixty-one dollars left.'

'A madman! A madman!' And Mr Rappaport was off, shedding clothes, howling for the water in the bath.

A week later (I was there), Rappaport casually told his father that he'd sold the bed.

'I made twenty-five hundred per cent profit,' he said.

'Uh?'

'I sold it for a hundred dollars.'

You could see the wheels whirling inside Mr Rappaport's head. You could hear them click into place. It was terrible to watch.

'Big deal!' Mr Rappaport finally announced. 'You know what happened, you fool? They opened up the asylum and they gave every madman a hundred dollars and told them to buy stupid beds. That's what happened! You idiot! Get out of here, you're driving me mad! Get out, get out!'

Mr Rappaport threw himself into his chair and stared, *stared*, at a programme on the cats of London on the television, slowly quietening down.

'He loves you, Rappie,' I said. 'He's shy, he's clumsy, he can't express his feelings.'

'Two minutes is up!' Mr Rappaport, that shy father, roared from the bathroom.

'Come tomorrow,' Mrs Rappaport said. 'It's enough for one day.'

She stood in the doorway, a nice woman really, who liked to go to her son's shop and browse around among his stock, looking over her shoulder all the time as though she expected her husband to appear out of thin air, bellowing and roaring. Her son would be wearing one of the jumpers she had knitted (all of them too long), and she would move around and touch the ormolu clocks, the French birds, the crystal doorknobs, the brass beds, the gold pelmets, the grandfather clocks, the hunting prints, the kerosene lamps, the tiffany shades, the old chests, the keys, the marble tables, the high-backed chairs, the lion's-head knockers, the chandeliers, the pewter pots, the copper pans, the silver spoons, the gold rings, the old pocket watches lovingly and elaborately inscribed.

And her son would follow her around, quietly explaining, 'That's Regency, mum, that's Louis XIV, that's Sterling Silver, that's . . .'

And you could see that Mrs Rappaport almost, *almost*, understood her son at last.

'Goodbye,' I said to Rappaport.

'You go,' he said. 'There's only enough water for one, and you can make it to the fort, you're stronger than I am, and Miss Cindy really loves you, it's you she loves, she told me . . . be happy together . . . be kind to each other . . . I'll try and hold them off while you . . .'

His voice gave out. He seemed to sink into the European pillows, to fade, to be no longer there.

I picked up the three top magazines from Rappaport's magazine box (I knew that would make him happy), and quietly tiptoed out of the room.

Outside, the sun was still drizzling. It was after six and the sky was dark, and the trees were black in the night, but I knew Rappaport would have liked the sun to be drizzling, so, for me, it was. He likes it to drizzle sun when he's dying. He's funny that way.

◆ *Pride and Joy*

◆

◆ I never had the pleasure of meeting Mr Ernest Hemingway, so all I know about him is what I've read, but the first time I saw Ned Matthews, that's who I thought of. Hemingway. Not that Matthews looked much like him. Hemingway wasn't that short. Hemingway had more hair. Hemingway sported a grizzly white beard, and all Matthews had was a moustache. But his chest was Hemingway, a broad barrel, stretching his shirt. And his walk. He walked as though he'd just shot a lion, a mixture of offhand and proud. And then there were his fingers. His fingers were definitely Hemingway. It was eight o'clock in the morning, the first time I saw him, we were all eating our breakfast, and the fingers of Ned Matthews' right hand were wrapped around a large glass of frothy ice-cold beer. You could see the bubbles rising in the glass and popping out on top. You could practically hear them too, it was suddenly that quiet.

Eight o'clock in the morning on an island on the Great Barrier Reef. A Hemingway time for a glass of beer.

He came up the centre aisle of the dining room, making for my table, at the far end of the room, furthest from the door, me and sixty other holiday-makers staring at his glass of frothy ice-cold beer, filled with the morning sun.

He wasn't alone. Right behind him came a boy who looked about sixteen, tall, with curly blond hair and a cocky smile. The smile was as much in his eyes as on his lips. He walked with an exaggerated swagger. He had a glass of beer in his hand too. And then came another man, taller than the boy, a thin, sinewy man with colourless eyes and his hair all shaved off at the sides and on top plastered down hard with oil. He wore a dirty tee shirt, battered jeans, no shoes. There was a beer in his hand too. The three of them came towards me in proud procession, through the hushed dining room, though now there were a few whispers.

'This free?' said Matthews, pulling out a chair. 'Help yourself,' I said, but he already had. He sat down, not giving me a second look. 'Billy, you sit here,' he said to the boy. 'Stan, over there.' He had that kind of voice that likes giving orders and was used to having them obeyed. The three of them made a lot of noise with their chairs, sitting down, getting comfortable, more noise than they had to. None of them looked over at me.

'Well, boys,' said Matthews, raising his glass. 'Bon appétit!' He drained his glass in one gulp. The thin man did likewise. The boy, I noticed, had to take a breath halfway down, but he made it, then banged his empty glass down on the table, sat back in his chair, looked serious, and then let out a great burp. Then he smiled at Ned Matthews, who smiled back, pleased with the performance. 'Only way to start the day, son,' Ned Matthews said. 'Yeah,' said Billy. Then the three of them lit up cigarettes. They were like three ham actors playing at being tough. For us? I thought. For each other? But it was too early in the day for games for me, and I went back to my cornflakes.

So that's Ned Matthews, I thought. That's what everyone's been waiting for. Well, well.

A waitress came over to take their order. She was a young girl, about seventeen, very pretty, without sophistication, not yet completely sure of herself. She dropped three menus on the table and then stood waiting, hands on hips, looking vaguely bored. Matthews reached over and picked up a menu. So did the thin man. But the boy left his where it was, turned around in his chair to face the waitress, who was standing behind him, and a little to one side, looked up, and gave her a cocky smile, his cigarette bobbing between his lips.

'What's ya name, honey?' he said. 'Why?' said the girl. 'I always like to know the names of the girls I sleep with,' the boy said. The girl didn't bat an eyelid, but her face turned hard. She stared straight back at him. The boy let out a small laugh, and then, slowly, so that it wouldn't look as though she had stared him down, he turned back to face his father. Very casually, he removed his cigarette from between his lips and gave him a big wink. Then he lolled back in his chair and took a slow, arrogant puff on his cigarette. 'Easy, son,' said Matthews, but his face was beaming with pride. I looked away.

But the performance wasn't over. Matthews had a loud voice, and I heard the rest. 'Girl,' he said to the waitress, 'let's have some eggs. Four eggs each. Fried. And some bacon. And some sausages. And a lot of toast. Hot.' 'Dad, I couldn't eat four eggs,' I heard the boy say. '*Four eggs each*,' Matthews repeated to the waitress. There was an edge of irritation to his voice. Not much, but it was there. 'And coffee,' he said. 'Black.'

The waitress went away. I turned a little in my chair, away from Matthews and his son and the other man, away from their games, and looked out of the window at the palm trees and the sea.

The sea was blue, the sky was another blue, the palm trees were green, and the buildings and huts scattered under them were white. It was a lovely place. It took an hour and forty minutes to walk around the island, an hour and five minutes to hike up to the top of the hill in the middle. The sea was warm, the bar was well stocked, the management put on barbecues and music at night, you could take a boat and hop around to other islands, if you wanted to. Or you could do nothing. Most people did nothing. It was a holiday place. I was there to sort out what I thought about a girl back home. Did I want her? Did I want her forever? I took a daily walk around the island, alone, just me and my thoughts, stopping off halfway for a swim. Captain Cook had been here before me and had left behind some goats, and their offspring watched me suspiciously as I sauntered past, an old man goat with a white beard and a dozen skitterish young ones. Sometimes I'd surprise them and they'd bound off through the long grass, making a hell of a noise. There were about eighty people on the island, sixty guests, twenty staff. And now there was Mr Ned Matthews and his son Billy and their hired man. It had been very peaceful up to now. And now?

Jim, a gardener and general handyman about the place, had told me about him. This was on my second day, when I had finished my walk around the island and was sitting under a palm tree, contemplating the flat sea, thinking about my girl. She was beautiful. She was magnificent. But. But what? 'Quiet, isn't it?' Jim said to me. 'Well, it is.' I said, 'but I like it.' 'Wait'll Ned Matthews gets here,' Jim said. 'Then things'll liven up a bit. This place is a morgue without him. Just you wait till he comes. Should be here any day.' He stared out to sea, as though expecting any moment something to appear. 'Who's Ned Matthews?' I said. 'Millionaire,' Jim said. 'Rich as blazes. Got himself a yacht, the *Southerly*. Beautiful.' 'What does he do?' I asked. 'Do? He don't do nothin'. He's a millionaire. He drinks, that's what he does. You'll see some real drinking when Ned gets here. I'll tell you what he does. He sails around from island to island, raising general hell. Should be here any day.' Again he scanned the horizon for some sign. 'I'll look out for him,' I said. 'Oh, you'll see him,' Jim said. 'You'd know he was here even if you was blind.'

Well, he was here, sitting at my table. I kept looking out of the window at the palm trees and the sea, waiting for the waitress to come with my coffee. I couldn't see the jetty, it was out of view. I took a sip of my pineapple juice. I heard Ned Matthews, in his loud voice, organising his labour for the day.

'That tide'll be out in about three hours,' he was saying. 'Stan, straight after breakfast, I want you to lash *Southerly* up tight. Get her high and dry. Billy, you can start stripping her underneath. I'll work on the pumps and the motor. I want to get her done in two days.'

'Okay, boss,' I heard Stan say. 'Yeah, dad,' the boy drawled. The waitress brought my coffee and I took it outside to drink in the sun.

Now I could see the yacht. It really was a beautiful piece of work. It was dead white, with gleaming brass flashing in the sun. It looked small, riding in the blue water at the end of the jetty, a toy, a rich man's toy. I sipped my coffee and lit a cigarette and thought about a millionaire's life of sailing from island to island, greeted everywhere with open arms, raising hell. Beer before breakfast. And the boy? I thought. Is he grooming him for that kind of life? Well, the boy seems to like it. Hell, at his age I was still at school. I was thinking about that when I heard a door slam and Matthews and his son and the hired man strode across the lawn past me and went out onto the jetty. They got to work without preamble. Matthews crushed out the cigarette he was smoking and stripped off his shirt. The Hemingway chest expanded in the sun. I watched him for a while and then I stood up and took my coffee cup back inside and then I went to renew my acquaintance with Captain Cook's goats.

He was Hemingway at lunch too, striding in with his glass of beer, his son and the hired man with theirs, down the centre aisle, a repeat of their morning's performance. They hadn't washed or changed, and seemed to wear the grease on their faces and hands like badges to an exclusive club. Matthews, as before, ordered for all three, in his loud, commanding voice. Billy was cocky to the waitress, exchanging winks with his father. 'Keep at her, son,' Matthews told him, flashing his wide, even smile, and then they talked about the yacht.

He wasn't Hemingway at dinner, though. He was Clark Gable. He came in alone, wearing a dark blue yachting jacket and trim grey slacks. He smiled to left and right as he came down the aisle, his eyes merry and sincere. His son came in a few minutes later, and then the hired man. Matthews let them order their own dinner. He was polite to the waitress. He ordered a bottle of wine and sipped it slowly. He even smiled at me. 'Nice weather,' he said.

When I had finished my meal, I went outside to smoke and to look up at the stars and listen to the palm trees moving about in the breeze coming in from the sea. I took a walk along the front beach. The tide was way out, and I saw the *Southerly*, out of the water, tied up to the end of the jetty. She really was a beautiful boat. The moon shone on the polished brass. The sails were the colour of rich cream.

After a while, I went in to the bar. Matthews and his son and the hired man were there, down one end. Matthews was talking to a fat stockbroker who had taken too much sun and looked scalded, like a lobster. He looked a little hemmed in by Matthews, and kept saying, 'Is that so? Is that so?' to everything Matthews said. The stockbroker was wearing a lilac shirt and canary yellow slacks and white shoes. He looked over-festive and a little uncomfortable. Matthews was describing the effects of certain drinks he had sampled in his time. 'Try this one,' he said to the stockbroker, and handed him something in a long-stemmed glass. The drink was bright green, with a white froth on top. Matthews handed one of the same to his son, and picked up a third. The hired man was drinking beer. 'Three of these and you'll roar like a bull,' Matthews said to the stockbroker. 'Cheers!' He drained his in one gulp. 'Cheers,' said the stockbroker, looking perplexed.

I bought myself a beer and sat down on a cane chair at the other end of the bar. 'Say goodbye to your hair,' I heard Matthews saying to the stockbroker, handing him another drink. This one was a vivid red. 'This little invention is guaranteed to take it out by the roots,' Matthews said. 'Is that so?' said the stockbroker. 'God's truth,' said Matthews' son, upending his own glass.

Matthews then ordered something that looked like milk, but came out of four bottles, then something pale blue, then he went back to the bright green. His son matched him drink for drink. 'I do believe I'm bringing up a little alcoholic here,' Matthews said, putting his arm around his son's shoulders. Billy seemed to swell with pride. Matthews laughed, and then broke away from his son and gave him a playful jab in the ribs. 'Watch it, old timer,' his son said. 'I can drink you under the table any day.' Matthews threw back his head and laughed, showing his white, even teeth. 'That'll be the day, son,' he roared, and then he turned to the bartender and shouted, 'Hey! How about getting off your fat behind and giving us a bit of service round here?' The bartender was standing not two feet away from him. 'Yeah, shake it up there,' Billy shouted. I felt I'd suddenly had enough of Matthews and his son, put down my beer glass, and went to my room to read.

Actually, I was tired. I was sharing a room with a retired Irishman and I wasn't getting much sleep. I had had the room to myself the first night, but the next day a new boatload of people had come and the Irishman was put in with me. He was an enormous man, weighed at least sixteen stone, moved slowly, as big men do, and was jovial, smoked cigars and told ribald stories. I liked him. He had been retired for four years, he told me, his two sons now managing his business, and he was on perpetual holiday, going where he fancied, doing a little oil painting to pass the time. He must have been over-tired that first night, because he went to bed straight after dinner, and he snored till five in the morning, louder than anyone I had ever heard in my life. He was like an engine. There were no pauses. At three in the morning I couldn't stand it any longer, and I sat up and shouted, 'For God's sake, stop that snoring!' But the snoring went on, and I felt a fool for shouting in the night, and the first thing I did after breakfast was go to the office and demand another room. 'I'm exhausted,' I told the manager. 'I didn't sleep three minutes all night.' The manager was a small man with a face like a nut, crinkled and burnt with sun. He nodded sympathetically. 'I know,' he said. 'You get one every now and then. The thing is, can you put up with it one more night? I haven't got a spare room in the place. There'll be one coming up tomorrow. I'll move you in there. But please, just one more night. I'm sorry. Believe me. My first wife used to snore, I know how it is.' 'Okay,' I said, and that night before going to bed I drank three large brandies and then two tots of rum, but there wasn't a sound out of the Irishman all night. Not a squeak. 'Listen,' I told the manager in the morning, 'don't move me out of that room. He didn't snore at all last night, so I think I'll stay. You know how it is on an island. I don't want to create bad feelings. He must have been over-tired, that's all. He didn't utter a peep all night.' 'Sure,' said the manager, and that night the Irishman outdid himself, not only snoring but moaning, grunting, and giving whistles. He sounded like at least three men. The next night he snored again, then for two nights he didn't, and then he came back again, worse than ever. He was unpredictable, there was no pattern to it. Some nights he snored, some he didn't, and between the snores and the anticipation I was getting little sleep.

Just after midnight, the Irishman came in. He sat down very carefully on the end of his bed, lit a cigar, and then told me three or four ribald stories. When he had finished his cigar, he went into the bathroom, came out in his pyjamas, got into bed, and began to snore. I put on my shoes and went out to the bar.

A party was in progress, with much shouting and laughter. The cooks were there, the gardeners and handymen, and all the waitresses. There were three or four holiday-makers, including the stockbroker, who was redder in the face than ever and had spilt something on his canary yellow slacks. Ned Matthews was in the middle of it, and next to him was his son. Billy had an arm around the waitress from our table, who was flushed with drink, but didn't look too happy. Everyone was drinking something purple. I bought myself a brandy. Jim the gardener pushed through to me. 'I told ya the place'd liven up,' he said. 'And we haven't started yet.' He downed his purple drink and waved the empty glass over his head. 'Tastes like paint stripper, but what the hell,' he said, giving me a wink. 'I'm not payin'. Listen, we're all moving down to the beach, in about an hour. It's all organized.' 'Not for me,' I said. 'I'm just having a couple of brandies and then I'm going to bed.' 'No crime to change your mind,' Jim said.

By half past one I'd had enough brandy to take the edge off the Irishman's snoring, but I could hear the party down at the beach. There was a lot of screaming and singing, and it seemed to go on all night. I slept two hours at most and woke up feeling hollow and haggard, not at all in the mood for Matthews and Billy and the hired man walking down the centre aisle at breakfast with their frothy ice-cold glasses of beer, but there they were, right on time, performing the ritual.

There was a lot of drinking that night too, and the next night, and the night after that, and each morning in they came, always in the same order, always with their glasses of beer.

The drink was showing on them. They were puffy about the eyes. Matthews appeared on the third day with a plaster across his forehead. The hired man had a bruised lip. But each ravagement, each wound, seemed to increase their pride. '*Bon appétit!*' Matthews roared, and down went the beer. Then he ordered the breakfasts. Four eggs a-piece, sausages, bacon, toast, black coffee. I watched the boy. How long can he last? I thought. How long can he keep it up?

Five days after Matthews had appeared, a new boatload of people arrived. I watched them getting off the boat. They were the usual crowd, middle-aged, cluttered with luggage, bright and bold in holiday clothes. Except for one. She was twenty-two or three, with dark hair to her shoulders, and looked like a princess. She stepped neatly ashore, showing lovely long legs, and then turned, and helped a grey-haired woman step down. 'Thank you, dear,' said the woman. 'Come on, mother,' said the princess, and together they walked along the jetty and under the palm trees across the lawn to reception.

The Irishman had added a fire engine to his nocturnal noises the night before, and I went off to have a sleep before lunch, on a quiet beach I had found on the other side of the island, away from everyone, just me and Captain Cook's goats.

At lunch-time, Matthews and Billy and the hired man downed their beers, lit their cigarettes, and waited for the waitress to come. 'When are we going to have some real drinking, dad?' Billy asked his father. 'I thought you told me we was gonna have some real fun.' 'I want to get the boat out this afternoon,' Matthews said. 'Then I'll show you some drinking.' 'Careful, old man,' Billy said. 'I don't want to carry you to bed like I did last night.' 'That's enough of that,' Matthews snapped. I sneaked a look across at Billy, but his face was turned away and I couldn't see his expression. But for a second the table was tense. Don't tell me Billy is outdrinking him, I thought. His own son. His own pride and joy.

He was Clark Gable again that night, in his yachting jacket and grey slacks, and from the dining-room windows you could see the *Southerly* afloat, about half a mile out. She looked beautiful. Matthews ordered a bottle of wine with his meal, and, when it was over, lit up a cigar.

After dinner, I took my usual walk along the front beach, the sea so flat and shining with moon it looked like mother-of-pearl. The palm trees stirred and rustled, and I wanted my girl. But forever? I lit a cigarette, and when it was finished went into the bar. Matthews wasn't there. It was quiet and pleasant. But the princess was there, with her mother. And Billy. Billy was talking to the girl. He looked very neat and polite. The girl was listening to what he was saying and nodding her head. She had wonderful eyes. Then Matthews came in, went over to them, and put his arm around his son's shoulders. I don't know what he said, but everyone smiled. He was a model of charm. Then he left them, went over to the bar, and came back with two of his green drinks. 'Compliments of the *Southerly*,' he said, and handed the first drink to the mother, and then the other one to the girl. And then, with a bow and a smile, he excused himself, and went down to the other end of the bar where his hired man was drinking beer. I bought myself a beer and took it to a cane chair in a corner. Billy and the girl were laughing together. He asked did she want a cigarette. Then the manager, in dark suit, came in and announced that the steeplechase game had been set up in the dining room, and would we all care to move in there? We moved in, taking our drinks. The princess went in with her mother and Billy. Matthews went in with the hired man.

The steeplechase game went like this: there were four wooden horses and they moved down a ten-yard long course, according to a throw of dice. You could own a horse for a race by successfully bidding for it, or you could just bet.

Matthews paid forty dollars for a horse in the first race. Billy moved it for him. 'It's your money if you win,' Matthews said. The winner got whatever was paid for the other horses. It was about a hundred dollars. The race was neck and neck right to the end, and then Matthews' horse flashed over the line.

'Drinks are on me,' Matthews announced. 'So long as it's champagne.'

He paid sixty dollars for a horse in the second race, which his hired man moved for him, and he almost won that one too, except right at the end it stalled and a real-estate agent in a gay madras cotton jacket ran past him to win. Matthews was charming in defeat. He presented the winner with a bottle of champagne and a cigar.

He stayed out of the third race, and only bet in the fourth, where he won, but for the fifth, the last race, he staggered us all by shooting the bidding up to a hundred and fifty dollars. The money seemed to appear in his hand out of nowhere, crisp, new notes. He handed them nonchalantly to the manager, and then poured himself a glass of champagne.

And then, more Clark Gable than ever before, he approached the princess's mother, and with a bow asked, 'Would you allow your daughter to move my horse for me in this race?'

He was incredible. It was like watching a snake, each move so deadly and calculated, impossible to take your eyes away.

'Of course,' the mother said. 'Cynthia?'

'I'd love to,' the princess said.

Matthews put his arm around Billy's shoulders, gave him a playful punch, then a wink. They stood together like that all through the race, both beaming, father and son. Billy, I saw, was looking quite flushed. With excitement? With drink?

And of course Matthews' horse won. It romped home. The princess cried with delight. Champagne flowed.

I looked at the girl and suddenly I felt immensely sad. Everyone was shouting and laughing. I wanted my girl. 'Champagne for everyone!' Matthews cried. I pushed past him and went outside.

There was a full moon. Ned Matthews' yacht rode calmly at anchor, bobbing slightly, a millionaire touch to the night. I wanted to be a million miles away.

I sat down under a tree, my back to the trunk, lit a cigarette, closed my eyes. Everything was mixed up inside my head, my girl, Ned Matthews, the princess, Billy, and over it all a great sadness. And then I must have fallen asleep, because the next thing I knew I was lying on the grass and someone was shouting.

I sat up. I looked at my watch. It was nearly three. The shouting seemed to be coming from the bar. I stood up. My head felt too heavy to hold. I stood for a while, blinking and swaying. Then I heard someone yell 'Help!' and then, quickly after, the sound of breaking glass. A lot of glass. I started to run.

The bar was in chaos. The floor was strewn with bottles, half of them broken. A window was broken too, the jagged glass glinting with moon. The hired man was sitting on a cane chair, his mouth open, a glazed look on his face. A couple of handymen were at the bar, not looking too good either. Our waitress was at a table, fast asleep. The princess was near the door. She was crying. The front of her dress was torn, and she was holding it together with both hands. Her face ran with tears. And, in the centre of the room, in the chaos of broken bottles, Ned Matthews and his son faced each other, their fists balled, their faces bleary with drink.

'You're a pig!' Billy shouted. 'A dirty pig!'

His father swung and hit him in the nose. Blood gushed out at once. Billy yelled 'Jesus!' and kicked his father as hard as he could in the ankle. His father swore, almost fell, but came back and landed two punches in his son's ribs. Billy fell down.

'Oh, you pig, you pig, you pig,' he moaned, on the floor, and then he started to cry.

They came in for breakfast right on time, in the usual order, Matthews, Billy, then the hired man, each with his glass of beer. Eight o'clock in the morning. Right on the dot.

They looked terrible. Matthews' eyes were rimmed with red. He hadn't shaved. There was a cut on his right cheek. His son looked half asleep. The bridge of his nose was puffy and his face was unnaturally white. The hired man looked grey. The silence in the dining room, as they came down the centre aisle – Matthews at one point stumbling and almost falling – was electric.

They sat down. 'Well, boys,' said Matthews, raising his glass. *'Bon appétit!'* Down went his beer. The hired man drained his quickly too, and then licked his lips, as though he could have done with another. Billy raised his glass, took one sip, and then put the glass down. 'You can finish mine,' he said to the hired man.

Ned Matthews looked astounded. 'Billy!' he snapped. 'Drink your beer!' 'Ah, I'm not in the mood,' Billy said. 'Billy!' Ned Matthews roared. Billy looked up at him, opened his mouth to speak, but then changed his mind. Something seemed to pass over his face. He looked away. His father stared at him. And then he laughed. He meant it to be, I'm sure, a good-natured, jokey laugh, but it wasn't. It wasn't like that at all.

Then the waitress came up to the table. 'Six eggs today!' Matthews snapped. 'Double sausages and bacon. And coffee. A lot of coffee. Hot and black!'

'Not for me,' said Billy, in a voice I had never heard him use before. A young boy's voice. 'Can I have,' he said, not looking up from the table in front of him, 'a cup of tea?'

It was very quiet, for what seemed to me forever, and then the waitress spoke.

'Sure,' she said. 'Sure. I'll bring it to you straight away.'

◆ *Sunday Lunch*

◆ This story is a salute, no more, no less, to that fabulous couple, Dora and Abe Besser. Absolute top people. 'Come to lunch!' Dora cries every fifth Thursday. 'One o'clock! Don't be late!' And then, in a whisper, just before she signs off, 'Tell me, how is your brother? Do you need money? Oh, the poor Bornstein boys.'

The poor Bornstein boys are my brother and me, orphaned at the respective ages of twelve and twenty-two, our lives a grey drudgery of sock washing, skimpy meals, unironed shirts, dust under the beds, the only sunshine the splendid Sunday lunches we go to each week, to this aunt, that aunt, a cousin, an old family friend, and every fifth week to the elegant home of the fabulous Bessers.

How to describe a Sunday lunch at the Bessers? What poems are required, what songs shall I sing? ('Ode to a Stringy Chicken,' says my brother. I'm ignoring him.) Shall I speak of the atmosphere? The fine conversation? The food?

Let's just go.

Punctually at one, my brother and I, hair combed, clean shirts, shoes gleaming, stand at the front door of the Besser residence. A golden suburban sun beams down.

'Ready?' I ask my brother.

He nods.

I press the bell.

Melodious chimes sound somewhere deep inside. We wait. We hear no footsteps, no sounds of any kind, but the Besser house, we know, is luxuriously carpeted, wall to wall, and this very second Dora or Abe (or both!) may be only inches away, about to swing open the door and receive their guests. I clear my throat. My brother scratches the tip of his nose. I give my smile muscles a quick flex. The front door remains closed. Another press?

No, not just yet. Give them a chance. I half turn, one hand in a trouser pocket, and survey the Bessers' front garden. It is immaculate. No fallen leaf sullies the manicured grass. No weeds bloom in the borders or beds. No, the garden is more than immaculate. It looks, actually, vacuumed, as though twice a day Dora Besser runs out with her Hoover and gives it a thorough going over. The flowers, the shrubs, the one tree in the dead centre of the lawn, are so neat they look like those painstakingly executed water-colour plates you sometimes come across in turn-of-the-century gardening books. Another press!

Once more the melodious chimes ring out, but this time, no sooner is my finger off the bell, than the door swings open.

The great Abe!

'Once is plenty,' he growls.

Before I can speak he has turned, gone, vanished, leaving my brother and me standing lamely at the front door.

Abe is angry.

I give my brother a furious glance (Why didn't you tell me not to press it again, you idiot!), and we steal inside, closing the door carefully behind us. Along the passage we go, on the deep carpet, not making a sound. Abe is angry! No one is making a sound. The house is as quiet as a doctor's waiting room. It's so quiet you could hear motes of dust falling, only there aren't any. We creep on, walking on toes.

We pass an open door. It is the Bessers' cosy dining room. In the centre stands a ten-foot long table, brilliant with polish, twelve chairs placed around it, a chandelier hanging above. Paintings adorn the walls. Cabinets crammed with crystal and silver gleam and shine. We continue on.

The next room is the lounge. Several months ago Dora Besser suddenly tired of her old lounge suite, sold it 'for a song' and made purchase of a lush settee and two armchairs, all plushly covered in fine green velvet. Fearing for the velvet, she caused to be sewn attractive floral slipcovers, but these too she feared for, and so laid upon them sheets of plastic, which proved, however, to be too cold to the touch, so now, as we pass, I perceive a scattering of newspapers laid out to relieve the chill. Adding a further touch of majesty to the room is Dora Besser's massive black grand. Upon it stand two silver candlesticks and between them a frowning photograph of Estelle, Dora's runaway daughter, married at eighteen to a Canadian, never seen again. It was she who played the piano. We tiptoe on.

The door to the next room is closed. This is the den. Abe's room. Faint sounds of television come from within. A chair creaks. We hurry past, hearts beating wildly.

Now we are at the kitchen, the heart of the house. But where are the smells of cooking, the pots on the stove, the plates on the table? Nothing. The room is bare. I look at my watch. Are we too early? No, it is eight minutes past one, good time. But is today Sunday?

'Stay here,' I say to my brother. 'I'll look outside.'

I open the back door and there is Dora Besser. She is on her knees, scrubbing the concrete with a brush. Her face is white. Her bucket clangs.

'Hello,' I say.

She starts as though shot. She leaps to her feet. She blinks. Colour jumps to her face.

'Oh, the poor Bornstein boys!' she cries. 'What's the time? I get so carried away with my work! Come, come! We'll eat. Where is your brother?'

She is wearing a shapeless grey dustcoat, I don't know what underneath. Her hair is hidden by a faded green scarf. She looks like a cleaner at a third-rate hotel. She was once a great beauty, my mother told me, and showed me a photograph of Dora aged nineteen. She looked like Ingrid Bergman. She was standing outside a restaurant wearing a fur coat and cap. There was snow on the ground. Her eyes flashed. Her smile took my breath away. She had been, my mother told me, the most sought-after girl in town, much wooed, gay, petulant, an easy laugher, intelligent, spoiled, a sun around which everyone revolved. She rode to the opera in a droshke, alighting to the sound of tinkling bells. She swept up long flights of marble stairs, her eyes flashing, her chin proud. She smoked cigarettes in a long holder. She read the latest magazines and books. The fabulous Dora!

'Hello, Mrs Besser,' says my brother.

'Oh!' cries Dora Besser. 'So thin! You're not eating enough! What are you feeding him?' she asks me, her eyes hard.

'Steaks,' I say. 'Vegetables. All sorts of –'

'It's a tragedy!' cries Dora Besser, smiting the side of her face with an open hand. 'Sit down, sit down, everything's ready. Tell me,' she asks me, in a sudden whisper, 'do you need to . . . wash your hands?'

'No,' I say.

'You don't have to be shy in my house,' Dora says.

'Really,' I say.

'And you?' she asks my brother.

'I'm all right,' he says.

'Good. Sit.'

We sit.

She runs to a cupboard. Plates clatter onto the table before us. Cutlery rings out on the cold Formica top.

'Salt?' asks Dora.

'Well . . .' I say.

'Here it is,' she says, plunging down a salt shaker in the centre of the table.

She opens another cupboard and inside I see four bowls of soup. I note, with trepidation, the absence of rising steam.

'I put them in here to cool down a little,' Dora says, sweeping the bowls to the table. 'Personally, I don't like it too hot. Start, boys, it'll get cold! Where is my husband? Abe! It's on the table!

He's having one of his moods,' she whispers to me. 'Don't be alarmed. We'll have a pleasant lunch. Abe! The Bornstein boys are here! We're eating already!'

I dip my spoon into my soup and bring it to my lips. I am not enamoured of lukewarm chicken soup, nor, I know, is my brother, but we eat nicely, smiling each time Dora looks at us.

But where is the great Abe?

'Don't worry about *him*,' Dora says, reading my thoughts. She inclines her head in the direction of the den, then twirls a finger by her right temple. Then she smiles. 'Enjoy the soup, boys,' she says.

'It's very nice,' says my brother. A fine career awaits him in the Diplomatic Service.

'It's a simple soup,' says Dora, 'but I always find it refreshing. Ah,' she says, 'you're here.'

The great Abe has come!

But what's this? He has entered without flourish, sans fanfare. Almost, in fact, slipped in. Where's the joke? Where's the greeting? Where's the friendly pat to the top of my brother's head? I hardly have time to smile politely before he's sitting. A spoon is in his hand. His gold cufflinks flash. He begins to eat.

I sneak a look at him. What an elegant dresser is the great Abe, but what would you expect from the owner of Star Modes, Children's Wear & Accessories? His shirt is silk, his trousers a pin-check tweed. I can't see his shoes. I lean forward a little, to catch a peep, but no, they're out of sight. I have a ruthless interest in the great Abe's feet. His feet are not like yours or mine.

Silence reigns. There is a certain tenseness in the air. We eat our soup. I think about Abe's feet. My interest in his feet dates from a phone call I received about three months ago. It was the fabulous Dora. Her husband was throwing away old shoes.

'The poor Bornstein boys!' she cried. 'It was my first thought!'

'Well, that's very kind of you,' I say, 'but, well . . .'

'Handmade!' she wailed. 'Like new! Black, brown, everything! He says suddenly nothing fits any more. Beautiful shoes.'

'Well . . .'

'The shoes are waiting! Bring your brother!' And bang she hung up.

Second-hand shoes? We went. Our plan was to take a pair each, whether they fitted or not, and in that way not offend Dora, and then to throw them away the second we got back home, thus not demeaning ourselves with cast-off footwear.

'Come in!' cried Dora. 'Here they are!'

There were at least a dozen pairs lying in a pile in the passage. We sat down and slipped off our shoes. My brother takes a size eight (wide) and I take a regular six, but both of us found a perfect fit, me a gleaming black calf made to measure in the Promised Land, my brother a brown suede with a pattern of little holes punched in the toe. (Lovely shoes. We have them to this day.) Dora Besser hovered over us, urging us to try them all, a soft white slip-on (too small for me), a heavy-soled red brogue (too big for my brother), a two-toned stroller that pinched us both, while the great Abe himself, for whose feet all these shoes had been expensively constructed, remained secret and aloof in his room. The den. (I could just imagine him sitting in there, his magic feet expanding and contracting, one minute a narrow five, the next a wide nine, up and down they go, a miraculous phenomenon, while he watched TV.) When we'd made our final selection, Dora made us a cup of tea (too milky), forced on us cake (stale), and then, without so much as a glimpse of the great Abe, home we went.

We eat our soup. The atmosphere is chilly. I don't dare look up. Then Dora speaks.

'Tell me,' she says, speaking loud and clear, trying for a touch of nonchalance, 'what is happening in the world of literature?'

'Well . . .' I begin.

'What, for instance,' she says, 'are you reading this minute?'

'This minute?' Will I tell her *Playboy*? 'Somerset Maugham,' I say.

'Maugham, Maugham,' says Dora Besser. 'I've read Maugham. That's *old*. I want to know what's *new*. Tell me, what should I read?'

Her eyes implore me to speak (while the tenseness continues). What is the magic book? What writer will suddenly alter the course of her life? Who has the secret, who holds the key?

I furrow my brow with thought. I rub my nose. I am on dangerous ground here. I have only to mention a name and she'll rush out and buy the complete works. The last time we came for Sunday lunch she asked me what and I told her Philip Roth. Three nights running she sat up late straining her eyes, and then came the phone call. She asked questions, she gave opinions, she delivered herself of a lecture on the state of the modern world. And then Abe came on the phone. 'Listen,' he growled, talking, I bet, out of the corner of his mouth, maybe even with a cigar in it, 'that Philip what's his name. Roth? Yeah. I'll tell you Roth. A *pisher*. He doesn't know nothin'. I knew forty years ago double what he knows now. Triple! Don't tell me Philip Roth. Listen, you all right for money? You need a little help?'

'Chekhov,' I say.

'Chekhov?' says Dora Besser. She looks astounded.

'The stories,' I say lamely.

'Of course,' says Dora, 'he *is* an attractive writer, but – Abe? Where are you going?'

Abe Besser has pushed away his soup. Before we know what's happening, he's gone. The great Abe! Fled!

I look down at my soup. The bowl is empty, but where else dare I rest my eyes? My brother the same. We hear a car starting up, then the noisy sound of it reversing at speed down the drive. Zoom zoom. Abe has gone.

Another silence falls. The awkwardness is terrific. But, when Dora speaks, her voice is curiously flat and matter-of-fact.

'You see what's happened, boys?' she says. 'My husband has left me.'

Who can reply to such a statement?

She stands up, takes away our soup bowls, clicking her tongue as she reaches across the table for her husband's ('Look, he hardly touched it.'), and then, when she has disposed of the bowls, she bends down at the oven, and takes out two plates of chicken, a drumstick on one, breast on the other, carrots and potatoes with both.

'Eat, boys,' she says, placing the plates before us.

'What about you?' I ask.

'How can I eat now?' she says. 'In such a situation? I'll smoke a cigarette. Do you mind if I smoke while you're eating?'

'Of course not!' I say quickly. My brother has his mouth open too, but I beat him to it.

'Life is a gamble,' Dora Besser says, and lights a long menthol cigarette.

I take a small piece of chicken. 'Delicious,' I say, and instantly wish I hadn't. She doesn't want to hear such things at a time like this!

'Eat, eat,' says Dora. 'Don't worry about me.'

Don't worry about her? I worry about her all the time.

Dora Besser, I want to shout, I worry about you madly!

I worry about you sitting all alone on those hard seats in those drafty halls, while string quartets torture the air. Tuesdays and Fridays are chamber works, full orchestral performances Saturdays and To Be Announced. I worry about you booking up for entire seasons, year after year. (I worry about Abe too, sitting out each concert in the car, furiously puffing a cigar. He went to one or two, but couldn't take any more. 'If you want my honest opinion,' he told me, on the subject of Brahms, 'it's a load of *dreck*.')

I worry about you, Dora, sitting up the back every Monday night at Adult Education, not knowing what questions to ask. (Abe stays home and watches TV.) We went over the syllabus together, looking for something suitable. 'Life is passing me by,' you said. I told you Domestic Science was cooking. I put you on to Archaeology and History of Jazz.

'You're not eating,' Dora says to me. I plunge back to my stringy chicken. Dora looks at her watch, then picks up the phone on the bench by the oven.

She dials a number while I attempt to insinuate my fork into a potato. Can't. It's a rock.

'Sonya?' says Dora. 'How are you? Fine, fine. Listen, my husband has run away, is he by any chance with you? I don't know. I've got the poor Bornstein boys here, eating a nice chicken, we were all having a pleasant lunch, suddenly he runs out. Yeah. The car. He's not with you? All right, you'll give me a call.'

She plonks down the phone, thinks for a minute, and then dials again.

'Mavis?' she says. 'How's things? Listen, is my husband with you? He just this minute ran away. I've got the Bornstein boys here eating chicken, suddenly he runs off. Yeah, give me a call if he should come.'

She stubs out her cigarette, lights another, consults a small address book, and then dials another number.

'Manya, is my husband with you?' she says. 'He has abandoned me. In the middle of lunch with the poor Bornstein boys, a nice chicken, he runs off without a word.'

When she has finished her call, she makes a fourth, a fifth, a sixth. My brother and I have finished our chicken. Only bones remain on our plates. We sit looking down at them. Dora dials a seventh number, drawing on her cigarette, her chin tilted up, as she waits for a reply.

'Sara,' she says, 'my husband has left me, is he with you? I'm distraught with worry. The poor Bornstein boys too. I've got them here, eating a chicken. Yeah, yeah. Give me a call, I'll be grateful.'

She dials again. By now everyone in town must know Dora Besser's husband Abe has deserted her, the poor Bornstein boys are there for lunch, the meal is chicken.

'Myrtle?' says Dora. 'The poor Bornstein boys are eating a chicken and my husband has run away. Is he with you?'

Has Star Modes bit the dust? I suddenly think, as Dora dials yet another number.

But he was in Miami last year! He came back brown as a nut, with the biggest cigar I've ever seen poking out of his mouth.

'Betty', says Dora, 'my husband has broken the marriage!'

I remember my parents taking me to see the Bessers when I was twelve. They were living somewhere else then. They're always moving. 'What do we need such a big house for?' Dora always says, just before they move. 'Two people. Simple tastes.' But the ten-foot-long table (never used) has to be housed, the massive grand, the lounge suite, the cabinets, the chandelier. From big house to big house they go. Are they bankrupt at last? I think. The fabulous Bessers?

'Tragedy has struck!' Dora announces to yet another friend.

He was about to leave for New York, that time my parents brought me to visit. I was awed. This man was about to fly to New York! And there he sat so calmly, riffling through his wallet. 'Excuse me, Mr Besser,' I said, 'but what's the first thing you'll do when you arrive?' My head swam with bubblegum and comics. 'The first thing?' said Abe Besser. 'The first thing I'll do when I get off the plane is have me a big crap.' Then he gave me a wink, and went back to his wallet. I was speechless.

Dora puts down the phone. She stubs out her cigarette. She stares down at the floor, a defeated woman. The light catches her cheekbones and for a second I see the Ingrid Bergman of old. My heart goes out to her.

Don't worry about concerts! I want to cry. Don't worry about Adult Education! Don't worry about Philip Roth!

But I don't say a word.

That dirty rat Abe!

How did such a little man (Abe is small) win the heart of the fabulous Dora? She must have been at the peak of her Ingrid Bergman days when he wooed her successfully. What did she see in him? He roared around on a motorbike, my father once told me. Big deal.

Suddenly Dora looks up.

'Boys!' she cries. 'Why didn't you tell me? Sitting here so quietly, not saying a word.' She swoops away our plates. The bones rattle into a bin. 'Apple compôte!' she cries, whisking out glass bowls from the fridge. 'Eat, boys. Pretend nothing's happening.'

Pretend nothing's happening?

A marriage broken!

A life in ruins!

'One more phone call,' says Dora.

She crosses her legs, wiggling a foot, waiting for the ringing to stop.

We hear a click. Someone says, 'Yeah?'

'Abe,' says Dora Besser. 'Come home.'

The great Abe?

Dora puts her hand over the mouthpiece and whispers to me, 'He's at the factory. He always goes to the factory. Abe,' she says into the phone. 'How long will you be? Ten minutes? Hurry. Lunch is on the table. It's getting cold.'

◆ Rappaport Lays an Egg

◆

◆ Business is brisk. All week the shop has been cluttered with people, people coming and going, inquiring, expressing interest, reaching, taking, at times so many it's been positively dangerous, valuable items in perilous sway, the magic eye front door buzzer (which upsets the canary in the room at the back) providing ceaseless musical accompaniment, an electronic French farce, buzz buzz, buzz buzz, goodbye to lamps and urns and brass beds and frolicsome garden statuary and even that hideous Victorian overmantle ten feet long at least with every available inch between and around the spotted inset mirrors knobbly with rudely-carved angels and lions and clusters of fruit, the whole business jet black with either age or grime (surely that wasn't the original finish), yes, even that's gone, sold, a little lady saw it and fell in love with it and had to have it and paid instant cash, likewise the hatstand with the three broken knobs and the alarming list, what a week it's been, seven thousand taken, maybe more, and now it's six o'clock, Friday, the week over and done, the CLOSED sign up on the door and on the road outside all Melbourne streaming home, cars, school-girls, a jangling green tram, in and out of the samovars and the art nouveau table decorations and the Staffordshire dogs in the window they rush and slip, while inside, Rappaport, sole proprietor of Rappaport Antiques, unmarried, thirty-three, stands with his friend Friedlander, who is two years older and looking for a job, Friedlander expressing amazement at the volume of trade, but on Rappaport's face, where there should be satisfaction, prosperity, glee, is indecision, gloom, possibly even (but it's a bit dark in here, Rappaport hasn't yet switched on the lights) a scowl.

A scowl?

'That lamp,' says Rappaport. 'You know that lamp I sold on Tuesday? You know the one. With the *spikes*. Sold it for two hundred and fifty and you know what? An absolutely identical one down the road, except the spikes weren't even as spikey, went this morning for – guess? *Four hundred*.'

'Gee,' says Friedlander. 'But listen, what'd you *pay* for your lamp?'

'I don't know,' Rappaport mumbles. 'Twenty, twenty-five.'

'Twenty-five and you got two fifty? A million per cent profit! What are you complaining about, for God's sake?'

'What I'm complaining about is ... *inflation*.' Rappaport hisses out the word. '*Galloping inflation*. Inflation is suddenly galloping so much it's practically insane to let anything go, at any price. Sell it tomorrow and you get double. *Triple* even.'

And Rappaport gives his moustache a mournful chew, his shoulders slumped, true misery in his eyes.

'Ah, stop grumbling, Rappie,' Friedlander says. 'Wow, you've just taken in seven thousand and – '

'Big deal,' Rappaport rumbles. 'And what about my *stock*? What about my *name?* Friedlander,' he confides, his voice down to a whisper, 'you know what this galloping inflation is doing to me? *I am no longer the biggest thief in town.*'

What a pronouncement! Friedlander has to take a step back. Is the man joking? Is this some new kind of antique-dealer humour? Friedlander doesn't know whether to laugh or cry, Rappaport standing slumped before him in his baggy Yves St

Laurent jeans, his Turnbull and Asser shirt, his Jaeger knitwear, his Bally boots, begging for sympathy. He laughs.

'Take me home, Rappie,' he says. 'Take me home to my wife and children. It's lentils for dinner again tonight, but I don't care, we'll put the children to bed and then afterwards Kerry and I will take up the lino in the kitchen and who knows, maybe we'll find some old newspapers we can read, and when we've read them we can burn them to keep warm, and then we'll draw our thin coats over our pale bodies and go to sleep.'

'Wait in the car, Friedlander,' Rappaport says, his manner suddenly icy. 'And don't slam the door! There's valuable stuff in there and I'm not in the mood for disasters.'

These drives in Rappaport's car. This year it's a Peugeot station wagon, bright green, a mighty console of heating and demisting knobs in the front, it's like flying a plane, also the latest in stereophonic push-button cassette players, the speakers set in the doors and on the floor a fine litter of Rappaport's musical tastes, Al Bowley and Noel Coward and the complete *oeuvre* of Frankie Laine, plus, to lend a little tone, a selection of Beethoven done on the moog. Friedlander eases himself in very carefully, not disturbing a thing, and a minute later in comes Rappaport, crashing and crunching and muttering oaths. Something falls over in the back. Rappaport's door won't close. A newspaper is sent to the boot, pages fluttering like a bird. Another oath. Another door slam. Friedlander sits very quietly, not saying a word. Rappaport slams the car into gear and off they go.

'That lamp,' Rappaport growls.

They have been driving together like this for more than a dozen years, the cars each year getting posher as Rappaport's fortune grows, but inside always the same, the same junk, the same newspapers and magazines, the same lightshades and vases and mirrors and prints (a fortune, a fortune!) placed so recklessly it's dangerous to sit, the same flotsam of vital addresses and messages and phone numbers and business cards, Rappaport's hurricane-struck filing system, impossible to actually put your hand on one that you want but nothing ever thrown out. And, for more than a dozen years, the same dialogue too. Anyhow, the same recurring themes.

'Real estate,' Rappaport breathes.

Friedlander doesn't say anything. If he walked, he'd be home in five minutes, but that's not the form. Over the years he's learnt, come to understand, that these drives are necessary, Rappaport the restless modern man needs to be in motion, behind the wheel, needs to have buildings floating past, tree-lined streets, bridges, traffic, the soft rumble of tyres beneath him, life in flux, before he can confide his heart's most secret woes. And Friedlander's role is to listen. Rappaport is the patient. Friedlander is Dr Freud.

'My father,' Rappaport mutters.

They turn right, then left, then right again, Rappaport doing no more than twenty miles an hour, eyes narrowed, his face hard, focused dead ahead. Friedlander, still silent, takes out his cigarettes, quietly, sneaks one to his lips, out of the corner of his eye watching Rappaport for some display of emotion. And ah, here it comes.

'Half a million!' Rappaport explodes. 'The place went for half a million and I could have got it for twenty-seven. My father.'

And looking out of his window Friedlander sees that this is where Rappaport has brought him, they are cruising past the lumpy grey building where Rappaport, as he has told Friedlander many times, could have made his pile.

' "It's not a proposition," he said,' Rappaport is rumbling. 'A proposition? The best part of town! Property's going up here a thousand a week!'

'Is that so?' says Friedlander.

Mr Rappaport is not enamoured of this son. The other, the doctor, can do no wrong, but for Rappaport his father has just one word. *'Doopeh.'*

The lumpy grey building slides slowly past, Rappaport grieving after it with his eyes. Half a million! And still going up! This is the building where Rappaport ran to his father, begged him on bended knees to help him out, swore by all that was sacred that here was the guaranteed sure-fire red-hot real-estate bargain such as comes up once in a lifetime, maybe less, and his father listened, thought, stroked his chin, and finally proclaimed, 'It's not a proposition.'

And then added, just to make things crystal clear between them, 'Doopeh.' And now it's worth a fortune.

But Friedlander doesn't feel sad. Truth to tell, all this money talk bores him slightly. This isn't the old Rappaport. He remembers how they used to rush to movies together, followed by gargantuan Chinese meals. Ah, those were the days! What's happened to that Rappaport? They haven't done a movie together for years.

'Hey, where are we going?' Friedlander asks. 'I'm supposed to be home.'

But Rappaport doesn't reply, and really Friedlander shouldn't have asked, because he knows where they're going. They're doing what Friedlander calls (but secretly) 'The Tour', that slow, mournful drive past all the properties that Rappaport at one time or another asked his father to help him with, and some of which he even put deposits on himself they were so good, and then had to sell, sustaining losses, shops, houses, building sites, every single one of which has at least quadrupled in value, but from Rappaport's father always the same word. 'Doopeh.'

And as the buildings float past Rappaport grieves and moans and chews his moustache, the car filling with misery, until Friedlander can't stand it a second longer and says, 'Rappie, I think you should have special T-shirts made up, you know, those printed ones, with your business philosophy written out on the chest.'

And he digs out a ballpoint pen, and on the back cover of a handy magazine carefully letters the legend:

BUY CHEAP
SELL CHEAPER
LIVE IN ETERNAL REGRET

'Friedlander,' says Rappaport, his voice barely audible, 'I can't tell you how nice it is to have you around,' and neither of them says another word until Rappaport pulls up, as he does so often after one of his mournful tours, in the driveway of his parents' comfortable suburban home.

Mrs Rappaport is on the telephone. She is gossiping. Smoke

from her menthol cigarette veils the room. Also steam from her cup of tea, which is by her left hand, and from which she takes small excited sips when she gets the chance. She is always on the telephone when Friedlander comes, a round, pleasant woman without a real care in the world. Friedlander gives her a polite smile as he goes past with Rappaport to the kitchen, where Mr Rappaport sits at the table, chewing bread.

'Dad,' says Rappaport.

They sit.

Mr Rappaport has always seemed to Friedlander a surly man, but this is probably not true. He's a serious man. Wide-shouldered. Feet on the ground. Bald. Also a scoffing anti-smoker so Friedlander doesn't take out his cigarettes.

'I sold that lamp,' Rappaport says. 'You know the one I told you about. The one I bought for twenty dollars. Sold it for two hundred and fifty. Business has been very good.'

Mr Rappaport doesn't say a word.

'And that hat stand,' says Rappaport, 'I sold that too. Five hundred. Cash.'

And in the quiet of the kitchen Rappaport runs through his week's dealings, explaining, adding, outlining future plans, his voice somehow a little high, a little slow, a little modest, even when the sums, to Friedlander at least, seem astronomical. Twenty minutes tick slowly past. Friedlander looks down at his hands. Mr Rappaport reaches for another piece of bread.

'Well,' says Rappaport. A silence falls. 'I'd better go,' Rappaport says. Friedlander starts to stand up. 'I'll see you, dad,' Rappaport says. Rappaport and Friedlander move towards the door. Rappaport gives his father a small wave. 'We're off,' Rappaport says. Mr Rappaport remains at the kitchen table, possibly nodding, it's hard to tell.

Back in the car, Rappaport speaks. 'Hey, my father was in a good mood today,' he says. 'He didn't call me *doopeh*.'

A week passes. Business remains brisk. Calling in on Friday around six Friedlander notes the absence of many large items, including the solid lead fountain with the three dolphins and the urchin on top which Friedlander had sworn no one in his right mind would ever buy, gone, carted away, and what's this? Where's the gloom, where's the depression, where's the talk of what galloping inflation is doing to the antique trade? Not a word. In fact, Rappaport is the opposite. He seems positively buoyant.

'My dad's helping me,' Rappaport says.

'What do you mean?' Friedlander asks.

'A shop,' Rappaport says. 'I've found this absolutely beautiful shop. My dad's going to help me buy it. I'm sick and tired of paying rent for this foul dump, and anyhow it's not big enough. I haven't got any room to move.'

'How much?' Friedlander asks.

'Auction,' Rappaport says. 'But don't worry, I know the area like the back of my hand, I know what things round there are worth, what they're fetching, it'll go for seventy, maybe seventy-five, absolute tops, and my dad's agreed to help me to eighty.'

'What do you mean, help?'

'Well,' says Rappaport, 'I'll put in five, he'll put up the rest. It's a tremendous investment for him. A beautiful shop. Just wait till you see it.'

Friedlander takes a step back and looks at his friend. The excitement, the joy. He's going to buy a shop. Look at him, Friedlander thinks. When did I last see him excited like this? Not for years. Not since we used to go to those movies together, rushing like lunatics to be first in. Or that time at the fancy dress ball, putting beer into champagne bottles and leaping onto tables with a single bound.

'Don't do it,' Friedlander says.

'What do you mean?'

'Don't go to your father,' Friedlander says. 'Look, how many times have you gone to him? And how many times has he turned you down? You know how it is. Listen, you've been in business – what? Ten years? Twelve? Have you ever been hungry, have you ever had to sleep out in the rain? So what do you want your father for, all of a sudden? Rappie, you're selling him your *individuality*, your *soul*, and all for a lousy shop. Don't do it.'

Rappaport doesn't say a word. Nor does he look at Friedlander. He drops his eyes, looks down at his Bally boots, begins to chew his moustache. A lengthy silence falls over Rappaport Antiques.

'Well, that's my opinion,' Friedlander says. 'You do what you want to do.'

Further silence. Further looking down.

'Look, I think I might walk home tonight,' Friedlander says. 'I need the exercise. See you, Rappie.'

And he tries for a smile but it doesn't somehow come off, and he goes out quickly, doesn't look back.

Hey, why the lecture, why did I explode like that? Friedlander asks himself, walking slowly home, and he goes over it all again, this way and that, and when he gets home he starts to tell Kerry about it all and halfway through he is suddenly struck by a completely different thought.

'Hey, I've made a big mistake,' he says. 'I got it all wrong. He's not selling his *soul*, for God's sake. Look, all these years Rappie's been after just one thing. His father's respect. That's what he wants, that's what's important to him. Not the shop, what's a shop? What he wants is for his father to say, "You're not a *doopeh*, you're a bright boy, and just to show you how much I think of you, here's seventy thousand." And I told him not to do it. I lectured him. I carried on like an idiot.'

'Phone him up,' Kerry says. 'Phone him up and tell him what you've just told me.'

'Ah, I can't,' Friedlander says. 'Not now.'

'Well, if you don't, I think you're a rat.'

'I know,' Friedlander says. 'Do you think I feel good? I just can't though, that's all. Hey, the auction! I'll go to the auction! Rappaport and his father, side by side! I must find out exactly when it is. That's one auction I wouldn't miss for the world.'

The auction. Father and son. Mr Rappaport stands stiff and straight in a dove-coloured raincoat, Rappaport has chosen a jacket featuring a muted check, both of them very serious, silent, Friedlander a few steps behind not daring to approach.

It's three o'clock on a Thursday afternoon and not a bad crowd here. Seventy people? Eighty? But how many are serious bidders, how many have just come for a look?

It used to be a butcher shop, these premises that Rappaport desires, you can still see some sawdust around on the floor. Also the old tiled walls, bleak and white, here and there one dropped off making a crossword puzzle pattern. Ssh, the auctioneer is holding up his hand.

The terms of sale are lengthy and then there follows a description of the premises, of the locality, of the business potential, of all Australia, it seems to Friedlander, who is nervous beyond words, and why? He's not a bidder. He looks across at Rappaport and his father and sees that both of them are white-faced, doubly serious, ramrod stiff, and he can't help feeling – what's this? – a certain pride.

Good luck, Friedlander whispers to himself.

A silence. A vacuum. God, it's horrible, Friedlander can't breathe, and then bang, it's away.

The bidding starts at forty thousand, in seconds is at eighty, then a leapfrog up to a hundred, a hundred and ten. There's a pause here, but not for long, up to a hundred and thirty it goes, and a minute later it's all over. Sold for a hundred and forty-eight thousand dollars, neither Rappaport nor his father having got a bid in, the pair of them as white-faced and ramrod stiff as before, but Friedlander can see that they're thunderstruck, crushed. He doesn't know whether he should go over to them or not. He does. He is ignored.

'Sorry, dad,' Rappaport is saying. 'I forgot to calculate for galloping inflation.'

Mr Rappaport at first says nothing. His face is blank. Serious. Bald. He looks slowly at Friedlander and then at his son. Friedlander steels himself for the word and finally out it comes.

'*Doopeh*,' says Mr Rappaport and walks slowly away.

Friedlander stands with Rappaport. What is there to say?

'Come on, Friedy,' says Rappaport. 'I'll drive you home.'

◆ A Fool in Winter

◆

◆ Will he die? I thought. Will he actually die? Will the spirit of gentle Vincent slip from his frozen body this icy night and fly up – invisible vapour – to the clear killing English winter sky? Wind howled. I sat in my warm house by the roaring fire and saw him there, gentle Vincent, in his large house, his twelve paraffin heaters going out, one by one. I saw the bathroom going first, icicles forming in seconds on the window, the long white bath as cold as death. Then the kitchen, the bedroom, the dining room with its cold wooden table and chairs. Do something, Vincent! I saw the cold advancing stealthily along the hall, the heaters there flickering, fluttering, going – a last thin plume of black smoke – gone. Now there was only the front room, where Vincent sat. Vincent! The killing cold leaned against the thin door. *Vincent!* He sat. I saw his cold white hands. I saw his gentle face. I saw his eyes.

He sat.

'Where are the car keys?' I asked my wife. 'I'm going down.'

'I am happy,' said Vincent, dappled sun falling through leaves onto his gentle face. He sipped his beer. Then he began to manufacture a cigarette with the fivepenny cigarette-rolling machine he had bought that morning, his lap strewn with papers and tins. Long grass hid his bare feet. An aeroplane zoomed low overhead, hidden by trees. A truck roared down the road, on the other side of the garden wall. Vincent didn't seem to notice these things. Nothing disturbed him. He creaked in his canvas chair, absorbed, at peace.

Summer in London comes to me each time as a miracle. I can hardly believe that it's happening, that it's here. Green sprouts from every crack, a haze of leaves hangs over the world. London is lush with leaves. Not just in the parks, but in the railway cuttings, on building sites, on rubbish dumps, all the ugly places. The grey walls disappear, the battered buildings soften; and our garden, where we sat, is magically changed from a damp, bleak space overlooked by windows on all sides, to a leafy, private place. I looked at Vincent, busy with his machine. He seemed delighted with it. He seemed delighted with everything.

At last he got his cigarette rolled, lit, burning nicely. He blew out a long plume of smoke. He sat back and looked up at the trees. Then he looked at me.

'I've just decided,' he said. 'First thing I do when I get back to New York is get rid of my apartment. Sell all my stuff. Who needs all that junk? Then I catch me a plane back here. I'm going to live in London.'

'What'll you do here?' I asked him.

'Don't worry,' he said. 'I'll find me an opening.'

'For ever?'

'Why not? Where in New York can you sit in a garden like this?' He turned in his chair to look around at the trees, his gentle eyes shining with a child's wonder. 'Man, it's so beautiful,' he said.

I drove him the next morning to the airport, Vincent in his faded jeans walking barefoot to the reception counter, his fivepenny cigarette machine bulging in the pocket of his battered blue shirt. His luggage was one small canvas bag. He didn't have a jacket or coat. His flight was called, we shook hands, and I went back to the car.

Another bum, I thought.

I had met him, briefly, in Tangier, where I was doing something for a magazine. At a café. A small, gentle-faced American, about twenty-five, with a copy of something by Kant on the table in front of him. 'How is it?' I asked him, pointing to the book. 'Well,' he said, 'I'm not really sure. I haven't opened it yet. I just like to carry a book around, you know. Makes me feel I'm doing something.' 'Been here long?' I asked. 'Eight months,' he said. 'Man, it's so beautiful. No hassle, no rush. If you want to sit, you sit. No one gives a damn.' He had also sat, he told me, in Spain, Portugal and Greece, but Morocco, in his opinion, was the best. The Arabs were great sitters, too. It was their way of life. 'You must be rich,' I said. 'Naah,' he said. 'Who needs all that? When I get down to nothing, I shoot back to New York and slave for a while. But not a minute more than I have to, believe you me. Man, that is some place. New York is the capital of hassling. You been there? I was *born* there. Who needs all that rushing? What's the point?'

I gave him my address in London, after we'd talked for a while, and told him to look me up if he ever got there – you know the way you do. Then I forgot all about him. Six months later, he phoned me up.

'Hey, I'm in London, man,' he said. 'Between planes. Okay if I come around?'

He stayed eight days. I showed him around a bit, we went to some movies, but mostly he just sat. In the garden. He didn't so much as glance at a newspaper, he didn't watch TV. He just liked to sit. His book this time was something by Spengler, he had it with him even while he ate, but he didn't open it. I was busy a lot of the time, so was my wife, but he didn't mind being alone. I liked his gentleness, I liked that look of childlike wonder in his eyes, his enthusiasm for the simplest things. He was so quiet, so gentle and peaceful, that when he left it was as though he had never been.

Summer in England. If there's a villain in this story, then that's what it is. The greenness, the long evenings, the soft air. Vincent fell in love with summer in England – as who doesn't? But he was different.

He went. And then the first leaves started to fall, the evenings grew shorter, the sun wasn't quite the same. We quit our London flat and rented a place in the country, a rambling house on the top of a hill. There wasn't another house in sight. I started to write a book. We had been there two months when it began to snow. The whole country went softly white. The view from every window was the same. Two days later, the phone rang. It was Vincent. He was in London.

'Hey, where are ya, man?' he said. 'I went round to your place, no one there. A guy upstairs gave me this number.'

'I'm in the country, Vincent,' I told him.

'Yeah?'

He sounded surprised, disappointed, and something else. Alarmed? There was a pause. Static crackled on the line.

'Why don't you come up for a few days?' I asked him.

'Yeah,' he said. 'I'll do that. How do I get there? Man, it's cold. You got a lot of heat up there? Hey, I'm literally freezing to death.'

I gave him directions, and then told my wife Vincent was back.

'He's coming up here,' I told her. 'Just for a few days.'

'Who's Vincent?' she asked.

'You remember. The sitter.'

'Oh, him,' she said.

Vincent arrived the next afternoon. I picked him up at the station. He had a little more luggage this time – four suitcases and a small trunk. 'Everything I possess in the world, man,' he said. Not quite everything. He had also brought a girl. A slender, gentle blonde with big eyes and long lashes.

'Sylvia,' he said, introducing us. We shook hands. Sylvia's long lashes went down shyly over her eyes like a pair of curtains. I helped Vincent put his bags into the car and then I started up the hill to our house.

Vincent sat very quietly, not saying a word, his eyes glued to the fields of snow stretching left and right. He seemed to me to look – what? Frightened?

My wife was upstairs with the baby when he arrived. Vincent strode into the house, slapping his hands to his upper arms like an Arctic explorer, stamping his feet.

'When's the heat come on?' he asked. 'This is really cold.'

'I usually do a fire round five,' I told him.

'Five?' he said, his eyes wide as he stared at the snow outside, the garden covered, the trees like black sticks.

'I'll make some coffee,' I said. 'Warm you up.'

My wife came down. We sat around the kitchen table, Vincent with both hands around his coffee mug, his head down low, as though trying to catch the steam. He was dressed in the same jeans and battered blue shirt, with a navy pea jacket over, the collar turned up. He looked very small.

'You've really come to England for ever?' I asked him.

'That's right,' he said. 'Got rid of my apartment. Had a big sell-out of all my junk. You should have seen it. I posted a few signs around the neighbourhood, that's all there was to it. Got about a hundred people. Descended like vultures. Make me an offer, I told them. If you can't buy it, take it. I don't want any hassling. I was cleaned out in less than two hours.'

'You were beautiful, Vincent,' Sylvia said, a look of adoration in her big long-lashed eyes. But, when I looked at her, she looked quickly down.

'Goodbye, New York,' Vincent said.

'For ever?' I asked.

'For ever.'

'Vincent always does what he says he'll do,' Sylvia said, reaching across for Vincent's hand. 'That's why I like him.' She smiled proudly at me, then at my wife, and then her long lashes came down.

'I'll start a fire in a minute,' I told Vincent, who was rubbing his hands. 'You look a bit cold.'

'Man, I'm freezing,' Vincent said.

'How long are they staying?' my wife asked me, later, with Vincent and his girl in front of the fire in the sitting room, and we were in the kitchen, alone.

'I told him a couple of days,' I said.

My wife looked at me. 'Why's he come?' she said.

'God knows,' I said. 'He must be crazy. I'll give him a couple of days, and then I'll sort him out. I can't work with him here.'

'Ssh,' my wife said. 'They'll hear.'

Why had he come? He had two thousand one hundred and ninety-six crisp green American dollars in a zip-up canvas belt around his waist, everything he owned in the world was in our house, and he had come to England, he told me, because it was so peaceful. It wasn't peaceful like Tangier, but maybe he'd had enough of that. The trouble with Tangier, he told me, was that you couldn't get to a decent movie.

'Man,' he said, 'in England you've got it all. Movies, the theatre, decent bookshops. There are some great restaurants too, you know that? But without that New York hassle. England is, like, civilized.'

'What'll you do?' I asked him. 'Take a flat in London?'

'Well,' he said, 'I've been thinking. Maybe we'll stay in the country. It's so peaceful out here. Maybe I'll buy me a cheap car and just tootle in every now and then, you know.'

His eyes sparkled with that child's enthusiasm. He looked very happy.

'What'll you do when your money runs out?'

'Oh, I'll keep an eye open,' Vincent said. 'Some kind of freelance job, maybe. Something I can do at home.'

Here? I thought. Is he reckoning on staying here? Our house was big, there were two spare bedrooms, two bathrooms, but I hadn't invited him, I didn't want him here. I could feel my book grinding to a stop, while Vincent sat.

Six days, seven, eight. He made no move. And his girl was the same. Vincent sat with a book by Hegel unopened beside him, and Sylvia sat with him, sometimes looking softly at him, sometimes just there.

Throw him out? I thought. Will I throw him out? He doesn't know a single person in England. What'll he do? It had started snowing again. The road down to the village was almost gone. And Vincent, gentle Vincent, was cold.

He was always cold. I made a fire for him every morning, and he sat by it all day and half the night, and still he was cold. He looked cold. He looked small and shivery. He was used, he told me, to New York heating. His girl was cold too, but she didn't say a word. She sat with Vincent, her feet tucked under her, both of them staring into the flames of our fire.

On the twelfth day, I heard her singing 'Bless This House' in an achingly clear soprano voice as she moved about in the bathroom upstairs, directly over where I was sitting, trying to write, and I went straight into the sitting room and told Vincent he had to go.

'Now?' he said.

He looked astounded, horrified, baffled, guilty – and very small, smaller than ever.

'Tomorrow morning,' I told him. 'I'll drive you to the station.'

He looked away, into the fire, then down at his feet.

'Is there a hotel anywhere round here?' he said at last.

'There's one in the village,' I told him. 'Do you want to go there?'

'Yes,' he said. 'I think so.'

He sat with his girl by the fire all night – we could hear them whispering, long after midnight – and in the morning I helped him with his bags and then drove them down the hill to the village.

It had stopped snowing. There was no wind. It was like travelling underwater, floating through glass, the only sound the swish of the tyres on the snow-packed road. We didn't speak. Vincent sat huddled in his pea jacket, the collar turned up. He seemed to take up no room at all on the seat next to me. Sylvia sat in the back, her eyes down, her long bashful lashes lying on her cheeks.

I helped them with their bags at the hotel, shook hands (Vincent's were like ice), told them to phone me if they wanted anything, and then drove home to our rambling house on the hill with its four bedrooms, two bathrooms, dining room and sitting room and study and kitchen, its garage and outbuildings, its acre of garden, its marvellous views.

'How are they?' my wife asked.

'They're all right,' I said. 'I left them at the hotel. Look, Vincent's got plenty of money. He'll sort himself out. If I hadn't thrown him out, he'd never have gone. For God's sake, I'm trying to write a book.'

'Well, you don't have to shout at me,' my wife said. 'I didn't ask him here.'

I stormed into my room and closed the door. Damn fool, I

thought. What the hell has he come to England for? Okay, he had a nice time the last time he was here. He sat in the garden. He admired the trees. So what? The man must be a complete idiot.

I had a lot of work to do, I had done very little during Vincent's stay, but for two days I couldn't get started. Nothing made any sense. There was something wrong.

On the third day, Vincent phoned.

'Hey, I've rented a house,' he said. 'Just on the other side of the village. Come on over, I've got it nice.'

There were dancing blue flames everywhere you looked. The house was a furnace.

'Paraffin!' Vincent cried. 'I've discovered paraffin!'

He was barefoot, wearing just his jeans and that battered blue shirt. His hair was tousled, his face was flushed with heat.

'Get that coat off,' he said. 'I'll show you round.'

It was a large house, with not much garden, but fine views of fields from the windows on one side and at the back. We went upstairs, Vincent throwing open door after door, and from each one coming a fresh blast of heat.

'Twelve heaters, man!' he cried. 'You like it? Come on, let's go back downstairs. I'll make some coffee.'

I had never seen him so animated. He was like a child with a new toy, a child at a fair, giddy and excited. His eyes bounced with pleasure, as he ran from heater to heater, checking the gauges, fiddling with the wicks.

We went downstairs. Vincent threw open the door to the front room. It was not a very large room, and he had two heaters in it. The heat was fantastic.

'Hello,' I said to Vincent's girl.

She gave me a broad smile.

'Vincent's made it nice,' she said.

Vincent ran out to make coffee. Sylvia was barefoot too. She was wearing a thin summer dress with a pattern of flowers. She looked very lovely and very serene, her long lashes coming down the second Vincent went out of the room. I was wearing a heavy jumper – it was snowing outside – and I could feel sweat starting to trickle down my back. I sat down. Sylvia didn't look at me or say anything. Then Vincent came back with a steaming pot of coffee on a tray, biscuits and cake. The heat throbbed in my face as I drank.

'Paraffin!' Vincent cried. 'Nothing like it! I get six gallons delivered every two days, right to the door. Each heater takes about half a gallon and burns for twenty hours, but you've gotta keep checking 'em because sometimes they burn more, like if you've got the wick up too high or something like that. I'm just getting the hang of it. I fill them all up first thing in the morning, and then I give them a quick check round ten, and then another one straight after lunch. Then I don't do a thing till round four, except maybe for little things. And then, before we go to bed, I fill them all up again to the top, check the wicks, and that's it. Pretty nice, isn't it?'

Two thousand one hundred and ninety-six crisp green American dollars, I thought. Minus twelve heaters. Minus six gallons of paraffin every two days. Minus food. Minus rent.

Vincent gathered up the coffee cups and took them into the kitchen. I could hear him washing them up.

'What's Vincent doing?' I asked his girl.

'Well,' she said. 'He's thinking.'

'Oh?'

'Vincent is a big thinker,' she said. 'He thinks a lot.'

She smiled at me, she looked suddenly very proud, and then she looked away.

'Is he going to take a job?' I asked.

'Well,' she said, 'I'm not sure.' She spoke slowly, the lashes descending often. 'Vincent is a very relaxed type of person. He hates to hassle. I like that. I think that's a good thing. I admire that a lot. Everyone should try to be like that.' Up, down, up, down went the lashes. 'You wanna sit nearer the heater?' she said. 'You want a little more warmth?'

'I'm okay,' I told her.

'We like it warm,' she said.

'How are they?' my wife asked, when I came back.

'Oh, they're fine,' I said. 'Absolutely fine. Vincent's even got himself a job.'

'He has?' my wife said. 'What as?'

'He's a wick trimmer,' I said, and went into my room.

They invited us to dinner. The house was as hot as the first time, the dancing blue flames just the same in every room. It was tropical. We ate in the dining room, seated around the long wooden table, three heaters pulsating. In between courses, Vincent tinkered with them like a Swiss jeweller building a watch. His fingers fluttered around the dials, making microscopic adjustments to the flames. I thought of him with his fivepenny cigarette machine that time in our London garden.

'Are you doing anything yet?' I asked him.

'How can I do anything?' he said. 'I've got my hands full with these heaters.'

He laughed, a happy child, and swooping up a big book on Toynbee he ran out to the kitchen to see if Sylvia needed a hand.

'Can't you talk to him?' my wife whispered.

'How?' I said. 'What will I say?'

And we invited them to dinner, Vincent and Sylvia insisting on walking up the hill. They arrived frozen, half dead. We ate in the sitting room, before the fire. I brought in an electric heater, too.

'You still like England?' I asked Vincent.

'It's beautiful,' he said, but in his eyes there seemed to me to be a hint of something else.

It was a hard winter. The days started in darkness and, before you knew it, it was night again. The sky was always grey. When you went outside, the wind was like a knife. It rained. The water froze. The road up to the house was so bad even the milk truck didn't come. We put bread out for the birds each morning, but some mornings it was too cold even for them. The bread lay untouched on the snow.

We didn't see or hear from Vincent for two weeks. I worked. It went well, but it didn't go as well as it should have. I spent a lot of time staring out of the window at the snow. One afternoon I saw a truck going past on the road. That meant the road down to the village was clear. I put on a coat.

It was a quieter Vincent who opened the door. He was still in his battered blue shirt and jeans, but, when I looked down, I saw he was wearing shoes.

'Come in here,' he said, opening the door to the front room. 'It's warmer in here.'

Sylvia had just washed her hair. She was sitting in front of a heater wearing a scarlet silk kimono. She had a heavy old-fashioned shawl over her shoulders.

'Hello,' she said, but she barely smiled.

'I'll make coffee in a minute,' Vincent said, sitting down.

He was down to five heaters, three downstairs, two up. When he wanted a bath, he moved a heater in. Same in the kitchen. There were no heaters in the hall.

'We're running out of money,' Vincent said.

I nodded. I wanted to shout, 'Get a job!' I wanted to grab him by the shoulders, shake him, wake him up, but I couldn't. He seemed, sitting opposite me, his hands hovering over the heater, quite defenceless, so frail that I thought if I touched him he'd fall.

'What'll you do?' I finally asked.

'I'm thinking,' Vincent said.

The next time I went they were down to two heaters, not using them at night. Vincent and his girl sat very still, hardly moving. Vincent's face was very white.

'I dreamt about Mexico last night,' Sylvia said. She reached over to take Vincent's hand. Vincent didn't move.

'Would you like me to make some coffee?' I asked.

He's going to die, I thought. Both of them. They'll find them here, just like this. Sitting. I stood up.

'We're out of coffee,' Vincent said.

I'd like to sit on a beach,' Sylvia said. 'I'd like to feel sand between my toes.'

I drove home.

'They're broke,' I told my wife. 'They haven't even got any coffee. They're just sitting there, slowly freezing to death.'

'What'll we do?' my wife asked.

'Nothing,' I said. 'I'm not going to do anything. Why should I? He doesn't like to hassle, why should I? God! Have you ever seen such a fool?'

I did nothing. For two days. Except stare out of the window. Except wait for the phone to ring.

'Phone them,' I told my wife. 'Ask them up for dinner. We'll have a proper talk.'

She phoned. The phone rang and rang and rang. They're dead, I thought.

'Relax,' my wife said. 'They've probably just gone out for a walk.'

We tried an hour later, and then an hour after that. Nothing. It was almost six o'clock, the sky quite black.

'Where are the car keys?' I asked my wife. 'I'm going down.'

I drove down the hill like a fool. I sped through the village. Vincent's face loomed in front of me, pale and frightened, his gentle eyes looking straight into mine. 'Stupid idiot!' I shouted. I turned into his street. His house was the last one in the street. I swerved into his drive and ran for the front door.

There were no lights showing. The bell sounded cold inside the house, ringing to frozen rooms. I went round the side and looked in the windows. Cupboards were open, drawers were pulled out. I ran round to the front again. Through the front door keyhole I saw Vincent's twelve fine paraffin heaters lined up in the hall, like a row of soldiers on parade, the little window in the front of each one black and blank. They had gone.

Vincent is in Mexico. His girl sent us a card. 'It's so beautiful here,' she wrote. 'Vincent says he'll write you one of these days, but he probably won't. He's not lazy, I don't want you to think that, but he just doesn't like to hassle. You know.'

And here it's summer. The miracle has happened again, and the world is leafy and green. I sit in the garden and marvel at the trees. Apples are ripening. Birds sing. The baby crawls about on the lawn.

◆ Skylight in Lausanne

◆

◆ Two on the dot (Sunday in Lausanne) Percival slides out of his shiny white Renault 4 with three clear untrammelled daylight hours in which to complete the work vital for first thing Monday morning, the finishing touches to a textbook on higher mathematics he has been fastidiously laying out for four months, sixty-four pages of close-set type studded with diagrams of bewildering complexity, rhomboids and parabolas and zigzag graphs, each diagram not only insanely tiny but aswarm with captions like bees around a hive, and, what's more, all in French, to Percival a foreign tongue. And all done in his poky two-room flat, wife and infant child forever underfoot, until this morning, the deadline so close that off on the train went his wife to her mother's, taking noisy Simon, won't be back till five (eight clear hours!), but just before they went there was a phone call, an equally fastidious fellow graphiste (a biology text) with the same deadline for Monday a.m. desperate for cross-hatching help. Eight hours minus five leaves only three, which is cutting it fine, but, well, a friend's a friend, and there's not all that much left to do. Okay, to work. Percival strides to the front door, one hand slipping into the right-hand pocket of his elegant new plum-coloured velvet jacket and – oops.

No key.

It's in the right-hand pocket of his other plum-coloured velvet jacket, upstairs, in the flat. Two jackets. He knew it was wrong to have two jackets. All his adult life (except for the past two weeks) he'd had just one – the one upstairs, the original – and been perfectly happy. That jacket. Bought it when he was eighteen, eighteen years ago, in far-off Australia, land of his birth. Got his first job wearing it. Then fired, similarly clad. Wore it to Europe. Travelled with it in Russia, North Africa, Yugoslavia, Denmark, Spain. Slept in it, ate in it, was hungry in it, hardly a moment out of it, happy or sad. His jacket. Wore it whilst courting the girl who is now his wife, and two and a half years of married life later she'd suddenly looked at it and said, 'It's worn out.' 'I like it this way,' he said. He showed by his expression that he didn't want to discuss the condition of his jacket, and one morning three weeks later woke up to be surprised by an identical jacket made by his wife's own hand. Absolutely identical. The cloth, the lining, the cut. Even the buttons. An immaculate forgery. She must have done it in the small hours, measuring from the original and not making a sound. 'Very nice,' he said, but he wasn't so sure, and look, now it's betrayed him, for the first time in his life he's got two jackets and he's locked out of his flat.

Well, let's not panic, he says. Percival lives in what was once a house and is now three small flats upstairs and the owner on the ground floor (Percival doesn't like the owner and the owner doesn't like him), but the girl in the flat to the right has got a skylight through which he'll be able to get to his bedroom window which is probably open, or, if not, certainly the kitchen window on the other side of the roof, and so he gives her bell a push. Buzz buzz.

Nothing.

Wait a minute, this is not necessarily a disaster, he tells himself. In the flat to the left lives the pastor who's got an attic which is sure to have a skylight through which he'll be able to get up on the roof, not the best part of the roof but possible to scramble from there to another part, and then to the bedroom window, or, if it's closed, the kitchen. Buzz buzz.

Also not in.

Relax, says Percival, they're no doubt simply out to lunch. The thing to do is to drive down to the railway station and treat himself to the London *Observer* (which is devilishly expensive and doesn't even come in these parts with the colour magazine like the *Sunday Times* does but that costs even more), but the *Observer* always cheers him up, and by the time he's given it a preliminary flick through and drives back they'll be there, one of them at least, and he'll get up through one or another of the skylights and onto the roof and into his flat and be hard at work on that mathematics text in no time at all.

The *Observer* today is inexplicably delayed.

Percival thinks, calculates, counts his money, thinks some more. Okay, damn the expense, this is an emergency. Let's have the *Sunday Times*.

Similarly delayed.

Buzz buzz.

The girl hasn't returned.

Buzz buzz.

The pastor's still gone.

Twenty minutes already down the drain and what'll I do?

On account of he doesn't like the owner and the owner doesn't like him, Percival a year ago quietly changed his lock, so he can't now go to the owner with his woes. His wife has a spare, but that's an hour and a half there and an hour and a half back, where's the gain?

Another buzz, another look in at the railway station, back again to the flat. This is madness.

He drives down to the lake. If you have to sit and brood, may as well do it somewhere nice. He looks at the mountains. He looks at the water. All very grand, I suppose, but what a vacuumed view. Not a person to be seen. Not even a dog. Percival has been fired eleven times for his slow-motion fastidiousness in a rushy world, but look at Switzerland. No litter, no graffiti, not even a poster with a corner torn off. All so circumspect and decent and even the stirring mountains tamed to fit. Is he happy here? He rubs his red eyes. Don't ask. He married a Swiss girl and now it's nearly forty minutes irretrievably gone.

Buzz buzz. The station. The lake. Percival is locked in a mathematical triangle as rigid as anything in his book. He taps his pocket for his pipe but of course it's in his other jacket. Bloody hell.

Suddenly the light seems to change (he's back at the lake), to become brighter, harder, ominously clear, and looking along the lake Percival sees at the far end that the sky has turned black. A wild woolly storm is plunging his way. Circumspect Switzerland will be ravaged in ten minutes at the most.

Percival's heart lifts up. He's excited. His nostrils flare with primitive joy. There's nothing he likes better than to drive hard and fast through sheeting rain, through crashing thunder, through battering winds, he'll drive to his wife's mother's and pick up the key and – but this is foolishness. This is no time for storms. He has to get to work. His excitement dies. He takes one last look then turns his back on the coming storm and drives once more to the flat. The pastor's still not there, the girl hasn't come back, and three minutes later rain crashes down onto the roof of his car, striking it like hammers, a Wagnerian din.

He sits.

No one's going to come rushing back in this rain, the pastor (who is meek) will wait under an awning, the girl (who is fat) will order another cake, and God it's cold in this car. Percival can hardly see out of the windscreen the rain is so heavy, and just like that his bowels give a twinge and he has to go.

No problem. The toilet is part of the building but entered from the outside, round the back. The owner has his own but the flats have just this. Percival runs through the rain, closes the door, and sits quickly down.

Ah.

And then he looks up and sees that this room has a skylight too. A pale page of sky, high over his head, awash with rain. But impossibly high, fifteen feet up at least, probably closer to twenty, and what's there to hang on to, what's there to grab with your fingers or toes? A radiator on one wall gets you up three feet, then there's the faucet tap over the old-fashioned seat, another six inches, but after that there's nothing. Featureless walls. Can't be done.

Percival stands up.

On the other hand, look. The room's practically a chimney, narrow all the way up, you can just about touch the opposite walls with your elbows, and perhaps, who knows, get your back against one wall, your feet on the wall opposite, and somehow, well, walk up.

And die, thinks Percival, listening to the rain.

He stands up on the old-fashioned seat. The skylight above looks no nearer. And is it big enough to get through when he – if he – gets up? He sees himself crashing down, feet first into the bowl, the terrible impact, up to his waist in –

Fifty-seven minutes gone, noisy Simon approaching fast. He places a foot on the radiator, gets the feel of it under his thin-soled shoe.

Percival is thirty-six years old, but looks older, looks, in fact, in his velvet jacket and his slim Prince of Wales check trousers (which are six years old) and his stiff-collared fine-striped shirt (three years old) and his neat muted paisley tie (eight) and his wispy beard and his balding pate, like an Edwardian cricketer, a bowler or batsman when the game was more leisurely, a gentleman's pastime, tallish, thin, measured in his movements, sport on the green. He puts his other foot onto the faucet tap over the bowl.

For a mathematics text?

Now there's a jump required, an initial push off (Or shouldn't I check first if the girl's come back? Percival asks himself. The pastor?), and when he does it, quickly, his foot spins the faucet tap, which must have been loose, into action. Water gushes splendidly down into the bowl. A veritable Niagara. What a noise.

Jesus, thinks Percival. Well, no time for that now. Fix it later. I'm off.

And he is. But carefully, slowly, his back, feet and hands discovering that these walls have a texture, slight irregularities even, but God it's murder. An inch at a time. Don't look down. And all the while that water crashing into the lavatory bowl.

Six feet up it suddenly occurs to Percival what an idiot he must look, and he blushes, and then frowns, feeling his new velvet jacket scraping against the wall. It's insanity. What'll my wife say if I get it torn?

Up, up.

This is no time to glance at his watch to see how he's doing but he does manage a slight peep up which shows him that the skylight is getting closer, and it also shows him that it's smaller than he thought, surely not wide enough to get his shoulders through. Don't think about it. We'll see. Whoops. A smooth patch. Percival freezes, locked in mid-air, his body a tight spring crying out to be unwound, pressed between the walls.

Slowly the water below becomes fainter and that up above more distinct, he can hear individual drips and splashes and runs underneath the steady pounding, and suddenly his head goes bang. The skylight. He's there. Except he's facing the wrong way to get it open, and it's thick with cobwebs and dust. What if it's locked from the outside? He ventures a push. Nothing happens. He has to readjust his feet. Another push. Impossible, the thing must have rusted solid, it's like an – aah, away it flies from his push in a cloud of dust and ribbons of cobwebs, and cold air and rain smash into his upturned face, unlocking from his nose a monstrous sneeze which, by rights, should send him plummeting to his death, but what saves him is one thin long-fingered Edwardian cricketer's hand which shoots out, pure reflex, and seizes the skylight's sill.

Now it's a scramble (but trying not to hurry), head and one shoulder out in the rain and the skylight just not wide enough to get the other shoulder through, his feet, of course, hanging straight down, there has to be a way to do this, take a breath, think, which he does, and by dropping his inside shoulder and swinging his body over to one side he gains an inch, a little more, and pop he's out. Half out, that is, up to his waist, legs still dangling, but the worst over and done.

Christ, thinks Percival. My clothes.

The slates are slippery and slick and he has to proceed in a crouch, the sky above ragged now, the rain easing slightly, down to a steady drizzle. He gets to his bedroom window but even without trying it he can see that it's closed. He tries it anyhow. Don't worry. The kitchen. The kitchen window is always open. More roof. This jacket is sodden. And look at these trousers. It's uphill now, to the ridge of the roof, but the second he gets his head over all is well. Ah, he says, smiling in the rain. Four beautiful inches of open space beckon from the bottom of the kitchen window, the end of the rainbow, money in the bank. Don't hurry, he tells himself. Almost there.

He hurts his shoulder reaching in to get to the catch, has to move cups and saucers and a vase of flowers out of the way, bangs his knee badly climbing over, jumps.

In!

Percival stands, in his flat at last, surrounded by Swiss silence.

Right, says Percival. Now I have to go and turn off that tap downstairs. But I'm not going to make the obvious mistake. The first thing to do is to get the key from my other jacket and put it in my pocket. Which he does. Right. He debates should he take off this sodden jacket and put on his old one. No, not now. This will only take a minute. Key safely in his trouser pocket, he goes quickly downstairs, out of the front door, to the toilet, the sound of rushing water clearly audible from six feet away. He reaches for the door. Which is, well, think about it, locked from the inside.

Once more across the slates, down through the skylight, but where before it was almost impossible, now it's true madness, his body completely fills the space, he has to go down blind. With the added complication of closing the skylight after him when he's in. How he does it he's not sure himself, but he does, hanging by his hands, feet and back trying to make purchase, get that firm brace. He's in. Skylight closed. Going down. Which is infinitely harder than going up, and slower, and how his bones ache. His shoulder, his banged knee. Down he inches, down to that endless Niagara smashing into the bowl, louder and louder.

Nine feet from the bottom his bladder starts to scream, which must be nervous tension, also the gushing sound, and he makes it just in time. Then he turns off the tap, firmly, and, first checking that he still has his key, opens the toilet door, goes quickly to the front door, up the stairs, opens the door to his flat, where the first thing he sees is noisy Simon, and then his wife, both in tears.

'You were supposed to meet us at the station,' his wife says, 'but I'm not crying about that. Or about a whole day spent with my mother telling me I was insane ever to marry you but it's still not too late to change my life. "He hasn't got any money and he'll never have any money and look how he dresses. Leave him, darling, leave him," she said. All day. I know my mother and I'm not crying about that. But when I got to the front door there was Frau Karr and her fat timid husband screaming at me that my husband was running on the roof and wasting water in the lavatory and slamming windows and locking doors and in exactly seven days we are out in the street.'

'They can't evict me,' says Percival. 'I'll get the police.'

'Don't touch me,' says his wife. 'Simon is hungry and tired and wet and cold and I have to feed him and bathe him and put him to bed and then make something for us. I can't talk now. And what have you done to your new jacket?'

The mathematics text.

It's eleven o'clock (still Sunday in Lausanne) and Percival sits alone at his table, his wife and child asleep in the other room, rhomboids and parabolas and zigzag graphs laid out before him, cold and meaningless under the harsh artificial light. His shoulder hurts, his knee. He rubs his red eyes. He has been sitting here for an hour and he hasn't yet made a mark.

They can't, he says. I'll get the police.

Midnight comes and goes and he has still done nothing, the Monday deadline as close as his hand. Come on, he says. There's not that much to do. Some cross-hatching, some arrows, some inking in. Come on. He selects a pen and dips it into his ink jar and essays some trial strokes on a piece of paper, getting the feel of the nib, but his mind isn't inking, it's carrying boxes of books down the stairs, this lamp, the baby's bed. To where? He sees in his mind a howling waste, an emptiness, Europe after all these years still a foreign place. Why did I come here? I don't know, but I know one thing. I'm not going to die in Switzerland. I didn't come here for that.

I'll smash all the windows, he thinks. I'll break the doors.

Two o'clock in the morning and he's still done nothing, he's still carrying boxes down the stairs. Frau Karr, he thinks. If she says a word, a single word, I'll throw her down the stairs. And then her fat little husband. And then we'll get in the car and drive away.

To where?

He stands in the doorway of the other room (it's three o'clock now, still nothing done), looking down at his sleeping wife. I'm sorry, he says. I'm a failure. Your mother is right. I'm thirty-six years old, I've been fired eleven times, and what have I got to show, what have I ever done? I really am very sorry and I wish I knew what to do, but I don't. I'm sorry.

And then he looks down at his sleeping son, at Simon's tiny hand peeping from under his coverlet, one or two fingers entwined in his golden curls, at his soft mouth, at his perfect ear, and he is swamped with sadness, and then with outrage, Simon hounded and homeless in the howling waste, bloody Switzerland, that damned Frau Karr. He closes his eyes. He takes a deep breath. He subsides. And then suddenly he smiles.

You should have seen me, he says, the way I climbed up that wall. Absolutely impossible. And I did it. Your father's a mountaineer.

He looks down, smiling and happy, at his sleeping son, and he knows now what he'll do. First I'll take all our things out of this flat and load up the car, but everything correct and in order. Nothing broken. No noise. Pay the rent. Shake hands, if I have to. Then I'll go into that toilet and lock the door and then turn on that tap and climb up through the skylight and go across the roof and in through the kitchen window and then I'll walk down the stairs and we'll drive quietly away. Goodbye Switzerland, who wants to live here?

Now let me tell you what will happen, he says to his sleeping son. When the girl goes to use the toilet she'll hear the water and think it's the pastor, and when the pastor hears it he'll think it's the girl, and their Swiss gentility will keep them from knocking on the door. They'll use the railway station. They'll do it for days and days.

Finally they'll realise there's no one in there, they're bound to meet outside the locked door, and they won't know what to do. They won't break down the door because they're Swiss, and the Swiss respect property above all else. And they won't be able to get down that skylight because it's impossible. Can't be done. Not by them. Not by anyone, he says proudly. Just me. Your dad. Your father is the only one who can do it. The only one in the whole world.

Bending down, he bestows upon his son's brow a gentle, delicate kiss, and then he goes quickly back to his table, picks up his pen, and starts to ink in. You might think that now, swollen with triumph and love, Percival will whip through his work in ten minutes flat, but not so. He'll be here till morning with this meaningless text, applying more detail than is strictly necessary but this is how it has to be done. This is Percival. Meticulous. A mountaineer of molehills. Fastidious to the very end.

◆ **Bannister**

◆

◆ It began easily enough. *We think Bannister is staying at the Royal Hotel in Copenhagen. Check it. If he's there, let us know. That's all. Don't talk to him. Just let us know. That's all we want you to do.*

So he flew to Copenhagen. A delightful place in summer. Ivy on the walls. Boats tooting down the canals. Pigeons in the sky. Green spires. Long, long days, and at midnight the sky still chalky with light.

He was twenty-nine years old, losing his hair, but not looking any the worse for it. His face was too youthful for such things to matter. It had an openness, his eyes a brightness. He was the sort of person you strike up a conversation with at a bar. Harry Garlick. Married eight months and four days to a girl with jet black hair. She saw him off at London Airport, wearing a shiny red raincoat. Eve. 'I'll be back end of the week,' he said. 'Write every day,' she said. 'Twice a day,' he said, and boarded the plane.

But Bannister wasn't at the Royal Hotel in Copenhagen. Garlick showed the photograph he had been given, thinking perhaps Bannister was there under a different name, but no, no one had seen him. 'Must have the wrong hotel,' Garlick told the desk clerk. 'Wild goose chase, eh? Well, not my worry, I'm not paying.' He laughed, and put back the photograph inside the wallet, sneaking a look, as he did so, at Eve's smiling face under perspex on the inside flap. He couldn't resist showing her to the desk clerk. 'What do you think?' he said. 'Beautiful?' Then he wired to London for further instructions, and while waiting for a reply wrote to his wife, sitting outside at a café with a bottle of Tuborg and smoking a cigarette, and in a small yellow pad he wrote down his expenses, to the penny. *One Tuborg. Three kroner fifty.*

One day away and already he pined for Eve. He saw echoes of her, hints and shadows, in the girls walking past in the street, that one had Eve's ankles, that one her way of walking, that one her shoulders, almost, almost, but none of them was Eve, and to escape from his growing frustration he took out the photograph of Bannister and stared at it, and for the tenth time he read through the two typed sheets of paper that listed all that was known about Bannister, or all that London wanted him to know.

A reply came from London the next day. *Bannister is in Berlin. We're not exactly sure where. Check these three hotels. Wire when you find him. Fly.*

The hostess on the aeroplane reminded Garlick of his wife, and he felt his stomach tightening with a desire for Eve. He ordered a whisky, not looking at the hostess when she brought it to him, and drank it down in one gulp, and when he felt better he took out his yellow pad and made note of his purchase. *One whisky. Two marks.*

Then he lowered the tray on the back of the seat in front of him and wrote a letter to his wife, seven pages long, telling her how much he missed her, what he had seen in Copenhagen – girls everywhere, and not one as pretty as you – and how was London, what was she doing? He wrote until his wrist ached, writing passionately and with great detail, and then he folded up the letter and stared out of the porthole at bank after bank of rolling white clouds and the sky bright blue above them, but all he could see was Eve walking beside him through Hampstead

Heath, her hands in the pockets of her Cossack-style coat, kicking leaves as she walked, laughing with her eyes, but out of the corner of his eye he saw the hostess's legs and this pained him so strongly for Eve that once more he took out his two-page dossier on Bannister and the photograph from his wallet, and first he stared at Bannister's face and then he read through the information and then he went back to the eyes in the photograph and stared at them until the photograph blurred in his hand.

Bannister wasn't at any of the three hotels in Berlin. Garlick showed the photograph to desk clerks, lift attendants, doormen, headwaiters, wine waiters, people in foyers, to the managers of the hotels, telling them what he knew about Bannister from the two-page dossier in his pocket, trying to make the man come alive for them, but no, no one had seen such a man. Garlick wired back to London. *Bannister not here. Detailed expenses following.* Then he wrote to his wife.

Stay there, London wired back. *Further instructions end of the week. Keep in touch with all three hotels. You're doing fine.*

Stay here? Garlick felt his heart sink. He wanted to get back to London, back to Eve. He saw Eve walking naked through the tall-ceilinged front room of their flat, her hair done up with a paisley scarf, a paint tin swinging in her hand. She was painting the flat white. She liked to work naked, and the scarf was to protect her hair. Peter, Paul and Mary played on the stereo as she slapped at the walls. Then he thought of the money he would get when this job was over.

He checked into a small hotel just off the Kurfurstendamm. A small green room with an adjoining bathroom. A bed, a chair, a wardrobe, a chest of drawers. A neon sign flickered against his window all night long. He wrote a long letter to Eve on the first night, another on the second, and on the morning of the third he sent her a card. *Wish you were here. No. Wish I was there.* He walked around Berlin, staring at the sights, slipping into bars for fast beers. He tried to go to movies, but they were all dubbed into German. He tried the three hotels, again and again. No Bannister. He continued to make careful note of all his purchases and expenses, newspapers, meals, cigarettes, cabs, writing neatly in his yellow pad in tight columns. *Overcoat drycleaned. Box of matches.*

But still no Bannister.

Then the word came to go to Paris. The Hotel Ritz. *Hurry.*

Garlick caught a night flight out of Berlin. Tempelhof was grey with rain and he had to run across the tarmac, the jets screaming in his ears, a sudden gust of wind flapping his coat as he ran. He fell into his seat, puffing for breath. 'Out of condition,' he said to the man in the adjoining seat, smiling widely, but the man, a German, looked pointedly away, not amused. Garlick fastened his seat belt, grunting. 'Getting fat,' he said. 'All that beer and sauerkraut.' The German looked straight ahead.

When the NICHT RAUCHEN BITTE sign went off, Garlick undid his seat belt and lit a cigarette. The German kindled a cigar. Garlick screwed up his nose. He got a sudden picture of Eve's fluttering fingers. How long they were, how fine. She seemed to bob down in front of him, on her knees in front of his seat, like a child, to light his cigarette with a long wooden match. 'I want lots of children, Harry,' she seemed to be saying. 'Lots and lots.' 'Can you wait about a year?' Harry asked her, ruffling her hair. 'Of course I can,' she laughed.

The hostess asked him did he want a cup of coffee, but he declined, and settled back in his seat, eyes closed. He began to doze. Who is this Bannister? he wondered. What's he doing running all over Europe? Bannister, Bannister. I don't even know his first name.

He took the airline bus from the airport to the terminus, and from there a cab to the Hotel Ritz. He noted the fare in his yellow pad. He asked the desk clerk was there a Mr Bannister staying in the hotel. His eyes felt grainy from lack of sleep. He showed the photograph. The desk clerk studied it. 'Ah!' he said. 'You have just missed him. He left yesterday.' 'He was here?' asked Garlick. 'But of course,' said the desk clerk. 'M. Bannister always stays with us.' 'Do you know where he went?' Garlick asked. 'Just a minute, sir,' said the desk clerk, and turned to look in the pigeon-holes behind him. Then he turned back to Garlick, a card in his hand. 'Ah!' he said. 'Here we are. Madrid. Hotel Carlos V.' 'Can I see that?' Garlick asked. The desk clerk handed him the card. It was typed. No signature. 'I want to send a wire to London,' Garlick said.

He was in Paris four days waiting for a reply. He moved into a room on the Boulevard St Michel. He felt exhausted. 'Too much bloody flying,' he said to himself. He began a letter to Eve but halfway tore it up and crumpled the paper into a ball. His fingers felt cramped. It was uncomfortable trying to write sitting on the bed with his writing pad on his knees, smoke from his cigarette getting into his eyes. He went out into the street and sat down at a café and ordered a double whisky and then another one after that, and when he got back to his room he didn't even have the energy to take off his shoes but fell fully clothed onto his bed and was asleep a half minute later.

He woke up in the middle of an argument. Eve was crying. 'Why can't I have a baby?' she was saying. 'Not now!' he shouted. 'Not now!'

He flew to Madrid. Bannister was not there. He was told to go to Lisbon. He took a train.

The sheets on Bannister had become edged with grime from handling, the paper weak along the folds. Garlick handled them carefully as he read them through yet again. *Bannister tugs the hair over his right ear when he is thinking or nervous.* The train rattled along, flying over bridges, casting a long shadow. *He is flat-footed. Portly. He suffers slightly from asthma. Eyes: the palest blue.* Out of the window, farmhouses and trees. *Almost without colour. Round-shouldered. A wide, vacant smile. No scars. No known birthmarks. Age: around fifty. Not certain. Could be younger. Swiss bank account. Where not known. Friendly manner.* The train dived into a tunnel.

In Lisbon, Garlick was told to go back to Paris.

On the plane from Lisbon, Garlick had a violent scene with his wife. He wasn't sure how it started. He saw her stubby fingers angrily butting a cigarette. He saw deep lines from her nostrils passing the corners of her mouth.

Once more at the Hotel Ritz. Not there. The card this time said Amsterdam.

This seemed to Garlick the final straw. Furious, he asked the desk clerk for a form to send a cable. He lit a cigarette and took out his ballpoint. *You can stuff the job. Go to hell with your Bannister.* But his mind filled with an image of the flat in London and he was seized with an intense claustrophobia and he had to close his eyes to fight it off. After a long minute, he opened them again. He took a long pull on his cigarette. He ran his hand over his face. It felt flabby under his fingers. Then he wrote *Bannister is in Amsterdam. Shall I follow? Waiting on your wire. Garlick.*

He smiled at the hostess on the aeroplane to Amsterdam. She was tall and blonde and her feet were elegantly long. He gave her a wide smile. She smiled back. 'Double whisky,' he ordered. 'And not too much ice.' 'Leave it to me, sir,' she said. Her cheeks dimpled. He watched her as she walked down the aisle. Neat. Full of poise and confidence. Did she know the passenger in seat 53 who had just ordered a double whisky was in her bed, kissing her white breasts?

He sipped his whisky, at the same time taking out the sheet of airline writing paper provided. *Flying to Amsterdam,* he wrote. *Whisky. Two francs. Cigarettes. Book of matches.*

Bannister's face, when he took it out of his wallet, seemed to be smiling at him. He smiled back. Then he put it back inside his wallet, next to that of Eve, but not looking at his wife's face as he did so.

He went from Amsterdam to Brussels, and from Brussels to Stockholm, and then down to Nice. In Nice he hired a car and drove down the coast as far as Barcelona, and then back again, showing his photograph along the way at eleven hotels, always without luck.

Driving back to Nice, Garlick discovered that he had begun talking to himself. He smiled. He didn't mind. 'Where are you, Bannister?' he said. 'What are you doing? Where is your home? Haven't got a home, have you, Bannister? No home for Bannister. No home, no home.' The words drifted into a song. Garlick felt quite happy driving along the coast, tooting his horn at every bend. He drove all day and into the night. He felt comfortable behind the wheel of his car, a Citroën DS. It was only when he had to get out, to eat, to buy petrol, that he was aware how fat he was getting. Just to walk across to a toilet made him short of breath. But he didn't really mind. He was happy.

The first time he made love to a girl – a German girl in a room in Monte Carlo – he felt a stab of something like regret, but not regret exactly. It was something he couldn't put his finger on. He got up in the middle of the night, grunting, and padded on bare feet to the bathroom, and there he stared at his face in the mirror above the hand basin, looking for some outward sign of what he felt inside, but there was nothing. Same face. Slightly blurred. He blinked. Getting fatter. He smiled. His face moved into lines, like a map. Then it became a blur again. Nothing. He went back to the bed. The girl stirred. Garlick bent down and kissed her shoulder. She put her arms around him. 'Liebchen,' she murmured. He saw her puckered nipples coming awake. He breathed deeply the perfume of her hair.

There was an American girl in Venice and a Swedish girl in Rome. The Swedish girl was delighted with Harry's double chin. 'You are so sweet, so chubby and soft,' she said. 'Out of condition,' said Garlick, smiling widely.

He sat at a café on the Via Veneto. The trees of Rome were turning yellow now. The first sharp edge of winter was in the air. Garlick sat with a campari, watching the parade of people moving both ways along the street before him, listening to the spirited bursts of conversation in this language he couldn't understand, the racket of Fiats and Vespas, and high up in the sky the drone of an aeroplane, that monotonous, ominous burr.

The scene vaguely amused him. He ordered another campari and lit another cigarette.

He showed his photograph in the Hilton, in a listless way, leaning against the counter, not expecting any response from the desk clerk, not in the least put out when there was none. 'Getting cold,' he said to the desk clerk. 'Time to head down to Greece. Sit in the sun. That's the life.'

He took a plane to Athens. It was still hot there. He sat in Constitution Square, sipping ouzo, eating olives. People were walking past his table, but he didn't really see them. A sponge seller approached him. 'Not for me,' Garlick laughed. 'What do I need a sponge for? Travel light, that's my motto.' He laughed.

'Here, buy yourself a drink,' he said to the sponge seller, handing him a pile of drachmas. 'Have a ball. Life is so short.'

He stayed three months in Greece, moving from island to island, up and down gangplanks, making for the nearest café, glad to sit down. In Mykonos a wind was blowing, the canvas awnings over the cafés fluttering wildly. Rhodes was noisy with scooters and tourists. Crete was dusty with heat.

He had a large white room in Hydra, overlooking the harbour, with a jingling metal bed. He stripped to his underwear and lay down, a cigarette between his lips. He had arrived an hour before and he was exhausted. His feet hurt. He lay on his back, breathing noisily through his mouth. He stared up at the white ceiling. Then across at the white walls. Then there impinged upon this white vision his crumpled coat, lying on the floor, where it had fallen, and he sat slowly up and put his feet down on the cold tiled floor and reached over for it. He emptied out the pockets. Money. A handkerchief. Tickets. His wallet. A wad of grimy paper. He threw the paper into a corner, wadding it first into a ball, and then he sorted out his wallet.

Money. Cards from thirty hotels. A photograph of a girl. He smiled at it. 'Must have slept with her sometime,' he said. 'Goodbye, my dear, whoever you are.' He brought the photograph up to his lips, kissed it, then tore it neatly in half. 'You were beautiful, Miss No Name,' he said, and as he sank back onto the bed the two halves of the photograph fluttered to the floor.

From Athens he flew to Rome, but didn't stay there. He sat in the airport lounge and waited for his connecting flight. He leafed through a magazine, smiling at himself as he turned the pages.

On board the plane to Zurich he lit a cigar. The hostess brought him a double whisky. He smiled at her. 'Have you been to Zurich before?' she asked him. She was short, with freckles in a band across her nose. 'Me?' said Garlick, smiling. 'Never. About the one place I've missed. How is it in Zurich?' 'Oh, it's like everywhere,' said the hostess.

From the airport, he took a cab to Bahnhofstrasse. 'Rahn and Bodner, that's what I want,' he told the cab driver. 'It's a bank. Ha ha. Quite a few banks in this town, aren't there?' 'Rahn and Bodner,' said the cab driver. 'Yes. I know it.'

The doorman at the bank bowed as Garlick passed him. He smiled. Garlick smiled back. He went to a table and sat down. He took out his ballpoint pen. He tugged the hair above his right ear. Then he wrote on the form a sum of money, then the number of an account, and its code. He signed the form Alexander Bannister in a hand not his own. He stood up, grunting, and walked over to a teller's window.

For a second, moving on his flat feet across to the window, he had the strangest feeling, as though if he stopped for a minute and thought, paused, considered, he would be lost. But he didn't allow this to happen. He pushed his form in to the teller. 'Ah, Mr Bannister,' said the teller, not looking at the form. 'Nice to have you here again.' Then he looked down at the form. 'And how would you like it, Mr Bannister?' he asked. And the man he was facing said, 'In dollars.'

♦ A Red Fox, a Polish Lady, a Russian Samovar

♦

♦ Rain against the window and on the cobbles below wakes Moses Bornstein in his strange bed. He is at once completely awake. He starts to sit up, then freezes, somehow embarrassed, guilty, alert for sounds from the rooms all around. Nothing. Rain. He steals out a hand and looks at his watch. By the light of the moon (which a moment later he discovers is a street light shining through the nylon drapes) he sees it is just after two. Rain bounces and runs. A summer shower, clearing the air. He lies and listens, his feelings a jumble, but not unhappy. Hey, he announces. I'm in Prague!

A teddy bear, a doll, a model aeroplane on a string. The room is chalky with light, enough to read by, or so it seems. Moses sits up, carefully. There are his clothes, arranged neatly on a chair. Next to it is his canvas zip-up bag. And over the chair his coat, with, in one pocket, the little blue book with the name and address of the people whose apartment he is in, the Lanskas, total strangers really, friends of friends; and all the other names and addresses, vague connections, not one name with a face to go with it, a string of names to make a string of rooms across Europe, a string of beds to sleep in, all the way to London. And there? Moses suddenly wants a cigarette. He slips his feet out of the bed.

Still not a sound. He tiptoes to his coat. The Lanskas. A tall, thin man with a tall, thin wife, both so earnest and serious. He puts a cigarette between his lips. Ashtray? He remembers there is one on the desk by the window. Parting the curtains he looks down at the glistening cobbles, the bouncing rain. Shutters, grey walls. I'm in Prague! Then he takes the ashtray and slips back into the bed. The scrape and flare of his match seem to him enormous, but no sounds follow, nothing but the rain. Whispering out smoke he is pricked again by that feeling that has troubled him in all the rooms he has slept in these past weeks – an awkwardness, a falseness. He feels an intruder. He blushes, and quickly draws in breath. The Lanskas. He does not know these people, they don't know him. He is eating their food, sleeping in their apartment . . . But the rain cheers him, its rush and run, and he announces again: I'm in Prague! But this time it's to his brother Ben, twelve thousand miles away, in Melbourne, and tapping his ash carefully but otherwise not moving he continues the letter he has been writing to his brother almost non-stop from the moment he sailed, filling Ben in on everything that has happened, everything he is doing and is seeing, his secret thoughts, his plans.

Moses is twenty-five, ten years older than Ben. For a year they lived together, when their parents died, a curious relationship, not quite two bachelors, not quite father and son, until Moses said he had to go to Europe. 'I'm going mad here,' he said. 'It's just impossible to do anything.' 'Such as?' Ben asked. 'I don't know. I just have to go.' 'How long you be gone?' Moses' uncle asked. 'Three months?' This was the uncle Moses was leaving Ben with. 'Well,' said Moses, 'I'm not sure. About six, I think.' Not looking at his uncle directly, because he knew it could be for ever. Certainly not six months.

Mrs Lanska is a translator, Moses tells Ben. She told me she likes Raymond Chandler. See? I told you to read him. She also likes Dostoyevsky, but I don't think you're ready for him. We're going into the country tomorrow to pick up her children, a boy and a girl. They've been out there on holiday for a week.

Actually, Moses adds, but not in the letter, this very minute I'm in the boy's bed.

Prague's not bad, he continues. I had a walk around this morning. Wenceslas Square. Then the old town, which is pretty interesting. Kafka's old haunts. Another chap I don't think you're ready for yet, but if you get the urge, feel free. He's in my books somewhere. Which I hope you're looking after, by the way. Don't lend them to anyone! If I come back and find you've been lending them to people, you're in trouble. Okay? I'll be here another day or two and then I think I'll head up to Berlin. I'm not sure. Or maybe down to Italy, give Rome a buzz. Hey, guess what I found in Athens? That old Coleman Hawkins record I've been looking for all these years. Haven't got anything to play it on, of course, but it's great to have it. Twelve thousand miles to buy an old Coleman Hawkins record in Athens! Well, like I always told you, travel broadens the mind.

A soft green afternoon, seventy miles from Prague. Woods and fields, and in the distance some hills. The Lanskas have a cottage here, a log cabin that once belonged to a famous general. Mrs Lanska explains to Moses that it was his headquarters during some campaign (she tells Moses exactly when and what, and Moses nods earnestly, though he does not quite follow or understand), the log cabin now added to all around with new rooms, but still intact, a cabin within a cabin, its rough outside walls now inside, strange to see. 'It's very nice,' says Moses politely.

There are people everywhere, and Moses is introduced to them all. Mrs Lanska speaks English, of course, but no one else does, and all Moses can do is smile as he shakes hands with a Russian illustrator and his wife, with Mrs Lanska's father, with the illustrator's mother, with a small Polish woman, with neighbours and friends who have cabins nearby and who have dropped in for the afternoon. Someone asks Moses what he does for a living, what his profession is. 'I used to be in advertising,' he explains through Mrs Lanska. 'I was a copy-writer.' This is not understood. There is a silence. 'Well, I'm just travelling at the moment,' Moses says. 'Ah!' someone cries. 'Tourist!' 'Yes,' Moses says, though it is not exactly what he wants to say. 'What I'm really doing,' he adds, but can't find the words to continue. Another silence. Then the Russian illustrator comes forward. He is very interested in Moses' jacket, pinching and fingering the cloth. Moses blushes, baffled by the etiquette of the situation – should he take the jacket off for the Russian to try on? The Russian is a burly man, his shoulders are wider than those of Moses, his back is barrel-broad, 'Ah!' cries the Russian suddenly, thick eyebrows shooting up. Something has occurred to him. He taps Moses on the chest with a stubby finger, runs off, and is back a moment later with a framed woodcut of yachts and gulls, which he displays proudly, tapping his own chest. 'Well –' says Moses, and is saved by the arrival of Mrs Lanska's children, the boy smiling and holding by its tail a wriggling water snake.

The boy is a long-legged nine or ten, with short hair poking up at the back, and his father's thin earnest face. His name is Milos. His sister is smaller, younger, with ribbons in her hair, two floppy yellow bows. Her name is Anna, and she comes up to Moses, completely unshy, takes him firmly by the hand and leads him off – Moses not at all sure what's happening – into the cabin. She wants to show him where they sleep. She and her brother have bunk beds. Hers is on top. Moses tries with signs and mime to explain that that's the best one to have. The boy stands by with his wriggling snake. The girl says something to Moses in Czech. Moses shakes his head. She says it again. 'I'm sorry,' Moses says. 'I don't understand.' The girl stares at him, a frown beginning to crease her brow. This is getting awkward. What to do? Moses thinks hard and suddenly turns and waves a stern finger at the snake. The boy laughs. Moses mimes a lightning bite to the throat, a slow, agonising death. Now the girl is laughing too. Then she takes his hand again and leads him outside, her brother and snake following. Behind the cabin, under a bush, there is a rabbit in a cage. 'Beautiful,' Moses says to the girl. 'Bella. He's very nice.' Then Milos says something to his sister who jumps up and the pair of them run away, leaving Moses alone. He lights a cigarette. He smiles at the Polish lady, who is sitting by herself on a hard wooden chair. She seems to smile back – something flicks across her face – then looks down at her lap. Moses strolls on a few steps, the sun warm on his back. He sees the Russian illustrator, strolling as he is strolling, a cigar between his lips, enjoying the afternoon. He salutes Moses with a grin. A door slams. Some other children run past with a dog.

No one seems to be doing anything. The illustrator's wife is sitting in a corner, under a tree, her head bowed, as though asleep. Mrs Lanska's father is reading a newspaper, or anyway holding it – his eyes are to the distant hills. Moses strolls quietly on, he can hear the hum of bees, and suddenly it comes to him that this is a scene from Chekhov, from those stories and plays he read to please his father, that same tranquillity, that same wonderful boring peace. 'Read Chekhov!' he hears his father shouting in his ear. He smiles. So he went out and bought Chekhov. Which his father snatched from his hands. 'What's this *dreck*?' he said. 'It's Chekhov,' Moses said. 'Chekhov?' said his father, flicking rudely through the pages. 'But it's in English. In English it's not Chekhov. You have to read it in the original. In *Russian*. In Russian it's poetry. In English it's *dreck*.' He threw the book down, stamped away. Moses brings his cigarette to his lips. And did you read Chekhov? he asks his father. In Russian or English? He smiles, seeing his father staring at the television at home, sullen if you spoke to him, those never-ending cowboys thundering across the screen, the room all gunshots and hoofs. And then he starts to remember other things about his father, and frowns, and then blinks, to clear his mind of such things.

Where is Mrs Lanska? Moses turns a corner of the garden, and there she is, with her husband. They are setting up a long trestle table. Moses strolls over. 'Can I help?' he asks. 'We will eat soon,' Mrs Lanska says, shaking out a large white table-cloth, briskly and earnestly spreading it over the table, crisply and quickly smoothing the folds. Then the illustrator's mother appears, a short fat woman with high cheekbones and small eyes, puffing and grunting and carrying by its handles a large samovar.

'For the tea,' says Mrs Lanska. 'She brought it with her. She says it's the only way to make tea. Do you know such things? It will take time. It has to be made hot. You will go for a walk.'

A samovar. His mother came from Poland with a samovar. It stood in the garage, never used, but once a fortnight his mother would bring it out, set it up on the kitchen table, and with rags and powder make it gleam. And then carry it, shining like silver, back to its place in the garage gloom. 'What are you polishing it for?' Moses would ask. 'I mean, you don't even use it for anything. It's ridiculous.' 'Leave me,' his mother would say. 'How can you know about such things?' She rarely spoke about Poland, except once or twice to say how beautiful it was in the snow, to walk in it, to see the sun shining on it, sparkling like diamonds, and how poor they were but how it did not matter. 'We were *alive*,' she would say, but when Moses wanted to know more she would shake her head, a distant look in her dark, always sad eyes. 'What would you understand? It was a different life.'

The samovar is placed on a tray in the centre of the table. 'Oh, ah,' grunts the illustrator's mother, and leaning over fits a long flue, a chimney, to the samovar's top. Then she sits down, with more sighs and moans, and from a leather bag on her lap draws out twigs and sticks, matches and paper, and slowly, carefully, snapping her twigs, crumpling her paper, prepares the samovar. She blows, she coaxes, she frets. This is a serious business. This is her domain. Ah, it's alight. And up comes the smoke, curling out of the flue. Moses stands and watches, entranced. He has never seen a samovar in use before. His mother's did not have a flue.

'Go now,' says Mrs Lanska. 'Your walk is ready.'

Moses walks with Mrs Lanska's father, a dignified old man with thick white hair. The illustrator and Mr Lanska walk behind, followed by two neighbours, then the children – the men and children sent away while the women prepare the tea. They set off along a path beside a field, making, Moses sees, for a wood. The path begins to climb. Mrs Lanska's father asks Moses something in French. Moses shakes his head. '*Deutsch*?' asks the old man. '*Etwas*,' Moses says. 'Ah,' says the old man, and then says nothing, content just to walk.

They are almost at the wood when Moses turns to look back at the view and sees, loping across a field below him, a fox. 'Look!' he cries. It is a red fox, or anyway orange in the afternoon sun, and it is making for a clump of trees, but in no hurry, running easily, cutting gracefully through the long green grass. '*Voilà!*' cries the old man. The children have seen it too, and they all stand and watch the fox's progress, until it slips under a fence and seems to melt into the shadows of the trees. Moses laughs. This is perfect! This is Chekhov! Impossible to imagine a more beautiful thing! Then the old man stoops and picks a wild flower from the side of the path, fits it into his buttonhole, and then they go on, through the wood and around, past another field, back to the women waiting in the garden.

And look. Sun streaks through the smoke from the samovar, making cathedral shafts down on to the table, which is spread with food. 'Sit, please,' says Mrs Lanska. There is heavy black bread, cut thick, pale butter, plates of sausage and sardines. Honey, fruit, saucers of preserves. The illustrator's mother hands him a cup of tea. It is very hot. 'Thank you,' Moses says. He is given bread, butter, sausage. From the trees come the chirp of birds. Dear Ben, writes Moses to his brother, I am having tea in a garden in the country, seventy miles from Prague. The sun is shining. I can't describe it. It is straight out of Chekhov. Including even a samovar which a stout old Russian woman is turning the spigot of this very minute, pouring out a cup of tea. Hot tea, practically boiling. And there is smoke drifting up from the samovar, out of a chimney thing on top, catching the sun. No, I can't describe it. Read Chekhov. 'Please,' says Mrs Lanska, and Moses looks up to see he is being offered the preserves.

And then he becomes aware of the conversation all around the table, the illustrator is laughing, Mr Lanska is shaking his head, one of the children is asking for something, Mrs Lanska and the illustrator's wife are both saying something, and immediately Moses gets that prickly feeling, that feeling of falseness, of intrusion. He looks quickly down at his plate, busies himself with his tea, feels in his pockets for his cigarettes. When he looks up again he sees that he is sitting opposite the Polish lady, who just then raises her head, and Moses looks directly into his mother's deep, always sad eyes.

'Oh, Moses, Moses,' she says. 'What are you doing with your life? What will become of you? It's time. Decide. Decide.'

♦ Her Life: A Fragment

♦

♦ Fiction is art, and art is metaphor, that resonant bell to the hearts of our lives, a game, yes, call it that, certainly there are a game's rules and pleasures, skills and prizes, that magic of making, of manipulation, of neatness and rightness, the heady presumption of morality proclaimed, whether stated or denied, yes, a game, an attractive and seductive series of moves. But it is more than that, much more, for if fiction is a game it is our most necessary game, and even more. It is our central concern, no less. But fiction is a game not always possible to be played. For sometimes . . .

Listen.

A hand taps on the glass.

This is on Broadway, at Seventy-First Street, where I am sitting alone, eating cheesecake and drinking coffee. Not very good cheesecake. American coffee. I have just come from seeing Rainer Werner Fassbinder's *The Marriage of Maria Braun*, also alone. Also not very good: a fudged metaphor that tolled no bells. And now it is six o'clock, the day darkening outside, and

suddenly sprung to new liveliness, a sudden liveliness of lights
and noise and traffic and people hurrying past. A hand taps on
the glass and I look up, and there is Betty Rosenfield, smiling at
me from the street. I smile back, and beckon her inside.

Would you like coffee? Cheesecake? Anything?

Betty is a friend I have not seen for a year, not since my last
visit to this city. Not a close friend. A friend of a friend. An
acquaintance. A Jewish lady of, I suppose, around forty, and I like
her. I like her plump size, her eager small eyes, her wide mouth
always smiling, her hands and shoulders and springy curly hair in
endless movement. Her Jewishness.

No, she doesn't want anything.

She's on her way to a Movement Class.

She's only got a minute.

She sits.

She smiles.

So? What have you been doing?

I tell her, and she listens, and I watch her eating my words, the
way New Yorkers do, insatiable for stories of other lives, and
when I finish – it doesn't take me long – I observe the protocol,
the required etiquette, I ask about her life, but at first, when she
begins, I don't listen, don't listen closely, that is, because New
Yorkers fill you up with their lives as water fills a jug, full and
overflowing and still no end, and the burden of such immodesty
is sometimes more than can be borne – it is hard to sleep
afterwards, in this city where sleep is essential – and anyhow I
am happy enough watching her shoulders and her hands and her
eyes and her smile, that bouncing Jewish warmth, but suddenly I
am penetrated.

Her daughter.

Death.

Diamonds.

Oregon.

She lays them before me, as one would lay cold objects, on the
Broadway table, first one, then the next, the next, heaps and
tumbles them before me in that rushy, gushy voice of Jewish
innocence, Jewish warmth, filling the space between the ashtray
and my cup. Fiction is art, and art is metaphor, and here are the

counters, the markers, the symbols of that attractive and seductive game, but no, not here, not now. These objects are beyond metaphor, beyond games. My role, if I have a role, is otherwise.

You heard about my daughter, didn't you? How she committed suicide? You didn't? This was four months ago. You sure you didn't hear? No one told you? Well, what happened was, all of a sudden she became, I don't know, listless, she wouldn't go to school, she wouldn't do anything, just hung around the apartment all day, until finally I said to her, I want you to talk to your father. So I phoned him. He lives in Chicago. Well, we were sitting there, waiting, my daughter and I, and I heard him knock on the door, and I went to let him in, and when I came back, with her father, she was gone. I was out of there less than one minute, and she jumped out the window.

How old was she?

Fourteen.

I light a cigarette.

You sure you don't want coffee? Anything?

She shakes her head, those springy curls, doesn't want coffee, doesn't need anything.

But smiling, always smiling.

Well, that's how come I went to Oregon. You have to understand, I've never dealt with death before, death was never part of my experience to date. I mean, I've even still got my parents, you know? Even all my uncles. Anyhow, this man. He invited me to Oregon, and, well, why not? I had to do something, so I figured, okay, Oregon.

Oh, but I have to tell you, I'm into diamonds these days. I mean, it's my new business. I sell diamonds. What do I know about diamonds? What's to know? Well, that's how I met this man. I mean, I didn't actually meet him, I just talked to him. Over the phone. First it was about diamonds, he wanted this, he wanted that, and then he started calling me up all the time, every day. To talk. No, nothing sexual, nothing like that. I'll tell you. He told me he was fifty-nine years old and his wife had just died and he liked talking to me because it eased his bereavement. Look, this man. A millionaire. More than a millionaire. The California legislature, a judge, everything. I checked it all out. It was true. He's in *Who's Who*. Anyhow, that's when he said come up to Oregon. He's retired to Oregon, a house on a mountain, in this really secluded part. You ever been to Oregon? It's very lovely. I mean, it's almost total wilderness out there. Rivers and all.

Well, it turned out he wasn't fifty-nine, he was sixty-nine, but so what? I'll tell you, though. I was there for two days. The first day I went into this little bathroom, I think it was a maid's bathroom, and I opened a drawer, I was looking for Kleenex, and you know what was there? A Smith and Wesson .45 revolver. Loaded. I checked it out. And then I found out that there was a loaded revolver in every room in that house. And this was a big house. Maybe twenty rooms. As well as the five rifles downstairs.

And you didn't leave then?

Well, revolvers, revolvers. We all have something. You know about the Doomsday Theory? Well, that was another thing. Under that house, there was a sort of another house, under the ground, concrete, and what was in there was ten thousand dollars worth of food. Water. Everything. Generators. Air.

But it was the second night, I'll tell you. That's when he showed me his collection. I can't tell you. Hitler's cap. Goering's boots. Soap, teeth, a flag with blood. A whole room, full of that. Nazi stuff.

He knew you were Jewish, of course?

She smiles, the hands fly, the shoulders.

I don't know, I just got out of there. Oh, and he had a wooden leg. Did I tell you that? That was the first night, when I knocked on his bedroom door – we had separate bedrooms – and he took a long time to come out. I should have known earlier, I suppose, from the way he walked. That limp.

So what did you do? I mean, when you got out of there?

Oh, that's when I met the Sheriff. He was wonderful. He had this enormous Yamaha, this motorbike, and we went everywhere, and, of course, I was terrified at first, I've never been on anything like that before, but then it was beautiful, I relaxed, I was, like, all of a sudden really in touch with nature, the wind, the air.

Oh, what's the time, I've got this Movement Class.

We stand up.

And now there's another man. I know, I know. We talk about Kafka. He phones me every day and that's what we do. We discuss Kafka. We've been doing it for almost a month. I said I'd meet him tomorrow night. I mean, I've never seen him. It's all just over the phone. Well, who knows?

We are in the street. She goes this way, I go that.

Look, Betty, if I write all this down, all this stuff you've told me, is that okay, would you mind?

She looks surprised, puzzled, but quickly there is that smile, that Jewish smile, beaming on Broadway.

No.

♦ *Outrageous Behaviour*

♦

♦ He had never slept in before, not ever, not once. Six mornings of the week he was gone before Moses woke up, out of the house just after seven, wearing, every day of the year, summer and winter, his gabardine coat, spotty, baggy, likewise his shapeless hat, and in his left hand his famous gladstone bag, the sides so broken from years of flinging it to the ground that it hung down from its handle like an accordion (on the ground it was a leather puddle, with rubbed-raw patches and deep cracks and the shiny handle foolishly swimming somewhere in the middle). On the seventh day, Sunday, Moses would wake to the clatter of the lawn mower on the lawn just outside his window, the old hand mower, on wet mornings to the high whirr of the blades spinning uselessly, the wheels locked and skidding, gouging deep scars in the grass, to sounds of puffing, grunting, a savage kick to get the wheels free, red-faced, impatient sounds, lasting rarely more than ten minutes, perhaps fifteen, the lawn an obstacle to be got over, finished, done, never mind the cruel scars, the untouched clumps, the wild, waving edges. He claimed he did it for pleasure, but the evidence was no. Or was impatience his style? Noisiness certainly was. He was noisy in the kitchen (this woke Moses up, if the lawn mowing hadn't), banging cupboards, slamming drawers, rattling cutlery and plates. When he clapped the kettle down onto the stove it rang like a cymbal. He ate noisily too. Listen to him drinking tea! He slept sometimes on Sunday afternoons – a *drimmel*, he called it, a little dream – hunched under a plaid rug on the settee in the front room, the rug pulled up tight, almost over his head. Then he would wake up, slouch to the bathroom, wash his face – another noisy business – run his fingers through what was left of his hair, and then, hands in pockets, walk around the house, poking his nose into every room, and then outside, a slow circuit, proprietorial, proud, a landowner surveying his property, checking out that everything was in order, nodding to a neighbour, looking up at the sky. And then he made some tea. His habits, his ways. But he had never slept in before, not ever, not once, and though Moses sensed there was something wrong he didn't know what to do.

'Dad?' Moses called softly. 'Dad? Are you all right?'

Sunday morning. Ten o'clock. A hot Melbourne morning in February, going to be hotter. Moses stood in the doorway of his father's room. 'Dad?'

He was barely visible. His head had slipped down, almost off the pillow, the big European feather pillow Moses' mother had brought from Poland thirty years ago, just the top, the very top, of his head showing over the lumpy eiderdown (she had brought that too), grizzled, grey. The pillow on the other side of the bed, her pillow, was untouched. Moses' father never ventured to that side of the double bed, never encroached a centimetre, hadn't from the day Moses' mother went to hospital, a year ago. Where, twenty days ago, finally, wasted, exhausted, frail beyond belief, having lasted longer than anyone had thought possible, the doctors, the specialists, the endless consultants – but not Moses, Moses believed nothing they said, they were just words, this was his *mother* – she had died.

Moses called again. Now his father began to sit up. 'Hey, you slept in,' Moses said, smiling foolishly, coming into the room.

There *was* something wrong. He looked dazed. His eyes were bleary, distant, not quite in focus. Moses had never seen his father like this before.

'What's the time?' his father said. 'It's late. I'll be late for work.'

There was something wrong with his voice too.

'Dad,' Moses said. 'It's Sunday. You don't go to work today.' Out came another foolish smile. 'It's Sunday,' he said again. 'You slept in.'

He looked pale, veined, his skin like antique porcelain crazed under the glaze, like the thinnest paper. His cheeks were frosted with bristles. His lips were dry. He frowned, not looking at Moses, ignoring him. He sat up properly. He pushed the eider-down away. His feet, his white feet, touched the carpet by the side of the bed. 'Late,' he said, and then he moaned. His hand came up to his brow. 'Headache,' he said. 'Terrible headache.'

'Go back to bed, dad,' Moses said. He heard his own voice coming out strange too, too high, too thin. 'Would you like some aspirin? I'll bring you a cup of tea. Go back to bed. Please.'

Moses hurried to the bathroom, then to the kitchen. Aspirin. Water. The kettle on the stove. Moses spilt tea leaves, couldn't see the milk. The kettle whistled, pluming out steam. Sugar. A spoon. He made the tea, put everything on a tray, lifted it care-fully, but when he came back to the bedroom, his father had gone.

Then Moses heard the front gate banging and when he ran outside he saw that his father was already halfway down the street, wearing his gabardine coat, his shapeless hat, his accor-dioned gladstone bag hanging from his customary left hand.

Mr Harris next door was washing his car, Mr Williamson in the next house was clipping his hedge, the Slaters were out, the Beatons, scrawny old Mr Thurgrove in number nine was stand-ing in his garden in a dirty singlet with his arms crossed, squint-ing into the sun. Everyone was out and busy and looking and talking as Moses went down the street, eyes down, trying not to run. Someone said 'Good morning,' someone called, someone waved. Moses ignored them all, his face on fire as he hurried past.

He caught up with him outside the Millers, jaunty Mrs Miller in a shiny bikini snipping at roses, the rhinestones on her sunglasses flashing. Moses put his hand gently on his father's arm. 'Where are you going, dad?' he said. 'It's Sunday. You don't go to work today.'

His father turned and looked at him, blankly, his eyes puzzled, vague, as though he had never seen Moses before. His mouth opened but no words came out.

'Come home, dad,' Moses said softly, keeping his hand on his father's arm, turning him around, and together they walked back up the street, Moses not looking at anyone, his father not saying a word.

Moses helped his father off with his coat, his jacket, back into his pyjamas. His father pulled the eiderdown up and was asleep at once. For a full minute Moses stood and looked down at his father, hardly daring to breathe, and then he tiptoed out. In the hall he stared at the telephone, stared and stared, but how could he call the doctor, how, what could he say, just twenty days after his mother had died?

Doctor Rose said he'd come at once, be there in an hour. Moses wanted to go outside and stand in the street, but he couldn't with the neighbours there. He tiptoed to his father's doorway, saw that he hadn't moved, was still asleep, and then tiptoed away. Where? The kitchen? The front room? He went out to the garden at the back. He stared at the lawn, at the scars, at the clumps. He wondered should he mow it, it was something to do, but he thought, no, not now. He checked on his father again. Still asleep. He sat on the back step and smoked a cigarette, and then another, and finally he heard a car, and then a knock on the front door, and as he went past his father's room to let the doctor in, Moses saw that his father had once again gone.

Doctor Rose, good Family Doctor Rose, wearing a gaudy Hawaiian-type sports shirt loose outside his trousers, wearing canvas espadrilles and no socks, wearing a thoughtful frown, caressed his thick black moustache with the edge of a thumbnail and said it was flu. He said if he didn't eat anything, not to worry, that was all right. He said to give him liquids, tea, orange juice, water, but only if he asked for them. He said aspirin, maybe, but don't wake him up especially. Let him sleep, he said. The best thing was just to let him sleep. He said he'd look in again in the morning, and in the meantime not to worry.

'But he keeps getting dressed,' Moses said. 'He keeps putting on his clothes and taking his bag and going off to work. He doesn't even know it's Sunday. He doesn't seem to know any-thing.'

'Watch him,' Doctor Rose said.

Moses watched him. The house was still. Moses sat in the front room, in the kitchen, in his room, smoking, trying to read, just sitting, every ten minutes tiptoeing to his father's doorway and looking in. His father slept and slept. The afternoon waned. Moses wondered should he phone someone, an uncle, a family friend, to tell them what was happening, but he couldn't bring himself to pick up the telephone. He didn't, somehow, trust his voice. And what was there to tell? That his father was asleep? Why alarm everyone? The doctor said it was flu. He said to let him sleep. He said he'd be all right.

But he looked at me, Moses said to himself, and he didn't know who I was. He didn't even know I was there.

The house, as the afternoon waned, as the sun retreated, as night began to fall, grew even stiller. The public, outside sounds – cars, hoses, mowers, people talking and laughing, children running, people walking past – gone now, replaced by private, inside sounds – Mrs Harris next door in her kitchen humming to herself as she washed up, a radio, someone's muffled TV. A door opened somewhere on an argument, and then closed again with a bang. Moses sat in the front room and felt the stillness deepen-ing, spreading around him like ink.

Silence.

The whole past year had been silent, but in a different way, a different kind of silence. A busy silence. Hospital visits. Going there. Coming back. Silent meals. Silent thoughts. And then, suddenly, twenty days ago – nothing. Suddenly nowhere to go, nothing to do. All those things, those routines – yes, they *had* become routines – taken away. Moses and his father sat in the house, like strangers on a ship, forced into each other's company. Moses didn't know what to say. His father said nothing. Another kind of silence. A vacuum. A void.

And now this silence.

Moses stood up. Oh, for God's sake, he told himself, he's only got the flu! He snatched up his cigarettes, lit one, blew smoke. His hands, he saw, were trembling. Stop it! he told himself. He went quickly to his father's room and stood in the doorway.

'Dad?' he said.

He was awake. He was looking up at the ceiling, not moving, his brow creased. The room smelled stale, close.

'You're awake,' Moses said. 'Do you want anything? How's your headache? Do you feel better?'

His father mumbled something but Moses didn't catch what it was.

'Stay there,' Moses said. 'I'll bring you a cup of tea.'

Moses helped his father sit up. His father brought his hands out from under the eiderdown and reached for the tea. His eyes were still dazed, bleary. He took two sips, three, and then fell back onto the pillow. He mumbled something. 'What?' Moses said, leaning closer to hear. 'What did you say, dad?' 'I want . . .' his father said, and then he was sick. He was violently sick, on the eiderdown, on the carpet, on Moses' hand. And then he fell back again, moaned, and closed his eyes.

Moses phoned Doctor Rose. He was there in twenty minutes, still wearing his gaudy Hawaiian-type shirt, but tucked inside his trousers now, a jacket over it. He had also put on socks. Moses' father was awake, but didn't say anything while Doctor Rose examined him, listened to his heart, looked at his eyes. 'He had some tea,' Moses said, 'but only a few sips . . .' Doctor Rose went past him and into the hall. 'I'll use your phone,' he said.

Moses sat with Doctor Rose in the front room, waiting for the ambulance. Moses smoked a cigarette. 'I know how you feel,' Doctor Rose said. Moses looked down at his feet.

It was the same hospital, the same wing. Moses was asked to sign some forms. A nurse asked if he wanted a cup of tea. Moses shook his head. He waited in a corridor. Nurses and sisters walked past quickly on the cold, squeaky floor. Twenty minutes passed, thirty. Then someone called Moses' name, and then a doctor, Moses didn't catch his name, a tall man with tired eyes, told Moses that his father had suffered a brain haemorrhage, something about pressure, impossible to do anything just at the moment, but he was comfortable, the best they could do. The doctor said to go home, get some sleep, come back in the morning. Moses asked when visiting hours were. The doctor said he could come any time.

Will he die? Will my father die? Is my father going to die? Impossible! Of course not! Don't be stupid! Moses refused to let the idea, the possibility, enter his head. Or, if it did, he pushed it immediately away.

He made himself busy. He made phone calls. He repeated, endlessly, what the doctor had told him, to uncles, cousins, family friends, everyone he could think of to call, standing in the hall at home, trying to be efficient, brisk. When he phoned Mrs Salter, an old family friend, and she began to wail, Moses tried to cut her short. 'They told me he's comfortable,' he said, and started to hang up, but she went on and on, and he couldn't. He tried not to listen, staring down at his feet, her wails and moans boring into his ear, impossible to escape, but finally she finished, and Moses, quickly, phoned someone else.

Who else? Who have I forgotten?

They were all his mother's family, the people Moses phoned, the uncles, the cousins, and the friends too, people Moses' father had never really liked, had never really had any time for, had tolerated at best, sitting uncomfortably in their houses, restless, impatient, or when they came here, the same, berating them when they had gone, mocking them, bored by them, but never to their faces, because who else was there, what else was there to do? He had no family here – his were in Israel, a brother, two sisters, cousins, a complicated family tree Moses had never been able to unravel properly and his father had never bothered to explain, a private world he kept to himself, reading their letters almost secretly, and never out loud. He had come here in the thirties, alone, intending to stay just one year, make some money, go back. Instead, lonely, friendless, a rough, wide-shouldered young man, already balding, already grey, whose pleasure was in his body – in Israel, or Palestine as it was then, he had worked in a quarry, splitting rocks in the sun, 'A beautiful life,' he told Moses over and over, 'a real life' – he married. Moses thought of getting in touch with Israel, a phone call, a cable, but he wasn't exactly sure how to go about it, whom to contact, and somehow all that seemed too dramatic. Not now. It was after midnight. Moses brushed his teeth and went to bed.

He phoned the hospital at eight the next morning and was told that his father's condition was unchanged. 'I'll be there in half an hour,' Moses said. He splashed water onto his face, didn't waste time shaving or having breakfast, ran down the street for a taxi. When he got to the hospital, hurried along endless corridors, past endless doors, and then slowed down, stopped, stepped carefully into the ward, he saw that overnight his father had changed.

His eyes were no longer bleary. There was colour in his cheeks. He was sitting up, or trying to. There was a nurse by the side of the bed, her hands on his shoulders, trying to get him to lie down. Moses' father was shouting at her, telling her to leave him alone. His language was coarse and obscene. Moses came slowly forward, not sure what to do.

The nurse turned and saw him. She was a small woman, in her forties, with a sharp, mousy face. 'Who are you?' she snapped at Moses.

'That's my father,' Moses said. 'I've come to see him.'

'Oh,' she said. Her face fell, but only for a second. 'Well, he's behaving *abominably*,' she said, her face hardening again. 'Dreadful man. He's upsetting everyone in the ward.'

'Dora! Dora!' Moses' father shouted. 'I'm coming! I'm getting out of this stinking place!'

'Listen to him,' the nurse said. 'I'm going to get the doctor.'

'Yes,' Moses said.

Moses advanced to the side of his father's bed. There were rails on it, like a child's cot. 'Dad,' he said softly. 'You mustn't shout. You'll only make yourself worse.'

His father ignored him, didn't even look at him. 'They can't keep me here!' he shouted to the ceiling. 'I've been here long enough! I'm coming, Dora! I'm coming!'

He fell back onto his pillows. He laughed. He shouted some dirty words. And then he began to sing. Moses stood speechless by the side of the bed. Then someone tapped him on the shoulder, and a doctor, a new doctor, asked him to step out into the corridor.

There was nothing they could do. The pressure was still there. They were waiting, hoping to take an X-ray. Something about tests. Meanwhile . . . The doctor said it was all right if Moses smoked.

When Moses went back into the ward, his father was quiet again. His eyes were open, but he wasn't looking at anything. He didn't seem to know that Moses was there. Moses sat on a chair by the side of the bed. At twelve o'clock a nurse told him to go and have some lunch.

Now they began to arrive, the uncles, the cousins, the people Moses had phoned. Moses' father seemed delighted to see them. He sat up. He laughed. He sang. His face was very red, his eyes faded but clear.

'Ah, the fat pig!' he shouted at Moses' Uncle David. 'How are you, you thief, how's business? Don't buy from him,' he told everyone in the ward. 'He's a *ganef!* Black market. Stolen goods!' He laughed. 'Well, you're not going to steal from me,' he told Uncle David. 'You're too late. I'm going. Dora? Can you hear me? I'm on my way!'

He berated, he ridiculed, he mocked. 'Ah, the little *pisher!* he greeted Moses' Uncle Abe. 'You've come just in time. He thinks he's a hot-shot,' he told the ward, 'a gambler. Ha! His whole card-playing isn't worth a *fortz!*'

Mrs Salter crept into the ward, a handkerchief to her eyes. 'The dirty tongue has come,' Moses' father said. 'Well, I don't need dirty tongues. You know what your dirty tongue can do?' He told her.

'Oi oi,' wailed Mrs Salter, 'what is he saying? He doesn't know what he is saying any more.'

Moses' father chuckled, and then he moaned. He was obviously in great pain, but he wouldn't lie down, he wouldn't stop. He seemed somehow very happy. Mrs Salter began to cry. A nurse came and asked her to leave.

'You better go too,' she said to Moses. 'Let him rest.'

'I'm all right here,' Moses said, not moving from his chair by the side of the bed.

The nurse drew the screen around the bed, sealing it off from the ward. Moses sat alone with his father. 'Dad?' he said. 'Dad?' His father stared up at the ceiling and didn't say a word.

Because I never mowed the lawn? Moses said. Because I never helped him in the garden? Is that why? Is that why he won't speak to me, or even look at me, not even once, just to see that I'm there? But he speaks to everyone else. And he hates them. Why not to me?

But it was no *pleasure* to work with him, Moses said. He never did anything properly. Bang, smash, he didn't care how anything looked. Chewing up the lawn. Weeds all over the place. And whenever I went out to straighten things up, he'd walk away. Or stand there, criticizing me. 'Where's your muscles? You call that an arm? Ha! I've seen better muscles on a *chicken*!'

What did he want from me? What did he want me to be?

Like him? Did he want me to be like him? I can't. That's just not me. He's got no ambition, he never wanted to be anything. Breaking rocks in a quarry in Palestine. I can't do that.

Moses sat and stared down at his hands. And there came to him a morning a long time ago – five years ago? six? – a cold morning, close to rain. Moses and his father were chopping down a tree. It was an old tree, probably dead, or if not, certainly dying, and anyhow it was in the way. It was where they were going to put a washing line. First his father chopped, and then Moses took the axe, and in ten minutes, working together, they had it down. It was hard work and they were both in a sweat. Rain began to spit. Then Moses' mother came out and saw them both standing there, and the tree on the lawn. She looked alarmed. She always looked alarmed. 'Moses,' she cried, 'it's raining! Put on a jumper! You'll get a cold!' 'Don't worry, mum,' Moses said, 'I'm all right.' He laughed. 'A bit of rain never hurt anyone,' he said. Then Moses' father clapped Moses on the shoulder and said, 'Not bad shoulders he's got, uh?'

'I'm sorry, dad,' Moses said, sitting in the dark. 'I'm sorry. I'm sorry.' He felt, suddenly, that spot on his left hand where his father had been sick, where he had brought up the tea. His hand, just there, felt scraped, scalded, burnt.

Moses came every morning, stayed all day, sat and sat. There was nothing the doctors could do. He slept longer and longer, waking up to laugh and sing and shout at whoever was there. He called them thieves, liars, gluttons, and worse. His face was tight with pain. He didn't once speak to Moses, and when he happened to turn that way, his eyes were blank.

Six days, seven days, eight.

On the ninth day he was asleep all the time, though once or twice he moaned, softly, with almost no power or strength. The doctors still hadn't been able to do anything. A nurse brought Moses a cup of tea. It grew cold on the floor by his feet.

At eight o'clock on the tenth morning Moses came into the ward and saw his father lying curled on one side, his eyes squeezed tight. Moses sat down beside him. The ward was very quiet. His father looked as though he was trying to push something out of his way, a massive boulder, a gigantic rock. He was pushing with every part of his face. His cheeks blossomed with thin red veins, a network, a map. He was like that for an hour, exactly the same, straining and pushing, but never once moving, and then his eyes came open a fraction. A nurse came in and very softly began to draw the screens around the bed.

In the corridor a doctor, a very young doctor, his stethoscope poking out of the pocket of his crisp, white jacket like a badge to an exclusive club, put his hand on Moses' shoulder and said he was very, very sorry. He asked Moses would he like to sit down quietly for a while. Moses shook his head.

Outside, on the steps, the trees across the road moving like smoke, Moses saw someone hurrying towards him. It was Mrs Salter. She was carrying, in one hand, a large black handbag, an enormous thing, and in the other a string bag filled with fruit. She saw Moses and her eyes turned instantly weepy and wet.

'What's happened?' she said. Moses didn't say anything. 'Oi oi,' wailed Mrs Salter, fussing for something in her handbag. 'Why didn't you phone me?' Out came a handkerchief. 'He's gone, he's gone, such a beautiful man,' she wailed. 'When will we see such a beautiful man again?' She dabbed at her eyes, her nose, but looking at Moses all the time. 'And what will happen to you now, a boy, all alone in the world? Oi oi.' Her hand took hold of the lapel of Moses' jacket. 'But why didn't you phone me, tell me, so someone could be with him there? From the family?'

Moses stared at Mrs Salter's face. He stared at her crabbed mouth, at her pinched, hard eyes, her sudden tears. Her hand on his lapel felt like a claw. He felt something rising inside him. He felt himself swelling and trembling. He saw himself pushing Mrs Salter, savagely, flinging her aside, her string bag of fruit flying down the steps, and her vile black handbag, and Mrs Salter too, her falsely snivelling face, her deceitful eyes, down the steps she crashed. He saw himself shouting at her as she fell. 'Hypocrite! Dirty mouth! Liar! Filth!'

And then he felt on his hand that spot where his father had been sick, that scald, that burn, that chastisement he knew then he would feel for ever.

His eyes fell. 'Excuse me,' he said to Mrs Salter, or maybe he didn't even say that. He went past her, his eyes on fire but not with tears – they would come later, when he was alone, when there was no one to see – eyes lowered he walked quickly away, down the steps.

♦ Africa Wall

♦

♦ Breakfast in Tangier for Isaac Shur was a short loaf of bread, a tin of sardines or tuna, half a small watermelon, sometimes too a bottle of Coke. No coffee. Isaac Shur had no facilities for making coffee, his apartment had neither electricity nor gas, and though he could easily have bought a small primus stove, he preferred to leave his life the way it was. Unencumbered. Uncluttered. Everything he owned in Tangier fitted into two small canvas bags. He could leave in a minute. He had a trunk of books and clothes with a friend in London, and at odd moments he thought it would be nice to have them here, to have all his things together, but then he thought of porters and taxis and the fuss at customs and the worry of thieves – everyone was a thief in Tangier – and he decided, no. He didn't really need all those books and clothes. He didn't need anything. He was happy the way he was. Perfectly happy. Isaac Shur had been in Tangier, now, for five months.

He bought his bread and his melon and his Coke and his sardines or tuna always at the same place, the first shop down the hill from where he lived. He was there every morning at seven o'clock. He ordered by pointing, miming, smiling, shaking his head. Isaac Shur knew a few words of Spanish, Arabic and French – the lingua franca of this once international city – but he rarely used them. Speaking in a foreign language always made him feel that he was at a disadvantage. The first words he said, in a café, or restaurant, or shop, were, 'Do you speak English?' and when the answer was no, or a puzzled look, or a shake of the head, as it almost invariably was, then Isaac Shur would smile, *that* fact established, made clear, out of the way, good. Then he would launch into his performance of pointing and mime, happier with this, really, than speaking in English. In the shop at the bottom of the hill he was served each morning by the owner, a short, shuffling, always smiling Moroccan, shapeless in a dun-coloured jellaba, the Moroccan's cheeks, at that hour, frosted with grey bristles. The owner welcomed Isaac Shur each morning like a long-lost friend, throwing out his hands, calling out greetings, smiling hugely. Isaac Shur would smile back, then without further ado begin his business of pointing and mime. There were two black cats in the shop, lying about on sacks or on the floor just inside the door, warming themselves in the morning sun. The shop smelled of fruit and oil and Arabic coffee and bread and dust, and there was another smell too, surrounding all these others. This smell was not just in the shop. It was everywhere in Tangier. Isaac Shur had sniffed it in Spain too, and in Greece, but in Tangier it was sharper, more pervasive, impossible to ignore. Its exact cause or component was to Isaac Shur a mystery, but he had a name for it. He called it, to himself, the smell of poverty. He planned one day to write about it. Isaac Shur was a poet and a playwright. His first play had been bought by the BBC. Three of his poems had been published in magazines, one in the *New Statesman*. He was twenty-six years old, an Australian.

Isaac Shur sliced his watermelon with the Swiss army knife he had bought in Copenhagen. He was sitting at the table where in half an hour he would begin work, his typewriter and papers pushed to one side, the door open, the windows open, the shutters folded back, his view of bushes and trees, his garden. Sun fell onto the tiled floor. A breeze passed through the trees onto his face. Isaac Shur looked at his watch. Ten minutes past seven. Good. He felt alert and alive, as he did every morning. This was the best time of the day. From now till ten. Three hours. After that it would be too hot, too hot to think, too hot to work. Three hours. Two and a half. Well, that was enough. That was plenty. He would work till ten, maybe even till ten-thirty, and then walk into town, have his morning coffee, buy a newspaper, a magazine, sit, stroll. Then lunch. Then . . . well, he would see.

Isaac Shur wiped the blade of his Swiss army knife on his jeans. He used this same blade for watermelon, bread, forking out sardines, sharpening his pencils. He finished his bread, washed it down with Coke. His apartment was really just one room, but large, and odd-shaped: where he slept was up two steps and around a corner. Sitting at the table, finishing his breakfast, he could see only the foot of his bed. His two canvas bags beside it. A spare shirt. The kitchen was a narrow space behind him, a sink and a tap. The toilet, behind it, had to be flushed with a bucket. There was an oil lamp beside the bed, another one here on the table. Isaac Shur's was the garden apartment in a block of three floors. Isaac Shur brushed the breadcrumbs from his table and from his lap, lit a cigarette, and stepped outside.

It was a walled garden, the wall made of grey concrete blocks, and along the top of it a glittering necklace of broken bottles and shards of sharp glass set in cement: the terrible teeth of all walls in Tangier. Isaac Shur ignored this. He had learnt not to see it. The garden was wild and unkempt, shaded and private, Tangier locked out. Except in one place, where Isaac Shur stood now, where the ground rose, affording a view beyond the wall, as though the wall were not even there, a view that sailed clear of the hill, past the rubbish dump just beyond the wall – a dusty, smelly mound of earth and iron and feathers and bones and newspapers and broken bricks and God only knew what else – sailed past all this, quickly, barely touching it, away, and then along a green valley, a soft green cleft that ran as far as he could see, into the fuzziness of distance, into the vague shape of hills.

Isaac Shur stood with his cigarette. The valley was why he had taken this apartment. He had looked along it, that first time, and

the doubts he had had about living in a place that had no electricity, no gas, that was half an hour's walk from the centre of
town, a walk he would have to do at least twice a day, probably
four times. But more than that, the place was so isolated, no one
he knew lived anywhere nearby, and the rubbish dump just outside . . . but then he had looked along the valley, that first time,
and all his doubts fell away. Yes, he had said to himself at once,
the decision made. I will work well here. I will be happy. This is
what I want. Yes. The valley was green at all times of the day, no
matter how hard the sun blazed down, and always that same
green, soft and hazy, an English green, the green of Hampshire
and Sussex and the other counties Isaac Shur had travelled
through. And though, at that particular time, he had felt no
especial rapport with the English countryside – regarding it
merely as pleasant scenery, as he had seen the countryside in
France or Denmark or Germany – now, seeing it in Tangier, it
struck a chord, it awoke something inside him, some memory,
some need. He never tired of it, he could stand for hours looking
along its greenness, his eyes endlessly travelling its hazy length.
Halfway along the valley there was a village, and then a second,
and then a third, three clusters of white buildings patterned onto
the green, but the second, Isaac Shur knew, was not a village but
a cemetery, the tricks of perspective and light housing the dead
as it did the living.

Isaac Shur threw away his cigarette. He turned his back reluc-
tantly on the view. Time to work.

Isaac Shur had begun, a week ago, a poem on his mother's
hands. His mother had died when Isaac Shur was twenty-two,
and then his father had died, a year later, a year to the day. Isaac
Shur's method of work was to write down, in grammatically perfect sentences, everything he could remember. His mother's
hands slicing bread. Putting on lipstick. Dialling on the telephone. Flying to her heart when she laughed. Her fingers. Her
wedding ring. Her nails. Her palms. His mother's hands
covered, so far, twenty-odd pages. Isaac Shur felt he had hardly
begun. There would be twice that number of pages again, at
least. And when that was done, when he had recalled everything,
he would put the pages away, unread, never look at them again,

and then he would write his poem. He wrote quickly but carefully, his letters large and well-formed, and when he heard the clamour at the gate, his mouth fell open, as though he had just been woken from a deep sleep. For a moment he didn't know where he was. And then he did, and he knew what was happening. It was the same thing that happened every morning. Isaac Shur rushed out into his garden, waving his hands, shouting.

There they were, as they were every morning, clambering over the gate. Two of them were already inside the garden.

'Go away!' Isaac Shur shouted. 'Beat it! Scram!'

The two in the garden stood there, smiling idiotically. Isaac Shur ran at them. They ducked behind a bush. A third dropped down from the gate.

'Get out of here!' Isaac Shur shouted, wheeling around. 'Leave me alone!' Now the other two were in too, not just smiling but laughing, dancing on thin legs, waving their arms. Isaac Shur ran at them, but they were too fast, they were always too fast, ducking effortlessly out of reach, and then standing still, taunting him with their idiotic smiles. He ran again, his hands grabbing empty air, and then he remembered, instantly panicking, that his door was wide open, the windows, the shutters. Two of them were already inside, the little one, the one he called The Hot Shot Kid, and the tall one, the one with the shaved head. When they saw him, they ducked behind the table, overturning his chair. Isaac Shur saw that The Hot Shot Kid had his Swiss army knife. And what else? What else had they taken? His papers lay in turmoil all over the floor.

Isaac Shur, in true anger now, slammed the door. Right! Rushing for The Hot Shot Kid, he stumbled over the chair. The tall one laughed, and then was gone, fast as water, out of the window. Then he appeared at another window, smiling like a loon. Isaac Shur ignored him. He advanced on The Hot Shot Kid.

'The knife!' he shouted. 'Put down that knife! Put it down!'

The Hot Shot Kid, for the first time, looked afraid. He was a small boy, about five or six years old. He looked over his shoulder, at the slammed door. The game had become serious. Isaac Shur lunged and grabbed him. He grabbed the knife. The

Hot Shot Kid broke free and ran for a window. Isaac Shur let him go. He was shaking. He was wet with sweat.

The shutters, the windows. He locked everything. He shot the bolt on the door. They were laughing outside now, calling out. Isaac Shur picked up his papers. The Swiss army knife was in his pocket. What else had they taken? His pencils, his pen? No. Nothing. It was all there. He picked up the fallen chair, sat down. They were throwing dirt now, at the shutters, at the door. In another minute it would be stones. Isaac Shur saw, when he lit a cigarette, that his fingers were trembling.

It was his fault, of course. He had encouraged them. The Hot Shot Kid lived in the apartment above. Two of the others lived in the block too. The rest were from somewhere around, local kids, playing most of the time on the rubbish dump. Isaac Shur had noticed them there, vaguely, on that first afternoon, when he had moved in. On his first morning in his new apartment, Isaac Shur, walking around his garden, had seen them standing at the gate, looking in. He had waved to them, and smiled, and then, having bought a too-large piece of watermelon that morning, he had offered them each a slice, and some Coke too. He had unlocked the gate. They came into the garden. Isaac Shur had felt sorry for them, for their thin legs, their thin arms, their ragged clothes. He had given them some bread too, bread and sardines. They were polite that first day, standing in the garden, looking in his open door but not going inside, and Isaac Shur had invited them in, showed them his typewriter, his pencils, his papers, his Swiss army knife, explaining to them, pointing and miming and smiling and shaking his head, his work, his reason for being here, his life. That was the first day. On the second morning they had appeared in his garden. The gate had been locked, they had climbed over. They were still polite, still well behaved, but smiling more now, laughing, friends. Isaac Shur shared his watermelon with them again. From there to how it was now had happened in a rush. And getting worse every day. Worse and worse.

Stones banged against his closed door. Isaac Shur sat furious at his table, puffing on his cigarette. Ignore them, he told himself. Don't make a sound. They'll go away. He reached for his papers.

With the door closed, with the shutters closed, it was almost too dark to see. Isaac Shur lit the oil lamp on the table. He picked up a pencil. Her hands when she sewed on a button. The way she held the needle. The little finger of her left hand. The needle dipping. Her hand pulling the thread tight. The oil lamp pushed out heat in solid waves. Isaac Shur unbuttoned his shirt, and then took it completely off. He flung it away savagely on the floor. And then his jeans too, his shoes and socks. He was enormously hot. He could hardly breathe. The smell of his crushed-out cigarette was foul in the room. He lit another. Now they were kicking his door, shouting wildly, banging the shutters with sticks.

Isaac Shur had written his play in London in a large cold room in Maida Vale, the upstairs front room in a cracked grey house of bedsitters, on the slum fringe. His view, when he looked, was of identical cracked houses both ways down the street, as far as he could see. His only heating was a tiny gas fire set in the wall. The windows rattled with wind. A draught blew under the door. The linoleumed floor was ice to his feet. Isaac Shur was cold when he went to bed at night, cold when he awoke each morning. He had written his play in ten days, then ten days more for a second and final draft, typing as fast as he could, cold all the time. His fingers were white with cold. Coming back from his literary agent, he had seen, at Oxford Circus, a large colour photograph, a poster, an advertisement, for South Africa. The photograph showed three girls in skimpy bikinis laughing and jumping into the sea, and Isaac Shur had felt his muscles tighten with pain, looking at those bare bodies. He had shivered violently. He had felt sick with cold. His literary agent phoned him that night, ecstatic with praise, and a week later the play had been bought by the BBC. Beginner's luck? Isaac Shur knew no other writers, he had no experience of rejection or waiting, and though he was, of course, delighted, delighted and thrilled, the full measure of his success was unknown to him. This is the way it happens, he thought. Good. He had been in London, then, for a month and three days. Before that, for a year, he had travelled, never staying anywhere longer than two or three weeks. A week in Vienna. Ten days in Prague. Three weeks in Copenhagen, two in Stockholm and Oslo. This was his first time in Europe. He wanted to see it all.

Two days after his play had been accepted, Isaac Shur was at the flat of a friend, a fellow Australian who had been in London for two years. This friend, Graham Tinsdale, was a film editor. They sat before a small fan heater. Wind rushed unimpeded through the bare branches of the trees in the square outside, the windows of the flat uncurtained, cold black rectangles of night. Isaac Shur told Graham Tinsdale the details of his sale to the BBC. Graham Tinsdale looked amazed. 'That's terrific,' he said. 'Are you going to do another one?' Isaac Shur looked at the black windows. 'I don't know how anyone can live in England,' he said. 'It's so cold.' 'Go to Greece,' Graham Tinsdale said. 'Greece is good in winter.' 'I've been to Greece,' Isaac Shur said. 'I think I'll go to Tangier.' Isaac Shur had no idea why he had said this. Tangier. He knew nothing about the place, he had no real desire to see it, it was just something that had come into his head. Tangier. He heard the wind rushing outside. He shivered. 'When?' Graham Tinsdale said. 'I don't know,' Isaac Shur said. 'Tomorrow. The day after. Listen, is it all right if I leave a few things here? They're all in a small trunk. Won't take up much room.' Two nights later Isaac Shur was in Paris, waiting to board the midnight train to Madrid. He stayed in Madrid for four days, and from there hitchhiked down, and the closer he got to Tangier the more he recognized that he was afraid.

Why am I doing this? Isaac Shur asked himself. Because I had said to a friend in London that I would? That was nothing. I could have stayed in Madrid. Madrid was warm. Blue skies every day. The Prado. Good wine. Isaac Shur hitchhiked down, through Valencia, and then along the coast, Malaga, Estapona, travelling not very far each day, staying in hotels, rooms, and each night the fear growing. Why? Why?

All new cities are fearful places, but Tangier remained fearful to Isaac Shur longer than anywhere else he had ever been. And not only at night but during the day too. He was frightened of the shopkeepers, the touts, the beggars, the endless boys forever plucking at his sleeves, always with the same litany: 'How are you, my friend?' What frightened him more than anything else was that he knew his fear was visible to all. He radiated, he knew, not only discomfort but vulnerability. It was in his eyes, in the way he sat at a café, in the way he walked down a street, in everything he did. He wondered should he go somewhere else, but he didn't know where. He could think only of London, but that was too cold. No, he told himself, I don't want to travel. Not yet. I've had enough travelling for a while. Hotels, rooms. I want to be in one place. I want to do some work. Then Isaac Shur began to meet people, Americans, mostly, people his age, other writers, painters, college dropouts, kids having a good time. He moved from the hotel where he was staying to a cheaper one, he established habits and routines, he settled into good work. He developed a manner of walking down a street, of sitting at a café, of not seeing those things that he didn't want to see, of ignoring the hands forever plucking at his sleeves, the litany of pestering voices. He erected around himself the necessary shell or disguise that everyone developed, he told himself, to exist in this city. He learnt to keep his right hand always in his pocket, tight over his wallet and passport and traveller's cheques. Very quickly, he did this without thinking; it became second nature to him.

A large stone slammed against Isaac Shur's door. The door shuddered, daylight, for an awful instant, showing all around. Isaac Shur leapt up from his table, a shout in his throat.

What was the use? What was the point? Isaac Shur knew that even if he chased them away, which was probably impossible, even if he sat them out, did nothing, waited, didn't utter a sound, it would make no difference. The best hours of the day were gone. His brain was in turmoil now. The morning was ruined. He looked at the last words he had written. They lay on the page. They meant nothing.

In the kitchen Isaac Shur splashed himself with cold water, combed his hair. He dressed again in his jeans and shirt. Passport, money. There was a wild scramble in the garden when Isaac Shur stepped outside. Isaac Shur didn't look up. He locked his door, unlocked the garden gate and locked it again, then pushed the keys deep in his pocket under his passport and wallet. Still not looking up, paying no attention whatsoever to the children waving and shouting and advancing and dancing back on their thin legs on the edge of his vision, he started down the hill.

Just before the shop where he went every morning he saw a woman sitting on the ground, a baby on her lap. The palm of the woman's held-out hand was as crinkled as a dead leaf. Isaac Shur kept his hand tight in his pocket over his wallet and passport and traveller's cheques. The only acknowledgement he allowed himself to make of her presence was a curt shaking of his head. Give to one and you give to them all, he had learnt long ago. They were endless. Anyhow, he told himself, I don't have any small change.

It was not yet ten o'clock, but the day was already hot. Dust swirled in the road. That smell that Isaac Shur called the smell of poverty filled his nose. July. August, Isaac Shur had been told, was the worst month. Everyone went away in August. August in Tangier was unbearable. Even the nights were hot. Isaac Shur thought for a moment of going to Portugal, a month somewhere on the Atlantic coast, but the idea of travelling again, just now, of finding a place to stay, of having to establish his habits and routines all over again, was annoying, too complicated, and he pushed it away. He would think about that later, another time. Instead, quickly, he thought about where he would go for his morning coffee.

Isaac Shur had no one particular place. He left it, each morning, for his mood to decide. Some mornings he enjoyed the Café de Paris, on the corner of the Avenue Louis Pasteur, diagonally across from the French Consulate. This is where he had sat that morning when the *New Statesman* with his poem in it had arrived, the magazine open nonchalantly at his page – or so he had hoped it looked – sipping his coffee, smoking cigarette after cigarette, his eyes casually moving over the elegant lamps and the mirrors and the burgundy-coloured leather seats and the waiters in their clean aprons and stiff white shirts and black bow ties, and the parade of people moving past in the street, and the French Consulate with its classical facade and the tall palm trees in the garden, the tall iron gates, the black official cars. Isaac Shur's eyes drifting over all this and then back, again and again, to his poem on the marble table. The Café de Paris was expensive, but Isaac Shur didn't mind that. On the mornings that he went there he usually bought *The Times*, and took his time with it, sitting there for an hour at least, reading every word, even the obituaries and Court Circular. At the Café de Paris Isaac Shur was always alone, and he liked that too. He enjoyed the quiet hour, his newspaper, his cigarettes, the coffee.

Or he would go to Claridges, which was further along the street, on the other side, and sit inside, on a stool at the bar, and have a croissant with his coffee, sometimes two, looking up from time to time to see himself reflected in the mirror behind the bar, his face serious and dimly lit amongst the bottles of whisky and brandy and liqueurs and gin. At Claridges Isaac Shur felt international, a seasoned traveller, mature and self-contained, someone who knew the ropes.

No, Isaac Shur wasn't in the mood for the Café de Paris this morning. Nor for Claridges. He continued down the street that led down to the Socco Grande, past the Minzah Hotel, where, Isaac Shur had been told, Ian Fleming had always stayed whenever he had been in Tangier. Isaac Shur had had his morning coffee there several times, in the garden, sitting under a vast umbrella by the blue pool. The doorman, a turbanned and costumed tall black African, stepped out of the way on the narrow pavement as Isaac Shur went past.

In the Socco Grande Isaac Shur saw the usual crowds milling around the usual dilapidated buses, the usual vendors with their portable stalls – the man who sold scissors, the cakes man, the man with the scarves and belts – and the usual beggars, the usual touts, the endless wheeling boys. Hands reached out for his arms, his shirt. Faces appeared, serious, smiling. 'How are you, my friend?' Isaac Shur walked not quickly but not dawdling either, crossing the large dusty square, his right hand firmly in his pocket, his eyes enjoying the scene, but his face fixed straight ahead. The cafés. The shops. The different sudden smells, of charcoal and meat, of noodle soup, of gasoline, of bread, of chickens, of dung.

Halfway across the square Isaac Shur saw, standing together, in their usual place, the fatimas. Isaac Shur had employed a fatima only once. An old Fleet Street journalist, a man who had stepped ashore at Tangier on his way to somewhere else in 1939 and never left, had told Isaac Shur about the fatimas. 'Go down there, Isaac,' he had said, 'and for three dirhams you'll get your

clothes washed and your floors scrubbed and your bed made –
they'll even cook your lunch. But don't pay them more than
three dirhams, understand? Not a penny more.' Isaac Shur had
gone down to the Socco Grande at eight o'clock in the morning,
pointed to the nearest woman, and then taken her back with him
to his apartment on the bus, a thin woman with lined hennaed
hands. Isaac Shur had sat in his garden in his shorts while the
woman washed his clothes and his sheets and his towel, washed
them in cold water, pounding and pounding them, and then
spread them out on bushes to dry. After she had scrubbed his
floors, she had come out to where Isaac Shur sat in the garden
and mimed eating, her thin hands flying to her mouth, and then
pointing at Isaac Shur, raising her eyebrows. At first Isaac Shur
had thought that she wanted to make him lunch. He shook his
head, no, he didn't want lunch, he wasn't hungry, he would eat
later. Then he realized that she was telling him that she was
hungry, that he had to feed her. 'Oh,' Isaac Shur had said, blushing red, and had run down to the shop where he bought his
breakfast every morning and he bought what he always bought,
a tin of sardines, bread, a melon. The fatima had eaten these in
the kitchen, crouched in the furthest corner, her back turned on
the open windows, the trees and bushes, the view. When she had
finished Isaac Shur gave her three dirhams and she had fallen to
her knees on the floor and blessed him, and at the gate had told
Isaac Shur, pointing and miming and smiling, that she wanted to
come again, that she would always come, that she would be his
fatima. Isaac Shur had wanted to give her another dirham, for
the bus, but his hand stayed in his pocket.

Isaac Shur entered the street that led down to the Socco Chico,
the arched entrance to the market on one side, with its wet smell of
flowers, a tight, steeply downhill street crammed with tourist
shops. He walked faster here, both hands in his pockets, the left
one touching his Swiss army knife, feeling its smooth, familiar
shape. A sudden gust of boys – three? four? Isaac Shur didn't look –
appeared around him, touching, laughing, crying out, and then
they were gone, and Isaac Shur was in the Socco Chico.

Saint-Saëns had written his *Carnival of Animals* here, in the
front first-floor room of the hotel to Isaac Shur's right. Tennessee

Williams, Isaac Shur had been told, had sat here too, often, at one of these cafés, and watching the endless parade had conceived *Camino Real*. And William Burroughs had sat here. And Paul Bowles. And a young Truman Capote. The whole world passed through the Socco Chico, if you sat here long enough. This, anyhow, was the constant refrain of the Americans, the painters and writers and college dropouts whom Isaac Shur had met and befriended, in particular, George Matthews, a black-bearded New Yorker who was Isaac Shur's closest Tangier friend. George Matthews was a great sitter. Four or five hours at a stretch was nothing to him. That was his norm. George Matthews would sit, sometimes, the whole day through, and then, after dinner, come back, around ten or eleven, and sit another three or four hours, ordering, from time to time, a cup of coffee or hot chocolate, smoking a cigarette or two, but mostly doing nothing, just sitting. George Matthews always had a book with him, Spinoza's *Ethics*, or something by Hegel or Toynbee or Kant, once it was Marx's *Das Kapital*, but Isaac Shur had never seen him reading. A book was just something that George Matthews always had with him, a justification for sitting, a prop. He had graduated from Columbia University, but not in Philosophy, as Isaac Shur had supposed. His thesis had been on how to win at Monopoly.

Isaac Shur saw George Matthews sitting at his usual table at the Café Central, his left hand resting lightly on a small green book. 'George,' Isaac Shur said.

George Matthews looked up. His black-bearded face, which always looked gruff, broke instantly into a naïve, innocent smile. 'Hi,' he said seeing Isaac Shur. 'Hey, sit down, whatcha doin'? How's things?'

Isaac Shur pulled out a chair. There were three other people sitting at the table, two painters named Vincent and Berkeley, and a girl everyone called Bunny. Isaac Shur said hello to them, and then turned back to George Matthews.

'Those kids,' Isaac Shur said. 'Those kids are driving me crazy. I couldn't do any work this morning. Again.'

'Naah,' George Matthews said. 'Kids is nothin'. Don't let 'em hassle ya. Kids is kids.'

'Not these kids,' Isaac Shur said. 'These kids are vultures. They won't leave me alone. You know what happened this morning? One of them grabbed my knife. The little one, The Hot Shot Kid. I went crazy.'

'Yeah?' George Matthews said. 'The Hot Shot Kid, eh?' He smiled. 'He's some kid. So clip him one in the ear, he won't hassle you no more.'

Isaac Shur lit a cigarette. 'A clip in the ear,' he said. 'If you can catch him.'

'Listen, don't let 'em hassle ya,' George Matthews said. 'You want hassle, go to New York. Man, that's the capital of hasslin'. Here, you just relax. Take it easy.'

'Yes,' Isaac Shur said.

The usual waiter appeared, the one everyone called Dopey because of his drooping lids and bald head and slow, faraway manner. '*Con leche*?' he said to Isaac Shur, not quite looking at him. Isaac Shur nodded. The waiter poured out the coffee and milk simultaneously from the two silver pots he always carried, hardly looking at the cup, but getting it, as always, exactly right.

'How ya doin' there, Dopey?' George Matthews said. The waiter smiled the faintest smile and shuffled away. 'Isn't he terrific?' George Matthews said. 'The most terrific coffee pourer on the whole damn continent of Africa. In the middle of an earthquake, I bet he still wouldn't spill a single drop.' He laughed, and then turned back to face the square, his eyes darting, taking in everything, vastly alive, endlessly amused, under his black brows. Isaac Shur sipped his coffee and smoked his cigarette.

Ten minutes passed, fifteen. There was some talk at the table, the sort of talk there always was, small talk, light gossip, never about work. Work was never mentioned. Work, if you did it – or didn't – was your own business, a private thing. When Isaac Shur's poem had come out in the *New Statesman*, he had shown it to George Matthews, here, at the Café Central, at this table, and to the other people who had been here too that day, one of whom, a thin, crew-cutted Canadian named Steven, was a writer, working on a novel. Isaac Shur, excited, had not only let everyone read his poem but then launched into an exposition of his method of work, how he filled page after page with sentences in prose, and then put them away, unread, in a drawer, and wrote his poem. When he had finished telling everyone about this – it was the first time he had ever explained his work to anyone in his whole life – Isaac Shur had expected that there would be some talk about it, that Steven, anyway, would talk about how he wrote, but there wasn't. No one said anything. The talk, when it began again, moved where it always did, into small things, light gossip, and Isaac Shur wondered if this was Tangier or whether all creative people everywhere kept themselves buttoned up. Whatever, Isaac Shur had never talked about his work again.

Another ten minutes, another fifteen. Isaac Shur had finished his coffee. He didn't feel like another. He didn't want another cigarette. A Moroccan youth appeared at the table, a regular at the square. Isaac Shur instinctively put his hand over his cigarettes on the table.

'Hi there, Muhammad,' George Matthews greeted the Moroccan. 'How's it going?' The Moroccan shook George Matthews' hand, and then slapped him on the back. He shook the painters' hands too, and smiled at Bunny, nodding his head seriously. Isaac Shur ignored the outstretched hand when it came his way, countering it with a short smile, a quick nod, then busying himself with a cigarette. George Matthews invited the Moroccan to sit with them. The Moroccan sat, smiling. After three or four minutes he stood up, shook hands with George Matthews again, with the two painters, nodded and smiled at Bunny and Isaac Shur, and left. Isaac Shur stood up too.

'Hey, where ya goin'?' George Matthews said. 'What's the rush?'

'Well, I thought . . .' Isaac Shur began, counting out the money for his coffee. 'I've got some things to do.' He nodded at Bunny and the two painters. 'See you,' he said.

'Wait a minute, wait a minute,' George Matthews said. 'Listen. Why doncha come round for dinner tonight? I'll fry up a chicken.'

'Okay,' Isaac Shur said. 'What time?'

'I don't know,' George Matthews said. 'Nine?'

'Fine,' Isaac Shur said. 'Nine o'clock.' Isaac Shur signalled to the waiter, pointing to his money on the table.

'Ya feel like Monopoly?' George Matthews said. 'I'm in the mood.'

'You're always in the mood,' Isaac Shur said, moving away from the table. 'See you. Nine o'clock.' And then, remembering, 'I'll bring the wine.'

It was half past eleven. Isaac Shur, both hands in his pockets, ignoring the bustling bodies all around, walked down the street that led from the Socco Chico to the sea. He would walk along the beach, he decided. He would sit somewhere quiet for a while and think. He would have lunch. He passed, on his left, the mosque, and saw, through the open door, the tiled mosaic walls, the fountain at the entrance, barefoot Moroccans ritually washing, and, further inside, others sitting cross-legged, silent in prayer. Isaac Shur decided that tomorrow he would go to Gibraltar.

Isaac Shur went to Gibraltar about once a fortnight, going on the ferry at nine o'clock in the morning, coming back around six, a two-hour trip each way. Once, suddenly impatient, excited, the prospect of that two-hour trip too much for him, too predictable, too slow, he had taken a cab to the airport, and flown over, and then, at five, flown back, the trip, this way, costing him five times what the ferry did, plus the cabs. It had been worth it though, to see Gibraltar from the air, the thrill of landing on that impossible airstrip, that tiny neck of connecting land, the sea on both sides, the plane coming down on almost no space at all; and then, coming back, for the first time he had seen Tangier the way he had been told by old residents it used to be, in the twenties and thirties, before it had been 'discovered', a magical city floating pale blue on its hills above the Strait.

In Gibraltar, Isaac Shur changed his traveller's cheques – the rate was better than what you got in Tangier, though lately it had been falling – bought a pile of the latest English magazines and newspapers, sometimes too a couple of books, then he had lunch in a Chinese restaurant, and then, in the afternoon, sat in his favourite place, the small park and sailors' cemetery at the end of the main street, and quietly read. In Gibraltar he also bought a bottle of duty-free whisky – Johnnie Walker Black Label or Haig and Haig Pinch – two cartons of Camel cigarettes, and a box of Havana cigars. Ramon Allones, usually. Sometimes Punch. Isaac

Shur was no great cigar smoker, but he liked the image of himself smoking a fine cigar in the afternoons whilst sitting in his garden looking across at the green valley and its three white villages. Every afternoon, around six o'clock, the day's heat dying, this is what he did. Unless the children came again. But usually in the afternoons they left him alone.

Yes, Isaac Shur said to himself, tomorrow I'll go to Gibraltar.

The street he was walking down suddenly widened, and Isaac Shur, looking up, saw the sea. Palm trees. Seagulls. The road was torn up here, pipes were being laid. There was the usual commotion of tractors and trucks. Isaac Shur, turning left, made for the beach.

He walked for about half a kilometre, and then sat down, on a bench under a tree. He lit a cigarette. Between the beach proper and where he sat there was a row of beach clubs, places where, for a small fee, you could use the changing rooms, hire a locker, shower, buy a drink at the bar, but the real business of the beach clubs was sitting. The beach at Tangier is wide, a long trek across the hot sand to the sea, and Isaac Shur had discovered, on the two or three occasions when he had been to one of these beach clubs, that hardly anyone ever actually swam. Swimming was too much trouble. It wasn't worth it. It was too far. It was a sweat. Instead, everyone just sat, sprawled in deck chairs, smoking, talking, sipping Cokes, for half the day, and longer. Isaac Shur, even when with his friends, or with people he knew, had quickly felt restless, awkward, and each time had left after less than an hour.

Isaac Shur walked the length of the road that parallelled the sea as far as it went, and then back, and lunched, alone, at a noisy café on the harbour. Calamari. A glass of white wine. Coffee and a cigarette. A television set on a shelf above the counter was showing an old film starring Montgomery Clift. The film, dubbed into Spanish, was probably being transmitted from Spain. Isaac Shur didn't know what the film was, he couldn't follow the story at all, but he watched it intently as he ate, not at all bothered by not being able to understand what anyone was saying, enjoying the shots of buildings and cars, the interiors, the details – the telephones, cigarette lighters, elevator doors opening and closing, the clothes. He debated having a second cup of coffee and sitting until the film was over, but the café was too noisy, people coming in and going out all the time, money changers, touts, prostitutes, beggars, and though he would have liked to stay, Isaac Shur knew that he would be pestered if he sat here alone too long.

Isaac Shur walked back through Tangier a different way, up through the French quarter, the New Town. In the windows of the shops he saw cameras and watches and tape recorders and handsomely packaged bottles of aftershave, and Isaac Shur felt growing inside him an acquisitive urge, a desire to own – what? He looked at playing cards, battery-operated record players, transistor radios, silk ties, pondering each item, considering. A Dupont cigarette lighter? A pair of French sunglasses? No, this is ridiculous, Isaac Shur told himself, as he did every day, I am not going to pay these prices. I can get all this stuff cheaper in Gibraltar.

No children rushed at him when Isaac Shur unlocked his garden gate. Nor were they on the rubbish dump. The day was hot with silence. Inside his apartment, Isaac Shur opened the windows but left the shutters as they were. He saw the pages lying on the table as he had left them, his typewriter, his pencils, his pen, and for a moment he thought of sitting down, continuing his work, but no, he was too hot, he was too tired, he shouldn't have had that glass of wine at lunch. He sat down on the end of his bed and took off his shoes and socks. It wasn't the wine. Not just the wine. He unbuttoned and took off his shirt. He thought, if I lived in town, if I didn't have to do that walk every day. He put his passport and wallet and traveller's cheques under his pillow. He was almost too tired to take off his jeans. There was no wind outside, not a breeze, not the faintest stir of air, but Isaac Shur smelt, for an unaccountable instant, that smell of poverty. It filled his nose, his head, and then was gone, replaced by nothing.

What woke Isaac Shur at five o'clock was the garden gate rattling. At first he thought it was the children, and felt himself stiffen. Then he remembered. Today was the day he paid his rent. 'Coming, coming,' Isaac Shur called, dressing quickly, but not bothering with his shoes and socks.

She stood at the iron gate, haughty and enormous, wearing the spotless dove-coloured jellaba of the finest wool she always wore on these visits, golden slippers peeping out. Isaac Shur unlocked the gate, smiling apologetically. She swept past him, down the three steps that led to the garden, into the apartment. Isaac Shur, relocking the gate, saw at the kerb the battered black Vauxhall in which she always arrived, her son – one of her sons – sitting at the wheel, staring dumbly through the windscreen straight ahead. Isaac Shur hurried inside.

This woman had once owned, Isaac Shur had been told, the most expensive brothel in all Tangier. Certainly she was rich. She owned, beside this apartment, two buildings in the town, one of them a shop, the other offices and apartments; her mouth flashed with gold; on her left wrist sat a large Swiss watch, there were diamond and gold rings on most of her fingers, and the Vauxhall was hers. Yet, when Isaac Shur had gone to see her, to negotiate the leasing of this apartment, gone with the English painter who was relinquishing the apartment and returning home, he had found her living in what looked like abject poverty, in three cramped and crowded rooms in the heart of the Medina. In the first room Isaac Shur had seen an old man asleep in a chair, two young girls sitting on a battered sofa, a baby lying on a scrap of blanket on the floor. Flies crawled everywhere. The only hint of affluence was a television set in a corner. The other two rooms were filled with beds. The smell was appalling. Isaac Shur had had to go outside, to conduct his negotiations in the street. The English painter had done all the talking, in Spanish mostly, but with a few words of Arabic and French. Isaac Shur didn't know the woman's name. He called her Fatima.

'Fatima,' Isaac Shur said, coming into the apartment.

She was walking around the apartment, looking at everything, the typewriter, the two canvas bags, the shirt on the bed, her head high, aloof, completely disregarding Isaac Shur. Isaac Shur remembered that his wallet and passport were still under the pillow, took them out quickly, and began to count out the money for the week's rent.

'Fatima,' he said, holding it out in his hand.

Still she ignored him, looking around the apartment. Isaac Shur placed the money where he always put it, on a corner of the table. He watched the woman's eyes taking in his newspapers and magazines, his bottle of Johnnie Walker Black Label whisky, the Ramon Allones cigars, his cartons of Camel cigarettes. Finally, she sat down in Isaac Shur's chair.

'Whisky,' she said.

Isaac Shur fetched from the kitchen a glass and poured it half full. He handed it to the woman.

'Cigarette,' she said.

He offered his pack of Camels, lit one for her with a match. The woman's face said nothing. She raised the glass to her lips. Then she heard something, they both heard it, a sound outside, a step. The woman dropped the glass of whisky to the floor. The cigarette fell from her other hand. She sat, silent, stone, her eyes on a corner of the ceiling.

Isaac Shur went to the door and looked outside. It was nothing. There was no one there. The sound must have come from the apartment above.

'Nothing,' he said, holding up his hands, smiling.

The glass was not broken. Isaac Shur poured the woman another drink, lit for her another cigarette. Once more he offered the week's rent. Again she ignored him, sitting straight in his chair, puffing on the forbidden cigarette, but not inhaling, blowing the smoke away. Isaac Shur watched the glass go three times to the woman's lips, but each time it seemed to him the level remained the same. Then there was another sound, and once more she let fall the cigarette and glass.

She stayed for half an hour, never once looking directly at Isaac Shur, but the money disappearing, as it always did, into her jellaba, and when he unlocked and opened the garden gate for her, she swept past him as though she had never seen him before.

Now Isaac Shur stripped again, and standing in the kitchen washed himself all over, shaved with cold water, regretted for an instant not buying one of those handsomely packaged bottles of aftershave, then dressed again, this time putting on his spare shirt, fresh underwear and socks. He rinsed out the glass the woman had used, poured himself a good measure of whisky, selected and trimmed a Ramon Allones, and stepped out into the garden.

Isaac Shur stood with his drink and cigar and gazed along the valley. He felt awake and alert, refreshed by his sleep, his wash and shave, but not as he felt in the mornings. This was a different kind of wakefulness. Or was it wakefulness at all? Isaac Shur thought of the poem he was writing, and at once his brain felt tired, sluggish, annoyed to be forced to think of that. Then of what? Isaac Shur saw, on the rubbish dump, The Hot Shot Kid, the one with the shaved head, another one of them too. He took a step back, quickly, not to be seen. There was a concrete bench under a tree. Isaac Shur sat down.

George Matthews had said that what Isaac Shur needed was a Spanish girl. Spanish girls, he had said, were the best. No complications. No involvement. They knew what was what. He had even picked one out for him, a small frizzy-haired girl with large dark eyes who worked in one of the tourist shops on the Avenue Louis Pasteur. 'Don't be silly,' Isaac Shur had said. 'What are you talking about, "don't be silly"?' George Matthews had said. 'There's nothin' to it. You just go in, give her somethin', I don't know, a bottle of perfume, somethin' like that, then, well, you ask her to come for a walk. Tell her you've got your own apartment, that'll do it.' 'I couldn't do that,' Isaac Shur had said. 'Anyhow, I don't know enough Spanish.' George Matthews had laughed. 'Listen, you don't have to *talk*, for God's sake,' he had said. 'Look, you just rub these fingers together – like this.' George Matthews rubbed his index fingers, two naked bodies, side by side. 'Says the whole thing.'

Isaac Shur wrote once a fortnight to a girl in Australia. They had gone out together for nearly two years, a blonde girl named Ann, an interior decorator, and Isaac Shur knew that all he had to say was 'Come' and she would be in Tangier in a week. He had sent her, from London, a pair of Victorian jet pendant earrings, and she had had herself photographed with them on, three small photographs, pasted on a card, a triptych, two in earnest profile, smiling in the one in the middle. Isaac Shur kept this in his wallet, and each fortnight, before writing to her, he would look at it, at the three faces. Isaac Shur told her, in his letters, what he was doing, what he was seeing, what he was writing, he said how much he missed her, he signed his letters 'love', and as he wrote, what he felt was certainly true, but afterwards, reading his letters over before posting them, he saw how careful they were. They were not his voice; not the voice he employed in his speech or his poems.

Isaac Shur watched his garden filling gently with night. When he stood to refresh his drink, he saw that the valley had almost disappeared. Faint lights in the villages were the only sign of its existence. His apartment, when he went inside, echoed with emptiness, the sound of his shoes enormous on the hard, tiled floor. Isaac Shur poured himself another drink. He threw away his cigar and immediately lit a cigarette. He stood in the centre of the room and looked at the unmade bed, his two small canvas bags, his things on the table, the empty chair. It was still early, not yet seven o'clock. George Matthews didn't expect him till nine. He debated an hour at the Café de Paris with *The Times*, or maybe a stroll down to the Socco Chico, see who was there, a cup of coffee, a cigarette. He remembered he would have to get a bottle of wine. He would get that at the shop down the hill. Gibraltar tomorrow, he remembered. A breeze stirred the trees outside in the garden. Isaac Shur crushed out his cigarette. He felt, suddenly, impatient. He put down his glass of whisky, crossed quickly to the windows and closed them, stepped outside and locked the door. He would buy that bottle of aftershave, he decided, as he unlocked his garden gate, in that shop on the Avenue Louis Pasteur, the shop where the Spanish girl with the frizzy hair and the large dark eyes worked. Yes. He would do that now.

Isaac Shur walked home from his evening with George Matthews. It was after one o'clock, the sky blown full with moon. On the Avenue Louis Pasteur he passed the shop where the Spanish girl worked, where he hadn't gone in, but his thoughts were not on that. Two Moroccans walked hand in hand on the other side of the street. A woman stepped out of a doorway just ahead of him. Isaac Shur, walking past, saw for an instant her eyes above her black veil, the white flash of a naked ankle. Then he was past, walking quickly but not outwardly hurrying, the street empty ahead.

They had played Monopoly, as they always did, five fast games, the board set up and ready when Isaac Shur knocked on the door. They had played during dinner, and then afterwards, game after game, sitting in that curious windowless room in the centre of George Matthews' apartment, a large photograph of Humphrey Bogart hung crookedly on one wall, Beethoven's Fifth booming on George Matthews' record player. He had brought the record player with him from New York. He was never going back there again. He was through, he said, with all that hassling.

George Matthews, as always, had won every game. After the fifth game he had suggested they switch to Scrabble, or chess, but Isaac Shur had said no, he was tired, he wanted to get up early, he had to work in the morning. 'Anyhow, you're tired too,' Isaac Shur had said. 'You're nearly asleep.'

George Matthews had been smoking kif all evening. His eyelids drooped. The smell of his many pipes was sweet in the air. Isaac Shur had never smoked kif, and whenever George Matthews asked him why, as he had again this evening, Isaac Shur laughed, smiled, sipped his wine. 'I haven't got anything against it,' he had said again tonight. 'I just don't need it, that's all. I'm relaxed enough. Come on, it's your go.' There was something childish about George Matthews, Isaac Shur had always felt, something lacking, some essential quality, but exactly what it was Isaac Shur couldn't pin down. But did it matter? Isaac Shur accepted him as he was, accepted the endless games of Monopoly, the endless sitting. He liked him. He was glad that George Matthews was here in Tangier.

A café was still open on the corner where Isaac Shur turned up to ascend the hill to his apartment. Isaac Shur saw Moroccans in drab brown jellabas slumped at the tables, felt them looking at him as he approached, his footsteps ringing loud in the night, and his impulse was to cross the road, but he didn't. Instead, he inspected them coldly as he walked past, his eyes moving from one face to the next, pleased to see each one looking down, looking away, turning from his hard gaze. No one spoke. Isaac Shur began the walk up the hill.

He passed the shop where he bought his breakfast every morning, the shop closed now, but a wan light dimly visible inside, oily and feeble through the dirty window. Isaac Shur felt in his pocket for his keys. He was almost upon her before he saw she was there, the same woman he had seen this morning, sitting exactly as she had sat then, as though she hadn't moved all day, and the baby too, sitting against a wall shadowed by the moon like a pile of dirty clothing thrown there on the broken pavement. Isaac Shur made to step around her, automatically, that reflex action he had done in this city so many times, but she moved, her hand reached out, and when Isaac Shur took another step, quickly, away from her, out onto the road, she came after him, he felt her fingers on the fabric of his jeans. Isaac Shur jumped as though he had been struck. 'Oh, go away,' he said, 'go away!' The sound of his own voice startled him. He hadn't meant to speak, to cry out. He heard his voice as though it had come from someone else, heard the sound of it, the tone. Isaac Shur panicked. He began to run, the key to his iron garden gate already out, gripped hard in his tight hand.

At two in the morning Isaac Shur awoke to hear a sound in his garden, a sound of scraping and chipping, a sound of masonry. He lay dead quiet, too terrified to move, his hands frozen by his sides, his heart thundering high in his throat. He listened, but he didn't have to listen. Isaac Shur knew at once what the sound was, without a second's doubt. Someone was taking away his wall.

Isaac Shur didn't move. He heard the grey concrete blocks being lifted away, one by one. He couldn't move. His fear was enormous. He lay, his heart hammering, naked in the dark. He thought of the oil lamp by the side of the bed, but he knew that to light it was for him, now, impossible. He couldn't move his fingers. He couldn't raise his hands. The room was as black with his eyes open as it was with them closed. Another block, and another. He listened, terrified, to the mortar being chipped away. And then he felt something else, inside him, beside the fear, a first prickle, and then stronger. He began to breathe hard through his mouth, his anger growing, his outrage, growing and growing, pushing aside the fear. He sat up. He stood up. When he opened his door the moon fell inside at his feet like a page of paper.

An old Arab sat cross-legged on the rubbish dump beyond the wall, scraping broken bricks with a knife and putting them into a burlap bag. Curled beside him lay a thin yellow dog, the colour of bad cream in the light of the moon. Isaac Shur stared at the Arab's thin hands, but the Arab's face, bent over his bricks, was to Isaac Shur in shadow, a blackness, a void.

Isaac Shur caught the four o'clock plane to Gibraltar the next afternoon, the connecting flight to London at half past eight.